"You got him to resign, presumably to live the rest of his life in exile, but that was never really the plan, was it?"

For the first time, Ross seemed to falter before answering. When he did reply, he looked away from her and down at the conference table. "No."

Louvois watched Steeby once more touch the admiral's arm, offering yet another unspoken warning. It was now obvious to her there had been some kind of animated discussion regarding how he would conduct himself, and it seemed he wanted the freedom to make whatever comments he found relevant or appropriate, regardless of how they looked from a legal standpoint. That much was clear. Perhaps it meant that deep down, Ross still valued the principles he had spent a career and lifetime defending. That sort of devotion was not easily dismissed. Such was the case for true believers, at any rate, and perhaps it held for those who had fallen into darkness and now struggled to find the light.

"It's details like this that aren't in any of Ozla Graniv's reports," she said. "Section Thirty-One planned to kill him, Azernal, and Quafina all along, right? Wait, I'm sorry. I meant the Uraei program had calculated its probability models and concluded keeping him alive posed too great a risk, predicting he'd present a problem at some point in the future. The expedient thing to do was just kill him and the others. No regard for due process, established law, or even common decency. A computer program acted as judge and jury before ordering you to be the executioner, and you nodded like a good soldier and said yes, because it was distasteful yet necessary."

At long last, Steeby went into protective lawyer mode. "Madam Attorney General, do you have any actual questions for my client?"

"Sure, I've got a few." Keeping her gaze fixed on Ross, Louvois asked, "Do you prefer your penal colonies on Earth? Or, would you rather we ship you off to Elba II or some other barren planetoid with a poisonous atmosphere so you can never go outside and breathe fresh air and feel sunlight on your face? I may not be able to prosecute a piece of software, but I can damned sure throw the book at you."

STAR TREK
THE NEXT GENERATION®

AVAILABLE LIGHT

DAYTON WARD

Based on
Star Trek: The Next Generation
created by Gene Roddenberry

GALLERY BOOKS

New York   London   Toronto   Sydney   New Delhi   Nejahlora

G

Gallery Books
An Imprint of Simon & Schuster, Inc.
1230 Avenue of the Americas
New York, NY 10020

™, ® and © 2019 by CBS Studios Inc. STAR TREK and related marks and logos are trademarks of CBS Studios Inc. All Rights Reserved.

This book is published by Gallery Books, an imprint of Simon & Schuster, Inc., under exclusive license from CBS Studios Inc.

First Gallery Books trade paperback edition April 2019

GALLERY BOOKS and colophon are trademarks of Simon & Schuster, Inc.

For information about special discounts for bulk purchases, please contact Simon & Schuster Special Sales at 1-866-506-1949 or business@simonandschuster.com.

The Simon & Schuster Speakers Bureau can bring authors to your live event. For more information or to book an event, contact the Simon & Schuster Speakers Bureau at 1-866-248-3049 or visit our website at www.simonspeakers.com.

Manufactured in the United States of America

10 9 8 7 6 5 4 3 2 1

Library of Congress Cataloging-in-Publication Data

Names: Ward, Dayton, author.
Title: Available light / Dayton Ward.
Other titles: Star trek, the next generation (Television program)
Description: First Gallery Books trade paperback edition. | New York :
    Gallery Books, 2019. | Series: Star trek: the next generation |
    Identifiers: LCCN 2018057860 (print) | LCCN 2018058982 (ebook) |
    ISBN 9781982113285 (ebook) | ISBN 9781982113278 (paperback)
Subjects: LCSH: Interplanetary voyages—Fiction. | Space warfare—Fiction. |
    Space ships—Fiction. | Star Trek fiction. | BISAC: FICTION / Science
    Fiction / Adventure. | FICTION / Science Fiction / Military. | GSAFD:
    Science fiction.
Classification: LCC PS3623.A7317 (ebook) | LCC PS3623.A7317 A97 2019
    (print) | DDC 813/.6—dc23
LC record available at https://lccn.loc.gov/2018057860

ISBN 978-1-9821-1327-8
ISBN 978-1-9821-1328-5 (ebook)

For Michi, Addison, and Erin,
for all the usual reasons.

HISTORIAN'S NOTE

This story takes place in late 2386, seven years after the *U.S.S. Enterprise*-E's confrontation with the Romulan praetor Shinzon (*Star Trek Nemesis*) and a few weeks after the *Enterprise*'s encounter with the Eizand people (*Star Trek: The Next Generation—Hearts and Minds*). Shaking the very foundations of Starfleet and the Federation is Trill journalist Ozla Graniv's bombshell exposé of Section 31 and its numerous clandestine activities, including the conspiracy to remove and assassinate Federation president Min Zife in 2379 (*Star Trek: Section 31–Control*).

1

Sitting in the open-air cafe that was one of his favorite destinations in New Glasgow's arts district, William Ross froze in the act of bringing his teacup to his lips. Suddenly, terrible truths and dark secrets rose from the depths of shadow and revealed themselves.

"... *massive release of previously top secret information detailing the actions of a clandestine organization that has operated without oversight or accountability, both within and outside the Federation government, for more than two centuries.*"

The screen mounted to the cafe courtyard's far wall depicted a dark-skinned woman sitting at a desk emblazoned with the Federation News Service logo. It was obvious from her delivery that she was reading from hastily transcribed notes rather than prepared copy, which would explain the frequent pauses as she glanced away from the pickup to consult whatever padd or other device she had brought with her to the desk.

Feeling his pulse begin to quicken, Ross lowered his teacup to the saucer on his table. All around him, disparate conversations and other activities faded as other cafe patrons turned from their meals or dining companions to direct their attention to the screen.

"*Known as Section Thirty-One, the group consists of covert agents overseen by civilian Federation officials as well as Starfleet officers, all working beneath the notice of normal chains of command. Supposedly formed more than two hundred years ago with a mission to defend Earth—and later the Federation—from internal as well as external threats, this group has reportedly carried out missions and actions of varying scope, many of which would be considered illegal against*"

Federation citizens or acts of aggression against sovereign governments both friendly and otherwise. The information purports that nearly every Federation citizen for the past two centuries has been under continuous active surveillance, their every action and communication monitored by an advanced artificial intelligence that culls through this collected information, ostensibly searching for patterns or indications of threats. Section Thirty-One agents then acted on that information, to include murdering anyone deemed a danger to Federation or Starfleet interests. Again, all of these actions were undertaken without any form of due process or accountability to higher Federation or Starfleet authority."

Ross forced himself to stay in his seat. His eyes narrowed and his jaw clenched as he watched the news anchor once more halt her report. It was obvious she was still processing the information she had been tasked to disseminate. As any good journalist would do in a similar situation, she likely was pondering dozens of questions, all while faced with presenting a calm, composed demeanor to the viewing public.

So, this is how it ends.

The thought taunted him. Ross should have known the tranquility he thought he had found after a lifetime spent in service to others—a peace he had not sought yet ultimately decided was the best option not only for him but for his family—would be fleeting, at best. Decisions and actions undertaken with noble intentions in pursuit of what he believed was a greater good, despite the heavy price they exacted on his very soul, were now coming back to collect on debts he owed.

You knew it would happen one day. You were just hoping you'd die before the bill came due.

After submitting his resignation to President Nanietta Bacco after she learned of his involvement in removing Min Zife from office, Ross was content to remain retired, enjoying the newfound freedom and relaxing life he found with his wife, Stefana, here on Caldos II. It also meant more time to spend with their son,

Zachary. Now a student at Columbia University, Zach made the trip from Earth between semesters and for holidays, during which father and son spent their mornings on the tennis court behind the house. Despite the age disparity between them—nearly forty years, as Zach kept reminding him—Ross still managed to hold his own during their spirited games.

Their choice of retirement destination saw to it that they and the planet's other inhabitants largely were spared from the devastating effects of the Borg Collective's final invasion of Federation space five years earlier. Escaping the Borg's notice and being spared destruction or heavy damage meant that Caldos was one of a handful of planets chosen to relocate survivors seeking refuge from numerous other worlds that were not so lucky. The influx of tens of thousands of people had not caused the undue burden many Caldos residents feared. With the help of Starfleet and Federation colony support, the refugees had a smooth relocation. New villages and smaller communities were established across the planet, growing and thriving in this new post-Borg reality. Life on Caldos took little time returning to normal.

All of that, along with the rest of the quiet, happy existence he had finally found after decades in service to Starfleet, was about to be taken from him. What could he do? Ross considered and discarded possible courses of action. After his forced retirement, he thought he might simply disappear into obscurity here on Caldos II. Originally a colony world before becoming a full member of the Federation, the planet offered plenty of opportunity for those seeking a quieter, slower life far away from the normal machinations of twenty-fourth-century politics and other concerns. It was close enough to benefit from regular security patrols and civilian merchant shipping while too distant from anything that might give Starfleet reason to establish a permanent presence here. If this world could not permit him to fade into the shadows of history, where else could he go?

Nowhere.

If the news reports were accurate, and Ross knew they were, there was no place for him to hide. He would be found, along with all the others.

On the viewscreen, the anchor again dropped her gaze to her padd as she cleared her throat. When she returned her attention to the pickup, Ross saw a new, fierce determination in her eyes.

"Included in the data release is a roster of individuals formerly or currently affiliated with Section Thirty-One. The list is . . . disturbing and includes many familiar names. People we've called heroes and saviors of our very way of life. If even a fraction of what's been documented in this information is true, it indicates a staggering, ongoing violation of our society's most basic tenets of civil rights and privacy, carried out by some of the very people entrusted to safeguard the society we all hold dear."

Once the dust settled and the trials were over and those found guilty—including him—were dispatched to Auckland, New Zealand, or some other penal colony, there would be precious few people to remember or care about the good done by him and uncounted others over the course of generations. Since before the Federation's founding, even before the first spaceships from Earth traveled beyond the confines of their own solar system to encounter representatives from distant worlds, Ross and others like him had toiled in secret. They had done everything in their power to ensure humanity's uninhibited idealism and naiveté did not leave it vulnerable to attack or exploitation by some unfriendly power.

Were many of the choices made and actions taken morally dubious and even illegal? Yes. Ross did not always possess knowledge or understanding of the reasons precipitating those deeds, and in the beginning he questioned the wisdom of the group's ability to operate with seeming impunity while appearing to violate the very core values they were sworn to defend. Even his military training and tactical experience, along with his preference for viewing many situations through the harsh, stark lens that was required to navigate such situations, had not been enough at first to make him comfortable with some of Section 31's methods and edicts.

However, decades in service to the organization, particularly during the Dominion War, had shown him the value of such an entity. Was it susceptible to corruption? Left unchecked and unaccountable, any group or individual ran the chance of falling prey to such darker impulses. While it could not be argued that it had on numerous occasions acted far outside the boundaries of Federation law, the results were indisputable.

Nor could they be hidden any longer, thanks to the efforts and tenacity of Ozla Graniv. Ross was familiar with the journalist's work, and knew that she had for some time been working to expose Section 31. The results of her tireless efforts—all of the group's virtuous deeds as well as its sins—now were being broadcast to the known galaxy. Victories once celebrated in silence would be held up for the people to see, and perhaps appreciate just how many times their mundane existences had come within a hairsbreadth of annihilation.

Of course, they also would learn of the extraordinary measures taken to protect their way of life, but would any of that matter? Ross guessed it would not, and to a point, he understood this reality. Most people, in his experience, tended to view the safeguarding of their liberty and security through filters that allowed them to ignore the often-messy processes that made such things possible. When confronted with the brutal truth of what was required to preserve the society they took for granted, many of those same people found themselves unable to handle such cold, unforgiving reality.

After everything was said and all its deeds made available for scrutiny by an uninformed and unappreciative public, that would be the legacy of Section 31.

"William Ross!"

Jerking at the sound of his name, Ross turned in his seat toward the source of the call to see a pair of Federation Security Agency officers, wearing their familiar gray uniforms, moving from the cafe's courtyard entry and out onto the patio. The woman who had shouted his name was staring at him as she moved past tables of customers, her right hand resting on the phaser holstered on her left hip. On her right, a tall dark-skinned man was also advancing toward him, though Ross noted that he had moved away from his companion and was now approaching at a different angle, placing himself between Ross and a gate leading from the courtyard to the adjacent sidewalk and street.

Ross glanced over his left shoulder to where he knew another gate led to a walking path and a nearby park. A second pair of officers in gray uniforms, a human male and a Vulcan female, waited there.

No way out.

There was another option. Reaching into his jacket, Ross tapped the communicator badge affixed to his inner pocket. It was not a Starfleet-issue device, and carried a few features not found in traditional units like the one he once wore on his own uniform. He tapped it twice, activating an emergency escape protocol designed to transport him to a safe house. In this case, it was a small cabin in the mountains two hundred miles north of New Glasgow. His getaway was at best a temporary measure, but at least then he would have time to plan his next steps, including what to do about Stefana and Zach.

Instead of watching the surprised faces of the security officers as he vanished before their eyes, nothing happened.

What the hell? The answer was simple, of course. *A transporter inhibitor. They knew I'd try this. Damn.*

Ross remained in his chair in the cafe courtyard as the woman stopped walking toward him. She drew her phaser and leveled it at him. To his left, her partner mimicked her movements.

"Remove your hand from your jacket, sir. Do it *now*."

Saying nothing, Ross removed his hand from his jacket, leaving it open with its palm facing the officer. He raised his left hand to show that it, too, was empty.

The woman waved her phaser's muzzle, indicating for him to get to his feet. "Stand up, please."

Ross rose from his seat as the woman's companion closed on him and reached for his left hand. He did not resist while the man fastened restraints around his left wrist, then joined his hands together.

"Admiral William Ross," said the woman, who now lowered her phaser. "You are under arrest for crimes against the Federation including treason, murder, conspiracy to commit murder, sedition, and conspiracy to overthrow duly elected officials of the Federation government."

2

Keeping her attention on her desktop computer terminal, Alynna Nechayev checked the power setting of the phaser in her hand. The vid feeds showed the locations of what she recognized as a team of Federation Security officers approaching her house from all directions. Dressed in dark clothing as they moved under cover of darkness, they were arrayed in a circle that tightened with every step forward. In ten seconds, agents would be stepping onto her front porch. She glanced at her phaser once more, verifying that the weapon was set to stun before reaching for the communicator badge in her desk's top drawer.

Whatever you're going to do, she prompted herself, *it's time to get on with it.*

On her living room's forward wall, the viewscreen was displaying a succession of photographs depicting various Federation officials and senior Starfleet officers connected to Section 31, as revealed by Ozla Graniv and her devastating information release. She already had seen pictures of friends and colleagues like William Ross, Tujiro Nakamura, and even the late Owen Paris scrolling across her screen. Additional footage from a news team as well as private citizens showed another fellow admiral, Edward Jellico, being arrested by Federation Security officers.

Reports of other Section 31 associates being hunted or taken into custody were also coming in from worlds across the Federation, the information gathering faster than the ability of news correspondents to disseminate it. From what Nechayev could tell, it was obvious that agents of both the Federation government and Starfleet were moving with all due haste not just to contain the situation but also apprehend anyone implicated in the scandal before those individuals could evade them. Even though her role with Section 31 was not as intricate or damning as that of some of her fellow Starfleet officers and other associates, Nechayev knew anyone with any connection to the organization would be a target. Even the most benevolent judge, civilian or Starfleet, would see her actions on behalf of the group as nothing less than treason, regardless of motive or justification. That much was evident by the agents now closing in on her.

Nechayev had no intention of being arrested in her own home.

A check of her property's passive sensor system was enough to tell her that in addition to the team of advancing security officers, the unwelcome party had also activated some kind of transporter inhibitor. She determined it to be a portable model deployed about twenty meters from her house, tucked away within a grove of trees in which she had opted to build her home in the Adirondack Mountain region of northern New York. Of course, no one was supposed to know about this place. It was one of two safe houses Nechayev had established years earlier, and she had transported herself here within minutes of seeing the initial news broadcasts detailing the revelations about Section 31. The personal transporter system tucked into a closet of her San Francisco apartment was shielded from scans and kept no logs, so anyone conducting a search would have no means of tracking her from that point. Therefore, that Federation law enforcement agencies had taken so little time to target their search on this location indicated just how much information about her the Section 31 data release had revealed.

How much more do they know?

Entering a string of commands to the desktop terminal's touch interface, Nechayev activated a dampening pulse from emitters situated around her property. It was not a lethal or even harmful strike against her uninvited guests. Instead, the pulse was enough to temporarily disable any electronic devices in a half-kilometer radius, with the exception of anything inside her house. On the terminal, she saw images of various agents halting their approaches, pausing to study their weapons, tricorders, or other equipment they carried. The pulse had worked, as further evidenced by the status readout informing her the transporter inhibitor was now offline. Nechayev knew she had only moments before the agents activated another such device, or simply threw caution to the winds and stormed her house.

Time to go.

Phaser still in hand, Nechayev slung over her shoulder a bag she had packed for contingences like this, containing a small assortment of clothing and other items of varying personal and tactical value. Satisfied that she had everything she planned to take with her, she activated her combadge, pressing its faceplate several times in a prearranged sequence. The device offered a reassuring beep, and a moment later Nechayev felt the familiar tingle of a transporter beam coalescing into existence and wrapping itself around her body.

Within seconds the cozy, warm confines of her living room and its view of the forest and mountains disappeared, replaced by a wall of transparent aluminum separating her from a patio overlooking a brilliant white sandy beach and the beautiful blue water of the Pacific Ocean. The waterfront condominium on Mexico's San Juanico coast was catching the day's last rays of sunlight as dusk approached. Nechayev wished she could enjoy the moment along with the feeling of tranquility this place always brought to her, but there was no time. Even with her shielded transporter system, Federation Security likely also knew about this safe house. They would be sending agents to this location, assuming they were not already on their way.

No sooner had she begun moving to her study with its own desktop computer terminal than an alarm sounded throughout the condo. The sensor system she had installed, a twin of the one monitoring her house in the Adirondacks, was always overseeing the house and surrounding beach. In addition to its surveillance abilities, the system was designed to mask her presence, preventing anyone outside the dwelling from determining her location inside the house. So long as she remained in here, she was invisible to tricorder or other scan readings.

Quickening her pace, Nechayev continued into the study, keeping her bag slung over her shoulder and the phaser in her hand as she reached the computer terminal and turned it to face her.

Damn it.

Twelve more security agents were converging on the condo. The only avenue of approach not covered was the one leading to the ocean, for obvious reasons. Even if she could get out of the house undetected, making it on foot to the boat dock fifty meters down the beach without drawing attention was impossible.

From an already truncated list of options, Nechayev was now reduced to one.

Like her home in New York, the condo was outfitted with a few extra features that would now come in handy. She pressed the control to summon a menu, then selected the electro-dampening system that already had served her so well.

The terminal chose that moment to deactivate, which was followed by the entire house going dark.

They've cut the power.

Rather than waste precious time trying to figure out how the intruders might have accomplished such a feat, Nechayev dropped her bag onto the desk before opening a compartment on its side and retrieving the second phaser. With practiced ease, she thumbed the weapon's power setting to stun. Even now, and knowing her likely fate, there were lines she would not cross. One such boundary was her refusal to kill Federation officers carrying out their sworn duty.

Hell of a time to develop a conscience.

Grabbing her bag, she slung it over her left arm and across her back before moving to open a door on the bottom level of the wooden bookcase set into the wall behind her desk. Inside the compartment was a squat, metallic container with a keypad embedded in its top. Equipped with its own battery, the device was immune from the power loss affecting the rest of the house. Nechayev keyed a command sequence into the pad before pressing a control labeled "Commit." In response to her instructions, a red indicator began flashing, and a digital readout started counting down from thirty seconds.

Definitely time to go.

Through the doorway leading from her study, Nechayev caught sight of a shadow darkening part of one window affording the spectacular ocean view. Then a figure moved into view, crouching near the transparent aluminum door leading to the patio. From her vantage point, she did not think she was visible to the intruder, but with the house's defensive measures now deactivated she knew she could be tracked. If the agent she could see was already that close, his companions were likely taking up positions at the condo's other entrances. A check of the computer terminal confirmed her suspicions. Each of the four doors was now covered by two figures, with the other four having assumed defensive positions at the corners of the yard surrounding the house.

There was no time for this. For better or worse, Nechayev was committed to her rash plan.

Counting seconds in her head, she increased the power setting on the phaser in her right hand, aimed at the window, and fired. The weapon's energy beam punched through the transparent aluminum, creating a hole in the barrier a meter across. Outside, the man preparing to make his entry flinched before stepping back but Nechayev was faster. The stun beam from the phaser in her other hand caught the intruder high in the chest, and he was thrown backward over the patio's short wooden railing. He was unconscious before dropping to the ground.

Elsewhere in the house, Nechayev heard the sounds of other doors being forced and voices filtering from adjacent rooms and hallways. Finally, someone inside the house shouted a warning that echoed in the darkness.

"I'm scanning an explosive device inside the house. Everybody out, right now!"

Ignoring all of that, Nechayev bolted from her study toward the patio door. Movement from outside made her point the phaser in her left hand in that direction without taking true aim, but when she fired she heard the sound of another person caught by the weapon's stun beam. She saw the agent, a woman dressed in a formfitting black uniform, fall backward onto the chaise longue positioned near the walking path leading toward the beach. Shooting again just to be safe, Nechayev continued through the door leading to the patio, thumbing the power level on her second phaser back to a stun setting.

Shouts from inside and around the sides of the house came from multiple directions, but rather than trying to evade them she chose a point of attack and pressed ahead. Even with their tricorders, the two agents on the north side of her house, a male and a female cloaked from head to toe in dark uniforms, were unprepared for their quarry to suddenly go on the offensive. Both of her phasers found targets, and the two agents collapsed to the grass. In encroaching darkness Nechayev saw several figures moving away from the house, seeking cover among the nearby trees. The area between her and the water was clear, and she backpedaled in that direction while keeping her phasers ready for new threats. The dock was within sprinting distance, even if she was getting a bit old for this sort of thing. If she could make it aboard the boat moored there, she would have options unavailable to her so long as she remained on foot.

Then the countdown in her head dwindled to zero.

Nechayev did not flinch at the muffled sound of the explosion that erupted inside her house. The charge she had placed inside her bookcase was not intended to destroy the entire structure, let alone harm anyone in the immediate vicinity. Instead, its purpose was targeted toward sanitizing her office and its contents, while the room's walls contained the blast and any resulting fire. Even those security agents already disabled and left unconscious as she made her escape were protected from injury, but anything stored in her office and of potential value to law enforcement officials was gone.

The voices coming from elsewhere in the deepening darkness were less frantic than before the bomb's detonation, and Nechayev surmised the team's leader now was attempting to account for the group's other members. She knew the momentary confusion would give her only seconds to act. It was the boat, now or never.

"Halt!" a voice shouted from somewhere behind her. "Stop right there!"

In reply, Nechayev fired one of her phasers toward the voice's apparent origin point before hastening her pace down the paved walking path leading from her house. There were no lights out here on the beach, but she knew she was visible to the team's tricorders. There was no longer anywhere left to hide, and the situation had devolved into a simple footrace.

It was a race she could not win.

That point was hammered home as the phaser beam caught her left arm. It was not enough to stun her, but still sufficient to send Nechayev tumbling to the sand. Her left arm had gone numb and she lost her grip on the phaser in that hand, and felt herself hit by a minor bout of dizziness and disorientation as the beam's effects impacted her nervous system. With only her right arm to help push her up from the ground, she struggled to turn herself toward her pursuers and succeeded in time to see three Federation Security agents bearing down on her. Fighting to a sitting position, she tried lifting her remaining phaser.

"Don't do it," snapped the trio's apparent leader, a human or at least humanoid male clad in his dark uniform. Nechayev saw the phaser in his left hand, aimed at her face.

"Admiral Alynna Nechayev," said the man's companion, a

slender Andorian female. "You are required to submit yourself to arrest for crimes against the Federation. These include murder, conspiracy to commit murder, sedition, treason, and conspiracy to overthrow duly elected officials of the Federation government. Drop your weapon and cease resisting, or we will be forced to incapacitate you."

Fools.

Did these officers think a simple information release would be enough to stop an entity as pervasive, elusive, and autonomous as Section 31? Stop an organization that had existed without peer since before the Federation's founding? Did they really think that, now exposed to the public, the agency no longer posed a threat? The situation was still evolving, and Nechayev was uncertain just what actions those within 31's highest echelons of power would take to preserve the organization's mission if not their own lives.

One thing she did know was that being in the custody of Federation Security was by no means a guarantee she was free from danger. Section 31's reach was as long as it was formidable, with assets embedded within the very fabric of Starfleet and the Federation government. If the decision was made to end her life, there was nowhere she could hide, and no one to whom she could turn for help. The only things offering her a chance at safety were her silence and her loyalty.

Nechayev raised her phaser.

The last thing she saw was the flash of three phaser beams washing away everything.

3

—

It was all Leonard James Akaar could do to keep his temper in check. A mix of anger, disbelief, and disappointment raged within him, threatening to erupt like torrents of water pushing through the widening gaps of a failing dam.

Steady, Admiral.

Sitting in his office at Starfleet Headquarters on Earth, Akaar regarded the image of Jean-Luc Picard displayed on his desktop computer screen. Despite their earlier, contentious exchange at the start of the *U.S.S. Enterprise*'s most recent mission, the captain's legendary self-control now was firmly in place as he relayed his after-action report. He presented everything in his usual matter-of-fact manner, waiting in silence for requests to elaborate or clarify. His expression remained fixed throughout the conversation. It was as if he was reluctant to revisit the topic of discussion that had so thoroughly incensed both men.

Of course, Picard could not know about the figurative bomb Akaar was about to detonate.

"Tell me about Min Zife, Captain." He leaned toward the screen as he spoke the words, clasping his hands and resting them atop his desk.

For the first time, Picard's expression changed. The shock was as evident as it was genuine. Although the captain did a commendable job schooling his features after those initial seconds, the damage was done. Akaar had what he wanted.

"What about him?" asked Picard.

Satisfied that he had the other man's undivided attention,

Akaar reclined in his chair. "He was removed from office. He didn't step down for the good of the Federation and then disappear quietly into exile. That's the story fed to the general public, but that's not what really happened. The truth is he was forced to abandon his office without due process, without articles of impeachment being presented, and without any sort of formal investigation into his actions. Yes, those actions were heinous and cost millions of lives, and President Zife deserved to face a trial for what he did and allowed others to do, but he was denied that, wasn't he, Captain?"

Though Picard said nothing, his haunted expression revealed he now was considering memories on which he had not allowed himself to dwell for some time. Akaar supposed that was fair, to a point. Along with the *Enterprise* and its crew, Picard had endured much in the years since Min Zife's removal from office.

Akaar was still learning the full truth of what journalist Ozla Graniv had wrought with her unflinching exposing of Section 31. Akaar had heard of the group, of course, but its ability to remain invisible even while working in plain sight to further its agenda had confounded him, as was true of anyone who attempted to shine a light on its activities. Graniv had outdone everyone, at great risk to herself as well as the two Starfleet Intelligence operatives, Julian Bashir and Sarina Douglas, the latter of whom had died as a result of upending Section 31.

Just one of the group's more heinous actions was its targeting of President Min Zife, though in retrospect Akaar could understand if not condone its actions. During the Dominion War, Zife had entered into a secret agreement to arm the people of Tezwa, an unaffiliated planet near the Klingon border. The scheme had somewhat noble intentions, with Tezwa being part of a defensive strategy in the event Starfleet forces were forced to retreat while engaging Dominion attackers. Nevertheless, Zife's actions violated the Khitomer Accords, the peace agreement between the

Federation and the Klingon Empire. If the Klingons had discovered this breach, they might have been compelled to declare war against the Federation.

The former president might have succeeded with his plan, except that some of those weapons ended up being used against Klingon vessels. Zife tried to cover up what he had done on Tezwa, but he was unable to escape the long reach and iron grip of Section 31.

"With Zife's crimes revealed and knowing that bringing them to public attention would only provoke the Klingons to retaliate against the Federation," Akaar continued, "you and a few other officers decided to take matters into your own hands."

"Reluctantly, but yes." Picard shifted in his own seat, clearly uncomfortable with the turn the conversation had taken. At the same time, and just as Akaar suspected he would, the captain did not look away from him, though when he next spoke it was with a more reserved, deferential tone. *"At the time, it was believed that forcing President Zife to step down and allowing him to live in exile was the best course of action for the Federation."*

"It was a damned coup d'etat," Akaar snapped. There was no other way to describe what had taken place. "You forced him from office at the muzzle of a phaser." Despite himself, he felt obligated to be honest about his own feelings, which had been simmering since the beginning of the seemingly unending rush of startling revelations he was still struggling to absorb. "Yes, the ends were justified, but the means were deplorable, and despite your best efforts, the whole story's public. Everything, Picard. It's all out there, including all the players. The next time you're able to access the Federation News Service, you'll be able to read how Section Thirty-One lied to your faces. Zife never went into exile, Captain. He and his collaborators were assassinated—murdered—right there in the Monet Room just as soon as he was done delivering his final speech."

When Picard's expression changed this time, it was to one of horrified incredulity. *"What?"*

He remained silent as Akaar updated him on the firestorm ignited by Graniv's report and the massive release of information obtained directly from Section 31's own records. The ramifications were only just beginning to be understood by Federation and Starfleet officials, to say nothing of allies and enemies alike. Of more immediate concern for Akaar was the sheer number of people the renegade group had recruited, corrupted, and even murdered in order to continue carrying out its singular mission of protecting at any cost the Federation from any internal or external threat.

"Members of my own staff have been implicated. Respected officers, like Edward Jellico, William Ross, Alynna Nechayev, Owen Paris, and you." Akaar shook his head as a renewed sense of frustration manifested. "You, of all people."

Picard's voice had regained some of its force. *"I'm not proud of my part in that affair, Admiral, and I'm prepared to answer for my actions, but I did not suggest, sanction, or stand by while President Zife was assassinated. That was not part of the bargain."*

On this point, at least, Akaar knew the *Enterprise* captain was speaking the truth. He had not been among those who planned and carried out Zife's execution, but he still was an integral part of the plot to have the president removed from his office. Under normal circumstances, that alone would be more than enough to have Picard tried, convicted, and sentenced to a lengthy prison term.

Circumstances aren't really normal these days. Are they?

"Jellico, Nechayev, and the others are bigger problems," said Akaar, "but you at least are out of reach and perhaps out of mind. I may be able to mitigate the damage."

Picard shook his head. *"I don't require another cover-up, sir. I will accept whatever punishment is deemed appropriate."*

If anything, Akaar thought he could sense the other man's relief at no longer having to carry the burden of this terrible secret. It spoke to Picard's character that his decision to participate in what he obviously knew was a criminal if arguably necessary act weighed on him even after all this time. Why had he not come forward? The obvious answer was that he knew doing so would only bring the very unwanted attention from the Klingons and other parties he and his coconspirators had sought to avoid.

Naturally, there were other concerns. The Federation was still dealing with the aftermath of President Nanietta Bacco's assassination the previous year along with the troubling circumstances surrounding the naming and proper election of her successor. Kellessar zh'Tarash, the current president, was approaching the first anniversary of her inauguration and was doing her level best to guide the Federation away from the seemingly unending chaos of multiple political and military impediments. The exposing of Section 31 and all the collateral damage it would cause was the last thing she needed, but there was no avoiding the storm now heading directly at her.

The others involved in Zife's ousting—Jellico, Nechayev, Ross, Nakamura—would be easier to prosecute, given their role in the covert action that had followed the president's removal from office. Ross, Nechayev, and Nakamura would face particular scrutiny, as they had delivered Zife to Section 31 agents, along with the president's chief of staff, Koll Azernal, and his secretary of military intelligence, Nelino Quafina. While there was sufficient cause to regard Nechayev and Nakamura as accomplices in the conspiracy to assassinate Zife and his aides, William Ross was prominently named as having deep ties to those who carried out the heinous act. Owen Paris, having perished during the Borg invasion, was beyond the reach of justice.

Picard, on the other hand, presented something of a problem. Well respected within the interstellar community, even more so than the admirals with whom he had conspired against Zife, the veteran captain's involvement in the affair, on top of all the other officers caught up in various Section 31 machinations, would be devastating to Starfleet's public standing.

There also was the simple fact that Picard and the *Enterprise* were weeks away at maximum warp, continuing their exploration of the Odyssean Pass. The mission had already yielded numerous results, including the discovery of several star systems with resource-rich planets. Early studies of the data sent back showed great promise for colonization as well as expanding Starfleet's reach into a largely uncharted section of the galaxy. Tasking another starship to take over the *Enterprise*'s duties would be time-consuming as well as require reassignment of other vessels to cover just this one shift in ships and crews.

Then, there was the reality that the public's reaction to these startling revelations could not be predicted. Akaar knew that the news about Zife in particular would draw all manner of responses, both positive and negative. The simple truth was that regardless of the legal issues surrounding their actions, Picard and the others had done the Federation a favor by quietly removing the president from office, and if he had been allowed to live in exile, that likely could be justified, both to Federation citizens as well as allies and even adversaries.

Another point to consider was that compared to the other facts now coming to light, the ousting of a corrupt elected official was but one small problem Starfleet and the Federation faced. Exposing Section 31's laundry list of crimes and the public's haunting realization that significant aspects of their lives had always been impacted by the shadow organization's activities would provide sufficient means for Akaar to insulate one starship captain, at least for the moment. Picard's involvement in the Zife affair could, in theory, get lost amid the shuffle to hold to account other, more visible members of the rogue group.

"The public doesn't need another scandal right now," said

Akaar, still glaring at Picard, "and particularly not when it involves one of the genuine darlings of Starfleet. That's you, in case you were wondering. So, we can't do anything to you publicly, but here's the reality: You can forget any thoughts or dreams about making admiral. I know you said you never wanted a promotion and you wanted to stay in command of the *Enterprise*. Well, this is for real now. Captain is the highest rank you'll ever obtain."

It was a tall order, Akaar knew, but removing Picard from the *Enterprise* in light of all his accomplishments and sacrifices on behalf of the Federation might cause more harm than good. Akaar was banking on being able to insulate the captain from the worst of the fallout, which seemed feasible in light of the coming chaos. There would be endless questions from all quarters. It would not take long for investigators and law enforcement officials, to say nothing of President zh'Tarash herself, to all but forget about Picard—and perhaps even some of the other players if there were any mitigating circumstances that might help justify their actions. Instead, attention and energies would be focused on the heart of the matter: that Section 31 could function with such unchecked abandon for so long and with such a horrifying degree of success.

Graniv's exposé provided the explanation and the missing piece of a centuries-old puzzle: Uraei, the artificial intelligence program at the heart of Section 31's operation, had been active since before the Federation's founding. Not everyone with ties to the group knew of Uraei's existence, a fact that would only serve to heighten the feelings of deception, betrayal, and helplessness sure to grip any sensible Federation citizen. No one would feel inclined to trust anyone, about anything.

Akaar could sympathize with such feelings, even as he was gripped by similar uncertainty. The full roster of Section 31 agents, operatives, collaborators, and benefactors included the names of people he had known for years, even decades. It would take months if not longer to comprehend the scope of damage inflicted by the group, and years to recover from its effects, but Akaar did not have that kind of time. He needed to begin formulating a strategy for moving forward from this debacle, and he could not do so without the aid and support of people upon whom he could rely.

"My biggest concern, Captain, is one of trust. Can I trust you?"

"Absolutely." Picard's response was as firm as it was immediate. Despite the humbling nature of the dressing-down he just received, the man's demeanor had hardened. There was determination in his eyes. It was a look Akaar knew very well and had come to believe with the same conviction rarely offered to anyone outside his close circle. His instincts told him Picard was being truthful and that despite the legal and moral quagmire in which he had willingly entered, his actions were born not of malice but rather an imperative to serve the greater good.

Akaar could work with that, but it did not mean bygones were bygones.

"You'll have to convince me, Picard. Until that happens, and assuming I can provide cover and keep you from getting filleted by the media, you're on a very short leash and I'm the one holding the other end."

Giving the *Enterprise* captain a final admonition to continue with his mission and to heed Akaar's warning, the admiral severed the communication. Only after Picard's face vanished from the screen did Akaar allow himself to relax. Leaning back in his chair, he closed his eyes and rubbed the bridge of his nose.

Damn it.

This business was going to end careers, and not just those of the people snared in Section 31's web. Those in positions of elected or appointed authority, both in Starfleet and the Federation government, would be called upon to resign. Some might even face criminal charges of their own. Akaar wanted precious little to do with any of that, but duty required he be in the thick of it.

As if on cue, his intercom sounded, followed by the voice of his aide.

"*Admiral Akaar, I have the Federation attorney general on an encrypted frequency. She wishes to speak with you immediately.*"

Sighing, Akaar opened his eyes and shook his head.

And so it begins.

4

As was typical within the first hour or two after the conclusion of alpha shift, the *Enterprise*'s crew lounge was crowded. All seats at the bar were taken, and except for the odd empty chair all tables were occupied. Other crew members simply stood near the bar or in proximity to one of the tables, or near the room's slanted, forward-facing observation ports. The windows offered the best view of the distorted field of streaking stars as the starship traveled at warp. When she came here, T'Ryssa Chen always tried to grab a table next to the windows so she could enjoy the unfettered view. It allowed her to think; it was contemplation, if not outright meditation.

"Trys?"

With a start, she remembered that she was not alone at the table, and further realized that her friend Dina Elfiki was prompting her for the third time. Sitting up straighter in her chair, Chen cleared her throat.

"Sorry, Dina. I . . ." She frowned, embarrassed by the lapse. "I suppose I was distracted for a moment."

"Are you okay? Am I not being good company? Do you want to be left alone?" Born in Egypt, Elfiki spoke with a slight accent, and her wide, dark eyes conveyed obvious concern.

Chen waved away the suggestion. "No, of course not. I'm sorry. I don't know why I'm acting like this."

Yes, you do, she admonished herself. *You're acting the same as pretty much everyone on this ship.*

Sitting across from her at the table, Elfiki brushed aside a lock of her shoulder-length dark hair. "You're probably just tired.

I know I am." She took a sip of her drink. "I've spent the last thirty-six hours working with my team and engineering to go over the entire computer core and all our backup systems, again, along with every kiloquad of data storage, *again*. We did the same thing with the computer systems aboard every shuttlecraft and the captain's yacht, as well as every piece of equipment that has any form of onboard computer or data storage capability, down to the last tricorder and isolinear optical chip."

"Again?" asked Chen. "Didn't we just do all that?"

"Commander La Forge asked us to go back over all of it. So far as I can tell, we've removed every trace of the Uraei program from every system aboard the ship."

Chen sighed. "You could've asked me to help, you know."

"I know, but you were busy."

"Recalibrating the sensor array." Chen rolled her eyes. "Given a choice between that or throwing myself into a plasma conduit, I'd honestly have to give that some serious thought." It was meticulous, demanding, and necessary work and it bored her to tears. Perhaps not so mundane as scrutinizing millions of lines of computer code in search of malicious software, but at least that task could be accomplished at a console rather than crawling through Jefferies tubes from access panel to access panel. "That program was pretty sneaky. An extra set of eyes couldn't hurt."

She had read the official report from Starfleet Command describing the Uraei program's full operational capabilities, dating back to its initialization in the twenty-second century. Experts at Starfleet Research and Development had created a series of charts and other reports outlining the artificial intelligence entity's operational parameters and scope, including a full listing of its core computer code. Despite her own computer training at Starfleet Academy and subsequent experience aboard the *U.S.S. Rhea* and later the *Enterprise*, Chen did not consider herself an expert in the field. It was all she could do to keep up with other, smarter officers with natural or proven aptitude in such arenas, such as her friend. During her own service aboard the *Enterprise*, Elfiki's talents, initiative, and even instincts had made the difference during several close calls and saved lives along the way.

"We went over everything," said Elfiki. "Every line of code. Every stored file. We traced every data transfer back to its point of origin, including the memory banks salvaged from the *Enterprise*-D. You know, the ones stored in the Aldrin City Starfleet Archives Annex on Luna. We didn't find anything. Whatever Data, Lal, and the others did at Memory Alpha and Memory Prime, it left no survivors. There's not a trace of Uraei anywhere. You'd think that would let me sleep better, but forget it. I'm going to be seeing code in my sleep for the next month."

Chen let her friend talk, knowing she had to unload on someone. The task given to Elfiki by Captain Picard, to rid the ship's computer of any possible hint of the Uraei software, was a tall order given the program's inherent pervasiveness. The work performed by her, Commander La Forge, and their respective departments was guided by the detailed reports provided by Data in the wake of his successful defeat of Uraei. Aided by former Starfleet doctor Julian Bashir and Section 31 turncoat Sarina Douglas, Data and his android offspring, Lal, had created and deployed a cure for the disease that was the Uraei program.

"Well, we're all alone out here," said Chen. "We have to be doubly sure there's no trap waiting in a computer file somewhere. We have to be able to trust the equipment we're using and that's keeping us alive, after all."

Staring at her drink, Elfiki released a long sigh. "Yeah. All we've got is the ship, and each other."

Here we go, Chen thought. *Now we're getting to it.*

"We haven't really talked about this," Elfiki said after a moment. "I mean, we've all been busy, or maybe we've just been burying our heads in our work to avoid confronting it." She glanced around the room. "Look at this place. It's a tomb in here."

Her friend was right. The general mood was more subdued

than what usually characterized the lounge. People seemed to be doing their best to act as though everything was normal, but Chen could feel the pretense. There likely was no one aboard the *Enterprise* who by now had not heard or read the revelations about Section 31, the Uraei program, and their actions going back more than two centuries. That information was readily available thanks to the efforts of journalist Ozla Graniv. What her report did not offer were the answers to questions plaguing the *Enterprise* crew.

"It's not every day you find out your captain helped unseat a Federation president, who was later murdered by a shadow agency answerable to no one," said Elfiki. "That sort of thing tends to make a lasting impression."

"We all know he had nothing to do with Zife being assassinated," said Chen.

Elfiki nodded. "Of course. But until that report dropped, we all just assumed Zife resigned of his own volition and for his own reasons. You have to admit it's a bit troubling to hear the captain was involved with unseating him. Sure, if you look at it from the larger perspective, it makes sense. I certainly wouldn't have wanted to make a decision like that, and if I was asked to help I don't know that I could go through with it. I'd like to think I'd make the right choice, for the right reasons." She shrugged. "Sorry, Trys. I'm not doing very well with this."

"It's okay."

The revelations about Picard's involvement in Min Zife's removal had coursed at warp speed through the ship. There was the expected initial shock and disbelief, followed by anger and a sense of supreme betrayal, and uncertainty as to what the future held. Chen had heard more than a few hushed conversations in crew common areas, laced with doubt that the man to whom they looked for leadership and guidance might not be worthy of that respect. On the other hand, that worry appeared offset by a larger portion of the ship's complement who continued to voice support for their captain, reminding newer crew members of Picard's numerous accomplishments and decades of faithful service. She had no idea if the captain was aware of these different perspectives, or if he would be comforted by the knowledge that there were those among the crew trying to put the entire sordid matter into some kind of perspective.

To his credit, Picard had made himself available to anyone who wished to discuss the matter in private. During Chen's own conversation with him, he reiterated that he was not proud of his role in the affair, but that the choices made at that time seemed the least objectionable of several bad options. Any other course would likely have inflamed tensions with the Klingon Empire, at a time when the Federation could scarcely afford such controversy. There was no legal justification for removing the president without due process, and certainly no moral reasoning to excuse what happened after that.

"You should've seen him, Dina," said Chen as she described the meeting. "He was ashamed. It's as vulnerable as I've ever seen him. He said he's spent every day since then trying to live with the idea that it was necessary if distasteful, and removing Zife from office saved countless lives, and living every day working to atone for what he did."

"Do you think he ever told anyone?" asked Elfiki. "I mean, I know he's a private person, but he has close trusted friends like anyone else. You think he told Doctor Crusher, or Admiral Riker? Someone?"

Chen shook her head. "He says he didn't. That's not really the sort of thing you want to share." According to the captain, until Graniv's report went public, the only people who knew the truth about what happened were those who participated, and then only with respect to their role. Of course, now that Section 31's involvement was known, it was obvious to her that the circle of conspirators was larger than Picard realized at the time.

"Let's face it," said Chen. "As bad as what happened to Zife might be, the more I think about everything Section Thirty-One's supposedly done, it's hard not to feel sorry for the guy."

"You've got a point," replied Elfiki. "The lives we all thought we were living, controlled to one extent or another by a computer program." Before Chen could respond, she held up a hand. "I know. Simplistic, but think about it. How much of what we've been doing—what we've been doing for *centuries*—is because we were all nothing more than puppets carrying out that thing's wishes?"

"I don't buy it." Chen punctuated her reply by downing half her drink. While there could be no denying Uraei's presence and impacts on so many aspects of life for all Federation citizens, she refused to believe it was all encompassing and all controlling.

She acknowledged the artificial intelligence operated using a sophisticated system of predictive algorithms based on statistics and probability and pattern recognition. It even manipulated situations and circumstances based on those predictions in order to reach desired goals. Despite all of that, Chen could not believe every accomplishment made and every success enjoyed for more than two hundred years was a predetermined outcome. Uraei's actions did not render irrelevant the thoughts, feelings, ethics, and morality of countless flesh-and-blood living beings. To accept otherwise was to reject everything any Federation citizen might believe or represent.

Leaning across the table, she said, "We make our own choices and take action based on what we believe is the correct course, using logic and reason but also emotion and even a moral code of some sort." Chen tapped her chest. "It comes from *here*, Dina. I have to believe that, or else . . . what the hell are we *doing* out here?"

After a moment, Elfiki nodded. "Yeah, and here's another thing. I can even believe the people who created what eventually became Uraei did so with the best of intentions, but we all know what can happen with technology. It grew too large and too powerful, to the point where its creators were unable to keep up with what they'd made."

"And now that it's destroyed, where does that leave us?" asked Chen. "It's only been three weeks since the news broke. It'll be months if not years before the full truth of what Uraei did is fully understood, and then where will we be?"

Elfiki played with her glass, spinning it in a circle on the table. "The same place we've always been, I guess. Uraei didn't make any of us join Starfleet, Trys. Now that it's gone, it's up to all of us to prove *we* determine the course of our lives, rather than some machine."

Before Chen could respond, the whistle of the ship's intercom filled the lounge, followed by the voice of the *Enterprise*'s first officer, Commander Worf.

"*Senior bridge officers, report to your stations. Captain Picard, please report to the bridge.*"

"They're playing my song," said Elfiki, pushing her glass toward the table's center before rising from her chair. "Thanks for letting me vent, Trys. I appreciate it."

Chen smiled. "Back at you." She gestured toward the ceiling. "When you get up there, be sure to let me know if it's anything interesting. You know, something juicy for which you need your friendly neighborhood contact specialist."

"Will do," replied Elfiki. As she headed for the exit, she cast a wry grin over her shoulder. "But, come on. Since when does anything interesting happen on *this* ship?"

5

Moments like these reminded Jean-Luc Picard why he eschewed promotion or retirement in favor of starship command. The anticipation at possibly being the first to lay eyes on some newly discovered world, intelligent being, or artifact such as the one the *Enterprise* now approached was always a palpable sensation. This was why he had joined Starfleet. The opportunity to follow in the footsteps of explorers he admired—Shackleton, Baré, Archer, and Georgiou to name just a few—as well as contribute to the rich history they helped create and preserve was all he ever wanted. Even now, after decades of such moments and no matter how many times he found himself in such a situation, that initial feeling was always the same. His heart beat just a little faster, his senses came alive, and even his breathing seemed to quicken, if only the slightest bit.

Not that anyone around him would notice such things. Discipline must be maintained, of course.

"At our present speed, we'll intercept the vessel in three minutes," said Lieutenant Joanna Faur, the *Enterprise*'s senior flight control officer. Shifting in her seat so that she could look over her left shoulder to where Picard sat in his command chair, she added, "Target shows no aspect change, sir."

"Thank you, Conn. Maintain course and speed." Picard studied the object now highlighted on the main viewscreen. Even with the computer's imaging software interpreting data routed from the *Enterprise*'s suite of sensors, the craft remained stubbornly cloaked in shadow. It was massive, all but filling the screen, and that was with magnification reduced to keep the entire vessel visible. Rather than being some form of cylinder or other simple, identifiable shape, the ship's large aft section was rounded, and nestled within it was a large orb-like section. As the hull extended forward it separated into three spires, one to either side of the orb and one below, which gave the entire vessel a vaguely claw-like appearance. The vessel's configuration resembled a living creature more than an artificial construct. In some ways it reminded Picard of Cardassian space station design, with their long curved struts serving as docking points for ships too large to make use of ports set into the station's central hull. Each of this craft's spires easily dwarfed the *Enterprise*. Though the dark material covering the ship's main hull and spires appeared smooth, he could see protuberances scattered all across its various surfaces.

"Why can't we see more of it?"

Occupying one of the science stations along the bridge's starboard bulkhead, Dina Elfiki replied, "The material comprising the ship's outer hull is muddying our sensors, sir. We're not blocked, but it's like our scans are being 'absorbed,' for lack of a better word. The readings are clearing as we get closer, though, so we should have a complete picture in a minute or so." A moment later, she added, "There's something else, sir. The closer we get, the more our long-range sensors are becoming clouded. It's as if the whole thing is acting like a scattering field."

Standing behind Picard at the ship's tactical station, Lieutenant Aneta Šmrhová said, "She's right, sir. Long-range sensors are being affected by this thing. If we keep closing the distance, they might become totally useless."

"Keep an eye on that," said Picard, his attention riveted on the screen as he marveled at the vessel's apparent size. "Just how big is it?"

Elfiki said, "The main hull section measures over six thousand meters across at its widest point. Each of the connecting spires varies in diameter between one and three hundred meters."

In a word, the craft was enormous, dwarfing even the mammoth Spacedock facility orbiting Earth. Even the *Poklori gil dara*, the giant weapon ship created by the Raqilan people and encountered months earlier by the *Enterprise*, was outsized by this vessel.

"What about those structures peppering its surface?" asked Commander Worf from where he sat to Picard's right. "Are they weapons? Have our sensors detected any threats?"

Glinn Ravel Dygan, the bridge's operations officer and the *Enterprise*'s exchange officer from the Cardassian Union, said, "There are no such indications as of yet, Commander."

"And still no life signs?" asked Picard. Elfiki's initial report at the time of the ship's detection offered no conclusions on that front.

"Not yet, Captain," replied the Cardassian. "Sensors are still encountering interference, but the scans we've been able to make show no biological readings, and no other signs of activity we might attribute to living beings."

Šmrhová asked, "Captain, should we go to yellow alert? At least until we can confirm there's no danger?" It was obvious that the security chief remained concerned about the effect of the massive ship's proximity on the *Enterprise* sensors.

"Make it so, but shields only. No need to take an aggressive stance just yet."

Picard knew Šmrhová, to say nothing of Worf, would prefer to bring the ship's weapons online, but also understood the need not to appear provocative without just cause. In the hours since scans first detected the unidentified ship's presence, the craft had offered no sign that it posed a threat. Attempts at communication went unheeded, and Glinn Dygan could not even confirm their hails were being received. For all intents and purposes, the vessel appeared to be a lifeless hulk, adrift in space.

He asked, "What about power readings?"

"Scans are detecting minor fluctuations, sir," replied Elfiki. "Whatever's generating power over there is doing so at a very low output level. Still no detectable means of propulsion, either. So far as I can tell, the thing's just drifting, and has been for a while."

"How long?" asked Worf.

The science officer said, "That much I don't know, sir. At least, not yet. However, sensors are showing massive damage across the outer hull's forward edge and flanks. If I didn't know any better, I'd say the ship encountered some kind of ion storm, though I'm also picking up indications of meteor or asteroid strikes, and most of it is centuries old."

"It appears we've found ourselves another mystery." Glancing to Worf, Picard could not resist adding, "And we know how well those always go."

For his part, the Klingon only grunted, almost under his breath.

In truth, Picard welcomed the energy now permeating the bridge. It was a welcome change from the status quo that had characterized daily duty shifts during the past weeks. While the *Enterprise* continued its exploration of the Odyssean Pass, there had been little to alter the routine or command attention in the weeks since the Section 31 revelations and the truth of his own actions had become public.

This, he decided, was exactly what he and his crew needed. An intriguing riddle to study and solve. What secrets did this ship hold? What civilization did it represent? Had its creators abandoned it, or had it never even possessed a crew? Where were those people, and which of the star systems still waiting to be discovered and explored did they call home? Might the vessel's point of origin be determined, providing the *Enterprise* yet another opportunity to seek out a previously unknown race? Picard felt his pulse quicken at the very thought.

We're explorers again.

"Interception in less than one minute, Captain," reported Faur.

Elfiki added, "Sensor readings are continuing to clear, sir. We're now able to penetrate the ship's hull, in some areas. It definitely possesses a form of faster-than-light propulsion, though it and the vessel's main power generation facilities are offline. Large portions of what I'm guessing is the primary section of the ship are heavily shielded, and our scans still aren't having any luck with those."

"What about those projections all along the hull?" asked Worf.

"They're an array of solar energy collectors, sir. I'm able to trace the routes of energy conduits from the collectors through what looks to be a sophisticated distribution network."

Rising from the command chair, Picard moved past the conn and ops stations until he stood just in front of Faur and Dygan. He crossed his arms, studying the image of the ship displayed on the viewscreen. He now could see that continuous updates from the *Enterprise*'s sensors were helping to provide a more complete picture of the apparent derelict.

"Are the collectors active?" asked Picard.

"Most of them, sir. Some are inert, either due to damage or some other issue I can't yet identify. So far as I can tell, they're the only thing generating any kind of power over there, though out here with no star systems in easy reach, they're not collecting much. Now that we're closer, I can also detect very low-level energy readings—likely automated monitoring and maintenance systems." When she paused, Picard turned to see her shaking her head before continuing, "It seems like an awful lot of work going on to support nothing, or no one."

Worf asked, "You still detect no life signs?"

"No, Commander," replied Elfiki. "Absolutely no bio-readings. The power being generated by the solar collectors is being channeled either to an immense battery storage farm, or what I can only guess is the ship's central computer system. Like everything else with this ship, it's huge. I've seen space stations that are smaller than the processing core. Even if we could understand whatever language or languages the builders use, the whole thing's shielded and I can't access it."

None of this made sense to Picard. "Why would someone send a giant computer core into space and leave it to drift unprotected, let alone without a crew? What's its purpose? Is it possible this is someone's equivalent to our Memory Alpha?" Just the mention of the Federation information repository made him think about the scandal surrounding it, Memory Prime, and all the secrets they once contained and that Ozla Graniv had released.

"Perhaps it has simply gone astray," offered Glinn Dygan from the ops station. "An unplanned circumstance that befell the vessel's creators."

"Makes as much sense as anything else," said Elfiki. "Whatever this thing is, it represents an information storehouse of unimaginable value, at least to someone."

Picard heard the excitement in his science officer's voice, doubtless buoyed by the chance she saw to delve into whatever it was the alien vessel was harboring and what it represented. He could almost see Geordi La Forge watching the proceedings from engineering, already reviewing sensor data as he prepared his own report about the vessel's construction, mode of propulsion, weapons, and whatever else it contained. His chief engineer would want to explore this new find, cataloging every millimeter and collecting whatever new insight he could glean from its technology.

"Well, this would seem to demand our investigation, wouldn't you say, Number One?" Turning from the viewscreen, Picard saw the look of grudging acceptance on his first officer's face and almost smiled before catching himself. "After all, we may be able to determine its owners and return it, or at least let them know where to find it."

As expected, the Klingon maintained his bearing. "Until we learn more, sir, I suggest the initial survey be limited to a minimal away team that we can retrieve quickly. Myself, Lieutenants Elfiki and Chen." His pause was brief yet still noticeable before adding, "And Lieutenant Commander Taurik, sir."

It was natural that Worf might worry about his suggestion, given the rocky course Picard's relationship with the assistant chief engineer had been forced to navigate weeks earlier. Most of that was Picard's own fault, far more than the position into which Taurik had been placed by Admiral Akaar during the *Enterprise*'s recent mission to the planet Sralanya and the revelation that humanity had somehow become regrettably entwined with affairs of that world's indigenous civilization, the Eizand. It was a secret tucked into the shadows of history for more than three centuries, dating back to first contact on Earth between humans and Vulcans in the mid-twenty-first century, and Picard and his crew had been the unlikely instruments of that secret's terrible extrication into the light.

Taurik, having come across knowledge about future events during the *Enterprise*'s encounter with the temporally displaced Raqilan weapon ship *Poklori gil dara*, was in a unique position to observe and report back to Akaar anything Picard and his crew might encounter going forward. The significance of anything else they might find out here remained to be seen, but the way Akaar had placed Taurik in the position of being a possible informant had infuriated Picard, to the point where he had for a time relieved the Vulcan engineer of his duties and confined him to quarters. In hindsight, that was a mistake. Picard had apologized to Taurik and pledged that they would work together to navigate whatever obstacles they might discover out here, whether or not such encounters were preordained by future history.

However, the simple truth was that whatever knowledge Taurik possessed, its possible relevance to everything they encountered from this point forward could not be denied. Having him on the away team made perfect sense in every respect, and Worf understood that without having to bring it up at every opportunity.

Picard ordered, "Assemble your team and continue your review of the incoming sensor data, and be ready to transport to the derelict in one hour."

"Despite the difficulties with our sensors," said Šmrhová, "transporters shouldn't be a problem. We'll have to be well inside their operating radius, but otherwise I think we'll be fine."

Elfiki added, "And with no life support over there, we'll have to use EV suits."

Growling almost but not quite under his breath, Worf said nothing else and Picard suppressed a smile. Everyone aboard knew of the Klingon's professed disdain for any situation that called for him to don an environmental suit. That contempt only heightened if a lack of gravity was a factor.

"Sorry, Number One." This time, Picard allowed himself a small grin. "However, this *was* your idea."

His expression unreadable, Worf replied, "Noted for future reference, sir."

Satisfied with himself, Picard directed Lieutenant Faur to take the conn before moving toward his ready room. Crossing the bridge, he noted his first officer had fallen into step just behind him, rather than proceeding to the turbolift to begin his away team preparations.

"Something else, Number One?"

His voice low, Worf said, "A moment of your time, sir."

Entering the ready room with the Klingon behind him, Picard proceeded toward his desk. He settled into his chair, gesturing toward the pair of seats positioned before him.

"Mister Worf?" he prompted when a moment passed and his executive officer said nothing. "Is something troubling you?" Then, before the commander could reply, he added in a somewhat lighter tone, "This isn't about the EV suits, is it?"

"No, sir." Despite the gruff response, it was obvious even the Klingon was aware of the humor generated by his dislike for the protective garments. "I wish to discuss another matter—one I have not seen fit to broach before now."

Sensing where this might be heading, Picard said, "My situation with Admiral Akaar, and my involvement with President Zife's resignation." He sighed. "I've been meaning to talk with you about all of this, but to be honest, I was . . . worried what course such a conversation might take. Given what Zife did and how it so grievously affected the Klingon Empire, I simply did not know what to say to you."

Worf's expression was unreadable. "At the time, we all willingly believed he chose to resign, for those very reasons. Given his character, I should have suspected there was something more to his decision. Do you regret your part in that action?"

"I regret that it came to that," replied Picard. "The usurping of law is not something I take lightly, Mister Worf. However, balanced against the potential loss of life on both sides of a renewed conflict between the Klingons and the Federation, I felt it was the best of several dreadful options. I regret that I did not foresee other forces dispensing their own brand of justice. In hindsight, it seems so obvious."

Casting his gaze to his desk, Picard ran his hand along its smooth, gleaming surface. "After all we've been through, both our peoples, to have the peace we worked so hard to create threatened by the actions of a few corrupted individuals is appalling. I regret that I descended to their level and employed their tactics to achieve a result I knew—somewhere, deep within my soul—was at best a temporary solution. And I regret that our decision now threatens the very peace I swore an oath to protect. I shudder to think what your people must now be thinking about all of this. I even considered reaching out to Martok directly so that we might discuss it."

Despite the past turmoil that characterized their previous encounters, Picard respected the chancellor of the Klingon High Council, and that admiration was only deepened by the fact that the chancellor viewed Worf as a member of his own family. To Picard, contacting Martok seemed the honorable course, but doing so would likely cause further turmoil within the halls of the Federation Council and Starfleet Command, two entities who currently wanted Picard's head on a platter.

Worf drew himself to his full height. "If President Zife had been our chancellor and acted to so egregiously dishonor the empire, he would have been discommended, and then killed on the floor of the High Council chamber."

Picard almost chuckled at that, but restrained himself. "So, you're saying—"

"In removing President Zife, you righted a wrong in the eyes of the Empire. I have every confidence Chancellor Martok will view your action as justified."

"Well, then," replied Picard. "If only the Federation Council and Starfleet Command could be persuaded to see things as Martok does."

"I have every confidence he will do whatever he can to see that comes to pass."

Now Picard smiled. "I wish I could see Akaar's face when that happens."

6

—◆—

Though the last rays of sunlight were fading as darkness moved in to cloak the city, Paris only now was coming alive. Standing at the curved, floor-to-ceiling window that formed one wall of her spacious third-floor office within the Palais de la Concorde, Phillipa Louvois took in the sight of the city's streets and buildings, framed by strings and swirls of multicolored lights. Her gaze followed a few of the lighted paths until it fell upon the Avenue des Champs-Élysées. With one of her windows slightly ajar, she could hear the sounds of music from somewhere nearby, perhaps the Tuileries Garden. Uncounted people wandered the streets, walking paths, and footbridges connecting the different neighborhoods and parks.

Some festival, Louvois reminded herself. *Starting tonight, I think. What festival? Some sort of arts and music thing. Hell, what day is it?*

A heavy sigh escaped her lips. Louvois was a devotee of various performing arts and had whiled away many a Sunday afternoon wandering the numerous galleries in Paris. She should know what was happening just a short distance from her office, but all of that now seemed so far away. For the past several weeks, either here in her office or for those few hours each night she managed to find her way to her apartment, work defined her existence.

It's not every day you get to prosecute dozens of people for criminal conspiracy.

The errant, cynical thought made Louvois cast her eyes back toward her desk, which seemed to mock her as it played host to a haphazard collection of padds, isolinear optical chips, her computer terminal, and even several reports printed on actual paper. The latter was because she had grown weary of staring at illuminated display screens for hours on end, be it her terminal, one of the padds, or the large viewscreen occupying the wall to the right of her desk. The screen was active and divided into four equal sections, each of which featured a different news feed. As was often the case, she left the sound muted, with the screen programmed to alert her if something requiring her attention was broadcast. It was the only way to maintain her sanity, given the device's penchant for alerting her about "breaking news" on what she guessed was an average of every four or five seconds.

Drawing a deep breath, Louvois released it over a span of several seconds, closing her eyes and attempting to find within her some reserve of energy that so far had eluded her. She was tired; it was that simple. A decent night's sleep, rather than whatever few fitful hours she managed to snatch after dragging herself home at the end of a long, draining day, was in order. A vacation would be better, but Louvois knew that would not be happening any time soon.

With resignation, she returned her attention to the window and for the first time caught her reflection in the tempered glass. The lines and bags around her blue eyes were more pronounced than she remembered them. Her red hair, which she had allowed to grow out to the point she now needed to keep it in a functional bun during workdays, was only now starting to offer hints of gray at the temples. At sixty-two years of age, she was getting a little old for these marathon sessions of grinding days. In her youth, as a young Starfleet officer and lawyer working in the Judge Advocate General's office on Starbase 11, long hours were nothing. Later, following a temporary transition to civilian law practice before returning to Starfleet, she advanced to her own JAG billet, where that stamina continued to serve her. The hectic pace slowed only after she opted for retirement from Starfleet, but that comparably relaxed lifestyle once again proved temporary before she felt herself drawn back to the world of Federation politics and legal affairs. Ten years of working for the attorney general, beginning in a small, claustrophobic office located elsewhere on the same floor that housed her current surroundings, Louvois once more turned that relentless drive for excellence toward making a difference in the only way she had ever known: by championing the rule of law. She had, for all intents and purposes, reached the pinnacle of her chosen profession. There were few places left to go from here, and she was content with that reality.

But, that vacation still sounds pretty damned good.

"Madam Attorney General?"

The voice, breaking as it did through the otherwise utter quiet enveloping the office, almost made Louvois jump. She was at least able to catch the audible gasp before it could further embarrass her before turning from the window. Standing at the entrance to her office was her personal aide, Jason Anderson. Despite the hour, the young human male was still dressed in an impeccable gray suit tailored to exacting precision for his tall, lean physique. Close-cropped blond hair remained neat and in place, and neither could Louvois detect even the hint of beard stubble, even though she knew his workday had started even earlier than her own.

How the hell does he manage that?

"Jason, I thought I told you to go home?" Stepping away from the window, Louvois moved toward her desk. "Is anyone else still out there?" After weeks of eighteen-hour days with no end in sight, she had finally relented earlier on this Friday afternoon, ordering her entire staff to vacate the premises and not return until Monday.

Anderson, always composed and polite, replied, "Everyone else is gone for the evening."

"And why didn't you go with them?"

"I leave when you leave, Madam Attorney General."

The man was unflappable. After graduating two years earlier from the Faculty of Law, Oxford, Anderson eschewed offers from a number of prestigious law firms on Earth as well as other Federation member worlds, applying instead for a position within the Office of the Federation Attorney General. Louvois was in the midst of settling into that very role when one of her assistants pointed out the man's application, which had impressed her enough to offer Anderson the position of serving as her personal aide. For someone just out of law school, the opportunity was on par with clerking for a justice on the Federation Judiciary Council. He was also one of the most dependable, loyal assistants with whom Louvois had ever worked. If he stayed the course, by the time Louvois left her current billet and her successor took over, Anderson would have secured a rather large, impressive feather in his lawyer's cap.

"Well, if you're going to insist on disobeying my orders, the least you could do is call me by my actual name when it's just the two of us in the office."

Without batting an eye, Anderson said, "Whatever you say, Madam Attorney General."

It was a game they had played on more occasions than Louvois bothered to count, and he was as steadfast in his professionalism as he was unwavering in his commitment to the job. As her aide, Anderson by far spent the most time with her on a daily basis. He was her sounding board when it came to discussing any and all legal matters, and a trusted confidant with respect to sensitive issues not unlike the one that had consumed Louvois and her staff these past several weeks. In most if not all respects, Anderson was her right hand. He would make an outstanding jurist in his own right, one day in the not so distant future when he was out from under the shadow of this office.

Louvois held up her hands in mock surrender. "Fine. You win. I'm leaving." She began sorting through some of the work on her desk, deciding what she would take with her for the weekend.

"I honestly wish you could," said Anderson, "but Admiral Akaar is requesting to speak with you. In person."

Halting her rearranging of the detritus littering her desk, Louvois considered the implications of such a call. The admiral would be aware of the time difference between San Francisco and Paris, and he was not in the habit of calling on anyone outside normal working hours unless the situation demanded no other course of action. She also knew that if anyone else on the planet would empathize with the pressure cooker in which she currently worked—if for no other reason than he was facing the same tests himself—it was Leonard James Akaar.

"In person? All right, authorize his transport, and then get out of here while you still have a chance."

She thought she may have heard Anderson chuckling as he exited the office. A few moments later—long enough for her aide to transmit the authorization code allowing the use of a transporter into the palais—the familiar hum of a transporter beam echoed within her office. On one of the two pads tucked into a niche in her office's far corner, a column of energy appeared, and Louvois watched it solidify into the form of Admiral Akaar. Though he was in excess of one hundred twenty years of age as measured on Earth, the Capellan still presented an imposing figure. His broad chest almost strained his formfitting Starfleet uniform, while his thick mane of gray hair draped across his shoulders. By the standards of his native species, Akaar was on the far side of middle age, though Louvois was certain he could best opponents who were decades younger.

"Admiral," she said as he finished materializing.

Akaar bowed his head in greeting. "Madam Attorney General. Thank you for seeing me on such short notice."

"The work day's over," said Louvois, stepping around her desk and extending her hand toward him. "Call me Phillipa."

Akaar stepped off the recessed transporter pad and took her proffered hand, his stern features warming as he did so. "Only if you call me Leonard."

"Deal." Louvois gestured toward the small bar in her office's far corner, set into the wall near a sofa, coffee table, and a pair of overstuffed chairs. "Care for a drink?"

"Just one?"

"Well, we'll start with one and see where fate takes us."

Accepting her offer of brandy, Akaar led the way to the sitting area, waiting until she decided on one of the recliners before settling himself onto the sofa.

"So," said Louvois after taking a sip of her brandy. "What's the emergency that brings you to Paris on a Friday evening?"

Akaar smiled. "It's still Friday morning at my office."

"And you're drinking already?"

"It promises to be one of those days."

Raising her glass, Louvois offered a humorless smile. "So I've read. You've certainly got your hands full."

"Admiral Ross arrived on Earth this morning." Akaar stared at the brandy glass he rested atop his right knee. "He was found on Caldos II. Interestingly enough, he's not the first excommunicated Starfleet officer to hide out on Caldos II."

"There are others?" asked Louvois.

"Oh, the stories I could tell. Another time, perhaps." He paused, taking a healthy swallow of his drink before adding, "To be honest, given what we know of Thirty-One's methods, I was surprised to learn Ross was still alive, with his apparent level of access and knowledge about the group's inner workings. The only thing that makes sense to me is that this computer program running the whole show must have concluded he might still be useful one day, and he's been smart enough to keep his mouth shut."

Finishing her drink, Louvois rose from her chair and crossed to the bar. She poured herself another glass of the brandy before bringing the bottle with her and placing it on the table.

"Ross can tell us all about it." She dropped back into the chair, mindful not to spill her drink. "I can't wait to have that conversation."

Akaar replied, "As we speak, he's being prepared for questioning by the Starfleet judge advocate general. I wanted to extend the same courtesy you've been given with Admirals Jellico, Naka- mura, and Nechayev, and observe this interview, as well. I know we've already discussed this and your office is still preparing to question all Starfleet personnel we've taken into custody, and I want our process to be as transparent as possible."

Louvois nodded. "I appreciate that, Leonard." The Federation Council had determined that the Office of the Federation Attor- ney General would oversee the criminal prosecution of Section 31 operatives, including all Starfleet officers. Given the severity of the alleged crimes and their potential impact upon the entire Federation, its allies, and even its enemies, Louvois and her staff were best suited to leading all criminal proceedings against the ac- cused, civilian and Starfleet alike. Every suspect would face a pub- lic trial, and she was adamant that everything be pursued by the book, with nothing left to chance or technicality. There simply was no other option; not with something on this scale. Nothing that might be viewed as an attempt at obfuscation or a cover-up could be tolerated, from anyone and for any reason.

For his part, Akaar had been forthcoming and eager to co- operate from their first conversation, held the very night Ozla Graniv's revelations were coming to light. Like her, he wanted a thorough, open investigation that could not be accused of bias or malice, or any attempt to cover up what Graniv had exposed.

"The Federation Security Agency and other law enforcement agencies throughout the Alpha and Beta Quadrants are still rounding up people, but we've already got a lengthy and impres- sive list of people to interview," she said before taking a sip of her fresh drink. "Some actual, honest-to-goodness heroes. Maybe even a legend or two. The list of accomplishments and acts of courage in the name of protecting Federation and Starfleet values is staggering, but none of it can shield them from what's coming." She made no effort to hide her disdain. "What a damned waste."

Akaar rested his left arm along the top of the sofa's backrest.

"Not everyone will have been involved with Thirty-One to the same degree, but we won't know that until the investigations are complete." The admiral shook his head. "Doesn't mean anyone will escape unscathed, either."

"A lot of them are still out there." Louvois paused, staring at the brandy she swirled in her glass. "How many have false identities or some other means of avoiding us? Alynna Nechayev had four different safe houses just on Earth. Hell, there may be other operatives who weren't even listed but are still out there." She shook her head. "Doesn't matter. We'll find every last one of them. No one will escape." Pausing just before taking another sip of her drink, she eyed Akaar. "No one."

His expression clouding, as though he had been expecting this turn in the conversation, Akaar stared at her. "Picard."

"Picard." With one long swallow she drained her glass before placing it on the table between them. "You need to order him back to Earth."

"He's eight weeks away, Phillipa."

"Then he should get started now."

Frowning at the remark, Akaar held up a hand. "Believe me, I understand the need for Picard to answer for what he did, but he wasn't a Thirty-One operative. He had no knowledge of what they did to Zife and the others."

"We'll know that for sure once all this is over."

Akaar set his unfinished drink on the table before shifting his seat on the sofa so that he now faced her directly. "You can't for a moment think he was involved with those people. Working behind the scenes, influencing Federation and Starfleet policy while being responsible to no one but those other thugs and criminals? We're talking about *Jean-Luc Picard*. You know better than that. How much has he sacrificed—how much has he *lost*—upholding Federation values while others paid lip service or actively worked to undermine them? This is the man who stood up to Starfleet Command and came within a hairsbreadth of sacrificing his career over the Ba'ku affair. And let's not even talk about what he went through with the Borg."

"Believe me," said Louvois, "I understand and appreciate all of that."

The very idea that Picard could be a willing participant in something like Section 31 was laughable. Of this, Louvois was certain, but she could not allow personal feelings to obstruct the duty with which she was now charged. She also knew that Akaar would likewise not permit himself to be so swayed, but that did not mean that he—or she—was immune to such feelings.

"Tell me you weren't as shocked as I was when you saw his name listed with the others," she said. "I've known that man for more than thirty years and even before I met him, his reputation was already formidable."

Leaning closer to her so that his elbows rested on his knees, Akaar said, "Then you know he's a man of principle."

"And yet you still chewed him out when you learned of his involvement with Zife's ousting," Louvois countered.

"Of course I did." The response was curt, with Akaar biting on every word. "He was implicated in helping to remove at gunpoint the duly elected Federation president. Duty required I address that, just as it requires you and I both to haul him onto the carpet and do everything in our power to get to the truth of what happened, and make sure that justice is done. But, if I truly believed Picard was someone who couldn't be trusted, who couldn't be counted on when we need him most, I'd have had his first officer relieve him on the spot, take command, and bring the *Enterprise* home."

Akaar leveled an accusatory finger at her. "I know about your relationship with Picard, and how you were the one who prosecuted him during his court-martial for the loss of the *Stargazer*. I also know that despite this, you and he became friends. You respect and trust each other, even when duty's placed you on opposite sides. If you'd had any doubts about him—*real doubts*—you'd have already made your demand to bring him back, rather than wait three weeks."

He's right. Damn him, but he's right.

"For a man like Picard to arrive at the decision to remove Min Zife from his office," Akaar continued, "you have to know what that did to him. How he wrestled with it. How it still haunts him." He leaned back. "And the truth is that while we can't condone the methods, we all know he and the others did the right thing, for all our sakes."

"It doesn't matter what we think, Leonard," snapped Louvois. She pushed herself from her chair and started pacing the length of her office, stopping at her desk before pivoting and crossing back toward the door. "My sworn duty is to uphold Federation laws, just as yours is to support and defend against all who challenge them and what they represent: *all* enemies, external *and internal*. The last thing we need right now is to act like we learned nothing from the Leyton affair."

James Leyton.

The name rattled around in her head as she continued to pace. Leyton, a former vice admiral who had served as the Chief of Starfleet Operations in the months prior to the Dominion War. During that period of uncertainty, as the Federation and indeed the Alpha Quadrant remained largely ignorant of the true threat posed by the Dominion, he had attempted to push Starfleet toward taking more proactive measures and prepare for the war he was certain was coming. While he had his supporters, both within Starfleet and the Federation government, Leyton encountered ongoing resistance to his ideas from President Jaresh-Inyo.

Driven by what he believed to be the good of the Federation, Leyton began manipulating Starfleet personnel and resources as he prepared to defend Federation security against the looming Dominion threat. As part of his plan, he directed the sabotage of Earth's global power distribution network, directing a group of elite Starfleet Academy cadets to carry out his plan. The resulting fear and the implication that the attack was the work of the Dominion, specifically a group of Changelings who had infiltrated positions of power on Earth, gave Leyton the leverage he needed to convince Jaresh-Inyo to declare planet-wide martial law. Having also orchestrated a sophisticated ruse to push a story that the Dominion was sending cloaked ships from the Gamma Quadrant as a prelude to full-scale invasion, Leyton was preparing to stage a coup to remove Jaresh-Inyo from power and assume control as a military dictator for however long it took to defeat the Dominion threat.

And where was Leyton? Louvois had no idea as to the disgraced admiral's current whereabouts. Following the completion of his five-year term of incarceration at the Federation Penal Settlement in New Zealand, Leyton seemingly faded into obscurity, eschewing any requests for interviews by journalists, historians, or would-be biographers. Given the circumstances of his fall from grace, Louvois was surprised to see his name conspicuously absent from those implicated by the Section 31 affair. Had he somehow become involved in that madness? She made a mental note to task one of her assistants to track down the elusive James Leyton.

"The threat Leyton and others feared was real," said Akaar, "but his actions were abhorrent, undertaken for the wrong reasons. You can't compare him to Picard." When Louvois started to protest, he added, "All I'm saying is that not everyone wrapped up in this shares the same level of guilt. In our haste to see that justice is done, we have to make sure that it's meted out in just portions."

Nodding, Louvois halted her current sojourn across her office. "You're absolutely right, but we can't make those determinations without first doing the legwork. Our search for the truth must be unrelenting. We have to use every legal means at our disposal, shine all available light into every corner, so that no one can hide. It all has to come out. Every last distasteful shred of truth has to be laid bare for all to see. Otherwise, we'll never be free of doubt or worry that something like this could ever happen again."

She turned to face Akaar. "The Federation Council has charged me with making sure all of that happens, but I can't do it without your help. Can I count on you, Leonard? Can I trust you to be objective? To carry out what I know is a dreadful yet necessary task as we put aside our personal feelings and loyalties, no matter the cost?"

The admiral stood, stepping around the coffee table until he was close enough to extend his hand to Louvois.

"You can absolutely count on me, Phillipa. Let's do this."

7

T'Ryssa Chen was smiling even before the transporter beam released her.

Aside from the illumination provided by the work lights built into her environmental suit and those of her companions, the room in which they materialized was cloaked in darkness. Chen noted assorted groups or clusters of soft, multicolored lights peeking out from the shadows, highlighting workstations or some other equipment. She turned, allowing her suit lights to sweep across the room around her. In addition to highlighting the other members of the away team, she saw rows of consoles lining the walls. What did they do? What onboard systems did they oversee? Overhead, a large dark sphere descended from the center of a ceiling festooned with what might be conduits and even ventilation ducts. The sphere was pockmarked with more than a dozen holes suggesting light emitters.

You've been here ten seconds, and already you're on overload.

"I can see you, you know," said Dina Elfiki, her voice subdued as it came through the communication system built into the helmet of Chen's environmental suit. *"Your helmet lights are reflecting off your teeth."*

"Can I help it if I get excited about these things?" She could feel her smile widening as she oriented herself within the space into which she had materialized, accompanying Elfiki along with Worf, Lieutenant Commander Taurik, and Lieutenant Rennan Konya as the first away team to visit the alien derelict.

At this point during her tenure as the *Enterprise*'s contact specialist, Chen had participated in several away missions and initial meetings with representatives of newly discovered civilizations. The anticipation she experienced at the start of such outings never failed to send a small thrill coursing through her. This was why she had joined Starfleet, after all, and her tour of duty with the *Enterprise* saw to it that such opportunities were frequent. As a cadet attending Starfleet Academy, she had devoured books and official logs detailing the missions of ships like the *Enterprise* and its predecessors along with various others that had contributed to the ongoing exploration of the cosmos. Her posting to such a vessel and being a part of the wonder that was "seeing what was out here" would always be exhilarating.

"Away team to Enterprise,*"* said Worf, who had stepped away from the group and allowed his suit lights to illuminate the area ahead of them. *"We have arrived without incident."*

"Sensors have detected no shift in the derelict's attitude or defensive status in response to your transport," said Captain Picard, his voice sounding small and distant in their helmets.

Worf replied, *"As our scans indicated, there is no internal atmosphere or gravity here. All interior lighting remains inactive. There has been no noticeable reaction to our arrival."*

Despite her anticipation at the idea of investigating the derelict, Chen, like the others, had held her breath during transport, half expecting some automated intruder control system to come to bear even before they finished materializing. Thankfully, nothing of the sort had come to pass.

At least, not yet.

Over their speakers, the captain said, *"Keep us informed, Number One. Picard out."*

With the connection severed, the team turned their attention to their surroundings. Elfiki already had her tricorder out and was using it to take a scan of the entire room. *"It's just as our initial scans detected, Commander. Our point of arrival appears to be some kind of centralized workspace, located in outboard section number one."*

Prior to the away team's departure, each of the three spires jutting forward from the derelict's central core had been labeled in order to give Worf and the others easy points of reference while navigating the alien ship. "Outboard section number one" or "OS-1" was the identifier given to the spire that internal scans of the ship determined to be its "lowermost" level, with OS-2 and OS-3 indicating the sections ninety degrees to either side of OS-1 should one view the ship from the front.

Elfiki added, *"There are what look to be power or equipment interfaces set into the bulkheads and even along the deck or ceiling."* She pointed ahead of her, into the near darkness. *"There's an access point at that end of the room. According to our scans, that leads to a central passageway running the length of this spire. We should be able to get anywhere using that."*

"Has anyone else noticed how clean everything is?" asked Chen. "For a ship that's supposed to have been adrift in space for decades or even centuries, there's no dust on anything, or even floating in the vacuum. If whoever was here abandoned ship at some point before life support failed, there should be some kind of dirt or dust somewhere, right?"

Elfiki said, *"Maybe an automated cleaning and filtration process is one of the systems that's still online."* When Chen directed a skeptical look at her, the science officer added, *"We've seen weirder things."*

Shrugging, Chen said, "Point taken."

"Commander Worf, you may want to see this."

It was Taurik, who along with Lieutenant Konya had moved away from the group to stand next to a console set into the room's far wall. The array of displays, indicators, and what Chen thought might be rows of touch-sensitive controls was obviously unfamiliar to her, but already she could see patterns in the layout. While Konya stood a few paces from the equipment, cradling his phaser rifle close to his chest, Taurik had extracted his tricorder from a pocket along his left thigh, and the device was open and active as he waved it in front of the console.

"This is the room's only active station," he said. *"If these readings are correct, this console oversees environmental controls for this entire section."* Moving the tricorder along the station's lower edge, Taurik held the unit steady for a moment before reaching out with his free hand to touch something underneath the panel. Chen watched as a rectangular panel or wing appeared from a slot in the wall, halting in place after extending approximately one meter.

"A place to sit?" she asked.

Konya replied, *"That means someone—or something—was supposed to operate this console."*

"Somebody expected this place to be used by something other than an automated process," said Elfiki. *"At least at some point. Maybe prior to the ship's launch, or once it reached its intended destination."*

Chen said, "Without more information, the only thing that makes sense is that this is some kind of spatial habitat, or maybe even a colony ship. If it's the former, then why is it out here in the middle of nowhere without any link to a home planet or other support system? If it's the other thing, and it was meant to transport a large group to some unknown planet or other destination, where are they?"

"That is what we are here to learn," said Worf. *"Commander Taurik, are you able to access the ship's main computer from this station?"*

The Vulcan engineer replied, *"Perhaps. A connection with the* Enterprise *computer would facilitate a translation protocol, but our scans show this system is heavily encrypted. There likely are security measures in place to prevent unwanted access, and until we learn more about its operation, there is no way to anticipate the risks involved to our systems."* He tapped a control on his tricorder. *"I may be able to use this as an intermediary option. Doing so presents a much lesser risk, as opposed to a direct connection with our computer. However, it will require all of my tricorder's processing capacity."*

"Use mine," said Worf, offering his own tricorder to the engineer. *"The* Enterprise *can monitor the process remotely."*

Chen watched Taurik pull a small adhesive strip from another pocket and affix it to the back of the tricorder before placing it on the console. He then set its controls to run a continuous passive scan. The unit flared to life and she saw indecipherable script begin to scroll across its compact screen.

"I have enabled access to the Enterprise's *library computer, in order to assist with building a translation matrix,"* said Taurik. *"However, the link will not permit any connection with this computer. If it detects any attempt at an unauthorized access, it will sever all activities and shut itself down."*

Worf said, *"This process is likely to take some time. We should use this opportunity to continue our sweep of this section."* From his study of the data collected by the *Enterprise*'s sensors prior to their transfer to the alien ship, he recalled a spacious compartment near the end of this spire with a large external access point. It suggested an airlock or perhaps even a landing bay, one of three such areas detected by scans. Though there appeared to be nothing resembling escape pods, the three larger sections contained what might be collections of smaller craft.

"Since this room is supposed to be the main control center for this part of the ship," said Elfiki, *"I'd like to stay here and check out the rest of the equipment. Maybe I can find something else that'll give us a clue as to where this ship's crew is."*

Worf agreed with her request, and instructed Lieutenant Konya to remain with her before leading Taurik and Chen out of the room and into the connecting corridor. As with the chamber behind them, the passageway was an amalgam of form and function, with curving bulkheads sweeping from the wide deck and a high ceiling. Different displays and access panels, all of them inert, were set into the walls, and Chen saw more of the strange spheres descending from the ceiling. So far as she could tell, they were identical to the one in the control room. She indicated one of the spheres with a wave.

"Please tell me those things aren't part of some kind of intruder control system."

Taurik replied, *"Though I was able to confirm that the device is composed of an array of energy emitters, its outer casing is constructed from a material that prevents my tricorder from conducting a thorough scan."*

"That's not a no, Taurik." Unsatisfied with her friend's report, Chen aimed her own tricorder at the nearest of the spheres. She frowned at the returns from her scans, which were coming back muddled and indistinct. Grunting in mild irritation, she tapped the device's controls.

"Is there a problem, Lieutenant?" asked Worf.

"I'm not sure, sir." She held up her tricorder. "Some new interference in this part of the ship. We weren't detecting it when we first arrived, but it's here now and seems to be getting stronger the farther we walk."

Examining his own tricorder, Taurik said, *"I have reconfigured my scan frequencies to compensate. It does not eliminate the interference, but instead mitigates it so that our tricorders remain usable."*

"Keep me apprised of any changes," said Worf, and Chen heard the apprehension in his voice. She knew the first officer did not like surprises or for anything to remain unexplained. It was a trait she shared, even though she tended to approach such things as mysteries to be solved, rather than potential threats to be countered. However, hard-won experience during her tenure with the *Enterprise* had shown her there was value in such diversity of attitudes.

Particularly when we're wandering around mysterious alien ships like this one.

The corridor ended at a massive circular hatch set flush into the far bulkhead. Directing her suit lights toward the door's polished surface, Chen noted that like everything else they had encountered to this point, the door gleamed as if it was brand-new, free of dust or grime. Extending her arm, she placed her gloved hand on the hatch's smooth metal, then used her fingers to trace the seams where it joined with the surrounding bulkhead, and moved inward to form an X. Chen imagined the door parting into four equally sized triangular sections as they pulled back into the surrounding wall.

"A little big for a personnel door," she said. "Maybe large enough for some kind of utility vehicle or other equipment for loading and unloading?"

Taurik replied, *"A logical assumption."* The engineer held his tricorder toward the door. *"According to my scans, the hatch is magnetically sealed. I am detecting no evidence of force field emitters. I suspect the compartment must be depressurized prior to opening any external hatches."*

Worf eyed the Vulcan. *"Can you open it?"*

"I believe so, Commander."

Reaching into the oversized pocket on his suit's left thigh, Taurik extracted a hand-sized rectangular object Chen recognized as a P-38. One of several useful components of a good engineer's tool kit, the device was designed to circumvent the magnetic seals on doors and assorted access panels. With practiced ease, he placed the P-38 near the hatch's center, just above where the seams met, before pressing one of the tool's control keys. Though there was no sound thanks to the vacuum enveloping the team, Chen still thought she sensed a slight metallic click as the seals locking the hatch were defeated. Then she saw the seams outlining the door's two lower sections widen.

"There you go," she said. "Nice job."

Retrieving the P-38, Taurik returned it to his suit pocket. *"The tool functioned as I expected it would, and per operating specifications."*

Chen could not help a small chuckle. "Ever the humble one."

With Taurik's help, Worf was able to widen the gap between the door sections far enough to get a grip on one edge. Then it was a simple matter of applying brute strength to force the door open. As they pushed downward on the hatch's lower sections, the upper portions corresponded by lifting up and into the recessed slots at the top of the doorway. It took only seconds to create a large enough opening through which they could pass. Worf, once more leading the team, was the first through the door, directing the light on his left arm ahead of him as he surveyed the new compartment.

"Definitely a landing bay," he reported.

He stepped farther into the room with Taurik following him and Chen bringing up the rear. Once through the entry, she saw the chamber was immense. Bulkheads rose toward a high, curved ceiling, along which she noted catwalks and observation stations behind transparent barriers. Across from where the team had entered the room was an opening in the bulkhead, which provided an unfettered view of open space.

"I guess that explains the door being locked," said Chen.

The majority of the cavernous chamber's deck was taken up by dozens of small transport craft, arranged in neat rows and, like everything else on the ship, looking polished and new. Each ship, perhaps half again as long as a standard Starfleet shuttlecraft, had a bulbous forward hull section sticking out from a bulky, utilitarian body supported by a triad of squat landing struts. A pair of large thruster ports capped off each ship's back end, with smaller thrusters positioned at various points along their hulls. The craft were constructed of a dark, mottled metal and highlighted with assorted markings and glyphs, which to Chen resembled the alien text scrolling across the screens back in the control room. A pair of oval-shaped viewing ports dominated the forward section, through which she could see nothing, and there were access hatches situated amidships on the port and starboard sides.

Aiming her tricorder at the craft nearest to her, Chen studied its readings and reported, "Magnetic clamps in the struts are anchoring them to the deck. No sign of faster-than-light capability, but I'm picking up a large power source at the rear, just in front of the primary thrusters. These things are definitely meant for short-range flights."

Taurik added, *"This vessel's size likely precludes landing on a planet's surface, and we have so far detected no signs of transporter technology. Therefore, it is logical to assume that these are transport craft intended for atmospheric flight to ferry passengers from ship to ground."*

"Okay, help me out here," said Chen, attempting to piece together the disparate parts of a riddle that seemed ready to spiral out of control. "Somebody builds a giant spaceship, capable of supporting however many thousands of people. They either don't make the trip after launching this thing, or else they were aboard at some point and opted to abandon it for reasons unknown. If it's the latter, I can understand leaving the door open in their haste to be elsewhere, but otherwise? Having an entire landing bay exposed to space seems rather odd to me. Plus, this deck is pretty crowded with ships that are only good for short hops. None of this makes any sense."

Without waiting for additional instructions, Taurik walked toward the open portal and the stars beyond it. He held out his tricorder, waving it in the direction of the opening. *"I am detecting damage to a control panel on the ship's exterior in proximity to the entry itself, and what would seem to be a manual locking mechanism for the door. It appears to have been accessed and tampered with in order to force open the hatch."*

"You mean like what we just did?" asked Chen.

"No. The methods employed here were much cruder, yet still effective. Further, damage to the mechanism looks to have been recently inflicted."

His concerned expression unable to be masked even by the restricted view offered by his suit helmet, Worf turned and scowled at the engineer.

"How recently?"

Pausing to once more consult his tricorder, Taurik replied, *"Within the last six hours, Commander."*

"Someone picked the lock to this door just before we got here?" It was a notion that made Chen's stomach quiver. "Out here in the middle of nowhere? Who?" She knew there was no way for Taurik to provide anything resembling an informed answer to that question, but she had to get it out there.

"Besides the door we used," said Worf, *"are there any other points of entry into this section?"*

Taurik said, *"Scans show two other hatches similar to the one we found, and three additional, smaller doors, which presumably lead to other corridors."*

"Worf to Elfiki and Konya. Are you hearing this?" The first officer's voice was taut and clipped, and he was turning and scrutinizing the bay around them as he spoke. Chen knew from experience his battle-honed senses were working to overcome his environment suit's restrictions, and she could tell by his expression that with each passing moment he was becoming more frustrated with his limited control of the situation.

"Elfiki here, sir," replied the *Enterprise* science officer. *"We've been listening this whole time."*

Continuing to survey their surroundings, Worf said, *"Remain alert. There may be someone else aboard the ship."*

Over the open comm channel, Rennan Konya reported, *"I've done another tricorder sweep, Commander. Still not reading any life signs, but I've taken up a defensive position near the door to this compartment."*

"Acknowledged," said Worf.

"Commander." It was Taurik, who had turned away from the open portal and was now aiming the flashlight on his left arm across the deck.

Looking where her friend was indicating with his wrist light, Chen frowned as she caught sight of the small ship tucked alongside the other craft occupying the bay. Unlike its companions, this vessel looked well worn. Essentially, it was a small, bulky cylinder with dull, dented, and scarred hull plates of varying colors covering its surface. Chen could see obvious welding seams where newer plates had been installed. Instead of landing pads or struts, the craft seemed to rest on its own hull. Its aft end terminated in a single thruster port, and a large window offered a glimpse into its single-person cockpit.

"One of these things is not like the others," she said.

"Indeed." Having moved to stand before the ship, Taurik was already examining it with his tricorder. *"My scans show it also lacks faster-than-light capability, but it does possess a compact fusion generator to provide power. I am detecting residual energy readings that indicate the craft was operational within the last six hours."*

Chen felt her stomach churn. "Just like the door panel." It was not until her right hand was resting on the pommel of her phaser that she realized she had reached across her body to where the weapon rested on her left hip. "Somebody's here."

"Our scans are still negative," said Konya over the comm link.

"My gut and this ship are telling me something else." For the first time, Chen felt a chill course down her body as she realized how vulnerable they were, standing exposed on the landing bay deck with no way to see more than ten meters ahead of them in any direction. Even the closest of the transport ships faded into the darkness that now seemed to press in on her.

Reaching for his tricorder's control pad, Taurik made some adjustment Chen could not see. *"I am attempting to scan for life readings, but I am encountering that same interference we detected earlier. It is a very strong reading, concentrated within this compartment."*

"Localized interference," said Worf, and Chen watched as the Klingon's shoulders drooped and his legs bent as he drew his arms closer to his sides. His phaser, to this point aimed harmlessly at the deck before him, was now raised. He began pivoting in a slow circle to his right, letting the light on his left arm sweep the area ahead of him.

Holy hell. We're being jammed.

The realization hit Chen mere heartbeats before she detected movement in the darkness, from between two of the unidentified transport craft. At first she thought it was just a trick of her suit lights playing against the darkness enveloping the bay, but when she flashed the beam on her left arm in that direction, she caught part of a dark figure moving out of sight.

"Commander Worf!"

Then something flashed, blocking out everything around her.

8

Chen had just enough presence of mind to duck as the yellow-green energy beam surged from the shadows. It passed over her head as she dropped to one knee, while instinct made her draw her phaser and snap a quick shot at the beam's point of origin. She missed whatever she was targeting, as evidenced by more movement in the landing bay's darkness. Their suit lights were inadequate for such a large space, leaving far too much concealment for their new adversaries.

Movement to her left, just on the edge of her flashlight's beam, caught her attention, and she fired her phaser in the direction of what she thought could be a large, bulky figure moving clumsily between transports. Another of the yellowish energy beams streaked across the bay in reply, passing wide to her left. Only then did Chen realize she was not the target.

"Taurik!"

The Vulcan was already moving for cover near one of the transports before Chen caught up to him. Lumbering across the deck as fast as her magnetic boots would carry her, she grabbed him by his right arm and pulled him down with her into a crouch just as another salvo of weapons fire traced across the open deck. One beam flashed close enough to her helmet that its reflection in her faceplate all but blinded her. She stumbled, releasing Taurik and using her free hand to brace herself against the parked ship.

"I hate this," she hissed through gritted teeth, hearing the echo of her exhaled breath within the confines of her suit helmet.

"Can't see or hear a damned thing in here. Commander Worf, are you all right?"

Why are you whispering? You're in vacuum, remember?

"I am uninjured," replied the first officer, his voice tense over the still-open communications channel. *"I have counted three assailants."*

Chen said, "I saw at least two more. How big was that ship of theirs, anyway?" It was smaller than a Starfleet shuttlecraft, and she guessed it could carry eight to ten humanoids of average size. Fewer, if they were wearing cumbersome environment suits like what she thought she had seen on one of the fleeting figures.

The lack of sound in the open landing bay was an obvious problem, but braced as she was with her left shoulder against the side of the transport, Chen felt a minor tremor in the craft's hull before sensing movement above her. Pushing away from the ship, she aimed both her flashlight and her phaser toward the top of the craft. Her beam highlighted an oversized humanoid figure bounding across the ship toward her. The attacker wore a dark environment suit, thick and padded and capped with a spherical metal helmet housing a tinted faceplate. In its left hand it wielded a large object that instinct told her was a weapon, and Chen reacted by firing her phaser. The assailant, seemingly caught off guard by her sudden movements, froze just long enough to make itself the perfect target. Chen's phaser beam struck it in the chest and the unwelcome visitor was knocked backward. It did not fall thanks to whatever gravity or magnetic boots were employed in its suit, but its body went limp in response to the heavy stun beam.

And then the lights came on, *everywhere.*

"Hey!" she snapped, holding up her left arm to shield her face from the sudden onslaught of brilliant illumination flooding the bay. Lighting panels recessed into the ceiling and high along the bulkheads chased away anything even resembling a shadow, revealing the entire chamber. If anything, the lights were too bright, making Chen wonder if the vessel's native species required such intensity as a natural consequence of their physiology. Thankfully, her helmet's sensors detected the increased illumination within the first few seconds and automatically darkened her faceplate to compensate.

Despite the new lighting, Chen still caught the telltale flash of a Starfleet phaser, Worf's, from somewhere to her right, and she turned to see the first officer aiming between two of the transports at something or someone out of her view.

"T'Ryssa," said Taurik, a moment before she felt his hand on her shoulder, pushing her down before aiming his own phaser over her head.

She dropped to one knee as her friend's weapon spat orange energy at another of the attackers. The beam caught the assailant just below its helmet, and Chen saw the expression of the being inside go blank. From this distance, she was able to make out the pale lavender skin stretched over a long, narrow skull with a large forehead that swept backward toward black hair. Its eyes and mouth were closed and it was obvious the alien was unconscious from Taurik's phaser beam. How long would that last?

"Above!"

It was Worf, shouting a new warning. She could not see the Klingon, but looking toward the ceiling told her what had drawn the first officer's concern. Scattered across the landing bay's ceiling were more of the odd spheres the away team had already encountered. Chen counted a half dozen of the devices just within her field of view. As opposed to their inert companions in the control room and passageway, these were active, spinning in place while varying numbers of their respective emitters now cast light in different colors. She watched as, while not synchronized with one another, the spheres spun in one direction before reversing course and then repeating that cycle at irregular intervals.

"Taurik?" was all she managed before the first sphere stopped its spinning and a beam of blue-white energy spat forth, aimed at a point somewhere on the landing bay deck. A momentary flash punctuated the strike before the beam vanished.

Movement to her left made Chen pivot in that direction, raising her phaser in time to see another of the dark, bulky suited figures emerging from between two of the transports. Its weapon was aimed at her, and there was no time to do anything before it fired in her direction.

Though she pivoted and ducked in a feeble attempt to avoid the attack, Chen still felt something punch into her right shoulder. Even though the energy beam struck her with force sufficient to loosen her left foot and its gravity boot from the deck and send a harsh tingle coursing across her entire body, it took her an extra second to realize she was not unconscious.

Or dead.

Since she remained awake and alert, she was able to hear the sounds of her own breathing drowned out by the droning alarm now sounding in her helmet.

"Warning," said the voice of the suit's environmental control system. *"Containment breach."* Those same words also flashed in her helmet's heads-up display, flashing bright red to make certain she did not somehow overlook the verbal advisory.

If that was not enough, Chen saw the hairline crack in her helmet's faceplate, just below her right cheek. It started near the edge where the transparent shield met the helmet housing, but it was already lengthening and spreading in a spiderweb pattern.

Acting on instinct, Chen pushed her left hand against the area of her suit where she had been struck. It was an all but useless gesture, she knew.

Emergency patch! her mind screamed at her. *Do it!*

During the next seconds, Chen felt Taurik pulling her with him toward one of the transports. At the same time, the alien that had attacked her seemed to have lost interest, breaking off its approach in hurried, even frantic movements suggesting it was desperately scrambling for some place to hide.

Overhead, another of the spheres flared to life, cycling so that one of its active emitters turned toward the alien. Through the steadily worsening cracks in Chen's helmet faceplate, she saw the device fire another beam of energy. The effects were not that of a weapon set on stun, and the alien did not simply go limp after being rendered unconscious. Instead, the figure was enveloped in the brilliant beam for an instant before disappearing without a trace.

Oh, holy shi—

"T'Ryssa."

It was Taurik, his voice level and firm as he continued guiding her toward the transport. Bending low, he pulled her with him so that they both could crouch beneath the craft's bow section. He had already holstered his phaser and was now extracting something from his suit's right-leg cargo pocket, and Chen recognized an emergency patch kit as the Vulcan applied it to her right shoulder. From the corner of her eye, she watched the repair compound go to work upon immediate contact with the suit's material.

"Warning," repeated her suit's monitoring system. *"Containment breach."*

"Taurik," she began.

Ignoring her, the engineer removed from his pocket a roll of transparent film, which he applied in hasty fashion to her faceplate. The flexible material began forming itself to the shield's contours, filling in any gaps while arresting and pushing together the existing cracks. Within seconds, the flashing alert in her helmet's display faded.

"Containment restored. Recommend emergency evacuation for proper repair."

With only her breathing to keep her company inside her helmet, it took Chen a moment to collect herself. Taurik's quick repair work was not a permanent solution to her problem, but it was more than adequate to alleviate the immediate concerns. She could function long enough for her and the rest of the team to return to the ship.

Only then did it occur to her that nothing else seemed to be happening out on the exposed landing bay deck.

"Are you all right?" asked Taurik, regarding her with obvious concern.

"Yeah. Thanks for that." Patting him on the arm, she dared to peek out from beneath the ship, stealing a glance at the nearest of the spheres. The mysterious device had ceased its movements, its emitters now dark once again.

"What the hell was that?" she asked.

Taurik replied, *"I suppose we can now conclude those devices are a form of intruder control mechanism."*

"Thanks for the update."

Deciding it was now safe to emerge from their hiding place, Chen moved out from under the transport while keeping her attention on the closest of the spheres. A quick glance around the bay told her that the other devices she could see had also gone quiet. When Taurik joined her, he once more was studying his tricorder.

"They appear to be inactive again."

Chen frowned. "That's what you said before." She tried not to dwell on the still visible cracks in her faceplate. The lack of immediate danger did not stop her from pondering worst-case scenarios, and she was more than ready to beam back to the *Enterprise*.

Taurik turned in abrupt fashion to his left, raising his phaser, and Chen followed suit. Both officers quickly brought down their weapons as they realized it was Worf moving toward them between two of the transports. He carried his own phaser at the ready, with its muzzle pointed toward the deck.

"Are you both all right?" he asked, eyeing the hasty repairs to Chen's suit and helmet.

Nodding, Chen replied, "Yes, sir. Thanks to Taurik."

"Glad to hear it."

It was the voice of Dina Elfiki over their comm units just before the science officer and Rennan Konya stepped into view from around another of the small ships behind Worf. Elfiki was heading directly toward them while Konya was making a more deliberate advance, turning and checking everything around him for additional threats. The security officer stole several anxious glances at Chen, and she saw the barely contained relief in his features. She waved in his direction before patting herself on her suit's chest to indicate she really was okay, and he offered a knowing nod in response.

"What are you two doing here?" she asked, looking to Elfiki.

The other woman's smile all but beamed through her helmet. *"Comms are still open, remember? We heard everything and came as fast as we could."*

Still studying Chen's helmet and suit, Worf glanced to Taurik. *"Commander, what is your assessment of what just happened?"*

The Vulcan engineer replied, *"It is obvious that some form of anti-intrusion system is active aboard this vessel. I am at a loss to explain how it functions, or why it did not activate before now."*

"Not just that," said Chen, "but only after those guys tried to ambush us. We've been here almost an hour. It had all that time to react to us, but it waits until a firefight before it decides to wake up? And what's with these other people, anyway? Why didn't we detect them earlier? Cloaking device? Jamming field? Magic?"

"Some kind of dampening effect," offered Elfiki. *"Maybe something built into their suits. I didn't get a chance to scan them before . . . well, before they were neutralized."*

Konya asked, *"And why weren't we neutralized, too?"* The security chief spoke while continuing to study their surroundings. *"Don't get me wrong, I'm happy to be overlooked, but it doesn't make much sense."*

"There will be plenty of time to analyze the entire situation," said

Worf before indicating Chen with a gesture. *"For now, though, we have more pressing concerns."*

And a whole lot of questions, thought Chen as she looked around the landing bay. Her gaze paused on the odd spheres, which once more hung inert above them like silent sentinels.

What the hell is going on here?

9

—◆—

"Requesting immediate retrieval."

Before Picard could acknowledge Worf's report about the away team's odd encounter and the near loss of T'Ryssa Chen, alarm klaxons sounded across the bridge and alert lighting flashed harsh crimson.

"Proximity alert," called out Aneta Šmrhová from the tactical station behind Picard's chair. "Deflector shields just went up."

"Stand by, Number One," said the captain.

Sitting in the first officer's chair and acting in Worf's stead, Lieutenant Joanna Faur called out, "What are we dealing with?"

"Our sensors only just picked it up," said Šmrhová. Picard heard the security chief curse under her breath before she added, "The derelict's hull is still interfering with our scans, but the new arrival has active weapons."

Picard turned back to the viewscreen even as its image shifted to reduce the size of the ship. The display now depicted an object just becoming visible around the vessel's far side. Watching as the screen shifted its focus from the drifting hulk to the smaller, far more maneuverable new arrival, he stood rooted at the center of the bridge.

"Magnify the image," said Picard. "Let's have a better look at it."

The image on the viewscreen zoomed forward, bringing the new arrival into sharp relief. Narrow and sleek, the vessel resembled some form of living creature more so than an actual spacecraft. Winglike projections extended from the ship's green-gray main hull, angled aft and giving it the appearance of a flying predator. Even its bow section furthered that imagery, looking to Picard like a bird's maw.

A maw with weapons turrets.

"Where did it come from?" he asked.

Šmrhová shook her head. "Unknown, sir. I'm picking up traces of a residual warp signature, but scans are muddled."

"Place phasers and quantum torpedoes on standby," ordered Faur. The flight controller pushed herself to her feet as she gave the order. "Conn, prepare for evasive maneuvers."

From the ops station, Glinn Dygan said, "The new vessel isn't moving to intercept us, sir. Its attention is focused on the alien ship."

"Are you sure?" asked Picard.

Šmrhová replied, "Confirmed, Captain. They're firing on the ship, and . . ." She looked up from her console. "Sir, sensors show the derelict is deploying its own defenses. I'm showing dozens of weapons emplacements protruding from all across the hull. However, power to those weapons is . . . well, it's pretty low, sir."

"What do you mean?" asked Picard. "Are you saying the ship doesn't have enough power to defend itself?"

"Not for any real length of time, Captain." The security chief tapped several controls on her console. "And from what I can tell, the ship's weapons are designed for use against larger, slower-moving targets. The attacking vessel is fast enough that it can likely avoid most of them, if its pilot has any skill at all."

Faur asked, "Is the away team in any immediate danger?"

"The vessel's hull is doing a pretty good job against the attacks. They could probably stand to move toward an inner corridor or compartment."

"Number One," said Picard, his attention still on the screen, "the derelict is under attack by an unknown party. Get out of that landing bay and into a more protected area until the situation is secure. We'll beam you off as soon as we can." He tried not to think about Chen, knowing that she and the rest of the away team could deal with her compromised suit for a few more minutes.

"*Acknowledged,*" replied Worf before the connection was severed.

On the screen, the attacking ship was making a strafing run across the derelict's hull. Picard watched streaks of yellow-green energy lance across space to impact against the massive ship's surface. From this distance, he could not tell whether the strikes were inflicting any damage, but then a salvo slammed into one of the collectors and Picard saw it break apart.

"The hull is strong enough to protect the ship itself," reported Šmrhová, "but the collector arrays and weapons placements are vulnerable."

Picard had seen enough.

"Hail them, Lieutenant. Conn, lay in a course to intercept." He waited a moment until Šmrhová indicated that a hailing frequency was established before continuing in a louder, more forceful voice. "Attention, attacking vessel, this is Captain Jean-Luc Picard of the *Starship Enterprise*, representing the United Federation of Planets. You are engaging in hostile action without provocation. Break off your attack, or we will be forced to intercede." Glancing over his shoulder, he looked to Šmrhová. "Anything?"

"They're receiving our hail," replied the lieutenant.

Faur asked, "What's their tactical capability?"

"Their ship is somewhat smaller and slightly more maneuverable. Sensors show a crew complement of nearly six hundred. Their shields and weapons are on par with ours, sir. We can stand toe to toe with them, at least for the short term." A series of beeps from her console drew Šmrhová's attention, and without looking up from her controls she said, "We're receiving a response, Captain. I'm pushing it through the universal translator." After a moment, she added, "Their reply instructs you to engage in unlikely anatomical acts with yourself, sir."

Despite the current tension, Picard almost smiled. "It wouldn't be the first time someone made such a suggestion."

"They're breaking off their attack," said Šmrhová. "And I'm now receiving an incoming hail, including a visual signal. The translation protocol's in place, sir."

"Let's have it."

The image on the viewscreen shifted away from the derelict and its attacker to display what Picard took to be a humanoid male. Dark hair framed a narrow skull with a large forehead that continued up and back in almost Klingon-like fashion, though the lavender skin was smooth rather than possessing any sort of prominent cranial features. Pale yellow eyes regarded Picard from beneath a pronounced brow, flanking a long, thin nose beneath which was a wide mouth teeming with sharp, gleaming teeth. His physique was slender, dressed in garments that appeared worn as well as haphazardly selected and thrown together. Long arms terminated in oversized hands with three digits flanked by longer, multijointed flanges. Though the alien's surroundings were cloaked in shadow, two other individuals were visible in the background, dressed as sloppily as their representative now standing before Picard.

"My name is Senthilmal, master of the Torrekmat civilian merchant vessel Zetoq." When he spoke, it was in a tight, clipped tone delivered in a deep voice that belied his stature. "Yours is a vessel and species I do not recognize, but you intrude upon matters that are not your concern. I know that you have sent a boarding party to the ship, but my people were already there. I am unable to contact them."

"They attacked my people," replied Picard, keeping his voice measured. "Their present status is unknown." It was a lie, but he suspected the truth might upset Senthilmal to the point the captain opted for even further provocative action.

"I offer you one warning to remove your party from the vessel, and your ship from the area, before I consider you a threat, and you force me to take appropriate action."

Ignoring the posturing, Picard replied, "Torrekmat? Is that the name of your people?"

"My people, my planet. What we call ourselves is no concern of yours."

"Why are you attacking that vessel?"

"It was adrift, abandoned. We claim salvage rights."

"So this isn't an enemy of yours?"

Senthilmal shrugged. *"I have no idea who owns the ship. We are independent salvage contractors. We find and acquire whatever we can and sell it to interested clients. Our scans show the craft is uninhabited. By all rights, it is ours. Just the metal in the hull will make us rich enough to retire."*

"Why were you firing on it?" asked Faur. The lieutenant had moved to stand next to Picard. "As you say, the vessel is abandoned and unoccupied."

"Its defenses presented a danger to my ship, but the risk is worth the reward."

He paused, and Picard watched him study something outside the viewscreen's frame. Then the Torrekmat's expression seemed to warm, and he leered at the captain.

"That ship of yours is rather nice, as well. It would command quite a price from any of our clients."

Picard offered no outward reaction. Keeping his voice measured, he replied, "Unlike your other prize, my ship is rather inhabited."

Again, Senthilmal shrugged. *"A minor inconvenience."* Then his features hardened. *"Besides, you have not heeded my warning, Captain, and I am not in the habit of repeating myself."* The transmission ended and the alien's face vanished, replaced by an image of his vessel.

"They're moving to intercept us," added Šmrhová. "And they're diverting additional power to their weapons."

Picard scowled at the new development. "Independent salvage contractors." He made no attempt to hide the disdain in his voice. "They're little more than marauders. Pirates." Senthilmal's obvious threat against the *Enterprise* and its crew was more than enough to convince Picard of the Torrekmat captain's intentions. "Warn them off, Lieutenant. Lock phasers on target, and await my command to fire."

Šmrhová said, "No response, sir."

So that's the way it's going to be.

"Fire a warning shot across their bow, Lieutenant. Close enough to let them know we're serious."

Šmrhová replied, "Aye, sir." A moment later, Picard saw the twin beams of orange energy streaking across space as the *Enterprise* unleashed a restrained example of its power. The phaser barrage cut across the *Zetoq*'s bow, but after a moment it was obvious the alien ship had no intention of breaking off.

Stepping backward between the conn and ops stations, Picard rested a hand on the shoulder of Lieutenant Gary Weinrib, the gamma shift officer who had replaced Faur at the conn station. "Evasive action, Lieutenant. Tactical, fire to stress their shields. I want them to rethink this idiocy."

The security chief responded by loosing several phaser shots at the *Zetoq* in rapid succession. Energy clashed against the Torrekmat vessel's shields, the effect obscuring the ship as it began banking to starboard.

Faur, who had moved back to the first officer's seat, consulted the console positioned in front of her chair. "They're moving to attack us from below."

"Incoming fire!" reported Glinn Dygan.

No sooner did the Cardassian offer the warning than the ship trembled beneath the force of the *Zetoq*'s weapons. Picard had expected the *Enterprise*'s shields to better weather any initial strike. A second salvo struck the deflectors mere heartbeats later, and this time alert indicators flashed across the bridge.

Šmrhová said, "They've routed power from their primary drive and various secondary systems to their weapons."

"Hit hard, and hit fast," said Faur. "They're gambling on being able to knock us out with a couple of quick strikes before we can react."

Looking over Weinrib's shoulder, Picard saw how the conn officer was maneuvering the *Enterprise* away from the attacking ship even as Šmrhová offered return fire to cover the starship's evasive movements.

"They're trying to cycle power between their weapons and shields," reported the security chief. "It's obvious they've done this before, but I think we can match them."

On the viewscreen, Picard saw the effects of Šmrhová's tactical plotting as a new round of phaser strikes slammed into the *Zetoq*'s shields. Instead of veering off in a bid to avoid further attacks, the Torrekmat ship instead turned toward the screen, banking up and over to its left as its forward weapons flared bright green.

"Evasive," Picard snapped, and Weinrib responded by running his hands across his station, his fingers tapping controls almost too fast for the captain to follow. The indicators on his console showed his deft command of the ship's maneuvering systems while providing Šmrhová ample opportunity to return fire.

Even his efforts were not enough.

"They're targeting the ventral hull," warned Šmrhová.

Weinrib, hunched over his console, snapped, "On it," but it was too late.

The next instant, the entire ship shuddered around Picard and the rest of the bridge crew. Consoles and displays around the room scrambled their readouts, and several went dormant as the overhead lighting flickered. Picard felt his stomach heave as the artificial gravity fluctuated, and he gripped the back of Weinrib's seat to steady himself. Instead of subsiding, the effect was magnified by a second salvo. The third caused Picard to lose his balance, and only Faur's quick, strong grip on his arm saved him from being thrown to the deck.

Glinn Dygan said, "Secondary hull shields are down. Hull

breach on decks twenty-two through twenty-four. Numerous warnings in the engineering section."

"Return fire!" Faur called out, but Šmrhová was already doing so. Phaser beams crashed into the *Zetoq*'s shields as the marauder ship now moved to retreat, and this time Picard saw the impact of the strikes against the other vessel's hull.

"Their shields are buckling," reported Šmrhová.

"Quantum torpedo," said Picard. "Target their propulsion section and fire for effect. I want that ship disabled."

The single torpedo, guided by Šmrhová's expert hand, found its mark near the *Zetoq*'s aft section even as the other vessel managed one final barrage from its own weapons. Faur had maneuvered the *Enterprise* so that its compromised ventral shields now faced away from the strike, which was still sufficient to once more rattle the deck beneath Picard's feet.

"They're moving off," said Šmrhová. "I'm picking up damage to their warp engines, or whatever they call them. There's a definite imbalance in the ship's primary power plant. Their shields are down and their aft weapons ports are offline."

"Any injuries?" asked Faur.

The security chief shook her head. "I can't tell. Our proximity to the derelict is preventing that kind of detailed reading."

Having moved back to the first officer's station, Faur called out, "Damage reports coming in, Captain, but engineering hasn't yet responded."

"Bridge to engineering," said Picard, raising his voice for the benefit of the intraship communications system. "Commander La Forge, report."

All around him, the lighting chose that moment to fade, throwing the entire bridge into darkness.

10

——◆——

To Geordi La Forge, it sounded as though every alarm indicator installed within the *Enterprise*'s main engineering section was being channeled directly into his skull.

"*Warning,*" said the voice of the ship's computer. "*Coolant leak. All personnel evacuate this section. Warning. Coolant leak. All personnel must evacuate this section immediately.*" The calm, composed female voice was completely at odds with the chaos unfolding around La Forge and his team of engineers.

Along the oversized chamber's far bulkhead, behind the massive warp core standing at the center of the room, he saw pale green smoke billowing from a ruptured conduit. His ocular implants allowed him to magnify what he was seeing, and he noted that the conduit had seven breaks just in that one section. There likely were others, he told himself, elsewhere in the room or even behind the bulkheads. The plasma coolant was escaping with enough force that it would flood this entire compartment within minutes, killing anyone who remained inside once he or the computer sealed the room. Worse, if left unchecked, the leak would eventually remove so much coolant that the warp core itself would be at risk of overload.

And that means a bad day for everybody.

"Everybody out!" Bellowing to be heard over the din, La Forge repeated his order while gesturing toward the exits. "Computer, execute emergency warp core shutdown. Authorization: La Forge theta-two-nine-nine-seven."

The computer, still audible even with all the other noise permeating the room, replied, "*Authorization confirmed. Commencing emergency warp core shutdown.*"

La Forge knew bringing the warp drive systems offline could be accomplished in under a minute with the main computer overseeing the entire process. The question was whether too much coolant had escaped to thwart this action.

"Computer, is everyone out of this section?"

"Affirmative. All personnel except for the chief engineer have successfully evacuated."

Sprinting for the nearest exit, La Forge charged into the corridor beyond. Behind him, the massive door leading into main engineering slid shut, magnetic seals activating as the oversized hatch locked into place, isolating the compartment from the rest of the ship. In the passageway, he counted eight members of his engineering staff: those closest to this exit when he gave the evacuation order. One of the engineers, Ensign Ryan Giler, was hunched over and coughing, and La Forge guessed from his pale complexion that the younger man may have caught a passing whiff of coolant vapor. Any more than that, he likely would be comatose if not dead.

"We need to get you to sickbay," said La Forge, resting his hand on the junior engineer's back.

"Ensign Kurtz," said another voice from behind La Forge. "Take Giler to sickbay."

Looking over his shoulder, La Forge saw that it was his other assistant chief engineer, Lieutenant Commander Linn Payne, giving the orders. She was a recent addition to the *Enterprise* crew during its last visit to a Starfleet starbase before returning to the Odyssean Pass. Though Payne was human, La Forge recalled she was a native of Alpha Centauri B, and she currently supervised the gamma shift in main engineering. She had been covering for Taurik's beta shift while the Vulcan was assigned to the away team investigating the derelict when the excitement began.

Ensign Nathan Kurtz, a blond human male, placed a hand on Giler's arm. "Aye, Commander. I'll take care of him."

"Keep me informed," said La Forge.

"Aye, sir."

Stepping away from the rest of the group, Payne brushed aside a lock of her shoulder-length brown hair as she regarded La Forge.

"Sir? Are you injured? Were you exposed to the coolant leak?"

La Forge shook his head. "No, I'm fine. Everybody here okay?" The other members of the group nodded, and he responded with a small, humorless smile. "Great. I don't know about the rest of the team. They used the other exits to get out. Can somebody check on them?"

Two of the junior engineers, Lieutenant Taro Trinell and Ensign Maureen Granados, raised their hands.

"We'll take care of it, sir," said Taro. The Bajoran woman patted her human companion on the shoulder. "Let's go."

As the pair turned and headed off in search of the rest of their team, La Forge moved to a nearby panel, pressing his hand to its smooth black surface, which flared to life at his touch.

"Computer, transfer engineering to this station. Show me the master situation monitor."

In response to his command, the panel displayed a smaller version of the master systems display constantly in operation in the engineering section's main work area. La Forge frowned as he noted far too many areas illuminated in red. At the same time, he allowed himself a small sigh of relief.

"Warp core shutdown complete," reported the *Enterprise* computer.

La Forge blew out his breath. "Days that end without a warp core breach are better than days that don't."

"Amen to that," said Payne, who had moved to stand beside him. "We still need to compile a comprehensive damage report."

"The computer's already on it." La Forge tapped the panel and its version of the master display. After he took a moment to absorb the information it conveyed, things did not look as bad as he at first believed. Aside from the coolant leak affecting the warp core, most of the damage inflicted upon the ship was limited in scope, though spread throughout the starship's secondary hull. From his initial review, nothing was beyond the ability of his engineers to repair.

Small favors.

"Bridge to Commander La Forge," said the voice of Captain Picard, transmitted through the intercom system. *"Geordi, we're registering a coolant leak in main engineering. Are you all right down there?"*

Tapping his communicator badge, the chief engineer replied, "I'm sorry for not responding sooner, sir. We had to evacuate due to the leak."

"Any casualties?"

"Everyone got out, sir. I've sent one of my people to sickbay to get looked at, and I'm verifying that we had no other injuries."

"We're on emergency power up here. I'm also seeing the damage reports, and I know about the warp core. How badly are we hurt, Geordi?"

"I haven't had a chance to run full diagnostics yet, sir, but I think we fared pretty well, all things considered. Warp drive's offline until we repair the ruptured conduits and replace the lost coolant, sir. That along with the various safety checks will take the most time, and of course we're without primary power until that happens. After that, there's still plenty to keep us busy, but it's nothing we can't handle with enough time. Did our friends decide to call it a day?"

"They've got their own problems," replied the captain. *"They've moved off, but they're still close enough that we need to keep an eye on them. Geordi, even with the damage they've sustained, I'm not comfortable with the idea of sitting here without warp power."*

La Forge replied, "Neither am I, sir." He exchanged looks with Payne, who had activated an adjacent wall panel and now was calling up various status reports and diagnostic routines. "We'll get on it as quickly as we can, and I'll keep Lieutenant Faur informed with regular updates."

"Thank you, Commander. Picard out."

With the conversation over, La Forge reached up to rub his temples. He could already feel a headache coming on, and the hard part was just getting started.

"I've stopped the coolant leak in main engineering," said Payne. "We still need to vent the compartment, after which we can further assess possible damage to the warp core support systems."

"Right." La Forge was well aware of the effectiveness of the automated diagnostic processes overseeing the *Enterprise*'s vast array of sophisticated onboard systems, but he did not place full faith in them. For him, they were a starting point, a means of determining where to begin the real work of diagnosing and curing whatever problems might ail the starship. It was an attitude he acquired during his years learning how to be an engineer while serving aboard the *U.S.S. Victory*, and he made sure his subordinates held the same appreciation for this approach.

"Okay," he said, tapping the wall panel one final time. "We've got a lot of work to do. Let's get started."

All around him, Senthilmal heard, saw, and felt his ship dying.

Coupled with the status indicators and monitor screens displaying cross sections of the vessel's interior compartments and systems, damage reports from the *Zetoq*'s engineering level were enough to tell him that he and his crew were in a precarious position. Lighting here in the control center was out, replaced by battery-operated illumination from various points around the room. The ship's secondary power generator was a stopgap measure at best, and would be exhausted within just a few cycles if the main engines were not restored to at least partial functionality.

"I need an updated report from the engineer," snapped Senthilmal. He watched as the *Zetoq*'s primary crew worked at their individual stations, several of which were hampered by any of the numerous system disruptions currently plaguing the ship. Stepping away from one of the consoles that remained functional, Jakev regarded him with an expression of frustration.

"Main propulsion is offline," he said. "According to Driva, the star-drive suffered significant damage. She was forced to take the entire system offline to prevent an overload. We are operating on reserve power and conventional propulsion until repairs are completed."

Despite his clouded features, Jakev delivered the report with a calm reserve, befitting his status as Senthilmal's second-in-command. Of course, even that title suggested more formality and structure than the *Zetoq* enjoyed. Senthilmal was the salvage vessel's undisputed master, but Jakev served as relief captain, a role that encompassed responsibility for the rest of the crew and their duties. For this service, he received a larger portion of any profits realized from successful recovery and sale of whatever the *Zetoq* might find wandering around out here.

"Have you dispatched a message back to the guild?"

Jakev nodded. "Yes. We have yet to receive a reply, but I did stress the need for assistance, not just for our repairs but also recovering the derelict."

"Very well." Senthilmal disliked the thought of asking other ships for aid, but understood and appreciated the need to observe the bylaws under which the *Zetoq* operated. Jirol Salvage Guild rules required the equal sharing of profits for any vessel participating in a recovery operation. It was this code that prevented merchant ships like his from descending to total anarchy and unchecked piracy, though the latter sometimes failed strict adherence. The guidelines also guaranteed assistance from other guild vessels in the event of emergency, such as that currently faced by the *Zetoq*. Senthilmal and his crew had on occasion answered distress calls from other ships even if no salvage was involved. They also had engaged in piracy in rare instances. It was not something he sought, and when it happened he endeavored to avoid crossing at least some moral boundaries.

Would you really have killed the crew of that other ship?

His threat to the alien captain was largely a pretense, a means of asserting control over the situation. Senthilmal suspected his counterpart on the other vessel either did not believe him, or instead was confident in his own ship and crew to prevent such action. That they could defend themselves had already been made quite obvious.

"We cannot simply sit here," said Senthilmal, struggling to maintain control over his own growing exasperation. "We are all but helpless against the other ship." Though the *Zetoq* retained use of most of its weapons systems, they—like the ship's protective shield generators—required power at levels that could only be supplied by the main engines. With the vessel operating on backup power, channeling that energy to the shields or weapons would only hasten the drain on that reserve.

Jakev replied, "The engineer reports that partial main power can be available in short order. However, she stresses that we still would be operating at restricted levels, and any attempt to exceed that limit would be dangerous."

"Such as taking the ship back into a fight," said Senthilmal. "Meanwhile, an enemy lurks within striking distance."

"The other vessel is also damaged. Our scans reveal their defensive shielding was compromised, and they have also deactivated their primary engines, presumably to undertake repairs." Jakev paused, and Senthilmal noted his frown. "However, their issues are not as severe as ours. They likely will have their systems restored well before we do."

"Meaning they can attack us at any time. And, they have also sent another boarding party to the ship. For all we know, they could be taking steps to secure it for their own claim." Senthilmal blew out his breath in renewed frustration.

He started to pace the command center, only to realize that his movements would hamper the efforts of his crew to carry out their repair tasks. Gesturing for Jakev to follow him, he moved toward the hatch at the rear of the compartment and continued on into the connecting passageway. Once they were out of earshot of his subordinates, Senthilmal turned and leaned against the metal bulkhead.

"Jakev, you saw the tactical scans of that ship. It is a formidable combat vessel. Even in its weakened state, it might well be capable of destroying us. We do not know their intentions, but our inability to contact our boarding party is concerning."

"The other ship has opened a communications link and asked if we require assistance." Jakev's features clouded in confusion. "If it is a ruse, it makes no sense to me. Why waste time with such deception if their intent is to finish us?"

It was a question that had bothered Senthilmal from the moment the communication was received. Who were these people, and from where had they come? Their ship was unlike anything he had ever seen, and it was indeed an impressive vessel. Had he and his crew happened across it, abandoned and adrift, it would have made for a profitable venture. Still, as remarkable a find as it was, it could not compare to the gargantuan ship fate had delivered to them.

The derelict was a unique discovery, far more imposing than any other craft Senthilmal and his crew had previously salvaged. It outsized even the largest space stations in orbit around Torrekmat or the other worlds in his home star system. How it had made it this far through the region without being detected until registering on the *Zetoq*'s scanners was a mystery all its own. Scans of the ship indicated extreme age, with no signs of life aboard. Those same readings revealed the presence of a low-level power source as well as a complex network of automated systems, but for what purpose? The answer to that question proved elusive, but Senthilmal had proceeded from the assumption that there would be plenty of time to investigate. Sweeps of the vessel's interior revealed metals and other materials with which he was unfamiliar, meaning their value could not be properly assessed until he and the crew of the *Zetoq* found a way to get it home, but just the ship's size hinted at more wealth than he ever thought possible during an entire career in this unpredictable and often thankless business.

Complicating matters was the derelict's outer hull and how it interfered with the *Zetoq*'s scanners, forcing Senthilmal to maneuver his ship closer than he would have preferred during a preliminary survey. When even that proved less than useful, he had taken the further step of dispatching a boarding party to give the lifeless hulk a proper inspection. Their excursion craft had made it aboard the larger vessel, but only after having to circumvent the locking mechanism on one of the derelict's landing bay hatches.

After an initial report of finding nothing out of the ordinary, or any clues as to what might have become of the ship's crew, Senthilmal had lost contact with his boarding team. That was when alarms indicated the presence of weapons targeting his ship, and he had no choice but to bring his own defenses to bear. It was in the midst of the ensuing confusion that the other ship appeared. Senthilmal was still angry that his scanners and crew failed to detect the new arrival until it was too late.

And how much of that is your own fault?

The question gnawed at him. Was he responsible for the skirmish that had crippled the *Zetoq*? Possibly, but why had the alien vessel not heeded his warning? Senthilmal had made a lawful claim to the dead hulk, adrift as it was in open space. Who were these other people, and what brought them here? Were their intentions malicious?

Senthilmal did not believe that to be the case.

"Their offer of assistance makes no sense if they seek to destroy us," he said, regarding Jakev. "They might well be just another band of salvagers." His words rang false even to himself. His conversation with the alien ship's captain was enough to convince him that the new arrival was a military vessel. The garments worn by the captain and others visible during the communication inferred a rigid, disciplined structure. Then there were the ship's impressive weapons, making it appear very much like a vessel of aggression. Might it be the first wave of some superior force bent on invasion, looking to seize control of this area of space and all who dwelled within it?

Again, that felt wrong to Senthilmal.

Jakev asked, "What do we do?"

"For now, we continue our repairs and keep trying to reach the boarding party," said Senthilmal. There were no other serious options, he knew. "And we monitor the other ship. Perhaps they pose no threat, but if they do, then we must be prepared to answer in kind."

11

—•—

"Good morning, Madam Attorney General."

Philippa Louvois nodded in greeting to the Federation Security Agency officer waiting for her before the door at the end of the nondescript, beige corridor. It was the fifth such passage in which she had found herself since arriving at the FSA detention facility in San Francisco. In some ways, the color reminded her of being aboard a starbase or a *Galaxy*-class starship, back when the design aesthetic for that model of vessel leaned toward calmer, quieter palettes.

She had always hated that design decision.

Louvois nodded to the security officer, a Vulcan female. "Good morning. I'm sorry, but I don't think we've met." Like her own escorts, the officer was different from those assigned to this detail during her previous visits. She also wore a standard gray FSA uniform with a high collar and a black belt around her waist, with a phaser holstered along her left hip. Her shoes were glossy black, almost like mirrors as they reflected the hallway's overhead lighting. She wore no rank insignia, but instead only a communicator badge affixed to her tunic above her left breast, shaped like the FSA logo.

"I am Officer T'thas. The admiral and his attorney are ready to receive you."

Looking over her shoulder, Louvois eyed her security detail. "Which of you gets to come with me first?" In accordance with the agreed-upon interview procedures, she was allowed to bring one of her escorts with her into the room.

"That'd be me, ma'am," replied Officer Jonas Voight, the human male who with his female companion, Margo Dempsey, had been with Louvois from the moment she entered the detention facility.

"I'll be here if you need anything, Madam Attorney General," said Dempsey, who Louvois now noticed wore her dark brown hair in a short, almost Vulcan style. The security officer's demeanor was also as calm and measured as that of T'thas. No, Louvois decided, not that controlled. Instead, Dempsey seemed to be forcing herself to maintain her outward bearing.

Maybe she just hates this detail. I know I would.

Setting aside the errant thought, Louvois looked to T'thas. "All right. I guess we should get started."

Turning to the door, which was just as beige and boring as the surrounding corridor, T'thas tapped a rather long code into the control panel next to the entrance and the door slid aside, revealing more beige covering the walls of the room beyond. Positioned at the room's center was a black conference table, with two black straight-backed chairs on the side closest to her and a second pair on the table's far side. Louvois ignored all of that as she focused on the room's occupants, and at long last got her first in-person look at her latest interview subject.

"Admiral Ross."

Standing behind the black conference table that was the room's primary furnishing, William Ross looked as though he had aged ten years just since being taken into custody. His once black hair was now liberally streaked with white, and the Starfleet-regulation brush cut she remembered him favoring had grown out long enough so that hair rested atop his ears. Though he was permitted grooming items while in custody, he apparently had taken to growing a beard, which, while trimmed, was also mottled with gray. Even with these differences, including wearing the regulation jumpsuit issued to all Federation Security detainees, Ross still exuded the unmistakable air of a career Starfleet officer. It was a trait one did not easily leave behind even in retirement.

"Madam Attorney General," said Ross, his voice flat and measured.

Standing next to him, a human woman dressed in the uniform of a Starfleet captain, her blond hair pulled back into a ponytail, extended her hand. "Madam Attorney General, I'm Captain Rebecca Steeby, Starfleet Judge Advocate General's Corps, representing Admiral Ross."

Stepping into the room and allowing the door to close behind her and Voight, she accepted Steeby's proffered handshake and returned the greeting. With the required pleasantries out of the way, Louvois selected one of the chairs on her side of the table, and Ross waited for both her and his lawyer to sit before following suit. Behind her, Voight took up a position in the corner of the room, where Louvois knew he would remain in silence until called upon. She opened her briefcase and extracted the padd she had prepared for this interview.

"Admiral, by order of Admiral Leonard James Akaar, Starfleet Commander, you've been recalled to active duty until such time as any legal proceedings involving you are concluded. Under authority granted to me by President Kellessar zh'Tarash, I hereby charge you with the crime of treason committed against the United Federation of Planets, along with sedition, conspiracy to illegally remove from office a duly elected civilian government official, and conspiracy to commit the murders of Nelino Quafina, Koll Azernal, and former Federation President Min Zife. You are also named as an agent in the organization known as Section Thirty-One, a rogue element operating without accountability or higher authority from the Federation government and outside Starfleet's chain of command.

"You are further named as an accomplice and even a motivator in the persistent, ongoing civil rights violations of citizens across the Federation, an exercise that has been in operation for more than two centuries. Your preliminary hearing as required by the Federation Uniform Code of Justice has determined there is more than sufficient evidence to merit trial, either in civilian court or military tribunal to be determined at a later date. This is obviously not a court of law, but I advise you this interview is being monitored and recorded, and remind you that anything you say can and will be used against you during any subsequent legal proceedings. With that in mind, is there anything you'd like to say before we proceed?"

Ross shook his head. "No, Madam Attorney General. I'm ready to answer your questions."

Before Louvois could begin, Steeby added, "Madam Attorney General, before we begin, I'm sure you've had time to review the pertinent passages of the Starfleet Charter, in which Section Thirty-One's authorization to act in the interests of Federation security is outlined. Surely that goes to answer at least some of your questions, and perhaps even alleviates the need for a lengthy interview?"

It was a nicely rehearsed response, Louvois thought, and similar to replies offered by attorneys of the other suspects she had already interviewed. She expected nothing less of a counselor bound to vigorously defend their client. Still, none of those earlier answers had impressed her, let alone convinced her to alter her interview approach, and such was the case now.

"Yes, Captain," she said. "Article Fourteen, Section Thirty-One. Perhaps one of the most ambiguously worded passages in the history of any governing document ever created and perhaps even the written word itself, which is truly saying something, and supposedly allowing for certain rules and regulations to be circumvented."

She made a show of consulting her padd before continuing, "'During times of extraordinary threat,' is what it says. What I didn't read while reviewing the charter is where it grants the authority to carry out wanton violations of Federation law while acting in the interests of that security. Perhaps I overlooked the relevant paragraph?" When neither Ross nor Steeby chose to respond, Louvois nodded before laying her padd back on the table.

"I'm not naive, Admiral. I know history is full of examples where rules were bent and even broken in service to a greater good. However, in many if not most of those cases, the ones making such unilateral decisions were always held to account by other parties. Whether those decisions were deemed justified or criminal was judged by someone in a position of authority over those individuals or organizations. If I'm to believe the rather broad wording of the Starfleet Charter, the very same document that spends an inordinate amount of text enumerating and describing in vivid detail the laws under which the organization and its officers will conduct themselves also gives itself a loophole whereby an off-shoot entity is free to divest itself of those same laws in the course of carrying out its duty.

"We're to further interpret that this aforementioned *independent agency* is directed or supervised by no one holding a duly elected position of authority, and neither is it accountable to such parties. Whatever methods it devises are justified under the broad term 'interests of Federation security,' without any sort of approval or guidance in the spirit of limited power and checks and balances under which our government supposedly has operated for more than two centuries. Does that about cover it? Perhaps the charter's framers were just naive in failing to foresee the need to protect against something like what you represent, Admiral."

Her response had the desired effect, as Louvois watched Ross and Steeby exchange meaningful looks before returning their attention to her.

Leaning back in her chair, she tapped one fingernail on the table while regarding Ross. "Admiral, is it seriously your contention that the Federation has faced existential threats to its very existence since before its founding, requiring the near constant deployment of an extralegal department of Starfleet Intelligence mandated to act without oversight or transparency?"

After appearing to consider her points for a moment, Ross replied, "Madam Attorney General, you've read Ozla Graniv's exposé, so you know she backed up everything she wrote with information directly from Thirty-One's files. Everything we've ever done is there: a record for posterity of each and every action undertaken to preserve the safety and security of every Federation citizen. There's really nothing more I can add to what you already know, or have at your disposal. The record speaks for itself, and I have no intention of denying or evading anything in it."

"Fine," said Louvois. "I won't hold any of this against you personally. Give me the name of your commanding officer, or whatever you call the person who issued your marching orders. I'll put their feet to the fire."

For the first time, the admiral smiled. Clasping his hands and resting them on the table, he exchanged a glance with Steeby, who nodded her consent for him to continue.

"The charter's description of Section Thirty-One is purposely vague, in order to grant it the greatest possible freedom to carry out its mandate, which is exactly what it's done since before the Federation was founded, Madam Attorney General. As for its internal organization, Thirty-One isn't set up like a conventional military or intelligence gathering unit. It's cellular in nature, to such an extreme degree that we each only know a handful of affiliated individuals. I oversaw such a group, but even I didn't have direct access to the highest levels of our chain of command."

"You mean Uraei," said Louvois. "The artificial intelligence who's been pulling Thirty-One's strings all this time. For over two hundred years, a computer program has been analyzing patterns and activity, making predictive calculations and acting on probabilities to shape the course of our history. We've all just been told that the freedom and security we enjoy has been engineered by a piece of software."

Ross frowned at this. "I don't honestly believe that's true, Madam Attorney General. We still made choices, either as individuals deciding what was best for our own lives, or about how to impact larger groups or concerns. The mistakes we made were our own, the victories we earned and the defeats we suffered came about as consequences of our own actions."

"Working within a framework Uraei established," countered Louvois. "All this time, you took orders from a soulless machine acting as much to protect itself as the Federation. Hell, protecting the Federation was really just a means of ensuring its own survival. It manufactured the situations necessary to facilitate wars based on lies, assassinations, and other covert and even illegal acts to avert perceived threats, even if such dangers were merely estimated by its own predictive algorithms. Truth and lies, peace and conflict, life and death were calculated out to however many decimal points, all in keeping with whatever that thing's master plan was supposed to be."

Louvois leaned across the table, closing the distance between her and Ross to the point that Steeby put a warning hand on the admiral's arm. For a moment Louvois was certain the lawyer would protest the action, but she instead remained silent.

"So, I know at least most of why the software did what it did," she said, her gaze fixed on Ross. "What I don't know is why you, or any of your colleagues, did what you did. What drives someone to violate the very laws and values they've sworn to uphold in the name of safeguarding them? What makes those laws and values worth protecting if they can be so easily cast aside as a matter of convenience?"

She waited for Steeby to intervene or object, and once again was surprised at how the captain seemed to be allowing her client at least some free rein. Had they discussed this prior to her arrival? Perhaps Ross had been adamant that he would not refuse to answer any questions put to him? It would be in keeping with what she knew of the admiral's character, or at least what she thought she knew.

"I won't argue its methods often appear distasteful to the outside observer," replied Ross. "But they were necessary. It's my belief that even the most unpleasant actions undertaken by our operatives were carried out with the noblest of intentions to protect the Federation from any and all threats."

"Including murder?" asked Louvois. She glanced to Steeby, who flinched at the blunt question.

"Admiral," said the attorney, her tone quiet but cautious.

Ross did not break eye contact with Louvois. "As I said, Madam Attorney General, to the outside observer, certain actions appear . . . distasteful, yet necessary."

"So, it was distasteful yet necessary to assassinate President Zife along with his chief of staff and his military security advisor." Louvois purposely chose to phrase her reply as a statement rather than a question, and once again received a tense look from Steeby. Even Ross blinked at the comment, which Louvois found surprising. Surely they both knew this was coming?

"You don't have to answer that," said Steeby.

Louvois relaxed, settling back into her chair. "See, that's the part that I still don't get. Removing Zife from office, a problem of gargantuan proportions all by itself, served your purpose. You covered up his involvement in giving those illegal weapons to Tezwa and saved the Federation from being exposed as complicit in their being used against the Klingons." Crossing her arms, she shrugged. "If we're being honest here and setting aside the legal issues for a minute, you actually did us all a big favor, didn't you?" She then narrowed her eyes. "You got him to resign, presumably to live the rest of his life in exile, but that was never really the plan, was it?"

For the first time, Ross seemed to falter before answering. When he did reply, he looked away from her and down at the conference table.

"No."

Louvois watched Steeby once more touch the admiral's arm, offering yet another unspoken warning. It was now obvious that there had been some kind of animated conversation between them regarding how he would conduct himself during the interview. She guessed he wanted the freedom to make whatever statements he thought relevant or appropriate, regardless of how they might damage him from a legal standpoint. That much was not surprising, as she guessed that deep down, Ross still valued the principles he had spent a career and lifetime defending. That sort of devotion was not easily dismissed. Such was the case for true believers, at any rate, and perhaps it held for those who had fallen into darkness and now struggled to find the light.

"It's details like this that aren't in any of Ozla Graniv's reports," she said. "Section Thirty-One planned to kill him, Azernal, and Quafina all along, right? Wait, I'm sorry. I meant the Uraei program had spit out its probability models and concluded keeping him alive posed too great a risk, predicting he'd present a problem at some point in the future. The expedient thing to do was just kill him and the others. No regard for due process, established law, or even common decency. A computer program acted as judge and jury before ordering you to be the executioner, and you nodded like a good soldier and said yes, because it was distasteful yet necessary."

At long last, Steeby went into protective lawyer mode. "Madam Attorney General, do you have any actual questions for my client?"

"Sure, I've got a few." Keeping her gaze fixed on Ross, Louvois asked, "Do you prefer your penal colonies on Earth? Or, would you rather we ship you off to Elba II or some other barren planetoid with a poisonous atmosphere so you can never go outside and breathe fresh air and feel sunlight on your face? I may not be able to prosecute a piece of software, but I can damned sure throw the book at you." Once again, she leaned toward Ross, pointing a finger at him. "You've got one chance here. Just one, to make things a little bit easier on yourself. You said we still made our own choices even with that box calling the shots. Sure, it may have engineered and even manipulated circumstances in order to bring about its preferred outcome, but it still required the actions of living, thinking beings to carry out its agenda. Give me something that shows actual people, either you or someone else, were behind at least some of this. Show me someone put real thought into these choices, weighed the consequences, and approached them with something resembling intelligence and even a conscience, rather than simply letting facts and figures make life-and-death decisions."

Any reply Ross may have given was interrupted by the muffled report of phaser fire from outside the room. Turning at the sound and rising from her chair, Louvois was in time to see the door slide open to reveal Officer Margo Dempsey standing at the threshold, weapon in hand.

"What's going—?"

The rest of her question died in her throat as Louvois noticed the prone form of T'thas lying on the floor outside the room. At the same time, Dempsey was stepping into the room and raising her phaser. At first Louvois thought the weapon was pointing at her, but the first harsh orange energy beam streaked past her left shoulder. The scream of its passing was made even louder as it echoed off the small room's walls. She flinched away from the attack, hearing the cries of pain from both Ross and Captain Steeby, but there was no time to look as Louvois saw Dempsey now turning the phaser toward her. Without thinking, Louvois reached for her padd on the table and with movement fueled by desperation slung it toward the security officer.

Her aim was horrible. Instinct made the other woman throw

up her free hand to protect herself, spoiling her shot and giving Louvois a few precious seconds to act. All but forgotten training kicked in and she lunged forward, intending to close the distance before Dempsey could reacquire her target, but she was too late. Another phaser beam crossed the room, this one striking Dempsey high in the chest, and her body went limp. Her expression slackened and she dropped her phaser before crumpling to the floor.

"I can't believe she didn't take me out first," said Voight. The security officer was crossing the room, his phaser aimed at the now unconscious Dempsey as he moved to secure her fallen weapon.

Louvois turned from the stunned security officer until her gaze fell on Ross and Steeby, and she felt her stomach heave.

"You weren't the target."

The single shot from Dempsey's phaser had taken both Ross and Steeby, who each now sported gaping holes through the middle of their torsos. The way the bodies were positioned, with Ross lying partially atop the captain on the floor beyond the conference table, suggested the admiral had thrown himself in front of his attorney in an attempt to shield her. The power setting of Dempsey's weapon made that a futile gesture, with the phaser beam drilling through Ross before inflicting similar carnage on Steeby.

"She didn't care about you," said Louvois, turning from the ghastly sight. "It's like she knew she'd only have that split second of surprise and wanted to make it count."

His face ashen as he no doubt struggled to process his partner's actions, Voight said, "I don't understand. Why would she do that?" He paused, and Louvois saw he was trying to make sense of it all. "Was she . . . one of them? Part of Section Thirty-One? Maybe she was trying to keep the admiral from saying too much?"

It was an interesting thought, but Louvois didn't buy it and neither did she recall seeing Dempsey's name among the list of Section 31 operatives among the information she had reviewed during the past weeks.

Wait . . .

Something, a teasing fragment of some half-recalled nugget of information, clicked, but Louvois was unable to make the connection. Retrieving her padd from where it had landed after she threw it at Dempsey, she activated the device and requested a quick scan of the Section 31 files she had brought with her for the interview. It took the padd only seconds to retrieve the result of her search.

"I'll be damned," she said, glancing first at the unconscious Dempsey before looking to Voight. "Margo Dempsey. Her husband is listed as having also been an FSA officer."

Voight replied, "Yeah. He was killed last year while on an escort detail. The detail's shuttlecraft crashed on its way to a conference on Bajor." He frowned, as though trying to remember details. "Something to do with all the fallout following Ishan Anjar being exposed as an imposter and a Cardassian collaborator back during the Bajoran occupation."

"That crash wasn't an accident," said Louvois, feeling her heart sink. "Thirty-One sabotaged it. The diplomat he was escorting was going to argue for Ishan's extradition so he could be tried in a Federation court, but the Bajorans wanted him first." According to the files she had reviewed, it seemed the Uraei program ordered the shuttle destroyed to make it appear the diplomat was the victim of a simple accident. The action required the deaths of everyone else aboard the transport, including Dempsey's husband. What the artificial intelligence saw as the endgame from such a heinous choice would require even more digging into the voluminous catalog of Section 31's sins.

Incredibly, Voight's face seemed to have grown even paler. "Damn. How did she find out?"

"Thanks to Ozla Graniv, the files are available to anyone,"

replied Louvois. "Anyone can read them. She probably did just that, and saw something about the shuttle accident."

Dropping the padd onto the conference table, Louvois ignored the sound of running footsteps coming down the corridor and forced herself to look once more at the lifeless bodies of William Ross and Captain Rebecca Steeby. Whatever secrets Ross may still have carried—any information that may have provided context or nuance or even sense to so many of the crimes committed by Section 31—had died with him, taken in a split second by the actions of a tortured, grieving widow.

Hell hath no fury.

12

—◆—

Picard entered the conference lounge to find Geordi La Forge along with Worf and the rest of the recently returned away team waiting for him. Worf was the first to rise in response to his arrival but the others mimicked his action and Picard held up a hand.

"Please, be seated." As everyone resumed their places, Picard took his own seat at the head of the curved, polished black conference table, with Worf on his right and La Forge to his left. Under normal circumstances, Picard would have requested Lieutenant Aneta Šmrhová to join them, but his security chief was where he needed her: on the bridge monitoring the *Zetoq* and ready to act should the Torrekmat salvage vessel decide to renew their earlier skirmish. Likewise, Lieutenant Joanna Faur was continuing to act for Worf, temporarily in command of the bridge and monitoring the situation with the *Zetoq* and the derelict.

"Welcome back, Number One," said Picard, pulling on the front of his uniform jacket as he settled into his chair before turning his gaze to Chen and Elfiki, who sat next to Worf and La Forge, respectively. "Good to see you two, as well. Lieutenant Chen, you seem none the worse for wear." He was more than a little relieved when the away team returned from the alien derelict. The situation could have ended under far worse circumstances, and he was grateful to have all of his people safely back aboard.

"They build those suits pretty tough, sir," she replied. "That, and Taurik was on the ball." Turning in her seat to where the Vulcan sat to her right, she offered him an appreciative smile.

Resting his hands in his lap, Picard said, "Indeed. I've reviewed

Commander Worf's report, and he indicates you're all quite eager to get back over there."

Though Worf's and Taurik's expressions and body language betrayed nothing, there was no escaping the obvious enthusiasm both Chen and Elfiki were trying to contain.

"Absolutely, sir," replied Elfiki. "We were only just starting to scratch the surface when . . . well, everything else happened."

Chen said, "Every question we thought we had before beaming over just generates three or four more, sir. We could probably spend weeks over there." With a sheepish expression, she added, "That is, if we can get other people to stop shooting at us."

Nodding, Picard directed his gaze to La Forge. "Speaking of that, what's the status of your repair efforts, Commander?"

The *Enterprise*'s chief engineer replied, "We're still assessing the full extent of the damage, sir, but we've regained access to main engineering and I've already got a team giving the entire warp drive a complete inspection. Commander Payne is leading that effort, and so far she hasn't found anything unexpected. I'm estimating we can have the warp core back online in about four hours." He sighed. "I hated shutting it down in the first place, but once the coolant leak started, it was either that or eject it."

Picard understood his engineer's frustration, minor as though he might make it appear. "Given the circumstances, Geordi, it was the best possible outcome, not the least of which was preventing any loss of life." He had been relieved to hear the official report from Doctor Crusher during the hasty meal they had shared with their son, René, an hour earlier: the *Enterprise* had suffered no fatalities during their skirmish with the Torrekmat ship. A handful of assorted injuries—none of them serious or life threatening—were already well in hand by the chief medical officer and her staff.

Small favors.

"The rest of the repairs are minor, but time-consuming," La Forge continued. "We should have all of those done within the current duty shift, as well. I've got people from the other shifts pitching in. We'll get it all done, sir."

"Thank you, Geordi. Keep Lieutenant Faur informed as to your progress." Leaning forward in his chair, Picard rested his forearms on the table. "Number One, I know you haven't had much time to get updated on our situation, but what about the *Zetoq*?"

The first officer replied, "Lieutenant Faur briefed me, sir. According to her report, the ship has maneuvered to the far side of the derelict. Our sensors are unable to get a clear reading of its operational status, owing to the interference we have been experiencing since our arrival. However, scans made prior to its withdrawal indicate severe damage to their main engines."

"They were even worse off than we were," added La Forge. "Their systems work differently than ours, but I know a warp core flirting with overload when I see one. Chances are good they had to power down to make repairs, the same as we did."

Picard asked, "And there's been no response to our communication attempts?"

Shaking his head, Worf said, "No, sir, but we continue to hail them and offer assistance, and per your orders we have stood down our weapons. The ship remains on yellow alert."

It was annoying that the Torrekmat vessel so steadfastly refused to communicate. Despite the posturing by its captain, Senthilmal, Picard found it hard to believe the crew of a salvage ship would so willingly engage in battle. There was the possibility the *Zetoq* was a simple pirate ship, preying upon weaker spacefaring craft before meeting its match with the *Enterprise*. Upon further review, Picard found the other ship's attack strategy lacking, the product of someone with little or no training in the peculiar art of ship-to-ship combat. Were Senthilmal and his people in over their heads, and now struggling with how to extricate themselves from their current predicament without appearing weak?

"Have they made any attempt to transport anyone over to the derelict?"

Worf shook his head. "No, sir. Their ship does not appear to possess transporter technology, and other than the craft we found in the derelict's landing bay, no smaller vessels have been detected. Their distance from the derelict is sufficient that extravehicular activity without a shuttlecraft or similar vehicle is unlikely."

Based on the away team's report of how they found the over-ridden landing bay hatch, Picard had ordered Lieutenant Faur to maneuver the *Enterprise* close enough to the derelict that the ship's sensors could examine the other docking areas. No sign of similar tampering had been found, and scans showed no other access points along the massive vessel's hull. Thanks to Lieutenant Šmrhová's analysis of the situation, Picard remained confident about sending an away team back to the ship, and the risk posed by Senthilmal and his crew was negligible so long as they had their own repairs with which to contend.

"If they really are salvagers or pirates," said Chen, "then they're not about to give up something like that ship. Not without some kind of fight."

"Agreed," replied Worf. "We did detect a low-power communication signal transmitted from the *Zetoq*, aimed back along their original approach vector. According to the star charts, there is a solar system along that route, but even the Federation probes sent to survey this region collected no useful information."

"That's why they sent us, Number One." Picard punctuated his comment with a small, wry grin. Automated survey craft sent to the Odyssean Pass had charted the area years earlier, in preparation for eventual exploration by Starfleet. The *Enterprise*, as the first ship to venture this far from Federation space, had the privilege of confirming or refuting the veracity of those probes' initial efforts.

And isn't that part of the fun?

Prior to undertaking their extended assignment to the Odyssean Pass, Picard and the *Enterprise* had been too long away from the starship's primary mission of exploration. The past several months, spent as they were weeks away from Federation space and the officials who occupied offices and desks of which he wanted no part, Picard felt more alive than he had in years. Aside from his marriage to Beverly Crusher and the birth of their son, there had been precious few causes for satisfaction, let alone celebration. Five years after the Borg Invasion and with recovery efforts still under way on worlds across the Federation, and in the more immediate aftermath of President Nanietta Bacco's assassination and consequences of that tragic event, Picard had given much thought to the next steps of his own life and career. The mission to investigate this largely unknown area of space was exactly what he had wanted—what he had needed—to remind him why he had joined Starfleet in the first place, and why he wanted nothing more than to command this ship with this crew, pushing back the veil of mystery that still shrouded much of the galaxy around him.

So, let's get on with it, shall we?

"Lieutenant Šmrhová is monitoring the *Zetoq* and will keep us apprised of any changes in its status," he said. "That leaves us a bit of leeway with respect to the derelict. Based on what you've been able to learn so far and considering the issues our sensors and tricorders have been experiencing due to the vessel's hull and shielding, there still may well be a crew or passengers or someone else over there and we just can't detect them. If that's true, then they may need our help. For that reason alone, I feel it's necessary to continue our investigation and be ready to defend the derelict should the Torrekmat decide to take further aggressive action."

"There's more to it than that, sir," said Chen. "The way that intruder protocol acted just makes no sense if we're assuming something that's purely automated. It had every chance to take us out from the minute we beamed over, and it never so much as hinted at being a danger. Only after the fight in the landing bay did it activate."

Elfiki said, "Or, it was active all along and we simply couldn't detect it."

"Regardless," added Taurik, "that it singled out the Torrekmat and not our away team is hard to ignore."

Worf said, "Regardless of the reasons, it seems likely Captain Senthilmal blames us for the loss of his people."

"We'll deal with that at a more appropriate time," replied Picard. "I'd rather postpone such a discussion until we have more information about what really happened, and why. In the meantime, dispatch a message to the *Zetoq*, letting them know we believe their people aren't dead, but simply missing somewhere on the ship. Perhaps we can convince Senthilmal to work together to find them." It was a long shot, he knew, but still one worth taking.

Looking to the captain, Taurik said, "The defensive actions definitely suggest an intelligence at work, sir; artificial, or otherwise."

Picard replied, "Which begs the question: Where did everyone go?"

"We still have no idea," said Elfiki. "Based on our initial sensor readings and what we saw during our first visit, this ship should be occupied. It's obvious it was designed for habitation, for a *lot* of people."

She nodded to Chen, who rose from her seat and proceeded to the viewscreen set into the wall at the table's far end. The contact specialist tapped a command sequence into the keypad situated next to the screen, using her other hand to brush aside a lock of dark hair that had fallen across her forehead. In response to her keypad instructions, the screen flared to life, and a set of technical diagrams illustrating the alien ship coalesced into existence.

"Scans show what look to be environmental and food processing systems, and berthing areas," said Chen. "Somebody built this thing to take a *lot* of people somewhere. We're talking thousands of passengers, but if the sensors are correct, then there hasn't been anyone aboard that ship in a long, long time."

She tapped the keypad again. The action triggered a zooming

effect as one of the diagrams enlarged, and kept growing larger until Picard saw what could only be compartments linked by passageways, conduits, and what might be ventilation ducts. While the layout was not comparable to most starships and other space-faring vessels with which Picard was familiar, there was still a con-sistency of design indicating an aesthetic and sensibility desired by someone planning to spend considerable time traversing the stars.

"It's worth noting that there's presently no power being directed to any of those areas," she said, "or what we think are the berth-ing sections or any other place aboard that ship that might serve as part of the support system for a crew. If someone was on that vessel and decided to leave, they didn't do it in a hurry. Everything we've found indicates it was programmed for automation and ac-tivities requiring absolutely minimal power expenditures."

La Forge, who like everyone else was studying the diagrams with rapt fascination, said, "Maybe they were forced to evacuate for some reason."

"We did consider that possibility during our survey, Com-mander," replied Taurik. "We found no evidence of a catastrophic event that might have precipitated a large-scale evacuation, such as hull breaches or other debilitating damage."

Chen added, "And then there are those fleets of smaller trans-port craft taking up space in the landing bays." She stepped away from the viewscreen, but did not return to her seat. "Speaking of power expenditures, this thing is definitely running on minimum. So far as we can tell, the network of solar collectors has been de-ployed for years, pulling in whatever feeble energy it can acquire as it drifts in interstellar space."

"Right now," said Elfiki, "the ship's collectors are just scraping by with whatever's available through simple chance. If our read-ings are accurate, the ship can proceed like this for another two to three years before its reserves are exhausted and it can no longer take in enough energy to function. The skirmish with the *Zetoq* didn't help them, in that regard. In addition to losing a few of the collectors, whatever power reserves the ship is relying on have to be at critical levels. Our sensor logs show that when the derelict deployed weapons against the Torrekmat, it did so to the absolute minimum extent possible. They've got to be pretty close to running on empty over there, sir."

Picard, his attention still on the viewscreen, realized he was tapping his fingers in absentminded fashion on the conference table. Halting the involuntary movement, he straightened in his chair and cleared his throat.

"One presumes the ship had an intended destination before encountering whatever fate befell it. I know you've already attempted to access its computer. If we continue that effort, we may be able to extrapolate its previous course, or even its point of origin."

Nodding, Elfiki said, "That was our thinking too, sir, at least before everything went sideways over there. Without gaining access to the computer, we have nothing. The ship's simply been drifting too long."

Taurik added, "The vessel's computer system is heavily encrypted and shielded, making remote access difficult at best, sir, but with time I believe we will be successful."

"A direct interface is probably the better option," said Chen. "We were already taking the first steps for that before we were interrupted. With the situation relatively secure, we should probably try again." When Picard cocked an eyebrow in her direction in response to her failing attempt to hide her renewed enthusiasm, she cleared her throat. "Just a suggestion, sir."

"Indeed." Picard shifted his gaze to Worf. "Ready to make a return visit, Number One?"

The Klingon replied, "We will complete our repairs before the *Zetoq*, and we are already in a superior tactical position. There is a window of opportunity to continue our investigation, and our transporters offer us an advantage so far as crossing to the derelict with little risk from the Torrekmat ship."

Picard asked, "You're not worried about whatever automated countermeasures may still be active?"

"I am always worried, sir." To his credit, the first officer offered his reply with an expression Picard recognized as Worf's own brand of deadpan delivery. "However, as has been pointed out, we were not targeted. I believe if we remain consistent with our earlier behavior, the risk to us is acceptable."

"As much as I'd love to go," said La Forge, "with that other ship hanging around, I'd prefer to stay here to oversee the remaining repairs, Captain."

Nodding in approval, Picard replied, "Very well. Mister Worf, prepare your team, and take an additional security detail with you this time. As for the rest of us, we'll continue working to get our house in order, and keep an eye on Senthilmal and his people."

13

"This whole ship is just one big, gloomy, unending maze, isn't it?"

With the lights of their environment suits guiding the way—her suit a replacement for the one damaged during their first visit—T'Ryssa Chen and Taurik moved into another dark, quiet room. Like the two compartments they had investigated since returning to the alien derelict, this one contained workstations lining the walls and other equipment, mounted on storage racks, whose purposes she could not begin to fathom positioned around the room. More conduits of varying size ran along the ceiling from wall to wall, with a few exiting and reentering the same bulkhead. At the center of the room and suspended from the ceiling was another large sphere. Like almost everything else in here, it too was dormant.

"There's a lot more going on here than the other sections," she said, aiming the suit light on her left arm toward a row of stations along the room's far wall. "Look at that."

Taurik replied, *"This should be the power distribution center we detected earlier. That would account for the higher level of activity here."* Holding up his tricorder, he walked ahead of Chen. *"However, these readings indicate the consoles here were inert until three minutes and seventeen seconds ago. There are also indications of damage to various subsystems, most of them located behind the bulkheads and closer to the ship's outer hull. One of the damaged exterior solar collector array mounts is positioned near this section."* He held his tricorder so that it faced the bulkhead. *"There are crawlspaces and access points similar to our Jefferies tubes. Their dimensions are such that they are accessible for an average-sized humanoid life-form to navigate."*

Upon their return to the mammoth vessel, Taurik and Chen had requested permission to inspect what the away team's initial scans had identified as a power distribution center located in close proximity to their arrival point. Indications were that the section contained access conduits and other links to the ship's central core. Accompanied by Lieutenant Rennan Konya, the pair had set off in search of answers to at least some of the questions the derelict posed. That left Lieutenant Elfiki to oversee the access and translation efforts begun by Taurik's tricorder hours earlier while continuing her own investigation. Worf and the other two members of the security detail Konya had brought with him were tasked with scouting the landing bay where the team had encountered the Torrekmat boarding party, making sure no other salvagers had escaped detection or made it back to their transport.

Except for the stations she and Taurik now studied, the room's other consoles were lifeless, and Chen's tricorder also showed very little power being routed to this section of the immense vessel. With his original tricorder still connected to the alien computer interface and working under Elfiki's watchful eye to decipher whatever language this vessel's technology understood, Taurik now carried a replacement unit. His gaze was locked on its screen, studying its readouts as it continued to collect information.

"Okay," said Chen as she watched him work, "so somebody expected actual people to be working on and taking care of these systems, at least on occasion. Even fully automated mechanisms still require diagnostics, maintenance, and repair, particularly during long journeys. Again, who builds a ship like this and then abandons it for no apparent good reason?"

Taurik replied, *"It would be illogical to theorize as to the builders' motives while possessing incomplete information."*

"Humor me. This place is starting to make me nervous." The lack of any other meaningful light sources and listening to the sounds of her own breathing inside her helmet had lost their allure during their previous visit. Though she typically experienced no problems with wearing the EV suits for protracted periods, her brush with calamity at the hands of the Torrekmat boarding party was still fresh in her mind. Coupled with the derelict and its inability to offer even the most rudimentary hints about its operation or how the away team might more efficiently carry out its investigation, the whole thing was beginning to wear on her.

"Once we are able to access the vessel's onboard computer systems," said Taurik, *"the odds of our learning its purpose and owners increase."*

Chen shrugged. "It might be nice if we could find a light switch too." That was another question prompted by their previous tour of the derelict. The lighting in the landing bay had extinguished itself, as abruptly and without explanation as it had activated. She suspected it was a power-saving feature, owing to the ship's current energy concerns, and yet it, like the entire incident with the Torrekmat boarding party, gnawed at her. Something else had to be going on, something that she and her companions did not yet understand.

"Enabling interior lighting and perhaps even activating or restoring the ship's life-support systems would also be useful." Taurik gestured to the room's active workstations. *"From my scans of these consoles as well as the one in the first compartment, they apparently are configured in a manner similar to our shipboard interfaces, allowing for the oversight of specific systems or broader oversight over a range of processes. If my supposition is correct, I believe it will be possible to access most of the ship's autonomous systems from any station of this type."*

To Chen, the console—like its companion here and in the other rooms—appeared to be constructed from a type of material that allowed for a touch-sensitive interface, though unlike the panels on the *Enterprise*, these were not flat black. Instead, she could see rows of controls, laid out in sweeping patterns that seemed more artistic rather than the products of practical design. It took her a moment to realize that the pattern here was very similar if not identical to the consoles she had already seen.

"If you're right," she said, "and the users could reconfigure these stations to serve multiple duties, then the central computer routes power and instructions to a particular console and unlocks specific controls and indicators, each of which can serve different purposes depending on the desired action and access requirements."

Taurik nodded. *"In some ways, their technology is equal to or even surpasses our own, while in others they seem to have a less advanced means of interacting with their computer-driven or automated processes. It is an interesting contrast in form and function. The ship's main computer appears to be far more advanced even than that of the* Enterprise. *Its central processing core, data storage facilities, and information transfer network are rather remarkable, and that is just what I have observed with my tricorder. It will be fascinating to get a direct look at its operation."*

Now consulting her own tricorder, Chen said, "For all the logic they seem to have put into their design, some of this makes absolutely no sense." She gestured to the conduits above their heads. "As far as I can tell, half of these ducts go nowhere and do nothing."

"One set of conduits is heavily shielded compared to the others," Taurik replied. *"According to my scans, they are a part of the computer's data transfer network, but the capacity would seem to be unusually large."*

Eyeing the sphere at the center of the room, Chen noted the various ports or emitters, fifteen in all, covering its surface. "Check out those openings. Is it just me, or are they angled so they cover every workstation in here?" How had she not noticed that before?

"You are correct," said Taurik. *"The configuration may indicate a purpose other than what we have already observed."*

The communicators built into their helmets chose that moment to beep for attention.

"Worf to Commander Taurik," said the first officer over the newly opened comm frequency. *"The translation process appears to*

have made a breakthrough. I am transmitting its data to you and Lieutenant Chen."

Both she and Taurik studied their respective tricorders as Worf sent the information to them. Even before the transfer was complete, Taurik was positioning himself before one of the workstations at the back of the room.

"I should now be able to access one of these consoles." With his free hand, the Vulcan engineer began pressing inert controls, his glove moving across the panel's smooth surface with increasing speed and confidence. A moment later, the entire console came to life.

"Now we're talking," said Chen. "Nice job, Taurik."

He gestured to the station. *"As we suspected, this room's primary purpose is to monitor and distribute power throughout this area of the ship."* Pressing another control caused a display screen to flare to life, now depicting a technical cross section of the derelict. *"There are control centers like this one in the other two spires as well as the ship's primary hull. As we also suspected, any of these centers can be called upon to oversee any or all of the other major ship sections. It would appear the designers of this vessel placed great value on redundancy."*

Now seemingly comfortable with the unfamiliar console layout, Taurik began pressing keys at an ever-increasing pace. With each input, more screens and indicators activated. A new diagram appeared on one of the screens, with several areas highlighted in bright yellow.

"That looks like a damage control readout," said Chen.

Taurik replied, *"You are correct. I have accessed the ship's primary computer interface, and I am now attempting to retrieve status information for all onboard systems."* He paused, dividing his attention between his tricorder and one of the screens that now was scrolling line after line of unfamiliar script. *"As we initially suspected, this vessel is centuries old. Five hundred and four years, according to information I have found in the computer's memory banks. Its builders named the ship the* Osijemal.*"* He pointed to the screen with its strings of indecipherable text. *"My tricorder has been scanning what I believe to be the ship's logs. This vessel was constructed and launched with the intention of carrying its passengers to a new world."*

Stepping up to the adjacent console and using her own tricorder, Chen began pecking at some of the now-active controls. "Wow. These data banks are very heavily shielded, and encrypted. Even the logs you found are pretty well locked down."

"Which I find unusual, given the lack of detailed information contained in these files. The entries themselves are very short, almost curt. System status updates, diagnostic results, and related reports dating back almost to the time of the ship's launch."

Chen tapped one of the screens. "I can't find a single piece of information indicating where the ship even came from. I guess we'll need to get into a navigational subsystem."

Over the open comm channel, Lieutenant Elfiki said, *"I'm trying to get into their main library banks, but there's still a lot of encryption to navigate. The storage and transfer capacity built into this thing is amazing. Whoever designed this system liked being able to move a lot of information very quickly."*

"There's something else," said Chen, her eyes catching one of her station's display screens, and she gestured for Taurik to look at it. "I just found this. This ship has what looks to be a transporter system, but it's more advanced than ours. It also seems intended strictly for use within the ship." She scowled, more to herself than Taurik or anyone else. "That seems odd. What, these people don't like walking? Or turbolifts?" When Taurik did not answer, she cast a sidelong glance in his direction. "Taurik?"

Though he seemed engrossed in his tricorder and the console before him as he scrolled through page after page of untranslated data entries, the engineer abruptly halted what he was doing. Even from where she stood to his right and with his face partially concealed by the contours of his suit helmet, Chen still saw the briefest of frowns cross the Vulcan's face as he consulted his scan readings.

"What is it?" she prompted. When he did not answer, she added, "Don't tell me; let me guess. You've found a mysterious computer file that reveals this whole ship's from the future and sharing any of the information in it could disrupt the timeline, so now we have to quarantine everything until you can be debriefed by the Department of Temporal Investigations." Her gentle ribbing prompted no response, at which point Chen reached out and put a hand on Taurik's arm. "Hey, you in there?"

As though only now realizing he had been ignoring her, the engineer turned to look at her. *"I apologize. It is just . . . I have encountered an intriguing anomaly within the status update logs. If I am reading this correctly, there are updates detailing repairs to various onboard systems over the course of the past five centuries, dating back to the* Osijemal's *launch."*

"Repairs? Made by whom?"

Taurik shook his head. *"I do not know, and neither is there any indication as to the identity of the individuals making these log entries. Indeed, each entry is recorded in almost identical fashion, listing the system repaired, the nature of the work completed, and what I presume is a date and time along with current system status. It is what I would expect from an automated process, but the nature of repairs in some cases indicates work that could not be carried out via simple automation."*

"What about some of this stuff?" Chen gestured to a cluster of still unidentified equipment staged around the room, much of which no longer sat in darkness thanks to illumination thrown off by the active workstations. "Controlled remotely, somehow?"

Taurik replied, *"A logical supposition, which our investigation should be able to confirm."*

Before Chen could reply, light flashing from somewhere overhead made her and Taurik turn from the consoles, and Chen looked up to see the previously dormant sphere hanging at the center of the ceiling now showing the first signs of life. Flashes pulsed within several of the orb's ports.

"Um," she said, "did we finally do something to piss it off?"

Taurik replied, *"I do not know what I could have done to trigger such a response."*

"Worf to Taurik and Chen. What's happening?" There was no mistaking the apprehension in the first officer's voice.

"The sphere at the center of this room has activated," reported Taurik. *"We do not know what caused this action."*

The pulsing ceased, replaced by three of the ports illuminating. Chen, waiting for the thing to start rotating and shooting death rays or whatever it might do, could not help but flinch when a bright blue-white beam of energy surged forth from the port facing them. She almost ducked, but Taurik reached for her arm and held her steady. It took her an extra moment to realize the beam had halted itself in midair, pulsing. Then the shaft of light bent and curled in snakelike fashion, hovering as if scanning the room.

"Taurik?" she prompted, even as she rested her right hand on the grip of the phaser holstered along her left hip.

Over the comm channel, Worf snapped, *"Commander Taurik, report."*

Without replying, the Vulcan raised his tricorder toward the beam and its emitter. Chen was about to give silent thanks that the beam had opted not to interpret this movement as a hostile action when it suddenly extended forward in their direction. Instinct made her push Taurik to one side before ducking to the left and rolling to the deck. She closed her eyes and clenched her teeth before realizing she should not have had time to do any of that before the beam struck her. When she opened her eyes, it was to see the beam, instead of lashing out either at her or Taurik, darting toward an active workstation behind them. Not striking the console, the beam had come to a stop less than a meter before the controls, its leading edge now dividing into smaller tendrils that extended to connect with the station's different panels and displays. In turn, the console's banks of indicators and readouts began shifting at a rate too fast for Chen to follow.

"This is incredible," was all she could muster. Despite her earlier shock, she still had not drawn her phaser, and now she opted to keep it holstered. Was that a mistake?

Rising to his feet from where he had fallen after Chen's push and moving several steps back from the console, Taurik once more held up his tricorder.

"Fascinating. This energy manifestation is acting in a most unusual fashion. My scans indicate it is conducting repairs to damaged systems."

Chen's eyes widened in amazement. "By itself?" She gestured to the tendrils. "Is it alive?"

"No." Taurik continued studying his tricorder. *"At least, it is not a life-form like any we have previously encountered. My readings show it to be pure energy, but it is obviously being controlled and directed by a very sophisticated transfer system. I am attempting to trace the beam to its point of origin."*

"Taurik," said Elfiki. *"Trys. The sphere in our room just activated. It's doing something very similar to what you're describing. It's like it doesn't know or care that we're here. The thing actually* moved around Konya *on its way to one of the consoles. It was all I could do to keep him from shooting the emitter."*

"It's acting with deliberate intent," said Chen. "Or an incredibly responsive computer program capable of making adjustments on the fly."

Ever calm and composed, Taurik replied, *"We still have no data to support such a hypothesis."*

As he spoke, the energy beam and its collection of tendrils, which now numbered six, continued to work at the pair of consoles. Overhead, other emitters activated, directing new beams to other stations and even some of the stationary equipment.

"Think about it, Taurik. It couldn't have anticipated us being here, so it's either programmed to act this way, or to improvise based on variations in expected results. Or it's alive." She glanced again at the sphere hanging from the ceiling. "Or *they're* alive."

Taurik remained impassive. *"We cannot rush to conclusions, including whether this . . . phenomenon . . . poses a threat. Careful examination is required."*

"I've got your careful examination right here." Holding her tricorder out in front of her, Chen took a tentative step toward the energy tendril hovering over the workstations. She was certain she felt the faintest of reverberations even through her suit's layers of protection, and then a subtle tingle coursing across her skin.

"T'Ryssa, what are you doing?" asked Taurik. *"This is not advisable."*

Without breaking her gaze from the energy beam, Chen replied, "I'm supposed to be our contact specialist. Well, I'm trying to make contact."

"Lieutenant Chen." It was Worf, his deep voice almost booming through her helmet speakers. *"Do not approach the beam. It may be dangerous."*

As though reacting to the first officer's command, the tendrils lancing across the workstations quickly receded back into the main beam, which then pulled away from the console and arced to its left until it now faced Chen.

Uh-oh. Maybe this wasn't the best idea.

"T'Ryssa," said Taurik, his tone one of warning.

"It's okay," she countered. There was no way to be certain of this, of course, and yet her gut told her she was in no peril. Surely, the thing could have taken aggressive action at any point since their arrival. Ample opportunity had presented itself.

No, Chen decided. *There's something more here.*

The tendril surged forward, enveloping her.

"T'Ryssa!"

Although she heard Taurik's shout of alarm, it seemed distant, overwhelmed by a rush of sound that filled her ears. Blinding blue-white light flooded her vision, and the tingle she sensed earlier now washed across her entire body. There was no pain, but instead it was as if she were being immersed in soothing, warm water. Her body relaxed of its own accord, and Chen was overwhelmed by a sudden sensation of falling.

Then darkness swallowed everything.

14

"T'Ryssa!"

With Taurik's voice echoing in his suit helmet, Worf aimed his phaser at the sphere at the center of the room. For their part, the tendrils of energy emitting from the device still seemed not to care about the strangers in their midst. Instead, they carried on with their tasks of interfacing with the various consoles and the odd piece of bulky equipment, each of which was active with assorted indicators and readouts flashing a litany of status messages or other information Worf could not yet understand.

Then, as mysteriously as the energy beams appeared, they retracted back into the sphere, and the emitters projecting them went dark as the entire device returned to its former dormant state.

"Commander Taurik," said the Klingon into his helmet communicator. "Report."

Having regained his composed demeanor following the momentary outburst, the Vulcan engineer replied, *"The energy beam made direct contact with Lieutenant Chen. It enveloped her and . . . now she is gone, sir."*

"Gone?" Lieutenant Rennan Konya, who until now had taken up a defensive position near the room's one apparent exit, elevated the muzzle of his phaser rifle so that it now aimed toward the sphere. *"Are these things weapons, or not?"*

Taurik replied, *"I do not believe so, Lieutenant. According to my scans of the computer system I am now able to access, there was a spike in activity within the central core that corresponds to Lieutenant Chen's disappearance. What we at first believed to be defensive weapons instead appear designed for matter-energy manipulation."*

"*You're saying she was transported?*" asked Dina Elfiki. "*Where?*"

"*Assuming that is the case, I am presently unable to answer that question, Lieutenant.*"

Worf lowered his phaser. "Stand by."

Contacting the *Enterprise*, he apprised Captain Picard of the situation. While the captain at first ordered the away team to return to the ship, the Klingon was able to convince him to hold off on that action.

From his location in the power distribution center, Taurik added, "*I still have not detected any readings that might be consistent with particle-beam weapons, Captain, and neither have I recorded any sign of . . . residual biometric readings.*" It was a very sterile way of reporting the lack of any trace remains of what might have once been T'Ryssa Chen. "*The same was true following the engagement with the salvagers in the landing bay. I am therefore unable to conclude that these devices are weapons. Instead, I believe the beam emitters are part of a sophisticated transporter system that is somewhat more advanced than our own.*"

"*But you've detected no indications of a typical transporter signature?*" asked Picard.

At Worf's prompting, Elfiki replied, "*Not yet, sir. It could just be that their system operates in a manner we're not able to detect using our typical settings. I think I can make adjustments to our tricorders to scan outside their normal wavelengths, and if we pick up on anything, I'll transmit those configurations back to the* Enterprise *so that the sensors can be modulated.*"

"*We'll scan the entire vessel, Number One.*" His voice, characteristic of the captain's unflappable demeanor, remained steady but even Worf noted the subtle tinge of worry as Picard considered the potential loss of a crew member. "*If Mister Taurik is confident she was subjected to a form of transporter beam, then it stands to reason she's there, somewhere, along with the Torrekmat boarding party.*"

Worf said, "If that is the case, she may still be in danger."

"*It is also possible the transporter, acting as it did, relocated Lieutenant Chen and the salvagers to a form of detention facility,*" replied Taurik.

"*We'll find her,*" said Picard. "*And the Torrekmat. Until then, proceed with caution. If anything else should happen, I want you off that ship immediately. Is that understood, Mister Worf?*"

"Understood, Captain."

"*Very well. Be careful, Number One. Picard out.*"

After instructing Taurik to remain where he was so that they could join him and notifying the security team in the landing bay to maintain their position, Worf led the trio out of the room and into the connecting passageway.

"*I don't like this at all,*" said Konya from his position behind Elfiki. Guarding their rear as the team moved, the Betazoid security officer made a point of turning himself at irregular intervals, examining their flanks and the passageway behind them.

For his part, Worf agreed with the lieutenant. Studying the corridor ahead of him, he caught sight of another of the emitters, suspended by itself at a junction in the hallway. This one was larger and possessed many more projector ports than the device they had left behind, but Worf noted a console set into the right bulkhead that seemed to be within the field for at least one of the sphere's ports.

"*It seems like an awful waste of resources,*" said Elfiki as they walked. "*Using transporters to move around? Even on a ship this size, turbolifts or magnetic rail tubes would be more efficient from an energy-cost standpoint.*"

Konya said, "*Maybe we're talking about a life-form that has limited physical mobility. Or, here's a thought: We beamed from the* Enterprise *into one of the spires. What if they're meant to be segregated from the rest of the ship for some reason, and the only way in or out is via transporter?*"

"My response to that is to wonder what's so dangerous over here that they have to keep it cut off from the main hull section," said Elfiki. *"Thanks, Rennan. I feel much better now."*

Worf suspected Konya was making an attempt to focus on their immediate mission in order to keep from dwelling on his concerns about Lieutenant Chen. The first officer was aware that the pair had resumed a previous romantic relationship that had endured its share of hardship. To their credit, neither officer had allowed their personal matters—either their own or each other's—to interfere with their duties aboard the *Enterprise*, and they had worked out whatever problems may have plagued them.

From firsthand experience, Worf knew that shipboard romances could be fraught with problems, not just with the relationship's active participants but also anyone who stood to be positively or negatively affected by it. He recalled those first awkward weeks aboard the *Enterprise*-D after he began a relationship with Deanna Troi, former ship's counselor. Years prior to her marrying William Riker and before his promotion to captain and their joint departure to a new assignment aboard the *Starship Titan*, the romantic affair between her and Worf could have made things uncomfortable with them as well as Riker. He and Troi had already enjoyed a previous relationship during his early assignment to her homeworld of Betazed, but years later, with Riker now serving as the *Enterprise*'s first officer and Worf as the ship's chief of security, Riker had said or done nothing that might be construed as jealousy or any other negative attitude toward Worf and Troi. Their relationship ended without fanfare, and the three of them remained friends, which was the best possible outcome.

Then came Worf's assignment to Deep Space 9, where he found Jadzia Dax.

Enough, he reminded himself. *Now is not the time to ponder your own past anguish.* However, Rennan Konya's current emotional state might become an issue, despite the security officer's best efforts to control or prevent such distraction. Worf would have to be mindful of such things, and be ready to assist his junior officer if the need arose.

Taurik was waiting for them at the entrance to the power distribution center, the lights from his environment suit illuminating that section of the passageway.

"Commander," said the Vulcan, offering nods of greeting to Elfiki and Konya.

Looking into the compartment, Worf asked, "Has there been any change?"

"No, sir. The device has remained inert since Lieutenant Chen's disappearance."

"And we're sure she wasn't vaporized?" asked Konya, his voice tight.

Holding up his tricorder, Taurik replied, *"I have scanned the sphere and found no evidence of a weapons system. So far as I am able to determine, it is indeed a form of transporter apparatus. This strengthens our theory that Lieutenant Chen and the Torrekmat boarding party must be somewhere else aboard this vessel. Even with the* Enterprise's *sensors, finding them may still prove difficult, given the interference we've already experienced and the areas of the ship that are more heavily shielded."*

"We conduct a standard search sweep," said Konya. *"I'll take the people I already have with us, and work our way from end to end."*

Taurik said, *"Without additional personnel, such a search could take days to complete."*

"Then let's get some more people," replied Konya. *"The sooner we get started, the sooner we find her."*

On its face, Konya's strategy was simple yet sound and one Worf would have suggested himself. "That is certainly an option, but we cannot bring over additional personnel without first verifying that this ship poses no threat."

Elfiki said, *"Based on everything I've found so far, sir, there isn't any real intruder control system. Yes, there are interior pressure hatches and things of that nature that allow selected areas to be* isolated from the rest of the ship, but I've found no evidence of, for example, interior security force fields or neutralization measures such as anesthetic compounds or nonlethal weapons placements."

"You can vent the atmosphere from a sealed section," offered Konya.

"Sure, but right now there's no atmosphere anywhere on the ship." Elfiki gestured as though to indicate the ship around them. "According to everything we've found, whoever launched this thing expected it to travel for extended periods—decades or more—without being crewed by living beings."

Worf said, "Even with what we've encountered, the ship's defenses against external threats would seem to be lacking."

"Maybe," replied Elfiki. "On the other hand, if it was originally supposed to be traveling at warp, the likelihood of encounters with other vessels would be much lower. The larger risk would be if its course took it into the path of an unanticipated obstacle, like the ion storm we think was responsible for most of the exterior hull damage."

"None of this is helping us to find Trys," said Konya, and this time Worf cast a long, meaningful look in his direction. To his credit, the security officer seemed to understand the implied warning, and in return responded with a subtle nod of acknowledgment.

"Commander Taurik," said Worf, "have you had any further progress interfacing with this ship's computer systems? Anything that might help us find Lieutenant Chen or the Torrekmat salvagers?"

The engineer replied, "I was searching for an internal sensor grid. I believe such a system exists, but I am not yet able to access it."

"Maybe I can help with that," said Elfiki. Then, she reached out and placed a hand on Konya's arm. "We'll find her, Rennan."

Nodding, the Betazoid forced a small smile. "I know." To Worf, he said, "What can I do, sir?"

Worf pointed to one of the room's active workstations. "You and I will begin examining this ship's technical schematics. Perhaps we can narrow down the possible locations where Lieutenant Chen could have been transported." He had started considering this possibility while listening to Taurik and Elfiki discuss the ship's internal systems. Even on a vessel this size, there would be areas impractical if not impossible to access. Conduits, waste management, hazardous materials, bulk machinery, and other aspects of a ship's operation that were no place for soft, fragile living beings. Perhaps those areas could be eliminated in a bid to speed up their search efforts.

It is not the most satisfying course of action, Worf decided. *But it is better than nothing.*

15

The room was huge, beautiful, and intimidating, all at the same time.

All around her, the immense chamber's walls were covered in bright, colorful abstract swirls that stretched up toward a curved ceiling into which was carved a series of ornate patterns. Large cylindrical columns stood at the room's corners as well as at regular spacing down the length of the room. Ahead of her, a dais dominated the room's far end. Atop the dais sat a long, narrow table that to Chen appeared cast as a single, oval-shaped piece of black obsidian glass. Instead of legs or a center support mount, the table seemed to float in midair. On the table's far side were seven chairs, somewhat recognizable in form and function and yet obviously designed for a specific physiology. Behind her, the room ended at what might be a large, heavy door, hexagonal in shape.

Set into the walls to her left and right and placed in a manner similar to the columns were large circular windows offering views of lush, rolling landscapes festooned with trees that were at once familiar and utterly alien. Rather than being dominated by green foliage that was a frequent characteristic of Class-M planets, the vegetation here ran a spectrum of colors including deep reds, vibrant purples, and stark whites interlacing and harmonizing with each other. A cloudless, pale green sky provided a backdrop to the entire scene.

For the first time, T'Ryssa Chen realized she was no longer wearing her environment suit, and neither was she dead. Figuring that she would already have died had the atmosphere here been poisonous, she drew a deep breath and felt cool, fresh air fill her lungs. She detected a pleasant scent, obvious but not overpowering, that she could not identify.

"Okay," she said to no one. "That's not so bad."

Looking down at herself, she saw that she was dressed not in the single-piece garment she was previously wearing underneath her EV suit. Instead, her ensemble consisted of a loose-fitting gown that fell almost to her ankles and a neckline that fell just below her throat. Long, billowy sleeves covered her arms, and she noted that the garment was translucent, with the skin of her arms just barely visible beneath the material. This prompted her to verify that she wore nothing else underneath the gown. The fabric was soft to the touch, featuring a swirling kaleidoscope of colors not unlike the patterns adorning the walls. Her feet were bare, and the floor was neither too warm nor too cold, and neither did it feel hard or unyielding. The only thing she could decide was that the floor was just *there*.

Along with her suit, her tricorder and phaser also were gone, and it was not until she reached for it that she noticed she also had no communicator badge. Whoever had brought her to this place had been quite thorough in separating her from her equipment, and Chen felt a momentary pang of unease at that thought.

That said, this obviously isn't any kind of prison cell.

How had she come to be in this place? She had not awoken from sleep. Instead, she was just . . . *here*. Her last memory was of being with Taurik, watching the strange energy beam carrying out its work. She had moved toward it, scanning it with her tricorder, and then came the light.

The light.

That brilliant, blinding light that had blocked out everything, and the cacophony that flooded her helmet and pushed away all other sounds. The almost electrical sensation enveloping her body. Falling. Had she been falling?

You were transported, but to where?

The *Osijemal*? It was the only answer that made sense, at least with respect to her understanding of transporter systems, but the scene outside this room's windows would seem to belie that. Holographic technology provided one possible explanation.

"All right," she called out, "if this is a holodeck joke, consider me amused and impressed. You can come out now."

Of course, nothing happened.

Her people would find her. Chen knew that her companions, especially Rennan, would not stop looking for her. She had to be somewhere on the ship. All she had to do was figure out where she had been brought, and perhaps that revelation would provide a means of contacting Worf and the others.

"The answer's in here, somewhere," she said, to no one but herself. "I just have to find it, so let's get to work. Think, Trys."

Chen decided to conduct a methodical search of the chamber, starting at the door. She did not expect it to open, either at her approach or when she pushed and pulled on it, and she was not disappointed. The door possessed no handle or other obvious mechanism, and neither did she see any sort of key or control pad anywhere along the adjacent walls. Satisfied that she was stuck here until such time as she located another exit, she began working her way along the wall, intending to proceed around the room in clockwise fashion until she arrived back at her starting point. She might not have a tricorder, but she still had her own senses. Somewhere in here was a clue to her location, and how to get out, and she *would* find it.

So resolute was she in her convictions that it took her another full minute, she guessed, before Chen realized she was no longer alone in the room.

The sensation of being watched fell upon her with no warning, and she turned from the wall to scan the chamber, at which point she froze. Staring at her from where they now occupied the chairs behind the polished, floating table on the dais were seven beings.

And just where the hell did they *come from?*

Chen had heard no door open, and no indication of a transporter beam in use. One moment she was alone, the next she had an audience. Had they been watching her all this time, choosing only now to reveal themselves? She decided to take it as a good sign that they had appeared behind the table, which now acted as a barrier between them and her.

Of course, maybe your place is supposed to be on *the table, with a nice Chablis.*

Pushing away the sobering thought, Chen concentrated on studying her new admirers. If the chairs were any indication, these were tall specimens, vaguely humanoid in appearance yet while possessing many distinct characteristics. Slender yet muscled physiques were hinted at or else peeked out from variations on the multicolored gown Chen now wore, their pale orange skin providing sharp contrast to the darker, bolder colors of their garments. While each of the new arrivals almost certainly represented the same race, Chen noted the variations in height and weight, but nothing immediately stood out as indicative of gender. Completely hairless, at least so far as Chen could determine, their skulls consisted of a large, bulbous dome flanked by additional rounded protrusions where one might normally expect to find ears. Dark eyes were set under a pronounced brow, from which descended an extended set of mandibles that ended with a chin that fell almost to the center of their chests. Atop that length of bone or cartilage lay another, smaller segment that terminated just above a wide drooping mouth. This segment also featured a quartet of small holes at its lower end, suggesting a nose.

Their arms, Chen decided, were quite interesting. Somewhat similar to a human's, they also featured a point of articulation between the shoulder and the elbow. Forearms flared out to form hands possessing seven phalanges. While the digits on either end of the hands were shorter than their companions, they did not appear to be obviously opposable. In fact, additional knuckles on each finger suggested a much greater range of motion than that of a typical humanoid hand.

Stepping toward the dais, Chen made a point to keep her hands where they could be seen. It occurred to her that these people already knew she was unarmed, but she figured the gesture could not hurt.

"Hello," she said, not expecting to be understood.

"Greetings," said the figure seated at the center of the table.

Well, that was easy enough.

While its voice seemed to possess a feminine quality—to her ear, at least, though she realized it was something she could not quantify—Chen remained uncertain as to the alien's gender. Perhaps this species' perceptions of gender differed greatly from how she understood them.

These are the kinds of things you learn when you're a contact specialist. So, go forth and contact, already.

"My name is T'Ryssa Chen, of the Federation *Starship Enterprise.* My people and I have no hostile intentions toward you. Our mission is one of peaceful exploration, studying newly discovered planets and—if appropriate—making contact with any civilizations we might find on those worlds. We found your vessel adrift in space, and when we detected no crew aboard along with damage to the ship itself, we wanted to see if we could determine its point of origin, and perhaps inform the people there of what we'd found." When none of the aliens said anything in response to her hastily concocted opening statement, she held out her hands. "Are you able to understand me?"

The alien offered a single, slow nod. "Oh, yes, we now understand you quite well. My name is Alehuguet. You have already learned that we call our vessel the *Osijemal.*" It gestured to the companions seated to either side of it. "We are the Conclave, representing the leadership council for our people."

"Who are you?" asked Chen.

"We call ourselves the Nejamri, and we have been monitoring you since your vessel approached to within range of our scanning capabilities. Along with the communications between you and your companions as you have moved about here on our vessel, we have also monitored your interactions with your fellow travelers on your ship. This, along with your own attempts to understand our languages, has greatly assisted us in constructing a translation matrix. It is not yet complete, but we have determined that it is sufficient for us to proceed."

"Fair enough." If she and the away team were going to wander around over here, trying to access the ship's computer and learn whatever they could about the people who built it, it was reasonable that these people would be just as curious about them.

Alehuguet continued, "According to our scans, your ship seems to carry representatives from many species."

"That's true," replied Chen. "I actually represent two different species: human and Vulcan. Most of the people on my ship are human or some close relation, and our Federation is a collective body consisting of civilizations on nearly two hundred distinct worlds." She indicated herself with a tap to her chest. "For what it's worth, I am a female of my species."

"As am I."

Chen asked, "We're still aboard your ship?"

Her face seeming to brighten as she regarded Chen, Alehuguet nodded. "Yes, but I suspect that you will have difficulty believing the truth about where you are. Our studies of your device's interaction with our computer have helped us select a word you can use to describe this place: Haven."

"Okay," said Chen. "Haven it is, then." Some kind of holodeck or other room that gave the illusion of being anywhere but on a spaceship. The need and benefits of such a retreat aboard a vessel during long-duration voyages were obvious, but she still did not understand the apparent drama surrounding this place. "Why am I here?"

Again, Alehuguet smiled. "Because, T'Ryssa Chen, we have been waiting a very long time for someone like you. We desperately need your help."

16

No matter how many times he strode into the hallowed Great Hall, Martok was all but helpless to resist the sense of pride washing over him. Here, cradled within the chamber's massive stone walls, was not just the legacy of the High Council but the very history of the Klingon Empire itself.

In particular, he enjoyed being here at times like these, when it was empty and he had it to himself. At this time of day, he was free to revel in the Hall's solemn nature without the activity of a council in full session, along with the annoyances that often accompanied such gatherings. Alone with his thoughts, Martok recalled his initial visit to the Hall, as a boy during a family excursion to the First City. Though not yet a blooded warrior while preparing to complete his first hunt, he remembered how his heart beat with anticipation and excitement upon seeing the storied chamber. Like the city itself, it represented all that it meant to be a Klingon. The stories told to him by his father and grandfather about the Empire's bravest warriors fired his imagination, and those flames were fueled as he laid eyes upon this hallowed sanctuary. As a boy, he never entertained the notion that he would see the inside of the Hall except as a visitor. The idea that he, the latest generation in a long line of simple foot soldiers from a common family born of the Ketha lowlands, might one day serve as a member of the High Council, let alone as its chancellor, would have been preposterous to that young boy so long ago.

It took us a long time, Father, but we restored honor to our house.
Even as a decorated, combat-tested general in the Klingon

Defense Force, and now occupying the highest seat of power in all the Empire, Martok still looked to his father, Urthog, for advice. Given the family's lack of noble blood, Urthog and his father before him had imparted an enormous amount of hard-won, commonsense wisdom, the appreciation of which in many ways was beyond the ability of those from more "accepted stock." In the years since his ascension to the role of chancellor, Martok had continued to seek his father's guidance. His aim was to ensure his reign over the Empire remained rooted in the best interests of all Klingon people, regardless of their societal status. He only wished his mother, wife, Sirella, and daughters Lazhna and Shen were still alive, so that he might benefit from their perspective as well. Regardless, he looked to their memories to help keep him on the correct path, their influence reminding him of why he was deemed worthy of such responsibility in the first place.

This is all your fault, Worf.

"You are not considering redecorating, are you? If so, I have some thoughts on curtains and new paint, and perhaps a plant."

The voice, deep and intimidating for those who did not know its owner, echoed off the Hall's high ceiling and slanted walls. With a smile, Martok turned far enough to his left that he could see with his one good eye K'shaf, a member of the council and one of his closest friends, regarding him from the chamber's entrance. So involved was he with his thoughts that he had not sensed the other Klingon's arrival. Were it anyone else, Martok might have cause for concern, but K'shaf had proven on occasions too numerous to easily count that he was worthy of unwavering trust.

As was always the case, K'shaf was dressed in an immaculate yet well-worn uniform featuring the vestments representing a long military career as well as his current political office. His long gray hair was pulled back from his face and secured at the base of his neck by a thick leather band. A wide, silver baldric hung from his right shoulder and across his broad chest to rest on his left hip, adorned with all manner of awards and devices that gave further testimony to his service and accomplishments. His ensemble was completed by the long, dark gray robe that was a match for the one Martok currently wore, as was the case with all active members of the High Council. The air of a politician was disrupted, however, by the scar running down the left side of K'shaf's face, a gift from a Jem'Hadar soldier during a brief yet fierce hand-to-hand battle at the height of the Dominion War when it seemed the Empire might well be conquered. Unlike K'shaf, that soldier had not lived to fight another day.

"Having seen the way you keep your office," replied Martok as he crossed the Hall's stone floor toward his friend, "I suspect it is your wife who sends along such ideas. Or perhaps your son."

K'shaf smiled. "My son has not yet even learned to walk or feed himself."

"And yet he is still not so slovenly as his father."

Laughing with a raucous ferocity only enhanced by the Hall's acoustics, the two friends exchanged their usual greeting, which involved each trying to knock the other off-balance. The short, mock skirmish ended, as it always did, in a draw, evoking more laughter. Clapping K'shaf on his left shoulder, Martok eyed his friend with a bemused grin.

"The session is not scheduled to begin until later this morning," he said. "What brings you here at such an early hour?"

"I knew you would be here, and that you likely would be alone. I know how you like to come here before each session, and that you prefer the solitude to the normal business conducted here." K'shaf's own smile widened. "I must say I find it hard to disagree with that stance."

The truth was that even now, years after the loss of Sirella and with his children all dead, Martok found himself on the constant hunt for reasons not to remain in the home they had once shared. If there was any location on Qo'noS that held less appeal for him, he had yet to find it. Why he hadn't relieved himself of the burden of the family dwelling and sought other, smaller accommodations somewhere else in the city's Old Quarter remained a mystery, except that it harbored far more pleasant memories than those that caused him pain and sorrow. Despite this, he found himself growing increasingly restless during those hours he spent there. Aside from sleeping and the occasional meal, he chose to occupy his time in other environs, such as his office or one of the libraries housed within the Great Hall or at one of the city's many taverns and gaming parlors. K'shaf often accompanied him on such ventures, and between them they were able to forget—at least for a time—the responsibilities they shouldered.

"It seems a bit early in the day for bloodwine," said Martok, before making a show of casting conspiratorial glances about the meeting chamber. "But it would not be the worst idea." After the pair shared another chuckle, he appraised K'shaf. "Something troubles you, my friend. Speak."

This time it was K'shaf who looked around, as though verifying there was no one to overhear their conversation. Indicating for Martok to walk with him, they began pacing a circuit around the Hall's perimeter. After waiting for several moments for the other Klingon to say something, Martok was about to prompt him when K'shaf at last broke the silence. When he did so, it was in hushed tones.

"This business with the Federation and the secrets that have been exposed. There has been much talk among the other councilors, but we all await your views on the matter and what you think it all means for the Empire."

With a sigh, Martok replied, "It has consumed my thoughts for some time, and I confess that I am conflicted. On the one hand, there can be no excusing the crimes committed by President Zife and those who aided him. The Khitomer Accords have been stressed and tried to the point that I fear they one day will simply crumble beneath the weight of our collective stupidity."

Enacted nearly a century ago, after the global catastrophe that had imperiled Qo'noS and every living thing upon it, the Khitomer Accords were the first of many tumultuous steps taken by the Federation and the Empire on their way to the present-day peace now enjoyed by both powers. Along the way, Federation scientists and engineers had provided all manner of expertise toward aiding the homeworld to recover from the ecological damage inflicted upon it following the destruction of the planet's moon, Praxis. The resulting atmospheric pollution, left unchecked, would have rendered Qo'noS uninhabitable if not for this intervention. While many Klingons bristled at the idea of humans coming to their aid—even now, decades later— cooler and more practical minds eventually prevailed. The bond forged during that effort only served to strengthen an alliance many on both sides would have dismissed years earlier as a naive fantasy.

Despite a promising beginning, the Accords would be tested numerous times in the decades since its enactment. Nearly fifteen years earlier they nearly collapsed altogether, when Chancellor Gowron opted to withdraw from the agreement after the Federation declined to participate in the planned Klingon invasion of the Cardassian Union. It was but a temporary setback, with the Accords being restored as the Federation and the Empire joined forces to fight the looming Dominion threat. The treaty remained intact, and the bond between the Federation and the Empire was perhaps as strong as it had ever been. At least, that was the case until the human journalist's startling revelations about secret agencies running amok, lashing out from the shadows while using vaunted Federation "morals" and "ideals" as cover for their actions. Martok knew with utter certainty that there would be no shortage of Klingons, including some who joined him here in this very chamber, who saw these new allegations as more than sufficient reason to once again question the necessity and practicality of the Khitomer Accords. It was this that had so occupied Martok's thoughts in recent weeks, during which he attempted to consider a broad range of viewpoints, both supportive and otherwise, regarding the Empire's long-standing if sometimes troubled relationship with the Federation.

"We have always known that humans and others like them can be as deceitful and dishonorable as any enemy we have ever faced," said K'shaf. "And yet, how many times have we stood shoulder to shoulder as brothers, facing off against some of those same enemies?"

Martok grunted. "If your argument is that humans are susceptible to corruption, I remind you of the circumstances in which I became Chancellor of the High Council." When K'shaf did not reply, Martok released a small chuckle, almost under his breath. "I often wonder if Worf, from wherever the *Enterprise* might be wandering the cosmos, ever laughs at the challenges and headaches he avoided by abdicating his own rightful ascension to the chancellorship."

Worf's challenge and defeat of the previous chancellor, Gowron, in the wake of the latter's shameful political maneuvering at the cost of far too many Klingon lives during the closing weeks of the Dominion War, should have secured his own rise to the role, but he had demurred. Instead, he recommended Martok to be the face of the Klingon Empire as it moved forward into a new age, throwing off the chaos that had plagued it from within. Gowron's corruption along with other internal strife, coupled with the deliberate sabotage of the Klingon government by the Dominion at the height of the war, had nearly torn the Empire apart. Worf viewed Martok as the one best suited to lead all Klingons out of that dark time. For someone with a humble upbringing and modest societal standing who wanted nothing more than to serve the Empire with honor, being asked to shoulder such responsibility was unheard of, and Worf's endorsement had caused no small amount of strife among the members of the High Council.

And yet, here I stand, though I doubt you are laughing today, my friend.

"Have we taken to hushed whispers uttered from the shadows?"

The new voice almost startled Martok but he was able to contain his reaction, and for the first time he noticed the figure standing just inside a nearby entrance to the Hall. It took him the briefest of moments to recognize it as Jo'shwar, another council member. Bald and burly, he moved with surprising stealth despite his bulk, allowing him to enter the room without attracting the notice of Martok or K'shaf. This was of somewhat limited concern to Martok, given the contrary stances Jo'shwar often took when the council was in session and various topics were subjected to rigorous debate. Though he was far from unreasonable or unyielding, he had already voiced fervent disapproval over the newly revealed scandal involving former President Zife illegally arming the planet Tezwa and how those weapons ultimately were used against Klingon forces. The issue had consumed much of the council's time and attention in the weeks since the allegations became known, and though Jo'shwar was not alone with his opinions about how or if the Empire should seek recourse against the Federation, his was one of the louder voices of dissent. To Martok's surprise, the other Klingon did not seem to be driven by an agenda of personal advancement or other gain. At least, he had never made known any such ambitions, and to Martok that was a reason to remain wary. Such opportunists seldom worked alone, or without significant planning to achieve their long-term goals. No, Martok had decided long ago, Jo'shwar was an adversary who bore watching.

How long had he stood there? What had he heard? These were

the questions that called for Martok's attention as he and K'shaf moved toward the new arrival.

"Good morning, Chancellor," said Jo'shwar as they approached. "I did not realize you were in private conference. I did not intend to intrude."

Hardly likely, Martok mused, but he kept the observation to himself. Instead, he forced a professional smile.

"Jo'shwar, you also grace me with your presence so early in the day. Perhaps we should not waste this energy we all seem to have, and convene the entire council so that we may get on with the business of the Klingon people."

Ever one to exploit any sort of potential tactical situation whether in battle or politics and likely thinking along the same lines Martok had considered, K'shaf said, "The chancellor and I were just discussing this pressing matter of what to do about our Federation allies. Another perspective is always welcome."

No fool himself, Jo'shwar could smell a trap being laid for him and rather than attempting to evade the topic, opted instead to charge ahead.

"I have already made my opinion quite clear." To Martok, he said, "With all due respect, Chancellor, peace treaties mean nothing if one of the bound parties engages in wanton treachery."

"Agreed," replied Martok. "However, we cannot condemn many for the actions of a few corrupt individuals."

Jo'shwar sneered. "The corrupted may not be so few."

It was but another variation on the same conversation already held several times during the past weeks, here in the Hall with the full council or with individual members in his office or while enjoying a meal in the city. While Jo'shwar had at first been a moderate voice during those discussions, Martok had watched as the other Klingon's demeanor shifted toward a more extreme position as time passed. Differences between them that he thought had been addressed seemed to be once more rising to the fore, much to Martok's worry. How far was Jo'shwar willing to push this increasing divisiveness, particularly with respect to the rest of the council?

"We have fought wars against the Dominion and the Borg alongside Starfleet vessels," said Martok. "A member of my family serves with distinction aboard the Federation flagship."

His sneer growing more pronounced, Jo'shwar replied, "Serving the whims of one who knew about this plot of Zife's. Picard has kept this secret for years. What other secrets does he harbor? Of how many other crimes against supposed Federation allies does he possess knowledge? Have you spoken with Worf, Chancellor? Does he still hold his captain in such high regard?"

"I don't need to speak with him to know the answer to such questions. Worf has stood by Picard since long before you or I even knew his name. His loyalty is absolute. What does it say of a human that a Klingon would respect him so?" Knowing what Jo'shwar was thinking and would dare not say, Martok leveled his eye at him. "Surely you don't think Worf, a member of my house and a warrior to whom I owe my very life, is somehow unable to judge a person's character and honor?"

K'shaf added, "And it is not just Worf who views Picard with such respect. Remember that he is one of the very few non-Klingons enshrined in the Hall of Warriors. That alone guarantees the respect of all our people until the end of time."

"Yes, yes. I have seen the statue. Placed there by Gowron, as thanks for Picard's service as Arbiter of Succession." Jo'shwar shook his head. "If only we could have predicted the shame Gowron would bring to the Empire."

"But we could not," snapped Martok, "and such hindsight does not negate Picard's status or honor, just as it does not diminish Worf's loyalty to him. Surely after all the trials the Federation and the Empire have faced together, these two have earned from us a measure of trust?"

He turned, indicating the Great Hall with a sweeping gesture. "We have all seen Klingons who acted in similarly despicable fashion put to death right here in this very chamber. What Picard and the others did to remove Zife from power is as close to being a Klingon as any human might hope to achieve."

Of course, he knew that Picard had not been involved in the late president's murder, but that was beside the point. For any Starfleet officer to even consider acting against a civilian Federation leader was all but unheard of. The known instances of such an outlandish action could safely be counted on one hand. For a man of Picard's character to involve himself in such matters spoke to the perceived severity of the circumstances at that point in time.

"You and I disagree on a great many things, Chancellor," said Jo'shwar, "but I confess I find your words on this matter quite compelling."

"Coming from you, that is high praise." Martok punctuated the reply with a leering grin, which evoked quiet laughter from both Jo'shwar and K'shaf.

The other council member raised a hand. "Even if you do manage to sway my opinion, others will not be so easily convinced. Many Klingons will want assurances that the Federation has not committed other acts of betrayal and aggression against us while hiding beneath the banner of peace."

"A view I can understand and appreciate," said Martok.

K'shaf added, "However, if the three of us, with our differing views and concerns, can have this conversation and see common ground before us, surely by working together, the entire council can reach consensus?"

"Listen to us," offered Martok. "Babbling on like politicians rather than warriors." The comment sparked more laughter, and he placed a hand on his companions' shoulders. "We will find a way to guide our people through this, my friends. There remain a great many questions, and together we will find the answers. On that, you have my word."

"And what if those answers force us to take action against our supposed allies, Chancellor?" asked Jo'shwar.

Drawing a long breath, Martok replied, "As always, we will do what is necessary to serve the Empire."

"Even war against an ally?" asked K'shaf.

"Perhaps," said Martok, "but it is our duty to ensure that is the proper course, for all our people, rather than merely the convenient one."

17

Less than five minutes had elapsed since Picard left the bridge in the capable hands of Lieutenant Joanna Faur and opted for the temporary refuge of his ready room. Lying on the couch opposite his desk, he closed his eyes, hoping for a brief respite. Fifteen, perhaps twenty minutes at most was all he would need to stave off mounting fatigue. The events of the long day had seen to it that regular duty shifts were off the table while the crew tended to the ship's various repairs. Add to that a missing member of his crew, and the day's stresses were becoming too much to bear, but he had no choice. His people were consumed with the tasks before them, acting with their usual high level of performance in accordance with his standards and expectations. Their tireless dedication had long ago won his trust just as he had earned their loyalty.

And yet, despite his fervent desire to continue leading by example and being worthy of that devotion, Picard felt fatigue threatening to overwhelm him. He could not remember feeling this way in quite some time. Of course, these were not normal times.

Just a few minutes, he told himself. *No more.*

For the first time in hours, he realized he was hungry. Aside from an all but forgotten meal shared uncounted hours earlier with Beverly and René, he had not left the bridge or his ready room. With an away team now back aboard the alien derelict, he would wait until Commander Worf provided the first substantial report on their progress before retiring to his quarters for a proper rest.

Or until Beverly relieves me of duty or shoots me with a tranquilizer.

Across the ready room, his replicator beckoned, but Picard decided he did not want to waste the energy required to move from the couch. Better to remain here, with eyes closed as he attempted to clear his mind for just a few precious moments.

His door chime sounded.

Damn.

Though tempted to do so, Picard could never ignore such a summons or, worse, order away whoever dared to intrude upon his feeble attempt at rest. The demands of command were as constant as they were unforgiving, and he knew that whoever waited for him on the other side of the door would not call on him without good reason. Resigning himself to the situation, he pushed himself to a sitting position, placing his boots on the deck and straightening his uniform tunic.

"Come."

The door slid aside to reveal Beverly Crusher, standing with arms crossed just to the side of the entry so that she could immediately see where he sat on the couch, as though anticipating that was where she would find him.

"You had to know I'd come looking for you."

Her tone was light enough that it evoked a small chuckle from Picard as she entered the room, allowing the door to close behind her. He shifted his position on the couch so that she could sit next to him.

"Is that professional experience talking, or a wife's intuition?"

Crusher offered a knowing smile. "Yes." Dropping to the couch, she situated herself so that she was resting against Picard's left shoulder. "We need to have a little chat, *Captain.*"

"I know what you're going to say."

"Well, that sounds like a great time saver, but I'm going to say it anyway."

"And you're right."

"Of course I am, but I'm still going to say it." She put a hand on his leg. "You need to stop doing this."

Picard sighed. This was an overdue conversation, and one he should not have avoided for this long.

"What am I doing?" he asked.

"Punishing yourself." When he opted to say nothing in response, Crusher continued, "I suspect you've been doing that in some manner since it happened. That's a long time to carry guilt, Jean-Luc."

"Not if it's justified. We've been over this, Beverly."

Crusher squeezed his leg, just above his knee, hard enough so that he looked up and his gaze met hers. "Yes, we've talked about it, to a point."

In the immediate aftermath of Ozla Graniv's exposé going public and the entire sordid affair being broadcast across the Federation—including distant starbases and starships like the *Enterprise* assigned to deep-space exploration missions—Picard had sat down with Crusher and admitted his role in Min Zife's ousting. Needless to say, the revelation came as a shock to his wife, who like the rest of his senior staff and a select group of other officers drawn into the Tezwa debacle assumed the president chose to resign due to his role in that mess. Learning their captain was involved in the illegal actions evoked a variety of responses, none of them more vocal than the one voiced by Beverly Crusher. While she allowed for his having kept the secret from her prior to their marriage, the idea of him not trusting her with his secret after that did not sit well with her, at least at first.

"My reasons for not telling you haven't changed, Beverly. You would have been duty bound to report me to Starfleet Command, and of course you would've refused to do so. I couldn't put you in that position. Not then, and certainly not after René was born." He rose from the couch and began to pace the ready room's length. "I knew what I was entering into when I had that meeting with Ross and the others. We all did. We all made certain there was no doubt about what we were agreeing to do." In particular, he recalled the uncertainty on the face of Edward Jellico during that meeting, and how he had to be convinced that quietly coercing Min Zife into resigning without making public the true nature of his crimes was the only apparent means of averting war between the Federation and the Klingon Empire.

"Even Jellico, who's as hawkish a military commander as I've ever known, wavered on this, that what we were proposing was the correct course. That's really the point that best illustrates the issue with what we did, Beverly." He paused his pacing, turning to face her. "No matter how aggressive he can be when it comes to matters of defense or security, he's never forgotten that Starfleet is subordinate to the civilian government. He was even more passionate than I was about trying to find some other way to go about the whole damned thing."

Since that fateful day, Picard had questioned, reviewed, and second-guessed the decision hundreds of times. Might there have been another way? With allies like Martok now leading the Klingon High Council, could some understanding have been reached? The chancellor was but a lone individual, and even his influence extended only so far. At the time, appealing to him carried with it the risk of other council members turning on him in favor of seeking vengeance upon the Federation for Zife's crimes against the Klingon people.

Not that any of this mattered in this new reality. Though no official statement had yet been issued by the Klingon government, unofficial reports forwarded by Starfleet Command suggested no small amount of turmoil within the chambers of the High Council. Picard could only imagine the stresses under which Martok now found himself. Though he would have plenty of loyal allies, there would of course be those who would see this as an opportunity to advance their own agendas, including removing Martok from power.

And they'd do so without the fuss of keeping everything secret. Klingon honor is a fascinating thing.

Crusher, who had remained silent on the couch for the minute or so that had passed since Picard resumed pacing, asked, "Is that why you're punishing yourself? Because you think Edward Jellico was a better person than you over this?"

The idea was something he had considered more than once, and every time he entertained the notion it only angered him. This time was no different.

"It's not about who's better," he snapped, instantly regretting the outburst. Drawing a deep breath and releasing it over several seconds, he continued in a more measured tone, "It's about right and wrong. That's what it's always been about. Everything else is just distraction."

"You all were right," said Crusher. "You were also wrong. It's that simple."

Picard scowled. "That should make for a grand defense at my court-martial when I'm tried for murdering a Federation president."

"They can't charge you with that, and we both know it." Crusher's voice was beginning to exhibit an edge, an obvious by-product of their having already had a variation of this conversation. "Damn it, Jean-Luc. You weren't in the room when Zife and the others were killed. You weren't even there when he resigned. A good lawyer could argue that you didn't even make the final decision to act. You're a captain. The others were admirals, and three of them were directly tied to Section Thirty-One."

"I'm the one who brought the evidence to them," argued Picard. "I set it all in motion. All the rest of it is semantics. Besides, those are officers I respect, or at least used to respect. They were friends, to one degree or another."

Now Crusher pushed herself from the couch, crossing the room and standing in Picard's path. As he stopped his pacing, her eyes locked with his. "Tell me you would've sanctioned Zife's murder, and I'll shut up about this forever."

"You know I'd never do that," replied Picard.

"I do. Stop punishing yourself." She pointed toward the port beyond his desk. "Do you think Ross or Nechayev or even Nakamura regret what they helped bring about? Of course not. They'll stand before a court and tell them they removed Zife for the good of the Federation and the safety of everyone in it."

Picard broke their eye contact, glancing at the carpet beneath their feet. "That was our argument."

"And yet here you are, letting it eat at you. Meanwhile, they had to have known even while you were discussing it how things would really go, and you know damned well they never felt an ounce of remorse. Not then and not now, other than the fact they were exposed by that reporter. They violated their oaths by allowing Section Thirty-One to corrupt them; by letting it subvert their loyalties and twist their perception of justice and morality. In their eyes, the ends justified the means, no matter the cost. They knew Zife and the others would be killed, and they never told you. They made you an unwitting accomplice the same way Zife did when he involved all of us in the Tezwa mess."

Reaching out, Crusher placed her hands on Picard's chest. When she spoke again, it was in a softer, almost pleading voice. "They made those choices, without your knowledge or consent. If you want to beat yourself up over your role in Zife's removal from office, that's fine. There's plenty there to pick at, but don't punish yourself for *other people's crimes*."

With a heavy sigh, Picard closed his eyes. "I wish it were that simple."

"Of course it's not simple," replied Crusher, pressing against him. "It's not simple because you have a *conscience*, Jean-Luc. You know what you did was wrong. Even though it likely saved countless lives, you knew what it would do to you, personally, but you took on that pain for the greater good. And it still haunts you, because you're a decent man, the man I love, but you can't afford the luxury of wallowing in guilt and self-pity right now. The crew needs you. They need to see what we've all come to expect from you: confident, in command, and there to lead us through whatever we're facing."

"I know."

While uncertainty in the face of adversity was not unknown to him, Picard was reasonably sure he could count on one hand the times during his life where he had been consumed with self-doubt to the point of near paralysis. Taking command of the *Stargazer* after his captain's death, following his rescue from the Borg Collective, and after the torture inflicted upon him by the Cardassian Gul Macet were perhaps the events that had taken him almost to his absolute limit. His trial by fire aboard the *Stargazer* and his worry in the face of that challenge could be chalked up to youth and inexperience, whereas the latter two incidents had robbed from him any semblance of control over his fate. He had been at the mercy of forces beyond his ability to fight, and both had driven him closer to his breaking point than even he wanted to admit. Though he had shared some of his feelings with Beverly, only in his private conversations with Deanna Troi and her successor as *Enterprise*'s counselor, Doctor Hegol Den, had he revealed the full truth. Still, he had found the strength to carry on even after those grievous offenses against his person. Why was he now finding it so difficult to persevere?

Because in those instances, you were the victim of circumstances, rather than the perpetrator.

The simple, blunt answer was enough to sap his strength. Picard was almost overwhelmed by a need to collapse, either on the couch or the floor, and it took physical effort to remain standing as Crusher rested her head on his shoulder. He reached up to stroke her hair as he felt her lean into him. Her presence was enough to push away his exhaustion, and to soothe the feelings of guilt and unworthiness now gripping him, along with helplessness at having to wait for word on the away team's search for T'Ryssa Chen. While Beverly might be able to offer only temporary respite from those pressures, for now it was enough. Standing with her, it seemed easier to forget about the reality still waiting for him beyond his door. The weight on his heart and even his soul seemed to lessen, if but for a moment.

Then, reality reasserted itself.

An alarm sounded in the ready room and his eyes snapped open. As he pulled away from Crusher, they had time to exchange the briefest of worried glances before the voice of Lieutenant Faur filtered through the ship's intercom.

"Captain Picard, please report to the bridge."

Forcing away his unwelcome feelings, he was moving even before the summons ended. The doors to his ready room almost failed to open in time as he twisted his body to avoid hitting them. Stepping onto the *Enterprise* bridge, he glanced at the main viewscreen and its image of the alien derelict still displayed upon it.

"Report." He could sense his composure and bearing returning as he moved toward the command chair where Lieutenant Faur was rising to her feet.

Faur replied, "We're at yellow alert and I've ordered the shields raised, sir. Several of the derelict's weapons systems have come back online. They'd been dormant since our encounter with the Torrekmat salvage ship."

"Are they reacting to us?" asked Picard as he studied the mammoth vessel.

At the tactical station, Lieutenant Aneta Šmrhová replied, "I don't think so, sir. Aside from closing to transporter range, we've taken no provocative action, but the *Zetoq* has begun moving from its previous location. They're not approaching us directly, but their course suggests they're trying to narrow the gap while maneuvering closer to the derelict."

"They likely know we sent over another away team," said Crusher, who had followed Picard from the ready room and now stood near its entrance at the perimeter of the bridge.

"Bet on it, Doctor. They've been using their sensors to keep an eye on us, and their scans were active when we beamed our people over. If they've scanned the derelict, they likely know about Commander Worf and the others."

Picard mused, "And if they still think we're trying to interfere with their 'salvage operation,' then they're not going to be very happy about that."

Shaking her head, Faur replied, "No, sir. Their lack of transporters is an advantage for us, though. If they want to board the derelict, they either have to dock or send people across in EV suits. So far, there's been no indication they're planning something like that, as they looked to still be dealing with their repairs, but that was before we sent our team back over."

"Hail them. Ask them if they require assistance, but do it in a way that lets them know we're aware of their movements." Moving so he stood just behind Lieutenant Gary Weinrib, the officer substituting for Faur at the flight controller's station, Picard said, "Conn, maneuver us so that the *Zetoq* understands we see what they're doing."

Surely Senthilmal was not ready for another confrontation? Picard could not believe the Torrekmat captain seemed bent on continuing along this course. While doubtless concerned for his own vessel, he also would be worried about his boarding party, which was still missing aboard the derelict. Even so, how could he not see that the *Enterprise* had taken every possible action to demonstrate a desire to avoid further hostilities, and even to establish more constructive relations? Was Senthilmal so singularly focused on the derelict and whatever value it might hold for him and his crew that he was blinded to everything else?

"No response to our hails, Captain," reported Šmrhová. "And now I'm detecting their weapons coming online." She looked up from her tactical console. "They're changing course to intercept us."

Picard looked over his shoulder. "What's our defensive status?"

"With the mains still offline, we'll have to rely on impulse power for shields and weapons. Given the *Zetoq*'s present condition, that should be sufficient." The security chief shook her head. "They have to know this, sir."

Releasing a small sigh, Picard returned his attention to the screen. On it, the *Zetoq* was growing slowly but steadily larger as it continued its approach.

Damn it.

"Sound red alert, Lieutenant."

18

Unable to stay seated or stand in one place, Senthilmal stalked the perimeter of the command center. He tried to study every screen, every indicator, every control. It was obvious from a simple visual scan of the various workstations that the *Zetoq* was still a ship in distress. A reasonable captain, to say nothing of an experienced engineer, would have no choice but to conclude that his ship was ill-suited for the task to which he had committed it.

None of that mattered. He could see no other choice.

"Senthilmal, this is a mistake."

The words, uttered so softly as to be almost inaudible, still made him jump, and he turned to see Jakev, standing less than an arm's length away. Senthilmal saw the look of unguarded concern on the face of his second-in-command. The younger Torrekmat's eyes shifted, as though looking to verify that none of the other crew members were eavesdropping on their conversation. Satisfied that they could speak without being overheard, he returned his attention to Senthilmal.

"Driva has cautioned us about undue strain on the engines. Her work is not yet complete, and she emphasizes these are temporary repairs. Taking the ship into battle at this stage is foolhardy."

"We cannot stand by while these newcomers take from us," snapped Senthilmal.

Keeping his voice low, Jakev replied, "They have made no further moves of aggression against us, despite having ample opportunity to do so. Indeed, they have offered to *help* us. What we are doing is *unnecessary*."

Senthilmal gestured toward the central screen, and when he spoke he was unable to keep the edge from his voice. "They have sent people back to the derelict. We still do not know what happened to our people. If we do nothing, they will claim what is ours."

The report from his sensor technician, Ledor, that she had once again detected the presence of life-forms aboard the abandoned hulk—life-forms consistent with those previously scanned aboard the alien ship that had challenged their claim to the derelict—was still too amazing to believe. How had the newcomers accomplished this feat? There had been no sign of their ship, the *Enterprise*, docking with the larger, drifting craft, and neither had scans registered any sign of smaller transport vessels crossing between the two larger ships. Did they possess some kind of technology that shielded or otherwise masked their movements? If that was the case, what other secrets did they harbor? What other weapons might they be holding in reserve, ready to deploy against the *Zetoq* or any other ship that presented a threat? And, as his own imagination had been asking him since their initial confrontation, what if these newcomers were simply the vanguard of an alien armada, bent on invading this entire region and subjugating all of the Torrekmat people? Senthilmal held no illusions that he and his crew could defend against such action, let alone against this single vessel they now faced, but neither could they allow such a thing to proceed unopposed.

And if they are being truthful, and mean no aggression?

If that was the case, then what had happened to his original boarding party? The small ship Senthilmal had dispatched to inspect the derelict upon their initial discovery was still aboard the alien vessel, so far as he knew, but all contact with his people was lost. Were they dead, or missing as the newcomer captain, Picard, proclaimed in his most recent communication? Instead, Picard blamed the derelict's own anti-intruder systems as the culprit, but that made no sense. Why would an automated protection system neutralize his people while leaving Picard's team unharmed? The explanation felt manufactured and weak, and yet there was something about the other captain Senthilmal could not dismiss. What if the newcomer was just that accomplished at deceit? What if all of this was just a trap, into which Senthilmal and his crew had stumbled?

These and so many other questions taunted him, but their answers remained stubbornly just out of reach. In truth, none of that mattered in this moment—not in the face of the simple fact that these interlopers appeared ready to take away that which he and his crew had rightfully claimed.

"What about their people aboard the derelict?" he asked. "Can you determine what they are doing?"

Still standing at the sensor station, Ledor turned to face him. "Not from this distance. The ship's hull is obstructing our scans. We need to move closer."

"And risk activating the derelict's defenses," said Jakev, and Senthilmal heard the caution in his friend's voice.

"Traek," he called out to his pilot. "Maneuver us closer to the derelict."

An older Torrekmat with deep lines creasing his face and hands, Traek was a veteran navigator, having served for many cycles in defense forces before taking a well-earned retirement and opting to sell his skills on the civilian market. Whereas younger members of the *Zetoq* crew might express worry or even fear in the face of new situations, Traek remained untroubled. At least, he presented that outward appearance, which usually was enough to put his companions at ease.

"Very well," replied Traek, manipulating his helm controls.

Senthilmal saw the change in angle as the *Zetoq* altered its course toward the drifting hulk. They were still much too far away to attempt a boarding without finding some way to link his ship to the other vessel's hull, but even from this distance the mammoth craft all but filled the screen.

"Senthilmal," said Ledor. The sensor technician had turned away from her workstation, and her features were clouded with worry. "The derelict's weapons systems are coming online again. I am detecting the presence of targeting scanners directed at us and the newcomer ship."

The drifting vessel's weapons had posed a moderate danger earlier, but that was when the *Zetoq* was operating at full capacity. With the main drive systems still ailing despite his engineer's best efforts, Senthilmal knew this meant his defenses were compromised.

"Traek," he called out to his pilot. "Can you evade those weapons?"

Not one for obfuscation, Traek instead preferred blunt truth regardless of the consequences. When he turned and regarded Senthilmal, it was with his usual expression of calm.

"Given the state of our engines, I am not certain. I recommend caution. We do not need to engage the newcomer ship. The derelict is much larger than either of our crews can explore without significant commitment of time and resources. Why not simply move to the ship's far side, and attempt a docking maneuver? If these newcomers truly mean us no harm, they will permit us to move away without engaging us. Were I their captain and faced with our approach, I would already be preparing my ship to defend itself."

At the sensor station, Ledor called out, "Senthilmal, the newcomer ship is moving now. It has altered its profile so that it now faces us."

"What about their weapons?" asked Senthilmal.

"Not as of yet, though their defensive shields are active."

"Senthilmal," said Jakev. The tone of his voice communicated his otherwise unspoken warning. After a moment, he added, "They are reacting to our approach. Nothing more. We are not yet ready for another battle."

"Neither are they," replied Senthilmal. "Remember, their primary means of propulsion also suffered damage during the earlier battle. For all we know, the only reason they have not moved to finish us is because they lack the ability. This may be our only opportunity to seize the advantage."

Jakev held up a hand. "If they are weaker than they wish us to know, then we can afford to wait for reinforcements to arrive. We were nearly evenly matched during the previous confrontation. With additional ships to help us, we might well be able to capture the newcomer vessel *and* take charge of the derelict."

It was not an invalid point, Senthilmal conceded. Despite the damage sustained by the *Zetoq* during its earlier battle with the *Enterprise*, they still were able to send a message detailing their current situation, including what was at stake. Additional Jirol Salvage Guild vessels were en route, but still cycles away from being able to provide any meaningful assistance. Until they arrived, Senthilmal and his crew were on their own.

From the sensor station, Ledor reported, "Senthilmal, the *Enterprise* is attempting to contact us again."

Ignoring Jakev's stare, Senthilmal turned toward the sensor technician. "Are they offering assistance again?" That the newcomers had so quickly and efficiently conjured a means of negotiating the barrier separating their language from that of Senthilmal and his people was another point of concern. Whoever these people were, they obviously commanded technology that at least in some ways was far superior to anything with which he was familiar.

"Yes. The message also states they are monitoring our movements. They are continuing to maneuver their ship so that it matches our approach."

Stepping closer to Traek, Senthilmal tapped the pilot on his shoulder.

"Arm weapons."

"Senthilmal," said Jakev, but offered nothing more when Senthilmal leveled a withering look at him.

"They say they are monitoring our movements. That is an implied threat."

"From their perspective, perhaps we are the ones acting questionably?"

Listen to him.

The warning came unbidden, catching Senthilmal by surprise. Was he acting recklessly? Why was he pressing this situation, while other options remained available? The prudent course was to wait for reinforcements. There was little to lose and everything to gain by exercising patience and reserve, at least for the time being.

Releasing the breath he only just realized he was holding, Senthilmal turned back to Traek, ready to order the *Zetoq*'s weapons on standby, but Ledor spoke first.

"The derelict! It is targeting us!"

Senthilmal did not have to say anything, as Traek was already reacting to the warning. His long fingers moved across his console with practiced speed and confidence, and the ship wasted no time reacting to his commands. The image on the display screen changed once again as the *Zetoq* banked away from the derelict, but even the seasoned pilot's skills did not allow the salvage ship to escape unscathed.

Everything around Senthilmal shook and rattled as the first salvo struck whatever remained of the *Zetoq*'s defensive shields. Alarms sounded around the command center, and indicators and status readouts flashed a host of warnings. His crew, hanging on to their consoles to avoid being thrown to the deck, turned to the task of dealing with the new alerts now demanding their attention.

"Shields are down!" called out Ledor.

Jakev moved around Senthilmal, pointing past Traek to the pilot's console. "Evasive action. Move us away from the derelict!" At the same time, he gestured toward Ledor. "Continue monitoring the *Enterprise*."

Even with several decks separating him from the ship's engines, he could feel their strain as they labored to obey the demands Traek placed upon them. Now more than ever, it was obvious that the *Zetoq* had yet to heal from its prior injuries. For the first time Senthilmal comprehended just how ineptly he had handled the entirety of the situation now engulfing him and his crew.

Fool!

"The derelict is firing again!" called Ledor.

Even as he gave the order for a new evasive course, Senthilmal realized he was already too late.

On the main viewscreen, Picard watched beams of brilliant yellow-green energy from two of the derelict's weapons placements converge on the *Zetoq*. The results were devastating and merciless as the double impact sliced through the rear third of the salvage craft's hull. A momentary flash of light accompanied the breaching of the Torrekmat ship's warp core, which expanded within a fraction of a second to envelop the entire vessel.

"Increasing power to forward deflectors," said Lieutenant Šmrhová.

As though anticipating Picard's command, Lieutenant Weinrib added, "I'm giving us a little more distance, sir."

The flight controller tapped a rapid sequence of commands to his console. From his vantage point standing just behind Weinrib, Picard saw the instrumentation relay the results of his maneuvering as the *Enterprise* retreated from the explosion and the conn officer used the hull of the derelict for cover. Though there was already considerable distance between the two ships, being caught in the open with compromised deflector shields invited further damage from the detonation's resulting shock wave. Even with Weinrib's fast action, the viewscreen still flared from the rippling effect as displaced energy washed across the forward shields.

"The *Zetoq* has been completely destroyed, sir," said Šmrhová.

"Sensors are registering debris, but the bulk of the ship was vaporized by their core breach."

Moving from where she had been standing near the door to Picard's ready room so that she was closer to the main viewscreen, Beverly Crusher asked, "Are there any survivors? Did any escape pods eject?"

Picard already knew the answer, but waited for Šmrhová to confirm it.

"Negative," replied the security chief. A subdued tone sounded from her tactical console, and she frowned. "I am detecting a small object moving on a straight-line course away from the debris field." After a moment spent studying her instruments, she said, "It's emitting a signal, sir. I think it might be a form of disaster beacon or buoy."

At the operations station next to Weinrib, Glinn Ravel Dygan said, "Perhaps it was launched automatically as part of whatever protocols were in place in the face of a warp core breach."

Still standing next to Picard, Lieutenant Faur said, "We could retrieve it." Looking to him, she added, "We'd need to maneuver away from the derelict to close the distance and account for interference from its hull for our transporters, sir."

Folding his arms, Picard rubbed his chin. "Can we intercept its signal, or access whatever onboard computer system it contains?"

"Yes, sir," replied Šmrhová. "We can scan its memory banks and transfer everything to a protected partition for later review."

"Make it so, but let's exercise caution. If it's broadcasting a distress message or other information detailing the *Zetoq*'s destruction, I don't want to do anything that might interfere with that."

In addition to simply not wanting to disrupt the final act of the salvage vessel's ill-fated crew, Picard hoped the buoy might show that the *Enterprise* played no role in the Torrekmat ship's final moments. How would messages dispatched by the *Zetoq* and the buoy be received by whoever intercepted the signal? So far, no reply had been detected, and sensors had not yet detected the approach of any other vessels. Would any would-be rescuers come looking to render aid, or simply to capitalize on the bounty left behind by their comrades? Perhaps, as Senthilmal had earlier hinted, they would just be looking for a fight, with an eye toward claiming the *Enterprise* for themselves.

That will be the day.

"Lieutenant Šmrhová," he said, "advise the away team about what's happened up here. Let them know we may need to cut their survey short." Though he loathed the idea of abandoning the search for T'Ryssa Chen, the safety of the entire crew and the ship had to take precedence. Picard took some solace in the fact that Chen would understand, and her Vulcan heritage might even prompt her to remind him that it was the logical course to take.

I'd still like to hear her say it.

19

—•—

T'Ryssa Chen stood on the balcony, looking over its ornately carved ivory white stone railing and down several stories to the bustling village square below her. Buildings, mostly one- and two-story structures of varying size with rounded tops, were situated in a pattern that seemed to spiral outward from the central open courtyard. A few taller buildings were mixed in with the rest, and Chen could see dozens more extending into the forest that surrounded the settlement. As with the foliage she had seen outside the chamber upon her arrival, the trees and other vegetation were at once familiar and alien. The entire scene was bathed by the rays of the brilliant sun overhead, and Chen watched uncounted people moving and convening about the village's open areas or along walking paths and vehicular thoroughfares. It was a welcoming sight and she could easily lose herself in its serenity, but there was just one problem.

"How the hell did I get here?"

As with her arrival in the lavish meeting chamber and her initial encounter with Alehuguet and the other Nejamri, Chen could not recall moving from there to here. Had she been transported? No, she decided. She would have remembered that. Further, she had no sense of missing time. One moment she was in the chamber, the next she was here.

But, wait. There was . . . something.

Disorientation? Chen did not feel dizzy or otherwise out of sorts.

"I love it here, this time of day."

Spinning on her bare heel, Chen turned to see Alehuguet

standing at the balcony's far end. Like her, the Nejamri wore the same light, flowing gown that gave the appearance of modesty while still hinting at the form hidden underneath. Chen still had not yet figured out how she had come to be wearing her own garment, and neither did she know what had become of her environmental suit or equipment. While she did not feel threatened or the need to carry her phaser, her tricorder might prove particularly useful.

Oh, and your communicator. It'd be nice to call home.

"Where are we?"

Moving closer, the Nejamri leader gestured toward the scene below them. "This is just one of the villages on our homeworld, Nejahlora. My family called it and the surrounding region home for generations. It is where I was born, but when I was younger, I moved away from here to explore our world. I lived in villages and cities of every size, including two of the largest population centers on the entire planet. Those were a wonder to behold. So many people, from so many different cultures and walks of life, all blending together to make something that was by itself something unique." She was smiling now, her gaze shifted in a way that told Chen she was recalling fond memories from long ago.

"So, this is a representation of your village?" asked Chen. "A digital facsimile? A holographic projection or something else?"

After a moment, Alehuguet's smile grew wistful. "Something else, T'Ryssa. Holographic representations are presented as a form of virtual immersion for the user or viewer. Nothing about you changes as you interact with the simulation and it evolves or transforms to meet your commands or responses."

Once more, she waved to the village below them. "This is indeed a computer-generated realization. Everything you see before you is the product of a very sophisticated software matrix; a central program continuously interacting with thousands of other, independent programs that in some ways are even more complex than the core process."

"You mean the people," said Chen. "Each person here is its own self-contained program."

"Each person here is their own person, T'Ryssa."

Chen frowned. "I don't get—"

Wait.

Before she could formulate the new question, the balcony before them disappeared. Indeed, her entire point of view seemed to shift as one instant she was above the village square and the dozens of Nejamri occupying it, and the next she was standing among them. Startled by the abrupt shift, she turned to find Alehuguet still standing beside her. The Nejamri leader began walking along one of the paths that curved away from the crowd and toward the buildings at the square's far end.

"Everything here . . . every person here . . . is what? Its own artificial representation?" She touched her stomach. It felt real enough, as did the fabric of her gown. "I'm not really me?"

Alehuguet's smile widened. "You are still very much you, T'Ryssa. At least, as close to you as our computer can re-create. The same is true for each of our people; more than sixty thousand Nejamri are here."

Sixty thousand?

A virtual realm all but indistinguishable from reality was a common experience thanks to modern holographic technology. Chen had spent her share of time on one of the *Enterprise*'s holodecks, either participating in training simulations or immersing herself in worlds based on historical reenactment or taken from the pages of a favorite novel. In each of those cases, there remained a tangible link to the world outside the program. It could be the voice of the ship's computer as she commanded or requested changes to the generated environment, or the simple act of calling for an exit and having a hatch appear to disrupt the illusion and lead the way to the corridor outside the holodeck's confines.

But . . . this?

Returning her attention to their surroundings, Chen now tried to study them in light of this new information. As with most humanoid races she had encountered, the Nejamri here represented a diverse cross section of their species. Tall, short, thin, bulky. Some were pale in complexion, while others possessed darker skin hues. The only constants seemed to be that everyone was dressed in some variant of the multicolored, wispy gown-like garment, and everyone was barefoot. Some, she noted, wore less, and in some cases much less, though such choices seemed not to raise any eyebrows or other looks of disapproval. Given the effort to create or re-create Nejamri society in such exacting detail, Chen made a mental note to inquire at some point about societal mores.

"All right," said Chen, holding out her hands so she could inspect them as she and Alehuguet continued walking the path. "So, these bodies of ours are avatars within a computer simulation. Where are we within the *Osijemal*? And how exactly are you able to hide more than sixty thousand life signs from our scans? This ship is obviously big enough to support that many people, but where are they? Are they shielded or cloaked?" Even with the disruption already experienced by the *Enterprise*'s sensors, Chen found it hard to believe shielding powerful enough to hide such a large population would not register in some other noticeable way.

For the first time, Alehuguet frowned, but it was only a momentary shift before her expression turned to one of enthusiastic realization. "Of course. Now I understand your confusion. Yes, you and I are standing here as simulations of our actual selves, but our consciousness remains intact and fully aware of what we experience here. However, our physical bodies do not exist outside the Haven."

Don't exist?

"Holy . . ." Comprehension dawned, slamming into her thoughts like a hammer striking an anvil. It all made sense, and yet at the same time it was insane.

"Our bodies. The transporter nodes we've found. Your computer and its immense data storage banks." Those and other fragmented thoughts spilled from her mouth, fighting for attention and scrambling to be voiced and heard. There were no visual or other sensory tricks at play here, providing an illusion of being in some other place. She was here; at least, her consciousness was here, integrated in some fashion with the *Osijemal*'s computer core in a manner far superior to any sort of virtual or artificial environment she had ever encountered. And her body?

"What did you do to me?" she blurted. She was certain she knew the answer, but she needed to hear it.

Alehuguet, in a manner Chen was finding increasingly frustrating, remained calm as she replied, "As with myself and everyone else on this ship, your body has been converted from its physical matter state and stored in our data matrix." When Chen had no reply, the Nejamri leader added, "We felt it necessary to show you what we have created, to demonstrate you are in no danger from us, just as you made every effort to show us we had nothing to fear from you."

"But . . ." Chen's initial attempt to pose the question died before escaping her lips, which she quickly found odd if what Alehuguet said was true and she really was not inhabiting her physical body. It was all too much to grasp, just yet. "But, how is this possible?"

"Long ago, we perfected the science of converting matter into energy. Your transporter is similar in many ways, but rather limited when compared to our technology, and is fraught with many risks that we have surmounted. For us, converting our bodies into components for data storage is just one part of a much larger, sophisticated process that enables transference of our consciousness into the Haven, where we live as though we still inhabit our physical forms. Meanwhile, our bodies are stored safely within the *Osijemal*'s data matrix, just as they were upon conversion."

Chen tried to imagine the level of complexity, energy, and even pure computer processing power and data storage required for something so ambitious. "I don't understand. You use a system like our transporter—much more advanced, of course—to convert your bodies into . . . something that can be stored in a computer, but your minds remain active and capable of everything you could normally do?" Then, she connected more dots, almost embarrassed at how long it took her to realize the link. "Of course. Your warp drive capability is limited. Even at warp two or three, it'd still take years to cross interstellar distances. Longer, depending on the circumstances. This ship is an ark, isn't it?"

Alehuguet nodded. "That is an apt description. The *Osijemal*, along with dozens of others like it, carry what remains of the Nejamri through the stars as we attempt to reach our new home. The responsibility for preserving our civilization has fallen to us."

She made no gesture, and neither did she issue any obvious verbal commands, and yet as soon as she finished her reply, the scene around her and Chen shifted. Gone was the village and its multitudes of people enjoying their simulated versions of life within the ship's mammoth computer. Now they stood as though atop an invisible platform, surrounded by space empty but for a single, dull green world before them.

"Nejahlora," said Alehuguet, gesturing to the lone planet. "As it was prior to the *Osijemal*'s departure. Even before I was born, my people knew our world was in its death throes. Uncounted generations of exploiting and polluting its natural resources had brought Nejahlora to a point where its ability to support life was endangered. The air we breathed and the water we drank were killing us, incrementally, with each successive generation."

Listening to the Nejamri's recitation, Chen realized they were moving closer to the planet. Even from this perceived distance, hundreds of thousands of kilometers away, she noted the telltale signs of extreme atmospheric pollution. What should be lush, fertile land and brilliant oceans instead were veiled by a dull, oppressive haze.

"The continents you now see were once far larger," said Alehuguet. "I've seen pictures and recordings of our world from generations past. The planet's polar ice fields were melted long before I was born, and ocean levels rose to consume many coastal regions. People moved inland to escape the rising waters, but the greater danger was the results of unchecked pillaging of natural ores and other raw materials used to build and sustain our civilization over the course of millennia. My parents were still children when the majority of our leading scientific minds reached the conclusion that the only chance of saving our people from total extinction was relocation to some other world capable of sustaining us."

Nejahlora receded from them, and Chen watched as other planets and what had to be the system's primary star came into view. In some ways, this sensation of unfettered movement through space was very similar to standing in the *Enterprise*'s immense stellar cartography center, with imaging software and displays that allowed for spectacular views and virtual flights of fancy such as what she now experienced. Chen counted a total of four planets orbiting the star, of which Nejahlora was the second out from the sun. The others traveled in orbits too close or too far from the star to provide for the sort of environment that had given birth to the Nejamri.

"None of your system's other worlds were habitable," she said.

"Precisely. Though the idea of converting the atmosphere of the third planet was apparently given great consideration and much time and resources were devoted to simulations to determine its feasibility, the plan ultimately was abandoned because it did not hold any of the raw mineral resources we required, and the other two planets were far too small and distant to support all of our people. Our own shortsightedness saw to it that most possible solutions were out of reach so long as we remained on Nejahlora."

The scene changed again, and now Chen saw dozens of ships like the *Osijemal* hanging in space near the planet. She and Alehuguet seemed to fly over the top of one of the nearer vessels, and Chen once more was awed by the size and complexity of the arks.

"When she was a young scientist," said Alehuguet, "what you would call my great-grandmother was one of many Nejamri working to find a world suitable for our needs. Deep-space telescopes were employed by all of our world's major governments, and the discovery of just such a planet was a joint effort among several nations. An automated survey probe was dispatched to that distant star system, and we had to wait years before it returned telemetry that confirmed our greatest hopes: the world was like Nejahlora in many ways, and was uninhabited. It promised us a second chance, so long as we could avoid making the same mistakes that brought us to this point. Armed with this information and the hope it represented, our people began constructing this fleet of ships to carry us to our new world. It was decided the best way to transport such a large contingent of people was to take advantage of our advanced matter-energy conversion and data processing technology. Supporting sixty thousand passengers for a decades-long journey would be impractical. Resource efficiency would only be marginally improved by placing us all in suspended animation. Because we are all stored in the ship's data matrix, we do not need food or medical care."

Chen smiled. "You don't get hungry, or tired, or sick. Or old."

"Precisely. However, the simulacrum stimulates various neural impulses in our brains so we feel as though we require food or sleep at the appropriate intervals. This allows us to interact with the program and each other in a manner very close to actual physical encounters. As for illness or injury, none of that exists here. Oversight processes ensure no one can come to harm within the Haven. This naturally means no one dies, either. When we arrive at our final destination, our technology will produce food from raw stores in the ship's holding areas, at least until such time as we establish an agricultural presence on our new homeworld."

"Amazing." Chen shook her head. "Existing as a computer program, or a pattern in a transporter buffer, for five centuries. I can't even imagine what that must be like."

"You think of your transporter and the computer immersion as two separate processes," said Alehuguet. "They do not have to be." She gestured around them. "It is not something we set out to do, of course. Like many scientific discoveries, it happened rather by accident, but once the feasibility was demonstrated, the technology to create such a virtual realm advanced and became more popular. At first its usage was limited to educational and entertainment pursuits, but medical professionals quickly realized it was a means of arresting a critical disease until a course of treatment or cure could be brought to bear. While it was never intended as a means of prolonging the life spans of perfectly healthy individuals, it provided us with the means to make the long journey from Nejahlora to the new world. Of course, fate saw to it our voyage continued far beyond even our most generous estimates."

Once again, the scene shifted around them, this time to depict a planet far different from the Nejamri homeworld. This one was all but cloaked in thick, dark cloud cover that prevented any sunlight from reaching its surface. So far as she could tell, the planet was dead.

"We arrived at the new world and I along with the Conclave emerged from the data matrix to take stock of the situation. What we learned was an asteroid struck the new planet while we were in transit," said Alehuguet. "The shock of the collision tore away the atmosphere, rendering the planet uninhabitable. Yet, we were here. Returning to Nejahlora was not an option, and other arks were already on their way. The *Osijemal* was among the first to leave home, but the construction and relocation process was to continue long after our departure, for as long as was necessary . . . and possible. After careful consideration, we dispatched a message to our homeworld, advising them of our intention to configure the *Osijemal*'s navigational systems to guide the ship to one of the other planets designated as potential alternate relocation options. The other arks would divide into groups and set course for the other planets. Our hope was that one of the worlds would meet our needs, and we would all eventually gather there. Once the configurations were made, we returned to Haven for the duration of the new journey."

Chen asked, "Are you still in contact with Nejahlora?"

"No." Alehuguet's expression turned somber. "Despite our advances in interstellar travel, our ability to communicate across such vast distances remained somewhat limited. One of our ship's automated functions was to deploy communications beacons that could be used to transmit messages, but it was one of the systems damaged by the interstellar storm we encountered during our journey. It also affected our navigational and propulsion systems. We have no idea if any of our subsequent transmissions ever reached Nejahlora, or the status of the evacuation operations, or if any of the other arks made it to their destinations or what they may have found."

Already considering the options at their disposal, Chen said, "If you can supply the navigational data, the *Enterprise* can chart the locations of those planets. We could send our own probes to investigate. They travel much faster than the *Osijemal*. One or two of the planets may even be close enough for us to conduct our own survey." She tried not to dwell too much on any possible issues this might raise with respect to the Prime Directive. That mandate against interfering with other civilizations was sacrosanct, with numerous oversight provisions even in the case of the other party establishing direct contact with Starfleet or Federation representatives.

But it certainly doesn't apply when they ask us for assistance, she thought, remembering her initial meeting with Alehuguet in the conference chamber.

"I'm sure we can get you back on the proper course, and even help you with your repairs. My crew would love the chance to see all of this." She gestured to indicate the space around them, almost laughing at the thought of Dina Elfiki diving headfirst into whatever energy beam converted her to a program fit for running around in this place.

Around them, the scene of space and the fleet of arks near Nejahlora disappeared, replaced by the chamber that had introduced Chen to the Nejamri. Once more, she stood before the table with Alehuguet and her companions.

The Conclave, Chen recalled.

"We did indeed request your help, T'Ryssa," said Alehuguet. Her reply was emphasized by a chorus of nods and expressions from her fellow Nejamri, some of whom seemed to be offering silent pleas for assistance. "Despite our advanced technology, the damage to our vessel has seen to it that we are trapped here, within the Haven."

Frowning, Chen asked, "If that's true, then I'm trapped here too?"

"Possibly, but I do not know for certain."

"You don't know for *certain*?" The question burst from her lips before she could stop it, and Chen paused to collect herself. Drawing a deep breath, she asked, "If you could bring me in, then why can't you send anyone out?"

Alehuguet replied, "Bringing you to us was admittedly a very risky action on our part, and not one we took lightly. The same was true of the other intruders, the ones who attacked you. The process required more power than we should have spared, but it was the only way to defend against those assailants and their weapons from possibly inflicting damage to some vital system or equipment. We also felt the need to protect you, as we believed you might be someone we could trust to help us. Thankfully, none of you were injured."

"So those salvagers aren't dead? They weren't vaporized?"

As though appalled by the very notion, Alehuguet recoiled and her expression blanched. "Fortunately, they are alive and in apparent good health. I wish I could say the same for their companions and their ship. Given their previous attacks on the *Osijemal*, we felt compelled to defend against further actions. I regret our choice resulted in that ship's destruction."

"But the salvagers already aboard the *Osijemal*; you brought them into the Haven?" asked Chen.

"Yes, but they do not enjoy the freedom we've given you. They've been placed in a detention facility, until such time as we can return them to their companions. We thought it the best decision at the time. Our primary concern was finding a way to effectively and quickly communicate to you the extent of our situation, so you could explain it to your companions. Our Haven has become a prison. Trapped as we are, we cannot properly repair our ship and continue our journey. We need your help so that we might finally reach whatever new home awaits us, and return to our physical bodies once our voyage is complete."

Trying to wrap her head around the magnitude of the request Alehuguet was making, it took almost physical effort on Chen's part not to laugh at what the Nejamri leader was proposing.

Oh? Is that all. Piece of cake, right?

20

—◆—

It was a common misunderstanding among those unfamiliar with such matters that Vulcans simply did not possess emotions. On the other hand, beginning in early childhood and learning over time to suppress them and disallow them from governing so much of their lives was expected of every Vulcan citizen. Indeed, achieving as much distancing as possible or even elimination of such impulses was a goal of many Vulcans. Some devoted their entire lives to that pursuit, facing formidable challenges and other tests to suppress their emotions and focus their minds to the reception of pure logic. The *Kolinahr* ritual was the pinnacle of this rigorous undertaking. So difficult was its attainment that very few mastered the discipline, and those who did were widely regarded as the most respected of all Vulcans.

Prior to his decision to join Starfleet, Taurik had given brief consideration to taking up the demanding ritual. Ultimately, he decided that being required to understand and control his own emotional responses while living among other races possessing diverse attitudes on the subject was the greater challenge. Other Vulcans, most far more accomplished than himself, had served with distinction among the Starfleet ranks and reported coming away with a greater appreciation for their non-Vulcan colleagues. Taurik thought it best to follow their example.

Because of this, he was able to empathize with Commander Worf's growing annoyance with the present situation.

"Have you found anything?" Every word was laced with barely tempered anger, and Taurik noticed the Klingon stood with clenched fists held at his sides. The first officer, despite decades of

service that required him to keep his own, far more violent baser instincts at bay while living and working in close proximity to humans, was not immune from the occasional outburst. Considering the present circumstances and how he must be feeling unable to do anything to affect them, all while being forced to continue wearing the environmental suit he likely found uncomfortable and restricting, for Worf this was a measured display.

"Not yet, Commander," replied Taurik. He turned from the workstation that had fought him at every turn in his attempts to unlock the secrets of the *Osijemal*. "Although we have been able to access some information, I have determined it to be of a 'general knowledge and usage' nature. Vast portions of the ship's main computer remain heavily encrypted and shielded, preventing us from conducting a comprehensive scan."

Worf muttered something that was not transmitted through his helmet's communications system, though his expression was enough to convey to Taurik that it likely involved his desire to express his mounting displeasure with the ship's builders.

"What about internal sensors?" asked Worf.

Shaking his head, Taurik replied, "They also remain inaccessible. Despite damage likely sustained during the ship's journey as well as the recent confrontations with the salvage vessel, most of those systems remain operational." That last part was perhaps unnecessary, he conceded, given their firsthand witnessing of the internal sensors and intruder control system's effectiveness. "As with much of the main computer, higher functions and the automated oversight processes are well protected."

"I just received an update from Captain Picard," said Worf. *"Their attempts to scan the ship's interiors are still being disrupted, either by its hull or other active countermeasures."*

Crossing the control room to join them, Lieutenant Dina Elfiki said, *"I swear, if I didn't know any better, I'd think this ship's computer was actively countering every time I try getting around a security block or encryption firewall. I'm not talking about its pre-*

*programmed anti-intruder processes, which have to be pretty sophis-
ticated given the reliance on autonomous operation. I mean, it's like
the thing is adapting to whatever I do, and maybe even anticipating me, the way a living being would."* She blew out her breath
hard enough to momentarily fog up the inside of her helmet.
"Damnedest thing I ever saw."

"An artificial intelligence with an ability to learn and evolve its
responses based on direct interaction," said Taurik. "My study of
the available sections of operating system software suggests just
such a process in play. Even the truly autonomous systems that
seem to require no outside decisions display similar characteristics."

If he was impressed by the complexity of the alien technology,
Worf chose not to share his opinion. *"There must be a way to gain
access to these systems. Without them, we will be forced to conduct
a manual search that could take significant time and effort to accomplish."*

Though the commander said nothing else, it was a simple
matter for Taurik to divine his true meaning. Worf was ready to
undertake that conventional search for T'Ryssa Chen at this very
moment, though he also was weighing the natural desire to determine the lieutenant's fate against the risks of having additional
Enterprise personnel aboard the derelict vessel. For Taurik, logic
provided one course: So long as any hope remained that Chen was
alive somewhere on this ship, then every effort should be made to
locate her in a manner that presented the least possible amount of
danger to those crew members charged with finding her.

"Even if the entire Enterprise *crew was brought over,"* said Elfiki,
"it would take hours."

Taurik replied, "I estimate seventeen point six hours, assuming our tricorders and other scanning tools encounter the same
issues we have so far experienced. This estimate does not take into
account any difficulties in accessing specific areas of the vessel's
interior, or so far unknown dangers that may present themselves."

"I might be able to help with that."

Along with Worf and Elfiki, Taurik turned to the workstation, his gaze now riveted to the image of T'Ryssa Chen on one of the console's display screens. Unlike them, she no longer wore her environmental suit but was instead attired in a loose-fitting, colorful gown. She appeared otherwise uninjured, and was even smiling at them.

"Lieutenant," said Worf as he stepped closer to the console. *"Are you all right?"*

On the screen, Chen nodded. *"I'm fine, sir. I'm in no danger, and neither are you. In fact, I've been making some new friends here. I apologize for taking so long to contact you, but it's been an interesting last few hours to say the least."*

Taurik cocked an eyebrow. "Hours? Lieutenant, it has been twenty-nine minutes and thirteen seconds since you disappeared."

"Huh." Chen shrugged. *"Okay, I'll have to ask about that."*

"Where are you?" asked Elfiki. *"Can you give us coordinates or some other clue as to your location?"*

Chen's smile returned, and even grew wider. *"Yeah, about that. If there are any chairs out there, you might want to sit down for this."*

Sitting at the head of the observation lounge's curved conference table, Picard regarded the split display on the room's main viewing screen. The leftmost image depicted Commander Worf, who now wore a standard duty uniform transported to him from the *Enterprise.* Now that the *Osijemal*'s life-support systems had been activated, at least in that area of the massive derelict where the away team was working, Worf and the others were free to move about that section unencumbered by their environmental suits.

On the right side of the screen was the image of a smiling T'Ryssa Chen. She appeared unharmed or otherwise unaffected by the incredible sequence of events that had transpired since her disappearance, though Picard had to remind himself that what he now saw was not actually Chen but instead a near-identical computer-generated representation of her. To him, she looked every bit as real as the woman he knew, or as finely detailed as a simulation of any person with which he had interacted on the holodeck. It was she, working with her newfound Nejamri friends, who had guided the away team through the process of activating the life-support systems.

"And you're certain you're all right, Lieutenant?" asked Picard.

Chen replied, *"Yes, sir. I admit it took some getting used to, and I'm still not sure how I feel about being stored as a computer file, but the Nejamri technology is amazing."*

Seated to Picard's right, Geordi La Forge said, "I could probably spend months over there poking around."

"You may get your chance, Commander." Picard, along with La Forge and Doctor Beverly Crusher, had listened with rapt fascination as Chen described her experiences aboard the *Osijemal* and the Nejamri's plea for help. His relief at seeing Chen alive and well was tempered by the remarkable story she had conveyed. Sixty thousand people, each existing as a consciousness disassociated from their physical body? Setting aside the philosophical, metaphysical, and even spiritual discussions such a scenario prompted, Picard found it difficult to imagine the sheer processing power required of any computer charged with such a daunting task.

"All right," said Picard, redirecting his attention to the viewscreen. "Lieutenant, are the Nejamri certain we can provide assistance without posing any danger to them?"

"They're sure they can guide us through repairing the systems that oversee their transfer process to and from the computer, but that's not even the top priority, at least not yet." Chen paused, looking somewhere offscreen before stepping aside to allow a new figure to enter the picture, and Picard and his officers got their first look at a Nejamri.

"Captain Picard, I am Alehuguet. It is an honor to meet you. On behalf of all my people, I appreciate your concern for our safety, and your willingness to help us."

"The honor is mine, Alehuguet." Picard almost stumbled over her name. He had asked Chen if the Nejamri leader preferred a more formal term of address, but the lieutenant assured him such conventions were unnecessary. After introducing Crusher and La Forge, he said, "We will render whatever assistance we are able. I assume you are aware of the other parties who've shown an interest in your vessel."

"*Indeed, Captain. The* Osijemal's *defensive capabilities are hampered by the damage it has sustained during our voyage, and were exacerbated by the arrival of the individuals looking to plunder our vessel. It is our hope we can address those issues in short order. As you might imagine, a great deal of power is necessary to sustain this ship. We never anticipated a journey of this duration, and the damage inflicted by the ion storm has only added to our problems. Our battery storage arrays are being taxed to their limits, and our solar energy collectors have been unable to draw in energy on a consistent basis. Once the* Osijemal *is returned to full operational status, these concerns will be nullified.*"

Chen added, "*Repairing or rerouting damaged systems will require more power than is available, sir. I suggested we might be able to set up a power transfer from the* Enterprise.*"

Shifting in his seat, Picard regarded La Forge. "Geordi?"

The engineer nodded. "In theory it should be easy enough. We'll have to make sure there are no compatibility issues, but I'm sure we can figure out a workaround if something comes up during our check."

"Will this impact our own repair efforts?"

"We can handle both, sir. My team's making good progress and we're still on schedule. I can delegate overseeing the repair duties long enough to tackle this. We'll get it done, Captain."

Picard knew better than to press La Forge for too much detail or explanation. None was needed. When it came to his estimates and evaluations of anything pertaining to the *Enterprise*'s operation, the chief engineer's word was his bond and it was a level of trust he had earned long ago.

"*Once the power situation is stabilized and they guide us through the necessary initial repairs,*" said Chen, "*the Nejamri can transfer enough engineers and technicians out of the Haven to finish the work. That's what they would do under normal circumstances if it was something they couldn't deal with from inside the Haven, but that ability was cut off after the damage inflicted by the ion storm.*"

La Forge perked up at this. "So, what we thought were simply automated processes were actually tasks being carried out by your people from . . . from within your computer?"

"*To a certain extent, yes.*" Alehuguet smiled. "*Many of the minor processes overseeing regular operations are indeed left to autonomous oversight systems, but even those could normally be overridden by one of our technicians if necessary. After the ion storm, that ability was severely compromised. However, our matter-energy conversion technology allowed us to direct a crude manifestation of some of our technicians into controlled energy streams, which allowed them to carry out some simple repairs outside our data matrix.*"

On the other side of the screen, Worf added, "*We observed this phenomenon ourselves, Captain. Based on Alehuguet and Lieutenant Chen's descriptions, it is also a very dangerous undertaking for the Nejamri.*"

"*Quite right, Commander,*" replied Alehuguet. "*It risks neurological damage to the individual carrying out that task. We only undertake such risky ventures when absolutely necessary. Your presence here is an enormous gift to us, Captain.*"

From where she sat to Picard's left, Doctor Crusher said, "Speaking of risks, I'm concerned about Lieutenant Chen. According to her report, you brought her into your computer matrix not through your normal transfer procedure, but rather something similar to what you've been using to make your repairs. I'm worried that this transfer may have unintended side effects."

"*I feel fine, Doctor,*" said Chen. "*Some initial disorientation when I arrived, and an occasional bit of dizziness when Alehuguet has moved us around, but otherwise, I'm okay.*"

Crusher glanced at Picard before replying, "That's good to hear, but I'll still want to give you a thorough physical once you're back aboard ship."

"Understood."

"There is another issue," said Picard. "The salvage merchants. They sent a distress message before their ship was destroyed. Our long-range sensors show no other vessels within scanning range, but they're still inhibited by our proximity to the *Osijemal*. We have to assume other ships will be coming to investigate." He was not comfortable with the *Enterprise*, still dealing with its own repairs, facing another possible confrontation while not operating at full strength. Likewise, the Nejamri vessel remained vulnerable until its own systems were restored.

"Captain," said Chen, *"if it helps, the people they sent aboard to inspect the ship? They didn't die in that firefight. The Nejamri brought them into the Haven too. They're in a sort of brig, ready for release back to the Torrekmat if other ships come calling."* She paused before adding, *"And assuming we can all be transferred out of here."*

"And if we're not able to retrieve you or that boarding party, whoever comes looking for the *Zetoq* will still be very unhappy. We need to be ready for that." To La Forge, Picard said, "Geordi?"

The chief engineer replied, "If we can prioritize getting the *Osijemal*'s defenses ready while we're conducting the power transfer, that should give us an extra advantage if someone else shows up."

"There are tasks we can perform to aid in that effort, Captain," said Alehuguet, *"and that ability will only expand as we regain power. However, we regret the destruction of the other vessel, and we do not wish to cause them further harm. I am hopeful this can be avoided."*

Nodding at the suggestions, Picard said, "We'll set to work immediately. Mister Worf and Lieutenant Chen, provide whatever assistance you can from . . . from where you are."

Once everyone on the viewscreen offered their acknowledgment and the communication was ended, Picard rested his hands on the conference table. The silence was fleeting, however, before Crusher spoke.

"I'm worried about Chen. Without being able to compare Nejamri physiology to ours, there's no way to know if whatever they did to her will have any sort of debilitating effects."

"I agree with your concerns," replied Picard. "For the moment, however, she seems fine, and she's now our liaison with Alehuguet and the others." He had not begun the day expecting to find himself and his crew in another first-contact situation. Though he welcomed the opportunity to meet representatives of a newly discovered civilization, doing so in a manner that placed any of his people at risk wore on him. "The fastest way to get Lieutenant Chen back to us is to help the Nejamri, so for now that's the priority." Once more, he looked to his chief engineer. "Geordi?"

The engineer's confidence was unwavering. "I'm on it, Captain."

"Very well, then." Picard rose from his seat, signaling an end to the meeting. "Make it so."

21

The conference room doors slid aside, and Phillipa Louvois walked in to see William Riker rising from his chair. He was the room's lone occupant, and she knew he had been waiting for nearly thirty minutes, but if that bothered him he offered no outward sign.

Remember, he's a hell of a poker player.

"Madam Attorney General," said Riker, his voice crisp and commanding. There was no particular warmth in his greeting, much as she expected. "I heard about Admiral Ross. I'm happy to see you're all right."

"Nothing a few stiff drinks and an enhanced security detail won't fix." In the wake of the attack on William Ross at the Federation Security Agency detention facility, security around all Section 31 suspects had been augmented and installations where they were being housed had been placed on heightened alert conditions. Access to any of the suspects, particularly those perceived as high-value targets, was now strictly controlled subject to approval only by her and Admiral Akaar.

Changing the subject, Louvois said, "Thank you for meeting me, Admiral. I know it was short notice, and you're very busy."

"I wasn't aware I had a choice. Admiral Akaar's *invitation* seemed rather clear on that point."

Years of ingrained Starfleet habits made Louvois take a quick appraisal of his uniform and general appearance. She was not surprised to see he presented himself as the epitome of a spit-and-polish officer, from the tips of his boots that reflected the overhead lighting to the tailored uniform and the precisely trimmed hair and beard. She noted there appeared to be more gray in his beard and at his temples than the last time she had seen him, which was not unusual for a man of his age. Still, the uniform suited him. She suspected that, like her, Riker would never be truly at ease when wearing civilian attire. When she dressed for work, her clothing was on par with a Starfleet duty uniform. Even her current ensemble of blue pantsuit, white blouse, minimal jewelry, and shoes designed for comfort was intended by her to feel somewhat like a uniform.

Old habits.

Louvois decided an attempt to lighten the mood was in order. Even with the possible directions their conversation might take in the coming minutes, it was her hope their meeting would not turn toward the adversarial. She offered a small smile, gesturing with the padd in her left hand for Riker to retake his seat. "Blame me for that, and I apologize for coming off as abrupt." She opted for the chair directly opposite Riker's at the table. "I can be a bit demanding when I'm pressed for time or resources."

"That, I remember." He returned her smile, and she recalled that wordplay and a natural charm were talents he wielded with formidable skill. "You made that abundantly clear the first time we met."

"Yes, I suppose I did." Louvois settled back in her chair, recalling her first memorable meeting with Riker, twenty years earlier. She was just beginning her assignment as a Starfleet Judge Advocate at Starbase 173, while Riker was first officer of the previous *Starship Enterprise.* What began as a routine stop for Captain Picard and his crew quickly morphed into her first true test as a Starfleet JAG, when she was forced to preside over the case that ultimately decided the android Data was not Starfleet property but instead a sentient being entitled to the same civil rights as any other Federation citizen.

It was a landmark ruling that looked good on her résumé, but one that had always made her feel uncomfortable. While she was impartial and even ambivalent to the case at its beginning, the trial as prosecuted by then Commander Riker and defended by Picard had been eye-opening in every conceivable sense of the term. That she had come so dangerously close to summarily ruling on Data's fate without that trial, if not for Picard's full-throated argument for his officer and friend, still made her uneasy whenever the topic was mentioned. In many ways, that single case had altered her attitudes and perceptions as a lawyer and—she hoped—a person.

"You and I never had a chance to talk after that business was concluded and the *Enterprise* left," she added. "And I never followed up. It's been a long time coming, but I apologize for putting you in that position. Even though the rule book was on my side, it was still a tremendous and unfair burden to put on you. And yet you were able to set aside what I only later understood to be deep personal feelings and carry out that assignment with complete professionalism. Your commitment to your oath is one of the things I've always respected about you, Admiral."

For a moment, it looked as though Riker would maintain his composed bearing, allowing no emotional response to what he likely considered unanticipated praise. Then, he visibly relaxed in his chair, and he nodded. "Thank you, Madam Attorney General. I appreciate that."

With that out of the way, Louvois knew it was time to get down to business. "As was the case then, the issues we're currently facing are equally unpleasant, if not more so. I think you'll agree we're dealing with nothing less than a full-blown crisis of confidence within Starfleet and Federation leadership. Everything we've been taught to believe and encouraged to trust has been called into question. Do I think we can survive this mess and push forward, perhaps learning valuable lessons along the way and discover how to do things better from now on? Absolutely. Will that be a painless process? Not at all. We've already seen how bloody things are going to get, Admiral, and it will all get much, much worse before it even thinks about starting to get better."

"I agree," replied Riker. He offered nothing else, and Louvois saw he had in subtle fashion resumed his former, reserved posture in his seat. The poker face had returned. He was no fool, she knew. Riker would wait and see where the conversation looked to be heading, weighing his responses and giving away nothing for free. These were not the actions of a man trying to hide guilt or anything of that nature. Instead, they were the practiced maneuvers of a skilled negotiator and an accomplished tactician.

"Before we get into this," she said, "I want you to know you're not considered a suspect in any of the allegations made by Ozla Graniv's report. I asked for this meeting as part of a fact-finding mission because of your relationship with one of the people who *is* implicated." She let the sentence hang in the air, allowing him to reach his own conclusion. It was a short wait.

"You mean Captain Picard."

No sense sugarcoating it.

"Yes," she replied. "Captain Picard." She tapped the table with one fingernail. It was time to start zeroing in on where she wanted this discussion to go. "How long were you his first officer?"

"Fifteen years." The reply was immediate, almost curt. While Riker maintained his bearing, Louvois did not miss the slight narrowing of his eyes and tightening of his mouth.

She said, "During your tour on the previous *Enterprise*, you were offered promotion and your own command. Twice. You were made such an offer even before you reported for that assignment. You declined each of those opportunities in favor of a lateral move from your previous role as first officer of the *Hood*. Why?"

For the first time, Riker frowned, allowing a hint of suspicion. "At that point in my career, I thought the *Enterprise* first officer's job would be more interesting."

"Any regrets?"

"None whatsoever." Leaning toward her, Riker clasped his hands before him and rested them on the table. "And before you ask, I don't have any regrets about passing up command of the *Aries* or the *Melbourne*, either. At that time, learning how to command a ship—how to inspire a crew to follow you anywhere you might lead—from a man like Jean-Luc Picard was an unparalleled opportunity. If I had it to do over again, I'd make the same choices without hesitation." He held her gaze after he finished speaking, and Louvois suspected another interviewer might have looked away or even flinched beneath his cold, penetrating eyes.

I'm a pretty good poker player too, Admiral.

"Your relationship with Picard—"

"*Captain* Picard."

Now we're getting somewhere, she thought.

"Your relationship with *Captain* Picard is well known. No one in their right mind would question your loyalty. Do you think he feels the same way toward you?" She suspected he might now be anticipating something along these lines, as evidenced by his once more relaxing just the slightest bit.

"I like to believe so," he replied.

"I'd think it was obvious." Louvois reached for the padd that until now had sat undisturbed on the conference table. She tapped a control and the device activated, and she called up a copy of Riker's Starfleet personnel record.

"Fifteen years working together," she continued, her eyes still scanning the file's contents. She had already familiarized herself with it, of course, as part of her preparation for this meeting, but having the text in front of her helped jog her memory with respect to details. It also provided her an easy means of controlling the conversation's tempo as she paused every so often to review a particular passage. "Putting your trust in one another, even putting your lives in each other's hands. It stands to reason you were his confidant on any number of matters. His sounding board; even his conscience. There likely would be a great many things he told you that he might not tell anyone else. Not even the ship's counselor. As captain, there would be precious few people with whom he would feel that sense of comfort and trust."

Riker's frown returned. "Begging your pardon, Madam Attorney General, but is there a point to this?"

"What can you tell me about his involvement in President Zife's removal from office?"

"Nothing. Like pretty much everyone else who wasn't in on it, I had no idea he was involved until I saw the news reports and read Graniv's exposé." He paused, glancing at the conference table separating them. "I admit it's pretty damning on the face of it."

"On the face of it?"

"Meaning you and I both know this wasn't just some power-hungry rogue group trying to usurp power for their own ends. There's no way Captain Picard would ever be a party to something like that. I think we both understand what he and the others were thinking at the time, given the shady deals Zife had conducted. What he did posed a direct threat to Federation security. I can't condone the methods and I hate to say it, but in this case the ends all but justified the means."

Louvois waited a beat before saying, "You seem rather certain of him. Captain Picard, I mean."

"I am."

"But he never confided in you about any of it."

Before answering, Riker drew a long breath, another indication he was growing annoyed with how the discussion was evolving.

"As I said, Madam Attorney General, he never said a thing."

"Why do you suppose that is?" asked Louvois.

As though realizing he needed to keep himself in check, Riker removed his hands from the table and rested them on the arms of his chair. "You'd have to ask him, but if it were me, I'd want to insulate my people from any fallout resulting from my actions. We both know what happened to President Zife was wrong, by any legal definition. What he did to precipitate all of that was also wrong, but exposing him publicly at that time would've only been disastrous for the Federation." His expression hardened. "But, there's no way Captain Picard would ever sanction Section Thirty-One killing Zife."

Louvois returned her gaze to her padd. "Still, it was his report to Admirals Ross, Nechayev, Jellico, Paris, and Nakamura that set the entire thing in motion. At best, he's an instigator of illegal activity. At worst, he's an accessory to murder."

Riker glared at her. "You can't be serious."

"At the moment, nothing's off the table." She set aside the tablet. "We're just getting started here, Admiral. Bodies are going to fall, en masse. I don't want that to happen, but I likely won't have a choice. All I can do is go where the evidence takes me, and proceed according to the law. I'm not happy about it, but that's the job. Right now, what I do know is that *Captain* Picard seems to be developing a habit of helping to remove duly elected heads of state. Zife was just the first one, but we can't forget Ishan Anjar, can we?"

It occurred to her in that moment that it was soon after the arrest of President Ishan that her path last crossed Riker's. There was an avalanche of debriefings, interviews, and paperwork that had followed that very unfortunate and very public removal of the Bajoran impostor who had risen to power while hiding behind an alias and after colluding in the assassination of President Nanietta Bacco. If not for Picard and his crew, with the able assistance of Admirals Akaar and Riker running interference for the *Enterprise* from the former's office at Starfleet Command, the truth about Ishan might never have come to light. The first anniversary of Bacco's assassination was looming, along with all of the events that had transpired in the months following her murder and dealt the Federation a black eye that still had not healed.

And now, here we are, getting punched again.

Seeing Riker winding up to rebuke her, Louvois held up her hand. "Ishan was a completely different situation. Picard did everything he could to make sure I had what I needed to bring a legitimate case for Ishan's arrest. We owe him a huge debt of gratitude for that, but it doesn't erase what he did with Zife."

"You're really looking to hang him, aren't you?" Riker had abandoned his reserved demeanor, and now leveled an accusatory finger at her. "After everything—*everything*—he's done. Everything he's given, everything he's lost, and you're still looking for a reason to destroy him."

Louvois did not flinch. "If I honestly thought that, he'd already be in a cell somewhere, but let's not pretend he hasn't bent or broken the rules when he decided it was necessary. While we're at it, the reason you and I are having this meeting alone in a conference room instead of an interrogation room with you in shackles is because so far as I can tell, you're not implicated in any of this."

"But you're not convinced I'm innocent."

"I don't know one way or the other."

Stopping long enough to let her own ire recede, she reached again for the padd. "Tell me, did he ever talk to you about any of the *Enterprise*'s most recent missions?"

If Riker was confused or surprised by the abrupt change in topic, he gave no outward sign. "No. We've not spoken in a while. He's out in the Odyssean Pass, and I've been busy with the *Titan*."

Calling up another file from her tablet, Louvois said, "Did you know you have a doppelganger in a parallel universe?"

"If you've read the *Enterprise*-D logs," replied Riker, "then you know we all have doppelgangers in hundreds of thousands of parallel universes. Maybe millions."

"I'm talking about one he encountered out in the Odyssean Pass." She divided her attention between him and her padd as she reviewed her notes. "Seems the *Enterprise* ran into a parallel-universe version of the *Enterprise*-D, commanded by that universe's version of you, from a time about twenty years in the past. Captain Picard wasn't there, because in that reality he never survived his assimilation by the Borg. He still helped you destroy the Borg cube that was set to attack Earth, but was unable to be saved.

So your field promotion to captain was made permanent, and the *Enterprise* sailed on."

Riker said, "I heard about it, but I haven't read the report."

"I know," replied Louvois. "Even if you had, you wouldn't know that after his encounter with the other you, Picard gave him the technical specifications for transphasic torpedoes, to be used against the Borg in his universe." She tapped the tablet. "He didn't mention that in his official report, but it is in his personal log as transmitted to the Starfleet Archives Annex at Aldrin City on Luna."

Now Riker's irritation was obvious. "You accessed his archived personal logs? Those are supposed to be protected for at least a century."

"Absent unusual circumstances, you'd be correct," said Louvois. "But I think we can agree the current circumstances are anything but usual. So I obtained a court order to access his records. My original intention was to search for any mentions of President Zife. You'll be interested to know that I found none. Not a single reference to the entire affair, recorded for posterity and future historians, which is the primary purpose for archived and protected personal logs stored at the annex. So far as I can tell, Captain Picard told no one about what happened. Not his wife, not you. No one."

Sighing in obvious exasperation, Riker leaned toward her. "What are you getting at?"

Louvois rested the padd on the table and then folded her hands before her. "Everyone keeps secrets, including Captain Picard. Including you. Until I know whether those secrets are relevant to this investigation, neither he nor you are off my radar or off the hook. Not by a long shot."

22

—•—

Standing with one hip resting against the master situation table that was the centerpiece of main engineering's primary work space, Geordi La Forge crossed his arms and reviewed the arrays of status readouts and indicators. From here, he and his team of engineers could monitor the current status of every shipboard system, as well as take direct action to access, override, or deactivate anything requiring attention or intervention. The station even allowed La Forge to circumvent—within certain limits—the *Enterprise* computer's vast array of autonomous systems in favor of direct human action. His influence over the starship and its thousands of interconnected, often interdependent, yet occasionally conflicting processes from this single station was about as close to being a god as any living being could get, at least so far as the realm of engineering was concerned.

Let's not get too carried away, Mister Chief Engineer.

"All right," he said, mostly to himself given there was no one else in earshot. "Computer, enable auxiliary shielding around the warp core."

The feminine voice of the *Enterprise*'s main computer replied, *"Auxiliary shielding activated."*

"Take all transporter, replicator, and holodeck systems offline. Activate the restrictions I coded for sensors, communications, deflector shields, and life support. Program La Forge Delta Lima Fourteen."

The computer responded, *"Program activated."*

Even without melodramatic comparisons between engineers and deities, this was where La Forge truly felt most at home. Though he had studied engineering while a cadet at Starfleet Academy, it was but one of several subjects in which he had immersed himself. His primary field of training, starship operations with an emphasis on helm and navigation, along with a natural curiosity, led him to engineering courses. To him, at least, the two functional areas shared a much more symbiotic relationship than even some of his fussiest teachers seemed willing to admit. When he pressed a control on a bridge console, he wanted to understand the processes and mechanics involved in carrying out the related instruction.

Initial assignments aboard starships only served to reinforce his beliefs, and the officers who oversaw his duty assignments saw that curiosity and channeled it, tasking him with ever increasing responsibilities as he moved between bridge duty and time spent belowdecks in engineering. It was a trend that continued upon his transfer to the newly commissioned *Enterprise*-D while he was still a young lieutenant. Under Captain Picard's command, a junior officer's education was an ongoing process, with La Forge taking advantage of every opportunity to expand his expertise and gain what would become an unparalleled working knowledge of the ship's every system. When the time came for Picard to appoint a new chief engineer following his first year commanding the *Enterprise*, he had without hesitation selected La Forge for the job.

And it's just been a hell of a ride ever since, hasn't it?

His mild, passing amusement at the wayward thought was pushed aside as La Forge continued to study the situation table. He had arranged the table's configurable display so that he now had a bird's-eye view of every system that would play a part in the upcoming task. All looked normal, or at least as close to normal as he could expect, given the circumstances. According to the information displayed before him.

So, why was he uneasy?

"Is something wrong, Commander?"

Breaking his gaze from the displays, La Forge saw Lieutenant Commander Linn Payne standing at the table's far end. The assistant chief engineer held an engineering padd in her left hand, and the look on her face told him she must have seen him poring over the situation readouts and his own troubled expression.

"No, Linn." Pushing himself from the table, he rubbed his temples. "I think I'm just tired. Been a long day."

The long hours since the *Enterprise*'s initial encounter with the *Zetoq* and the time spent overseeing repairs coupled with the new need to help the Nejamri restore power to their vessel was beginning to take its toll. On long days like this, the strain of his ocular implants resulted in headaches. While easily treated, they were still annoying and contributed to his overall fatigue and, ultimately, his mood.

"For what it's worth," said Payne, stepping up to the situation table and laying her padd on its surface, "I've double-checked all the configurations for the navigational deflector. Everything looks fine."

La Forge nodded. He had already seen her preliminary report, verifying she had made a comprehensive check of the tasks he had laid out as part of the team's preparations.

"I know, but whenever we try to figure out a way to marry up normally incompatible technologies, I get a little nervous. We can get a little creative around here, sometimes, and there's always a risk whenever you try to make a piece of equipment do something it's not designed to do."

After discussing the power transfer issue with Taurik and T'Ryssa Chen and—by extension—the Nejamri technicians still trapped in their vessel's mammoth computer matrix, it quickly became apparent that the logical course of action was to utilize the *Enterprise*'s primary deflector array. Designed to direct energy at modifiable frequencies, it was the one piece of equipment best suited for transferring power from the starship to the *Osijemal*. La Forge and Payne had worked together to create a configuration for the deflector's emitters that would allow it to engage several of the Nejamri ship's solar collectors. In theory, the effect would be no less stressful than if the massive vessel had moved to within fifty million miles of a primary star, allowing its collectors to absorb the transferred energy and quickly replenish its flagging battery storage farms.

"Okay. Let's do this," he said, returning his attention to the situation table.

"La Forge to away team. Are you ready over there?"

Standing before the workstation console that had served them to this point, Taurik and Dina Elfiki exchanged glances. Giving both the console readouts and her tricorder a final look, she shrugged.

"As ready as we'll ever be, I guess."

Standing a few paces away from the console, giving him and Elfiki room to work, Worf nodded at the informal report before tapping his combadge. "We are ready, Commander."

In truth, there had been little for him or Elfiki to contribute during the preparation phase for the attempt to transfer power from the *Enterprise* to the *Osijemal*. Commander La Forge and other engineers oversaw the needed modifications once it was decided the starship's main deflector would be utilized for the effort. Meanwhile, T'Ryssa Chen reported that Nejamri technicians and other specialists, working as they were able from within the giant ship's computer system, took on the process of verifying the vessel's solar collectors could handle being linked to the *Enterprise*. Taurik's and Elfiki's roles had been limited to carrying out whatever instructions or duties asked of them by T'Ryssa, who communicated information from the Nejamri about those tasks requiring physical interaction with equipment or other systems.

Releasing an audible yawn, Elfiki then made a show of stretching her arms high above her head. "I cannot tell you how happy I am to be out of those EV suits. After a while, those things start to smell like feet."

"Agreed," said Worf, making no attempt to conceal his relief at also being freed from the suits.

Likewise, Konya chimed in, though his tone was more playful. "Maybe your feet." The comment earned him a withering glare from Elfiki.

"You're one to talk," replied the science officer. "Your quarters smell like a locker room that hasn't been cleaned since we left Earth."

Konya smiled. "It's all part of my rugged masculine charm."

"I suspect Trys is happy her nose takes after humans." Elfiki matched his grin with one of her own. "I can't imagine her putting up with you if she had Vulcan olfactory senses."

Taurik, studying his tricorder's status readings while listening to the banter, replied, "The scent of unwashed feet is not an odor I would normally employ for such a comparison. I understand that even with their internal temperature controls, environmental suits can still be so restrictive as to cause perspiration, which naturally is absorbed by our undergarments and the suit's interior lining. Nevertheless—"

"Joke, Taurik." Elfiki chuckled. "I was joking."

Cocking his right eyebrow, the Vulcan replied, "As was I."

Elfiki laughed again, before landing a playful slap on his arm. "Best straight man on the ship, bar none." They both went back to their final checks and neither spoke for a few moments before she asked, "What do you suppose it's like?"

Taurik, engrossed in his review of the workstation displays, turned to regard Elfiki. "I beg your pardon?"

"Inside the computer," replied the science officer, tapping the console to emphasize her point. "Do you think Trys is okay?"

"Her last report indicated she was suffering no adverse effects to the transposition." Closing his tricorder, he added, "Though I am concerned about the disorientation she mentioned. We have no comparable experiences by which to judge what she has undergone. There may well be ramifications we are unable to predict." He had been mindful to pay attention to her during their communications while completing the various preparatory tasks, listening and watching for any signs of strain. Of course, he knew he was watching an artificial representation of her, but if she was suffering from any sort of neurological stress it would likely manifest itself in her speech patterns.

Elfiki patted his arm again. "Yeah, I'm worried about her too."

"Me three," added Konya. "I'll be happy when she's out of that thing and back here with the rest of us." He looked to Worf. "Right, Commander?"

"Indeed." The first officer had remained relatively quiet over the past hour, allowing Taurik and Elfiki to concentrate on assisting with the preparations. With Konya and his security detail remaining on the alert on the off chance there might still be some rogue Torrekmat salvagers wandering around somewhere on the ship, that left Worf alone with his thoughts. While he was not one to show his feelings with regard to such matters, Taurik knew the Klingon was very protective when it came to his fellow crew members. That sense of responsibility, already an intrinsic component of his duties, was only heightened in situations such as this, with an away team separated from the *Enterprise* and susceptible to possible danger. Worf had not allowed himself to relax since Chen's disappearance, and even word of her being alive and safe—in a sense, anyway—had done little to ease the obvious worry he was able to hide from everyone.

Almost everyone, Taurik thought.

"All right, everybody," said La Forge over the communications channel, which remained open throughout the preparation steps. *"Let's do this."*

Every time T'Ryssa Chen was certain she had become accustomed to her current situation, something happened to remind her that everything around her was artificial. None of it was real, and yet, *everything was real.*

This time, it was Alehuguet whisking her away from the simulated environment of the control center for the *Osijemal*'s solar energy collection arrays. There, Chen had watched dozens of Nejamri technicians conducting all manner of inspections on the ark ship's automated systems. Like everything else she had encountered since being transferred to this place, the room looked, felt, and even smelled real in every detail. Everywhere she looked, her surroundings defied her attempts to find flaws or any indication it was all simulated.

Gone was that control room, replaced by an even larger chamber, stuffed almost to overflowing with computer stations, display monitors, and immense equipment she did not recognize. Chen's first impression was that of a large power plant, and she quickly realized this must be the *Osijemal*'s primary energy production facility.

No, it's a virtual representation of it. Welcome to the grand illusion, remember?

"Just when I think I've got a handle on this place, you throw me for another loop."

Standing next to her, Alehuguet replied, "I apologize, T'Ryssa. I keep forgetting that all of this might be overwhelming to a newcomer."

As part of her acclimation process, Chen's movements within the Haven were in line with the limitations of her physical form. That meant walking or making use of ground, water, or air vehicles, which were abundant here. Only Alehuguet and the other Conclave members along with a select group of engineers and other technicians overseeing care of the *Osijemal* were permitted to move unfettered through the computer matrix, eschewing conventional modes of transportation in favor of near godlike abilities to change locations almost instantly.

From their vantage point, standing on a catwalk running along the immense chamber's ceiling, Chen had an unfettered view of the scene below them. She noted that most of the compartment's space was given over to rows of what she guessed were power generators and other support equipment. Each generator, more than twenty in all, towered above the Nejamri working around them.

"This is the primary power facility," said Alehuguet. "Each of the other hull sections has its own dedicated plant that can be operated independently if the need arises, but everything is overseen from this central point."

Chen asked, "And this is the same size as the real plant? I mean, the *actual* plant?" She shook her head. "It's enormous, but it'd have to be if you want to drive a ship this size."

Smiling, Alehuguet nodded. "When the software to represent the *Osijemal* interiors was being developed, there was consideration given to making these spaces smaller than their actual counterparts. The decision was made to keep everything at the same scale, so that everyone could interact with it just as they would in physical form."

"I've been meaning to ask about that sort of thing." Seeing Alehuguet's confused expression, Chen gestured to the scene around them. "What I mean is, given the power requirements to create and maintain all of this, why not take shortcuts for the sake of practicality? Indeed, given the power issues you've been having, it seems wasteful to continue running the simulation, or at least a good portion of it. If your consciousness exists within the computer matrix, why not just communicate directly with one another, without all of this?"

Alehuguet replied, "You are still thinking of the Haven as a simple computer program in which information is transferred from point to point, and that can be deactivated and stored for later use. While that is true to an extent, you and I are very much more than that. We cannot simply be stored. Our minds are far more sophisticated than a piece of software. They cannot be held in limbo or paused, at least not for any significant period of time, before becoming susceptible to irreversible damage."

"That sounds like our transporters," said Chen. "At least to a degree. They can hold someone in a dematerialized state for extended periods, but the person being transported has no awareness of time passing, and it's not something we normally do because of the risk of something happening while that person's pattern is held in the transporter buffer."

She recalled the most famous example of such an extended "interruption" of a normal transporter process. Famed Starfleet engineer Montgomery Scott had reconfigured the systems of a damaged vessel so that after dematerialization he and another Starfleet officer could remain in the transporter buffer with no pattern degradation until someone answered their vessel's distress call. Anticipating a delay in rescue, Scott also had linked the transporter to the ship's auxiliary power systems, which were undamaged and in theory could operate for decades without interruption. It was a fortunate bit of off-the-cuff contingency planning, as what Scott anticipated to be hours or days at most turned out to be seventy-five years. While the transporter pattern of the other officer had not maintained its integrity, in effect killing that person without his ever suspecting a thing, Scott survived and was found by the *Enterprise*-D. When he was extracted from the transporter buffer, it was as though he had not aged a day, and had no conscious awareness of time's passage. So far as Chen knew, the engineer suffered no ill effects from his ordeal, and his experience had been a favorite discussion topic among other engineers in the ensuing years. Recalling the incident made her focus on one particular detail.

Alehuguet cast her gaze downward, as though recalling an unpleasant memory. "There was a time, soon after we began developing this technology, where the process was much more limited. We were able to transition the consciousness of test subjects into those first, experimental simulacrums, but they contained no virtual realm in which to interact. The subjects were aware of their surroundings, at least as they described it, but there was nothing there except darkness and the voices of others participating in the tests, those monitoring the experiments, and the responses from other programs running within that test matrix. We soon discovered even limited time spent in such a state began to have detrimental effects. One such experiment ran into difficulty, whereby the test subjects could not be extracted. They were trapped in there for many cycles as engineers attempted to retrieve them. By the time they were retrieved from the simulation, their minds had been so affected that they required extensive psychological care. Some of them never recovered, and it is an obstacle we were never able to overcome."

"Stimulation," said Chen. "A mind transferred into an environment like this still requires constant stimulation, just as it would receive while in a real body. Our senses provide constant input to our brains, most of it without our conscious realization. Take that away, and those parts of the brain begin to . . . atrophy?" She was not certain she grasped the entire concept, or understood the mechanics involved, but she thought she understood it enough to appreciate what Alehuguet described. Perhaps the Nejamri brain was different enough from those of the humanoids with which Chen was familiar that it presented an even greater cause for concern?

"We eventually came to understand that if we do not exist here or in our physical forms, there are inevitable harmful side effects." Alehuguet indicated their surroundings. "All of this is as much a life-support system as atmosphere and environment would be for our bodies."

"And you never anticipated a power failure?" To Chen, it seemed an obvious problem. "I know you have backup batteries and you'd normally be able to use your solar collectors to recharge everything, and we're working on fixing all of that. But, if we hadn't come along to help you, what would've happened?"

"Ordinarily, emergency procedures would have activated, and certain key individuals would be returned to their physical bodies to assess the situation. If necessary, the entire community could be extracted from the Haven, and later returned once the emergency passed."

Now Chen understood. "But with the damage the *Osijemal*'s sustained, that couldn't happen."

"Exactly." When Alehuguet smiled this time, it was smaller and tinged with sadness. "If you had not found us, T'Ryssa, it is very possible, even likely, that our power reserves would have dwindled to nothing and our existence ultimately ended, and we would have been unable to do anything about it. You and your companions already have our undying gratitude."

It was still much to consider, Chen admitted to herself. More than a half million people, powerless to do anything except await their own extinction. What must that have been like?

"In case you are wondering," said Alehuguet, "this is knowledge we chose not to share with the entire community. We felt it better to allow them to live their lives as though everything was normal. Knowing the truth would have served no purpose and likely would have undermined the social order."

Chen could see her point. "I have to say, I don't know that I would want to know something like that. I can't imagine having to make that decision for an entire civilization."

Placing a hand on her arm, Alehuguet replied, "Thanks to you, they never will."

Taurik chose that moment to make his presence known.

"*T'Ryssa, the* Enterprise *reports they are ready to begin the power transfer.*" Thanks to yet another of the Haven's vast array of support features linking it to the *Osijemal*'s actual physical equipment, the Vulcan's disembodied voice was all around them as he spoke.

"Showtime," said Chen.

Standing with her eyes closed, Alehuguet appeared to be in a type of trance, but Chen knew from having witnessed it earlier that the Nejamri leader was in contact with other members of the Conclave as well as those engineers and other technicians involved in the coming activity. Instant communication via dedicated channels was yet another feature of living within the Haven.

Neat trick, but I still want my body back.

No sooner did she entertain that thought than Chen found herself moved from their vantage point. Now she stood alongside Alehuguet on the floor of the enormous energy generation complex. The generators, if that's what they were, loomed above and around her, arrayed in rows in every direction to the near exclusion of all else. Though they stood silent like soaring guardians, she could sense the power inherent in each one. A ring of workstations encircled each generator, once again reminding Chen in some ways of the *Enterprise*'s main engineering section or even the bridge. Unlike the consoles she had seen during the away team's investigation of the *Osijemal*, here everything pulsed with activity, and Nejamri engineers hovered over many of the workstations. She noted that none of them wore the flowing, brightly colored garments that were the norm for Alehuguet and everyone else. Those were gone, replaced by dark green coveralls with padded elbows and knees, and boots covering their long, narrow feet. Several of the engineers carried handheld instruments and other devices of varying shapes and sizes, none of which Chen could even hope to identify. All of it was so real that for the briefest of moments, she was once more able to forget that everything around her was nothing more than an elaborate computer simulation. So uncanny were the representations that it was easy to fall victim to such a perception.

"The power transfer is beginning," reported one of the engineers, who stood before a large console upon which was displayed a schematic indicating a progress scale. Within seconds, the scale began shifting its status readings, and Chen thought she even heard a few of the nearby generators start rumbling to life.

Here goes nothing.

23

Picard long ago had learned the often unexplainable art of communicating with the vessel under his command, utilizing his senses to detect even the slightest deviation or variance. Just as he prided himself on being able to read the smallest changes in attitude or emotion from his crew, so too did he place great value on the gift of listening and hearing what his ship told him. From the slightest pitch in the warp engines to the tiniest shift in artificial gravity, or even the almost imperceptible lag in the computer's response to a question or command, he listened, and saw, and felt. It was not mechanical skill or researched knowledge that provided this ability, but instead simple experience that could come only from the special bond created between a starship and its master, as well as the people it shielded and protected from the stark, unforgiving reality that was space travel.

It was because of this keen hyperawareness of his ship and its particular quirks that while sitting in his chair on the *Enterprise* bridge, Picard needed no status indicators or reports from his officers to know when the power transfer began. No alert tones sounded, and there was not even the slightest change in the overhead lighting. Instead, with his hands resting on the arms of his command chair, he sensed the subtlest of tremors beneath his fingertips as energy was diverted from the starship's powerful warp engines to the main deflector array.

"Transferring at one-quarter capacity," reported Geordi La Forge over the open intercom.

Sitting next to him in the first officer's chair, Lieutenant Joanna Faur said, "Our systems are reading normal, sir, but I'm not seeing anything from the *Osijemal.*"

On the main viewscreen, Picard watched as six different beams of white-blue energy lanced outward, away from the *Enterprise* and toward the mammoth *Osijemal*. He had ordered the ship to retreat from the ark far enough that the main deflector could target multiple solar collectors scattered across the larger ship's surface. The image on the screen showed how each of the beams directed itself to a different collector array.

"Geordi?" prompted Picard.

The chief engineer replied, *"Everything's in the green on this end, Captain."*

"Our readings here show no change, sir," added Worf.

"I'm going to try modulating the frequency, and increase the rate of transfer to one-third power," said La Forge. *"Stand by."*

Now the change in the *Enterprise*'s power output was more pronounced, as evidenced by the increased reverberation Picard felt in the arms of his chair. The omnipresent hum of the starship's engines also shifted, albeit slightly, in response to the increased demand. On the screen, the energy beams increased in brightness and intensity, as well as shifting their color so that the bluish tinge became more pronounced. A moment later, the captain heard a series of tones emanating from the science station along the bridge's starboard perimeter.

"Sir, we're starting to register feedback from the *Osijemal*," said Ensign Oliver Trimble, the junior science officer serving in Dina Elfiki's stead while the lieutenant was aboard the Nejamri ship. "The collectors are absorbing and directing the energy we're transmitting to the vessel's battery array."

Over the intercom, Worf reported, *"Status readings are showing that here too. All indicators are well within operational parameters."*

Acknowledging the reports, Picard said, "The frequency modulation seems to have done the trick, Mister La Forge."

"I wish it was that simple, sir," replied the chief engineer. *"There doesn't seem to be one frequency that does the trick, and when it shifts we're showing some feedback from the transfer."*

"Is there a danger to the ship?" asked Faur, earning her an appreciative nod from Picard for her astuteness.

"Good question, Lieutenant. I'm applying a dynamic modulator to automatically rotate the deflector's resonance frequency nutation. It's not perfect, but the computer can make the adjustments faster than I can, and hopefully anticipate any problems with feedback or any other unexpected issues."

While the strategy La Forge suggested was in service to upholding one of Starfleet's most inspiring values—coming to the aid of those in distress—like perhaps too many inventions it had its roots in more martial uses. It reminded Picard of similar tactics used to modify weapons and shields, though it was one he had not considered in quite some time. It originally was a tactic born of inspiration, or perhaps desperation, during an encounter with the first Borg ship to infiltrate Federation space on a mission to attack Earth. The previous *Enterprise*, dispatched to confront the enormous vessel, found itself in pitched battle near the Paulson Nebula, with the starship's shields and weapons all but useless against the relentless, ever adapting enemy. Elizabeth Shelby, at the time a lieutenant commander as well as a Borg tactical specialist from Starfleet Command and traveling with the *Enterprise*, hit upon the idea to randomly manipulate the ship's phaser resonance frequencies in a frantic bid to thwart the Borg vessel's tractor beam. The unconventional approach worked, giving the ship time and opportunity to break away from the battle and seek temporary refuge within the nearby Paulson Nebula.

Forestalling certain other unfortunate events, Picard thought. He could not help the feeling of helplessness and guilt the recollection provoked, re-igniting sobering memories of his subsequent capture and assimilation by the Borg, and the assistance they had forced from him as the Borg cube decimated dozens of Starfleet vessels before coming within a hairsbreadth of conquering Earth.

Stop it. The Borg are gone. You've atoned for those sins.

Shelby's initial, instinctive gambit quickly became the cornerstone of a whole new series of methods devised to defend against Borg weapons, despite the Collective's unerring ability to adapt itself to any technology employed against it. None of those had been foolproof, but their use had bought critical time and opportunity that, in the final analysis, contributed at least in part to final victory over what many historians already called Starfleet's most intractable foe.

Over the intercom, Worf reported, *"Enterprise, instruments here are beginning to register a more pronounced feedback reading."*

Before Picard could respond, new alert tones sounded from the science station, and Ensign Trimble turned in his seat. "We're showing that too, sir."

"Internal sensors are starting to react to the feedback, sir," added Faur. "Automated safety protocols are kicking in to avoid potential overloads."

"Mister La Forge, status?" asked the captain.

There was a lag before the engineer replied, *"We're seeing the feedback too. The modulation routine is attempting to compensate, but there may also be an oversight feature somewhere within the Osijemal's systems."*

Instead of Worf responding over the open communications channel, it was Lieutenant Commander Taurik. *"Commander La Forge may be correct,"* said the Vulcan. *"According to the Nejamri technicians, their systems are reacting as though this was an unauthorized infiltration of their onboard systems."*

"It might be because we're pushing the energy at the collectors, rather than allowing them to absorb it passively," replied La Forge. *"I may be able to adjust the deflector's resonance frequency to compensate for that too."*

Picard waited for an update. Seconds passed, during which he could hear the chatter of both Worf and La Forge along with their respective teams as they continued to work. As was normal during situations like this, he forced himself to remain still, reining in wayward feelings of restlessness and uselessness while allowing his people to work. It was a frustrating sensation, one he had never quite conquered in all his years occupying a captain's chair, but one he knew must be observed if his crew was to function.

"The feedback is diminishing," said La Forge after nearly one minute of silence. *"I've reduced the transfer rate back to one-quarter, and that seems to have evened things out a little. I'm going to keep it at this level for the time being, sir."*

From the *Osijemal*, Taurik said, *"We are being notified that the Nejamri engineers are working to reconfigure processes here. They believe they can override the safety protocols and allow the transfer to proceed unimpeded."*

"Excellent," said Picard. "Is there anything else we can do, Mister La Forge?"

Before the chief engineer could respond, everything came undone.

"Power surge!"

Standing well away from the workstations, Chen could only watch as a half dozen Nejamri engineers converged on one console, upon which now flashed a variety of status displays and other schematics indicating the rise of a serious problem.

"It is not a power surge," said one technician, pointing to a monitor as she spoke. "But the system perceives the energy transfer as one." Reaching forward, the female Nejamri tapped several controls. "See? One of the flow regulator circuits is not functioning. Without it, that conduit is unable to direct the incoming energy stream at a controlled rate, so it's pushing it back the way it came."

Another of the engineers, a short, squat male, asked, "How did this escape our notice before now?"

"The physical component is damaged," replied the female tech. "And it is in an area we cannot reach from within the Haven." She pressed other controls. "Shut down that conduit and reroute the incoming flow to an alternative channel."

It was only when she found herself standing right behind the engineer that Chen realized she had advanced on the cluster of Nejamri workers. Peering over the nearest technician's shoulder, she tried to get a better look at the workstation. Despite the indecipherable native script, she still could make out a few of the readouts showing a number of areas bathed in harsh crimson.

"Lorrander," said Alehuguet, who also had moved closer so that she might better observe the proceedings. "Should we notify the *Enterprise* to stop the power transfer?"

"I do not believe that is necessary," replied the female engineer. "We should be able to redirect the incoming stream without interrupting it. The problem is that our own system is treating this like a security breach, rather than the simple act of the collector's absorbing solar energy. The components were not designed for this sort of direct energy transference, but the *Enterprise* engineers are attempting to govern the transfer with their equipment."

Chen said, "But there's an obvious incompatibility getting in the way."

"Correct," replied Lorrander. "Your engineers are quite talented, and so are ours, but that still may not be enough to overcome all of the differences in our respective technologies. It is quite a unique challenge." With her left arm, the engineer reached behind herself to scratch just beneath the area corresponding to a typical humanoid's shoulder blades. The extra joint appeared to make the action far easier than those occasions Chen felt the need to scratch such an itch.

And how does a computer program get an itch, anyway?

It was an odd thought, but one Chen could not resist. Was the Haven's computer matrix so sophisticated that even mundane realities of daily life like unwelcome itches, aches, and pains were part of the programming? What about runny noses, acne, or the gunk that formed in her eyes when she slept? Did a computer simulation really need to go into that much detail?

Maybe not the best time for this sort of thing, Trys.

"Taurik, can you hear me?" she called out, knowing her voice would be routed through the Haven and to the proper communications channel linking her with the away team. "They're having some trouble in here with what sounds like the solar collectors' power-flow regulation. They're trying to craft a workaround, but part of the problem is a damaged component they can't reach. Is that something you can check out?"

The Vulcan replied, *"We are attempting to do just that, T'Ryssa. It appears the mechanism in question is located at a junction from which energy absorbed by numerous collectors is channeled before being routed to the battery storage facility. According to the schematics at our disposal, accessing it requires us to disassemble several other components. It is a process that will take some time."*

A new round of alerts sounded from the console, prompting Lorrander to assume control of the workstation while her companions scrambled for adjacent terminals. Several of the monitors within Chen's field of view changed to varying shades of red as numerous indicators flared to life.

"I think we may be past that, Taurik."

La Forge leaned over the master situation table, his hands moving as though of their own accord as he tried to head off what he could see was about to happen, but his gut was already telling him he could not stop it.

"Computer, disengage the transfer!"

Why had the automated systems not already done this? There was no time to ponder the answer to that question, and La Forge pushed it aside as he hovered over the instrument panels. Both hands worked at different tasks as he tried to get ahead of the power surge rushing back through the tenuous connection linking the *Enterprise* to the *Osijemal*. Even as he entered frantic strings of commands and willed the computer to carry out his instructions, he could see nothing he did was coming fast enough.

"The link's still active," said Linn Payne from where she hunched over the table's opposite side. "I think the power spike overloaded the frequency modulation."

La Forge replied, "I'm trying to reconfigure it manually." If he could find a frequency that the Nejamri ship's technology did not understand or could not process, that might be enough to cancel the transfer and, more importantly, sever the connection between the two ships.

It's not going to work.

"I'm trying to bring the deflector offline, but the power spike's causing some kind of lag," said Payne.

The table's displays were illustrating that, along with the computer's representation of the six beams of energy projecting forward from the *Enterprise*'s deflector array. Even with the transfer being conducted at one-quarter of the deflector's ability to transmit energy, the feedback coming their way still posed a threat to sensitive relays and other components of the ship's systems. Trying to get any of his commands to register, La Forge watched the streams turning red as they moved from the *Osijemal* toward the *Enterprise*.

"I've got it!" Payne shouted. "The deflector—"

It was too late.

The first indications came just heartbeats later, in the benign form of green status indicators on the situation table shifting to red. What followed was a series of alarms erupting from various consoles around engineering. Other members of his team were already moving to address the new alerts, silencing the blaring tones and reporting status amongst themselves. Thankfully, it took them only seconds to remove the annoying drone of the alarms, allowing La Forge to hear snippets of the various updates exchanged by his team members. He listened for anything that might hint at a truly serious issue, but the status reports scrolling across monitors on the situation table told him the *Enterprise* had managed to avoid serious damage.

"Relay overloads and circuit burnouts all through the deflector array," reported Payne, her fingers sweeping across her console. "Some of the adjacent sensor nodes are affected too." She looked up from the table, her expression that of irritation. "The computer finally disengaged the deflector and severed the power transfer."

La Forge grunted, shaking his head. "Better late than never."

"Bridge to engineering," said the voice of Captain Picard over the intercom. *"Status, Mister La Forge?"*

Continuing to work as he switched to diagnosing the litany of new issues now confronting him, the chief engineer replied, "Feedback from the power transfer is giving us some grief, Captain. Mostly overloads and the like; nothing we can't handle, thankfully, but the main deflector's offline until we repair the damage or route around it."

Neither he nor Picard needed to say out loud what that meant, even in light of their current circumstances. With the deflector array out of commission, even temporarily, the ship's defenses would be compromised, and traveling at warp speeds was all but impossible without the array to scan ahead of the starship and warn of obstacles or other dangers in its path. Returning it to full operation was of paramount importance.

"What caused the feedback?" asked the captain.

For the first time since the new problems surfaced, La Forge halted what he was doing. Planting his palms on the situation table, he leaned forward so that he rested on his arms. "Right now, my best guess is some kind of automated response from the *Osijemal*. According to Taurik, the Nejamri found some damaged equipment on their end that regulated incoming power flow, and other processes jumped in to compensate or protect against what they interpreted as an attempt to breach their system. It's not something anyone anticipated, sir."

This, of course, did nothing to ease La Forge's frustration at the entire situation. He *should* have anticipated it, along with any other possibility no matter how unlikely or even outlandish. As chief engineer, it was *his job* to plan for such eventualities, and he had failed. He and his staff had only just completed the repairs from the ship's previous skirmishes with the Torrekmat salvage ship, and now he had thrust more work onto them.

Quit whining, he told himself. *Get to work.*

"I've already got teams assessing the damage, sir. I'll have an estimate to you within fifteen minutes."

Over the intercom, Picard replied, *"Understood. In the meantime, the power transfer wasn't a complete waste. Sensors show it restored thirty-six percent of their battery capacity."*

Across the table from him, Payne said, "Well, I guess that's something."

"It gives the Nejamri a little breathing room while we figure out how to do this the right way," replied La Forge. "But before that, we've got some cleanup to do."

As though mocking his intentions, the ship's red alert klaxon began wailing and echoing through the engineering section.

"Bridge," he called out. "What's happening?"

Picard's voice, now taut and clipped, replied. *"We have company."*

24

Three ships, approaching in a loose formation, appeared on the bridge's main viewscreen. While each was similar to the *Zetoq* in its basic configuration, Picard noted a number of differences in their overall composition that altered their respective silhouettes.

"Sensors show variations in mounted weapons along with other equipment like grappler systems, extendable docking collars, and even remotely guided cutting and welding tools," reported Ensign Jody Fraser from the tactical station. "Their weapons are comparable to those on the other Torrekmat vessel, Captain, and they're active. Time to intercept is two minutes, seventeen seconds."

"Thank you, Ensign," replied Picard from where he stood between his command chair and the conn and ops positions. He turned and offered a reassuring glance over his shoulder to the young woman.

A young, blond human woman assigned to beta shift, Fraser had reported to the bridge less than thirty minutes earlier, called to duty by Lieutenant Faur so that Aneta Šmrhová could take advantage of a brief yet overdue and much-deserved respite after manning her station for two full duty shifts and well into a third. As expected, Šmrhová had protested, but Picard made it official by ordering her off the bridge with orders not to return for at least four hours. It was a command he expected her to disobey given the sudden turn of events, and his suspicions were rewarded a moment later when the starboard turbolift doors opened and the security chief all but ran onto the bridge. Stopping just outside the car, she regarded Picard.

"I know you ordered me to rest, sir, but—"

With a knowing look, Picard gestured toward the tactical console. "By all means, Lieutenant." To Fraser, he said, "Ensign, I won't turn away good help. Take the auxiliary station."

"Aye, sir," replied the security officer as she moved to the console opposite Šmrhová's.

Wasting no time taking up her station, Šmrhová reported, "The ships are maintaining course and speed, and I'm detecting sensor sweeps from the lead vessel. They know we're here, sir."

"Raise shields," ordered Picard, knowing the lieutenant would make the necessary adjustments to account for the main deflector array's current unavailability. "Phasers and quantum torpedoes on standby."

Sitting in the first officer's chair, Lieutenant Faur said, "They're scanning us, sir. Passive sensors, it looks like. Sizing us up, I'm guessing."

"Hail them," said Picard. He suspected the new arrivals would be anxious after doubtless scanning what little debris remained of the *Zetoq*. There was nothing to be done about the destroyed salvage vessel, but the last thing he wanted now was another confrontation while the *Enterprise* was operating at less than peak efficiency and he had an away team still aboard the *Osijemal*.

On the viewscreen, the image of the three approaching ships was replaced by that of another Torrekmat. A female this time, at least so far as Picard could tell; her physique was broader and more imposing than Senthilmal's had been, though her brow and nose were much less pronounced. Her hair was lighter in color and long enough that it rested atop her shoulders. At the center of her large, smooth forehead was an ornate tattoo or some other type of mark, its white hue contrasting with her lavender skin. Her eyes likewise were a bright white and seemed to stare out at the screen with a visceral intensity. Also unlike Senthilmal, her general appearance was not at all disheveled, and her dark, utilitarian garments were clean and free of frays, tears, and stains.

"Greetings," Picard began. "I am—"

"I am Brinamar, master of the salvage vessel Utenla, *and I know who you are, Captain Picard,"* replied the newcomer. *"Senthilmal's report was fragmented yet still informative. I suppose it was the best he could do before his ship's distress buoy was launched and you destroyed his vessel."*

Picard, avoiding the bait, chose his words with care and kept his tone subdued. "If you did intercept the *Zetoq*'s buoy, then surely it reported that the ship was destroyed after a failure in its warp-core containment system caused by defensive weapons fire from the derelict and not the *Enterprise*."

"A system that was originally damaged during a battle with your vessel, following your attempt to seize the derelict after Senthilmal and his crew made their claim."

"An unprovoked attack on my ship." Picard stepped between the conn and ops stations, keeping his gaze on Brinamar. "Let us be quite clear on this point. We discovered the derelict adrift. Our scans detected no signs of life aboard. Only after I sent a team to investigate was the presence of anyone else detected. Senthilmal's boarding party was using technology to mask their movements aboard the derelict, and they attacked my people. Then the *Zetoq* arrived and attempted to assert a claim. We have no interest in salvage rights, but we have since learned that there are crew and passengers aboard that vessel. All of this could have been prevented if Senthilmal had simply chosen to talk to me, rather than attack the derelict and my ship."

Brinamar's eyes narrowed as she regarded him. *"And yet, you are still here, and you still have a boarding party aboard the derelict."*

"Yes. We are attempting to render assistance. Their ship is damaged and they are unable to make the repairs without help." After weighing the pros and cons of trying to explain the Nejamri and their predicament, Picard opted against it, at least for the moment. It was still a lot for him to understand and fully appreciate, and he was uncertain he could communicate the situation to

Brinamar in a manner that would not serve to further inflame the current tensions.

"I do not know who you are or what you represent," said the female Torrekmat, after a moment of scrutinizing Picard as though trying to bore through him with her eyes. *"However, your life-form and ship design are unfamiliar to us, which leads me to believe you are a long way from whatever world you call home. Senthilmal's report refers to something called a 'Federation,' but beyond your single vessel I see no evidence of such a union."*

The veiled threat was not lost on Picard, but he elected to ignore it. "We are its first representatives in this region of space, and I assure you ours is a mission of peaceful exploration. Our discovery of the derelict was a matter of happenstance. Our only interest lies in aiding the crew to repair its damage and helping them continue their journey."

"They're scanning us again, Captain," reported Šmrhová from behind him. "More comprehensive sweeps this time, with an emphasis on our defenses."

For the first time, Brinamar smiled, but there was no humor or warmth behind her expression. Instead, Picard sensed callousness tinged with more than a hint of menace.

"That sounds very noble on your part, but I assure you my people and I are motivated by vastly different concerns. The derelict represents a handsome profit for whoever returns it to our homeworld. As for you and your ship, Jirol Salvage Guild rules require us to seek compensation for the loss of the Zetoq and its crew, as well as the extra time and resources we are expending in order to complete his salvage claim. Senthilmal's report and my own scans tell me your ship should more than cover the debt."

Beginning to tire of the conversation and bravado, Picard replied, "Did Senthilmal's report mention how well his ship fared when he decided to test mine?"

"Senthilmal was a fine salvager," said Brinamar. *"Very reliable, and always brought tidy profits for the guild. However, being*

a civilian pilot, he was not known for his tactical prowess. I am not surprised you bested him, as he possessed no real experience in such matters. "She stepped closer to the screen. "*I do.*"

The communication ended without warning and her image disappeared, replaced by the trio of approaching Torrekmat ships. Punctuating the conversation's termination was a new red alert siren.

"They're breaking formation," called out Šmrhová. "Accelerating and moving to intercept us."

Moving toward his chair, Picard ordered, "Target their engine sections and prepare to fire on my command. Conn, evasive action. They're going to try flanking us. Don't give them the chance."

"Aye, sir," replied Gary Weinrib, still substituting for Faur at the conn station. The lieutenant's fingers moved with rapid precision over his console, and the results were immediate. Picard saw the image of the *Osijemal* seem to fall toward the bottom of the viewscreen as Weinrib pushed the *Enterprise* up and away from the gargantuan ship in search of maneuvering room. Calling up a tactical display on his command chair's left armrest, Picard noted the positions of the derelict as well as the *Enterprise* and the three Torrekmat ships, already seeing the beginnings of Brinamar's opening gambit.

"Incoming fire," said Faur.

It was all the lieutenant had time to say before everyone on the bridge felt the impact of disruptor energy against the *Enterprise*'s shields. Along with inertial damping systems, they absorbed the brunt of the strike, which was followed just seconds later by another volley.

"Shields at eighty-one percent," said Glinn Ravel Dygan from the ops station. Like Šmrhová, he had been working steadily for hours but declined the opportunity for a rest interval, citing his Cardassian physiology as giving him an advantage so far as managing fatigue was concerned. "Two of the ships are attempting to converge on us from port and starboard angles."

Picard said, "Watch the third ship." His armrest display

showed him how it hung back during the initial attack, and now was maneuvering to approach the *Enterprise* from below.

At the conn station, Weinrib saw the strategy for what it was and was already adjusting the starship's course and attitude in response to the incoming attack. Watching the evasive counter take shape, Picard glanced over his shoulder at Šmrhová.

"Fire at will, Lieutenant."

The security chief was ready, unleashing multiple strings of phaser fire from the emitters on the top and bottom of the *Enterprise*'s primary hull. She had taken the time to plot strikes against all three ships, and scored hits on each one.

"Strikes on their deflector shields," reported Fraser from the auxiliary tactical station. "Their shield generators aren't as good as ours."

"Continue firing," replied Picard. Maybe sustained phaser strikes would convince Brinamar and her people to reconsider their strategy, but he doubted it. Even as he gave the command, he was monitoring the actions of the ships, and a glance at his armrest console showed him how the third vessel was breaking away from its companions. Now it pursued a direct course toward the *Osijemal*, but he had no time to give it much thought before Faur was calling out a new warning.

"Here they come again." Faur's right hand played over the compact console positioned next to the first officer's chair. "Routing power from noncritical systems to the shields." At the same time she made the report, Šmrhová was releasing new volleys of phaser fire at the incoming vessels.

"They're covering for the other ship," said Picard. "Trying to keep us occupied while they make a move on the *Osijemal*." He looked to Faur. "They may be trying to insert a boarding party. Warn the away team."

Rising from his seat, he crossed to the conn station and put his hand on Weinrib's shoulder. "Move to intercept that ship. I want them to wave off. Lieutenant Šmrhová, stand by to fire as we adjust our course, and continue targeting the other ships."

His various commands prompting acknowledgments, Picard watched as the viewscreen's angle and aspect shifted in response to Weinrib guiding the *Enterprise* back to the *Osijemal*. At the same time, Šmrhová continued firing at all three Torrekmat ships, scoring new hits on each vessel's shields.

"One of the ships is breaking off," said Faur. "Looks like we punched through their shields. Sensors are also picking up hull damage."

"Any damage to their life support?" asked Picard, keeping his attention on the viewscreen.

Faur replied, "Negative, sir."

"Targeting the second ship," reported Šmrhová, and Picard saw phaser beams lancing toward the salvage vessel to find its shields. Energies collided once again, and the craft seemed to slow its advance before banking up and out of the viewscreen's frame.

"Their shields are failing," said Fraser. "No hull or other damage I can see, but they may be rethinking their strategy."

Šmrhová added, "They're not moving off. They're falling in behind us. Transferring additional power to rear deflectors."

Her report was followed by another impact against the *Enterprise*'s shields accompanied by renewed alerts sounding across the bridge. Picard felt the deck waver beneath his feet but maintained his balance long enough for inertial damping to compensate for the sudden strike.

At the conn station, Weinrib shook his head. "Damn it!" With a glance over his shoulder, he added, "Sorry, Captain."

"They hit us full on with that one," said Šmrhová. "Our shields are at sixty-five percent."

Glinn Dygan said, "A few more shots like that, and they could go altogether."

"I'm returning fire." A moment later, Šmrhová looked up from her console. "Their shields are down, and they're moving off. Looks like they're maneuvering toward the other ship."

Listening to the report, Picard looked at Weinrib's console, noting the position of the three Torrekmat ships, including the one still making for the Nejamri ark. "Conn, continue on intercept course. I want that ship before it can target the *Osijemal*."

"Captain," said Fraser. "Sensors are showing something happening aboard the *Osijemal*." She looked up from her console. "Their weapons are coming online."

Once more and without warning, Chen felt herself bracing against a sudden shift in her perspective. Gone was the enormous power generation facility and its attendant Nejamri engineers. Now she found herself standing in the midst of an imposing collection of transparent bubbles, floating around her and gathered like a cluster. There were hundreds of them, including below and above her, stretching at least a hundred meters in every direction from where she stood alongside Alehuguet.

"What the hell . . . ?"

Each of the bubbles appeared to contain a curved console, mounted with a chair similar in design to what she had already seen around the ship and obviously constructed to accommodate Nejamri physiology. Inside many but not all of them were Nejamri, several of them dressed in green coveralls similar to those worn by technicians at the power plant. Others wore variations of the casual garment that seemed to typify "normal" Nejamri fashion. As she watched, each bubble, or pod, moved independently of the others, spinning in place or rotating on first one axis, then another. The pods' transparent material did not offer indications of what each occupant was doing, at least until one of the closer ones spun and tilted in such a way that she could observe the information and graphics displayed on its interior.

"This is our weapons control center," said Alehuguet. "Each pod controls a turret mounted on the *Osijemal*'s exterior. Working in concert, they form our primary means of defending the ship."

No sooner had Chen received word from Taurik that one and perhaps two Torrekmat salvage vessels were maneuvering toward the *Osijemal* than she found herself whisked from the power plant to this new location.

"Taurik?" she called out. "The good news is that the power transfer from the *Enterprise* wasn't a complete failure. With what we were able to supply its batteries, the *Osijemal* is able to bring more of its weapons to bear."

"Commander Worf has notified Captain Picard," replied Taurik. *"I will attempt to keep you apprised of the situation."*

Turning to Alehuguet, Chen said, "I'd like to see what's going on." She waved above their heads. "You know, outside." One of the pods close to them was unoccupied, and when the Nejamri leader made no objection, Chen climbed into it. The seat, though intended for a body shape different from hers, automatically contoured itself to fit around her, cocooning her and acting as its own harness and restraint system as the chair moved closer to the pod's control console.

"If only I could find a decent mattress that did this," she muttered.

Without her conscious command, the pod's canopy flared to life, providing Chen a detached perspective of what she quickly realized was the view as seen from one of the weapon turrets on the surface of the *Osijemal*'s hull. Above her and in the distance, she saw the *Enterprise* angling itself away from battle with a Torrekmat vessel. A second ship was moving away from the skirmish while a third was careening toward the *Osijemal*, and it was obvious the *Enterprise* was moving to intercept it.

The cannon corresponding to her pod was not active, but others in her field of view fired at the oncoming Torrekmat ship, which dodged most of the beams. A single impact against the vessel's shields caused a collision of energies but the ship kept coming. Then it fired its own weapons, and Chen saw the results of that attack as twin energy beams ripped into the *Osijemal*'s hull.

One of the Nejamri gunners was able to respond, aiming his weapon at the attacking ship and scoring direct hits on its forward shields. The salvage vessel broke off its assault, a maneuver that brought it into line with another turret that also found its mark. Chen watched as the Torrekmat ship's shields flared one last time before failing completely just as it fell victim to yet another defensive strike. With nothing to soften the blow, the full force of the turret's strike tore into the attacker's hull.

"Cease fire," said a male voice that seemed to resonate through Chen's pod.

The command came just as the Torrekmat ship, still suffering from the effects of the weapon's strike, altered its course in what she guessed was an attempt to retreat. Then she threw up her hands to protect her face as a blinding white light erupted from the vessel's aft end. From her vantage point she saw hull plates buckling and rending apart, the explosion shredding the salvage vessel and casting debris in all directions. At such close proximity to the *Osijemal* the results were immediate, with shrapnel ripping into the ark's hull. Smaller explosions and even puffs of released atmosphere appeared around dozens of impact sites, and the displays inside Chen's pod began flashing in ominous synchronicity.

Pushing herself from her seat, Chen exited the pod and saw Alehuguet standing in the midst of the cluster, eyes closed. Her brow was furrowed and her narrow jaw clenched as she "communed." When her eyes opened, her worry was evident.

"We did not intend to destroy that vessel. Only to disable it."

Chen nodded. "I know, and no one can fault you for defending yourselves."

"We do not wish to destroy life," said Alehuguet, as though not quite hearing Chen. "Some of us did not even want the *Osijemal* to carry weapons, but there were those who foresaw their unfortunate necessity." Sadness clouded her features. "They were correct."

"Alehuguet," said Chen, adopting a more forceful tone. "They attacked without provocation. They're only here because they want to lay claim to your ship, rip it apart, and sell its components. They don't give a damn about you or your people, or mine for that matter."

"*T'Ryssa,*" said Taurik, his voice seemingly all around Chen. "*Are you there?*"

Keeping her gaze on Alehuguet, Chen replied, "I'm here. What's going on?"

"*The salvage vessel's destruction has inflicted considerable damage to the* Osijemal'*s outer hull. We are still awaiting reports from Nejamri engineers, but it appears at least one power distribution hub was destroyed. Captain Picard reports* Enterprise *sensors are detecting a new, accelerated power drain.*"

Alehuguet said, "That is what I am being told as well."

Even as she spoke, the pod cluster surrounding them vanished, replaced by nothing but unending blackness. Suspended around her were those Nejamri tasked with manning various turrets, many of them looking confused at the sudden change. Then they too began to vanish until only Chen and Alehuguet remained.

"What's happening?" asked Chen.

Looking around them, Alehuguet seemed just as confused, and Chen thought she even saw the first hints of fear darkening the Nejamri's features.

Then she vanished, leaving Chen alone to drift in nothingness.

"Alehuguet!" she shouted. There was no echo, and her next cry was cut short before she felt the first odd tingle playing across her skin. Holding up her hands, Chen watched as they began to . . . *dissolve?*

"What's happ—"

25

Darkness. Wherever T'Ryssa Chen looked, she saw nothing but darkness.

"Where am I?" The words themselves seemed to be swallowed by the unrelenting blackness around her. Had she even spoken them aloud? How could she not be sure? Something felt wrong in this place. No, she decided. Everything felt wrong. Waves of what might be dizziness and disorientation seemed to wash over her, exacerbating her sensation of vertigo. She reached for her face, but there was no sensation of skin against her fingertips. Moving to touch her chest, she felt no garment beneath her hand. There was nothing.

She was *nothing*.

"Alehuguet? Are you here?" When no response came, she repeated the call and received the same result. "Taurik? Can you hear me?"

Silence. So all encompassing was the quiet that it took Chen an additional moment to realize she couldn't even hear the sounds of her own breathing, which she realized made sense since she did not really require oxygen in this place.

Haven. Where's the Haven?

Chen recalled those frantic seconds as everything around her vanished, including Alehuguet and the other Nejamri. It was like someone was turning off lights and forcing everyone to leave a room. No, she realized, it was more than that. During those final moments and for the first time since entering this realm, she truly felt as though she had entered an artificial, digitally rendered construct. It was comparable to standing on one of the

Enterprise holodecks and ordering the computer to end a program. Upon executing such a command, everything vanished, broken down into strings of data as it was pulled back to the data storage file from whence it came. Only those interacting with the simulation remained, left with nothing save the holodeck's cold, barren grid.

Here, she did not have even that.

I'm still in the Haven, she decided. Aside from a bizarre dream or perhaps some sort of unlikely mental breakdown, it was the only solution that made sense. Beyond that, whatever happened had to be an unexpected turn of events. Chen recalled Alehuguet's look of confusion and even worry just before she vanished along with their surroundings. This was not a normal occurrence, catching the Nejamri leader off guard.

"So, what the hell am I supposed to do?" She had not really expected an answer.

Alehuguet answered anyway.

"T'Ryssa, are you all right?"

Without warning, she appeared before Chen, or at least from Chen's apparent perspective, looking exactly as she had the last time they were together. She had not coalesced into existence or materialized as though via a transporter beam. Instead, she was simply *there*, her orange skin and brilliantly colored dress standing out against the black around them. A minor shift in sensations, maybe just in the way she heard the Nejamri's voice in the void, made Chen look down at herself. This time, she saw her body, still dressed in the loose-fitting gown. Looking around, she waited for other elements of the Haven to reappear, but the darkness persisted.

"What happened?" she asked. "Where are we?"

Alehuguet replied, "You are safe, at least for the moment." She spread her arms, gesturing to the unyielding black around them. "Most of the Haven has been taken offline. The last attack inflicted significant damage to the ship's power distribution network. The added strain of the battle and our existing issues is causing an accelerated drain in our secondary power source. Until the damage is repaired, all we can do is cut back on everything but the most essential support processes overseeing the Haven."

"So, where is everyone?"

"Our minds are active and supported by the computer matrix, but everything else has been deactivated. It is, at best, a way to extend our remaining power reserves, though at their present levels they will soon be exhausted."

Chen turned the problem over in her head. There was a solution, of that she was certain. "Can the damage be repaired?"

"It requires physical action," replied Alehuguet. "Without assistance, we will soon deplete our remaining power supplies." She paused, uncertainty and fear taking over her features. "When the computer deactivates, it means . . ."

Chen shook her head. "We won't let that happen. Captain Picard won't let that happen. Do they know?"

"Communications were severed as part of the damage," said Alehuguet. "However, we can still monitor your companions' activities. They are aware of the problem and investigating possible solutions, but they have not yet determined the full extent of the damage. Until communications are restored, we cannot assist or guide them."

Listening to the Nejamri's description of the situation, Chen was already thinking ahead. "Wait. They don't know everything you told me." She indicated the space around them. "I mean, I didn't have a chance to tell them how the Haven really works, and how you can't simply go dormant or whatever you call it. They don't realize the danger you're in." To her, the solution was simple. "Give me the information you need them to have to make the repairs, and send me back."

"That could be dangerous for you, T'Ryssa. The process we created to bring you into the Haven was untried, and I was reluctant to place you at risk in the first place, but as was the case with the Torrekmat salvage team, at the time there seemed to be no other alternative."

"Okay, but it worked, didn't it? Can't you just reverse the process and push me back out? In fact, send the Torrekmat with me. Maybe we can convince them to talk to the other ships and call off their attacks. As for the risk, if we stay here we're dead anyway, right? I can't just stand here . . . sit here . . . *whatever* . . . and do nothing. We have to try." She was all but dizzying herself, trying to process everything her brain threw at her as she searched for solutions. "Hell, is there enough power to get all of us out?"

"No." Alehuguet's shoulders sagged as though a great weight had just been placed upon them. "Even if the process worked, it would take more power than we have."

Chen said, "What about just sending a handful of engineers to help with the repairs?"

"Yes, that may be feasible, but we must keep the number of people being transitioned as small as possible." Forcing a smile, Alehuguet said, "You are very brave and selfless to risk yourself to help us, T'Ryssa. Thank you."

"You can thank me once this is all over."

The longer Taurik studied the information before him, dividing his attention between his tricorder and the Nejamri computer console, the worse the situation became.

"The distribution hub is shot," reported Dina Elfiki from where she worked at an adjacent console in the control room. Like Taurik, and thanks to the translation protocols his tricorder helped to forge during their first visit to the *Osijemal*, she now appeared almost as fluent and confident while operating the Nejamri technology as she was with the starship console interfaces with which they both were familiar. She tapped one of her workstation's screens. "There should be a regulator and switch in this component here, but it was destroyed by shrapnel. This junction is one of three directing power from the main battery plant to this spire. With that circuit fused, the hub is just draining power unchecked. If it's not fixed, it'll bleed the batteries dry."

Standing along with Rennan Konya behind Taurik and Elfiki, Worf said, "That area of the ship is not easily accessible." He moved closer, indicating another of the monitors that currently displayed a schematic cross section of the *Osijemal*. "That is a maintenance conduit, but it appears to be blocked by hull damage."

"If we can clear a path," said Elfiki, "that conduit is big enough for someone to get in there even while wearing an environment suit. It'll take time, but it's not impossible." She placed a hand on the workstation. "What about T'Ryssa and the Nejamri?"

Taurik replied, "The loss of power will obviously bring down the *Osijemal*'s main computer." He gestured toward his own console. "I have detected a marked decrease in energy usage since the attack. It appears that some form of power reduction protocol has been put into effect."

"Have you been able to contact T'Ryssa?" asked Konya.

Taurik said, "There has been no response to any of our queries since the attack, Lieutenant. The onboard computer is still active, but its processing activity has also diminished. I suspect this is also part of the power-saving measures."

"If the ship loses all power, and the computer deactivates," said Elfiki, "what happens to Trys and the others? They're not programs, Taurik."

"I suspect such a situation would be . . . unfortunate for anyone housed within the computer matrix."

"Unfortunate?" Konya almost spat the word. "Are you kidding with this?"

Worf placed a hand on the security officer's arm. The simple action was enough to incite the Betazoid to clear his throat and offer a meek wave.

"My apologies, Commander."

"I understand your frustration, Lieutenant," replied the Vulcan.

Worf said, "If you are correct, then maintaining at least some power is the primary concern."

"Agreed," replied Taurik, "but I suspect that will not be without some difficulty." Given the last attempt to transfer energy from the *Enterprise*, he suspected Commander La Forge would not be anxious to put the starship into that position again, but there were few alternatives to the current situation. "We may be able to supplement the ship's battery plant with portable generators, or perhaps by connecting the power systems of a shuttlecraft or runabout in some manner directly to the *Osijemal*, but I do not know if we can provide energy equivalent to what the computer is now using."

Before Elfiki or Worf could respond, they all reacted to a new sound from overhead. Taurik looked up to see the sphere at the center of the room coming to life, spinning on its support arm as several of its emitters illuminated. He realized it was his first time hearing the device in action, now that he and the away team were working without their EV suits. It was, he was forced to admit, a rather intimidating display.

"Anybody want to guess what it's doing?" asked Elfiki.

Seconds later, the device ceased swiveling, and six emitters began flashing, each adhering to its own pattern and tempo. Despite his years of training to suppress the instincts that drove emotional reactions, Taurik still flinched when the emitters unleashed their own beam of blue-white energy, aimed not at any of the consoles or equipment but simply the floor. Upon striking the metal plating, each beam expanded, bloating and stretching outward, and Taurik realized they were assuming humanoid form. The beams faded, leaving behind T'Ryssa Chen and five other humanoids Taurik recognized as Nejamri. Each was dressed in a dark, single-piece garment while a few carried satchels or packs of various shapes and sizes slung over shoulders or across their backs. Chen, meanwhile, wore her environment suit.

"T'Ryssa?" said Taurik.

Before she could respond, the sphere activated again, discharging another half dozen beams of energy aimed just to the side of the newly arrived group. Within seconds those flashes solidified into six more figures, all Torrekmat. Like Chen, they wore environment suits but theirs were larger, almost oversized garments identical to those worn by the boarding party the away team had encountered in the *Osijemal*'s landing bay. Taurik also noted all six were armed, with weapons secured in holsters at their waists.

"Don't move!"

It was Konya, who had retrieved his phaser rifle from a nearby console and now had the weapon tight into his right shoulder, peering down its length as he advanced on the new arrivals. Worf and Elfiki followed suit, drawing phasers from their holsters and moving to support Konya.

While the Nejamri all complied, each raising their arms to show they carried no weapons, Chen and the Torrekmat seemed not to hear the command or even notice the away team's presence. None of the Torrekmat attempted to bring their weapons to bear. Instead they stumbled one or two steps, before each began collapsing to their knees. Chen turned until she faced the away team, and Taurik saw her confused expression as she raised her right hand in a weak, listless wave.

"*Hey, guys,*" she said, her voice muffled by her EV suit's external communications unit. To Taurik, she sounded dazed, or somehow impaired. Could she be injured?

Then she, too, crumpled into a heap on the deck, leaving only the Nejamri to stare at Taurik and the others with silent uncertainty.

Darkness. Wherever she looked, Chen saw nothing but darkness.

No, that's wrong. Faint, reddish-white light teased the edges of her vision, and she became aware of a distant, low-pitched hum.

Other sounds, electronic tones and what she thought might be voices, teased her as awareness returned.

Chen opened her eyes, beholding the blurry, rather unremarkable ceiling of the *Enterprise* sickbay.

"Lieutenant?" said a voice from somewhere nearby.

Feeling the bed beneath her, Chen blinked several times in rapid succession in an attempt to clear her vision. The sensation of rousing from sleep was already fading, and her hands moved without her conscious thought until she felt them resting on her chest. Beneath her fingers she felt the material of a blanket draped over her body. Then a shadow fell across the bed and she turned her head to see Doctor Tamala Harstad standing next to her. The dark-skinned assistant chief medical officer reached out to place a hand on her shoulder.

"How are you feeling?" she asked.

It seemed an obvious question, though Chen realized she did not quite know how to answer it. She frowned, searching for her last memory before . . .

Before what? The question almost screamed at her from the recesses of her sleep-clouded mind.

"I remember floating in darkness," she said. Words did not want to cooperate just now. "Not falling, but simply . . . existing. Surrounded by suffocating void. Why?" Her thoughts were a jumble, at least at first, but already Chen sensed clarity returning. "Wait. Alehuguet." She glanced around sickbay, seeing no sign of the Nejamri leader. That made sense though, shouldn't it? Alehuguet could not be here. She was still trapped, inside the . . .

"Captain Picard," she snapped. "I need to speak with Captain Picard and Commander La Forge." Pushing herself to a sitting position, she pulled aside the blanket and swung her legs off the bed. That sudden action proved to be a mistake as a wave of dizziness washed over her. Harstad was there to prevent her from tumbling to the deck.

"You're going to want to take it easy for a bit," cautioned the doctor. "The disorientation should pass in a few minutes."

Sensing new movement in her peripheral vision, Chen looked up as Doctor Beverly Crusher and Captain Picard entered the ward from her office.

"It's good to see you, Lieutenant," said Picard.

Crusher moved to examine the medical monitor above Chen's bed. "You had us worried for a while, but we did a complete scan and found nothing out of the ordinary. It seems your little trip—or whatever you want to call it—left no lingering or debilitating side effects."

"Other than my being dizzy and wanting to throw up all over your boots, I feel great," replied Chen. Despite her quip, she actually was feeling better than just a moment earlier. "Okay, maybe I'll spare them."

Crusher put a hand on her back. "I appreciate that. Even though we've found no indications of anything wrong, I want to keep you here awhile longer, just to be sure. There's no way to anticipate what long-term effects your transition to and from their computer system may have."

"I feel fine, Doctor," replied Chen. "Honestly. Don't get me wrong; the whole experience was weird, but at the same time it was . . . *amazing*." She was surprised to realize she found herself missing the Haven and Alehuguet and those few Nejamri she had met. It was almost as if she had left a part of herself in that artificial realm and among those people, all of whom were still so real in every perceivable sense. There was an entire civilization waiting inside that computer, waiting for . . .

"Waiting for us," she exclaimed. "Captain, the Nejamri. They need our help."

Picard replied, "We know, Lieutenant. Commander La Forge and his people are already working with the Nejamri engineers who came with you, trying to figure out how to repair the damage to the *Osijemal*."

"You don't understand, sir," replied Chen, shifting so that she could place her feet on the floor in preparation for leaving the bed. "Their power. It's their power that has to be restored, and fast."

"Geordi knows, T'Ryssa," said Harstad, resting a hand on her shoulder. "You did everything you could. Let Geordi and the others take it from here. You need to rest."

Picard said, "Mister La Forge has already redirected his team's efforts back to solving the power restoration issue." He paused, as though gathering his thoughts. "It may prove a challenge, with the Torrekmat ships still nearby. They seem bound and determined to continue pursuing their salvage claim against the *Osijemal*."

"The salvagers Alehuguet sent back with me," said Chen. "Where are they?"

"Under confinement," replied Picard. "Not the brig. We've given them quarters and they're receiving meals, and Doctor Crusher has already verified that they also seem to be suffering no ill effects from their experiences."

Chen nodded. "They've seen the Haven and at least some Nejamri, too. They know this isn't just some derelict."

Crusher said, "The other Torrekmat ship captain, Senthilmal, mentioned some kind of guild, of which his ship and the others were members. Surely they have rules or a code they follow when it comes to their work? Unless they're simple pirates."

"It may not be that simple," replied Picard. "They've lost two ships and hundreds of people because of the *Osijemal*. We can't count on them being so understanding."

Pushing herself to a standing position, Chen tensed as a minor bout of dizziness manifested itself. It was enough to make her lean against the treatment bed. Inwardly, she cursed herself. There was no time for this. Too much was at stake, and she had no time for her own problems. Closing her eyes, she drew a deep breath and waited for the disorientation to pass.

"We have to try, sir," she said, her voice taut. "I promised them. I promised . . . her."

She imagined Alehuguet, standing in the center of that village she had seen upon her arrival in the Haven, the town square bustling with Nejamri enjoying the life they had fashioned for themselves while enduring their protracted journey to a new home. All of that now hovered at the edge of oblivion.

As was so often the case, Picard's voice cut through her anxiety, asserting practiced, paternal calm.

"Then let's make sure we don't break that promise, Lieutenant."

26

Centered on the viewscreen in the *Enterprise*'s conference lounge, Brinamar regarded the six members of the *Zetoq* boarding party. Picard had ordered them released from security confinement and brought here so that they might talk freely with the Torrekmat ship captain. While they remained under the watchful eye of Lieutenant Rennan Konya and a security team, none of them seemed interested in provoking a confrontation. The strategy of simply talking seemed to be working, at least for the moment.

"You are uninjured?" she asked. Her relief at seeing the boarding party alive and well was evident, which Picard chose to take as a good sign.

"We have been treated well," replied Gerat, the group's leader. Like his companions, the tall, lanky Torrekmat had been given Starfleet coveralls to wear in lieu of their cumbersome environmental suits and their other sweaty, filthy clothing. "First by the Nejamri aboard the *Osijemal*, and now by these newcomers." He glanced to Picard before adding, "Their captain speaks the truth, Brinamar. The first thing they did upon our arrival here was verify that we were unharmed by our experience aboard the derelict. We have been fed and given comfortable quarters in which to rest."

Picard, standing with Worf behind their Torrekmat guests, stepped closer to the screen. "And they are free to return to your vessel at any time. I also reiterate my earlier offer to render whatever medical or engineering assistance you may require."

Clearly taken aback by this development, Brinamar replied,

"You seem eager to offer aid now, Captain, whereas earlier you were doing your level best to destroy us."

"No," Picard said, refusing to be taken down this path. "The loss of your vessel and the *Zetoq* is the tragic result of our not communicating with one another. It is something I deeply regret, but when you attacked my ship you left me no alternative. Let us not compound that horrible mistake by making another. You've scanned the *Enterprise*, Brinamar, so you know its capabilities. I would prefer to help you rather than fight you." He paused, considering his next words with care. "I also wish to help the Nejamri, and the truth is that I believe you can assist us in that effort."

"These Nejamri," said Brinamar, shifting her gaze to Gerat. *"You are certain they are real beings, and not elaborate computer programs?"*

Turning, Picard indicated for his other guest to approach the screen. A broad-chested Nejamri, dressed in the dark garment that to the captain seemed akin to a set of mechanic's coveralls, made his way forward. Despite Picard's still progressing familiarity with his species, the Nejamri's orange features conveyed nervousness and uncertainty. It was obvious the engineer was uncomfortable being called upon to speak in this manner, let alone on behalf of sixty thousand of his fellow travelers. At Picard's urging, he directed his attention to the viewscreen.

"My name is Yidemi," he said. "I am part of the Nejamri community traveling aboard the *Osijemal*. It has been the only home we have known since before you were born. It protects us, and sustains us as it carries us to what we hope will be our new home. When you attack it, you attack my family. You forced us to defend ourselves, but we mourn the taking of life. On behalf of all Nejamri, I apologize for the loss of your people. We wish you no further harm."

To her credit, Brinamar's stance and expression softened upon seeing Yidemi, and Picard thought he may even have sensed a hint of embarrassment from the Torrekmat. To him, it was obvious she was struggling with conflicting emotions, troubled by the tremendous misunderstanding that had occurred here and the resulting loss of life. She doubtless counted friends among those caught up in the destruction of the two Torrekmat salvage vessels. The question now was whether she would let misplaced pride and a need to somehow avenge those deaths guide her next actions, or would she see the necessity in setting aside that tragedy in order to move forward?

To Picard's considerable relief, Brinamar seemed to choose the latter.

"You must understand, I am a salvage merchant. It is a simple life, but one I enjoy. Most of our work is uneventful, never taking us beyond the boundaries of our own star system. Our claims tend to be disabled or abandoned merchant vessels and heavy equipment left behind on our system's uninhabited planets, moons, and asteroids. I cannot truthfully say that no others in our guild have acted in dishonorable ways when conducting salvage, but I can say I have not. However, when Senthilmal transmitted information about your ship, I admit I was overcome by the possibilities it offered. A vessel such as yours represents more profit than my entire crew would otherwise earn during our lifetimes." She paused, looking away from the screen and shaking her head. *"But not this way."*

"It doesn't have to be this way, Brinamar," said Picard. "Not anymore. Help us help Yidemi and all his people on the *Osijemal.*"

Returning her attention to him, Brinamar sighed. *"Even if I decide to assist you, I cannot speak for the other ships that are on their way here. There are those in the guild who will see this as a matter of seeking restitution for our lost ships and crews. They may also be tempted by the* Osijemal, *and even your vessel."*

Picard replied, "We certainly can't offer you anything that can replace your lost people and ships, but there are other compensations we can offer."

"As can we," added Yidemi. "We would be more than happy to show our appreciation for your assistance."

"Surely we can come to some agreement," said Picard, "but time is of the essence. If you do intend to help us, then it has to be now. We have much work to do."

"Then we should begin," said Brinamar. *"We can discuss the other matters later, once the work is complete."*

Smiling, Picard nodded. "Agreed. Thank you, Brinamar."

Buoyed by the conversation and the Torrekmat captain's pledge, Picard allowed himself to savor the moment. Out of tragic misunderstanding, he along with Brinamar and Yidemi had managed to find consensus. Could something more substantial grow from this tenuous accord? There was no way to know for certain, and more immediate concerns demanded their attention.

One thing at a time, Jean-Luc, Picard reminded himself. *One thing at a time.*

"That is one damned big ship."

T'Ryssa Chen almost laughed at Joanna Faur's comment as she stared through the *Araguaia*'s cockpit canopy at the *Osijemal*. The massive ark ship dwarfed the runabout, crowding her field of vision to the exclusion of all else. It was difficult to look at the vessel, which made even the *Enterprise* seem small and weak in comparison, and not feel insignificant. Even the viewscreen images she had studied did not properly convey the ship's sheer mass.

"The inside's just as impressive," said Chen, dividing her attention between the cockpit's instrument panel and the view outside the runabout. "And that's before the whole computer-generated, simulated life thing."

Faur asked, "Was it really as impressive as you described? I guess I'm still trying to equate it to something like our holo-decks."

"In a way, the Haven *is* a holodeck," replied Chen, "but it's so much more. The Nejamri exist, work and play, love and hope and dream, living out their lives just as they would if they were back on their planet. Only the computer keeps them from acknowledging the true passage of time, and their lives keep them occupied to the extent that it's so easy to forget it's not real." Catching herself, she smiled. "But it *is real*."

Behind them, a voice said, "For us, it is real in all the ways that matter."

Chen shifted in her seat to find Yidemi standing at the back of the cockpit. The Nejamri engineer was smiling, his gaze fixed on the *Osijemal* as the *Araguaia* closed the distance.

"It was an amazing experience," said Chen, "even for the short time I was there."

"And I am thankful you suffered no ill effects," replied Yidemi. "Given the complexity of properly mapping and supporting the processes and needs of the brain, the scientists and engineers who created our technology never anticipated its use on someone of another species, but the computer's ability to process and adapt to new situations and inputs is one of its many strengths." He paused, his smile widening. "It is amazing that despite the vast distances that separate our worlds, and that of the Torrekmat, we have so much in common."

Faur replied, "We've found that to be the case when making contact with all manner of new species. And the similarities extend beyond physical characteristics. More often than not, we discover numerous shared values and beliefs, or they're at least something we can recognize. Bridging the gaps is a lot easier when each side is committed to understand the other."

"Do you encounter those who are more difficult to understand?" asked Yidemi. "Or perhaps they are simply unwilling."

"Unfortunately, that happens from time to time too," replied Chen. She paused, reaching up to rub her temples. It was only a small bout of dizziness, but enough to make her collapse a bit into her seat. Despite her concentration on her console, Faur noticed the gesture.

"You okay?" she asked.

Chen swallowed. "Yeah. Doctor Crusher told me to expect a little lag here and there, more as an effect of the meds she gave me than anything else." The *Enterprise*'s chief medical officer had released her from sickbay under the condition that she return if she felt it necessary, but the truth was that despite the fleeting sensation, Chen was feeling more like her old self.

"La Forge to Araguaia,*"* said the voice of the *Enterprise*'s chief engineer over the intercom. *"We show you on final approach."*

Tapping a control on her console, Faur said, "Affirmative, Commander." She paused, checking her instruments. "I'm preparing to orient us for the docking maneuver. Or whatever you want to call it."

"Unconventional insertion?" offered Chen.

Both women heard La Forge chuckling in response to the comment, but he otherwise chose not to acknowledge it. *"The hole they've cut in the hull doesn't leave you a lot of room to maneuver, Lieutenant, but the computer should be able to handle it, if you want."*

"I prefer to do my own flying whenever possible, sir," replied Faur. "That said, this isn't the sort of thing I usually do. We'll see how it goes."

Working to restore power to the *Osijemal* or at the very least arrest its accelerated energy loss, La Forge and Taurik had collaborated with the five Nejamri engineers who had transitioned out of the Haven's virtual realm and returned to their physical bodies. Between them, the group concluded that Taurik's original idea of using a shuttlecraft or runabout's main drive system offered the most stable source of energy with sufficient means to meet the ark ship's immediate power requirements. Disassembling, relocating, and reassembling such a system would prove a time-consuming process. Even drawing or replicating all the requisite components from the starship's expansive supply stores would take longer than La Forge preferred, coupled with the additional burden of having to run diagnostics and fine-tuning adjustments on the untested equipment prior to bringing it online. From a time and safety standpoint, simply slaving a shuttlecraft or runabout directly to the *Osijemal*'s main systems to serve as a substitute power source was the option that would take the least time and present the fewest risks.

All that was needed was to cut a hole in the side of the Nejamri ship. This unusual strategy would allow the *Araguaia*, chosen for this special assignment, to maneuver inside and in close proximity to the larger vessel's central power-distribution hub. This would bypass the various safeguards and other protective systems, thereby avoiding issues the *Enterprise* had already experienced.

"Once we have completed the installation, the immediate danger to my people is removed," said Yidemi. "We will be able to complete our repairs and continue our journey, but not before our people can thank you for all you have done to help us."

Faur turned in her seat. "Yidemi, I have to ask what made your people decide to make the voyage in this manner." She gestured toward the canopy as the runabout continued its approach. "We've encountered ships where the crews travel in suspended animation, and others where the crew and passengers who embark on the journey eventually leave the vessel and its mission to their descendants. In some cases, several generations pass before the ship reaches its destination. What motivated your people to decide on creating the Haven and making the trip that way? Given how large the *Osijemal* is, you could've easily supported your population."

"Those and other theories were considered," replied Yidemi. "However, the consensus among the populace, even before people were chosen to embark on this or one of the other ships, was that we did not wish to travel in hibernation, unaware of what was happening around us as we moved among the stars. Neither did we wish to spend the remainder of our lives simply maintaining our vessel and preparing to give it to successive generations, who would know of our planet and culture only what we could teach them during the voyage. Like everyone else aboard the *Osijemal,* I wanted to help establish our new home and live my life there. Then I could rest knowing the future of our people was secure for those who would come after us. The Haven provided us the best solution for all involved."

Nodding, Faur smiled. "When you put it that way, it makes perfect sense."

"I'm telling you," said Chen, "you're going to love these people."

"I hope I get to meet more of them." Faur returned her attention to her console as an alert tone sounded in the cockpit. "Okay, we're lining up for final maneuvering." She tapped several controls in rapid succession. "*Araguaia* to Commander La Forge. We're ready when you are, sir."

Over the open communications channel, the chief engineer replied, *"At your discretion, Lieutenant. See you inside."*

Beyond the canopy, Chen now could see a large hole cut through the *Osijemal*'s dense outer hull. Maintaining station just to the left of the runabout as it made its final approach was the *Utenla.* The salvage vessel commanded by Brinamar had done an exceptional job utilizing a pair of laser cutting torches mounted on omnidirectional swivels just beneath the ship's bow. According to the sensor readings Chen now studied on her own console, the opening was large enough to accommodate the *Araguaia* while providing limited clearance on all sides. Beyond the hole, support structures, conduits, and even a section of passageway had been cut away, also by the *Utenla,* so that the runabout could maneuver into the *Osijemal* and position itself at the location designated by Yidemi and his team of Nejamri engineers. To make the hole any larger was to introduce unwanted structural issues within the ark ship, something all parties wished to avoid. Though a sound plan on the face of it, this meant Faur and the runabout's computer now were tasked with guiding the *Araguaia* through very tight quarters on the way to its destination. While Chen had to admit to a bit of nervousness at the unorthodox methods in play here, she detected no such anxiety from Faur.

"Please tell Brinamar and her crew it looks like they did an outstanding job with the preparations," said Faur into the open link. "This is going to be a piece of cake."

"I'll pass that on," replied La Forge.

In truth, the same job could have been performed either by the *Enterprise* or a team of engineers in work pods, but Captain Picard instead used the opportunity to solicit the assistance of Brinamar and her crew for the effort. Chen knew he hoped to establish a bond with the Torrekmat ship captain and hopefully wipe away the remaining tensions between them. The strategy seemed to be working, and it was obvious during her interactions with Picard that Brinamar appeared grateful for the opportunity to move beyond the unpleasant nature of their introduction to each other, and Senthilmal's behavior before her arrival.

Completing her final adjustments using maneuvering thrusters, Faur brought the *Araguaia* to a position just before the gap in the *Osijemal*'s hull. The runabout's nose was close enough that Chen was sure if she reached through the canopy she could touch the ark ship's surface. Then, without waiting for further instructions, Faur tapped the thruster control and held for the briefest of moments, edging the *Araguaia* forward.

"Here we go," she said.

With the runabout now in motion, the flight control officer ceded control of it to the onboard computer, and Chen tried not to tense her muscles as they entered the gap. She watched as the inner hull and support structure drifted past the cockpit canopy, noting how sections of severed access conduits and other passages had been sealed off to prevent loss of atmosphere. Indeed, this entire area of the *Osijemal* had been cordoned off from the rest of the ship so that both Nejamri and *Enterprise* engineers could work without risking danger to other personnel elsewhere onboard.

"Told you," said Faur after a minute of flying in silence. "Easy as pie."

"I thought you said piece of cake?" asked Chen.

"Well, now I want pie."

Their giggles evoked a confused look from Yidemi, who said nothing from where he stood behind the women. His own gaze remained fixed on the view outside the runabout, watching as the craft maneuvered deeper into the ark ship.

"Don't worry, Yidemi," said Chen. "We're almost there."

Ahead of them, the makeshift tunnel ended and expanded to a larger compartment, a chamber that had just about enough room for the runabout to hover in as Faur oriented it according to La Forge's instructions.

"Rotating forty-seven degrees starboard," Faur called out, her attention once more on her instruments.

Rising from her seat, Chen looked through the cockpit and down to the deck where eight figures stood near a hatchway, watching the *Araguaia*'s landing. Four wore Starfleet environment suits while the others sported gray, bulkier garments with larger, bulb-like helmets and small rectangular packs strapped to their backs. One of the Starfleet figures, likely Commander La Forge, waved toward the runabout as Faur made the final tweaks and the craft settled to the deck.

"And that, gentle beings, is how we do that," said Faur, her fingers busy entering commands to power down the *Araguaia*'s engines.

Yidemi offered, "Excellent piloting, Lieutenant Faur."

"Thank you." She smiled. "We aim to please."

"Nice job, Lieutenant," said La Forge over the comm link. *"Suit up and come on out. We're on a short timetable."*

Chen frowned, exchanging glances with Faur and Yidemi. "You mean shorter than we thought?"

"You got it," replied the chief engineer. *"Captain Picard just told me there are five more Torrekmat ships inbound, and they're not answering hails. Things are about to get crazy all over again."*

27

Regardless of identity or relationship with the person elected to serve that role, one did not simply drop in on the President of the United Federation of Planets. Beaming into the chief executive's office literally was impossible, owing to the multiple, redundant transport inhibitors monitoring it and its adjacent rooms. While the option was available for other offices within the Palais de la Concorde, it was a privilege restricted to a very small list of approved individuals, and that access varied depending on the person and destination.

The Federation Security Agency had removed such options for the president, without exception. Anyone with business in those chambers underwent a thorough vetting and screening at three different checkpoints before any meeting began. In the event of an emergency that brought with it a need to evacuate, a personal escape transporter was hidden behind the west wall of the president's office. It could only be enabled by the president, her chief of staff, or the head of her personal protection detail. Once employed, the system was programmed to direct the president to one of seven different secret locations scattered around Earth, with the location changed at random intervals by the on-site, non-networked computer system overseeing encrypted communications and data transmission throughout the premises.

The elaborate security measures exempted no one, not members of the president's own family, or close friends, and not even the admiral commanding all of Starfleet.

Passing through the third checkpoint, Leonard James Akaar was permitted to board the turbolift that carried him to the building's presidential level.

"Good morning, Admiral," said Rasanis th'Priil, the Andorian *thaan* who was weathering his first year as the president's chief of staff, upon the lift doors parting to reveal the lavishly decorated foyer to the executive suites. He wore a dark gray suit that complemented his vibrant blue skin and shoulder-length, stark white hair. As was almost always the case when Akaar saw him, th'Priil carried a padd tucked under one arm. So far as the admiral had been able to determine, it was the Andorian's constant companion. Noting the admiral's gaze, he patted the device.

"A chief of staff's work is never done," said th'Priil. "Even before entering politics, I prided myself on my organizational skills, but my life prior to all of this was nothing compared to what I now deal with on a daily basis."

Akaar suppressed a smile. It was common knowledge that the chief of staff's very existence revolved around the nonstop stream of messages, news releases, and other detritus through which he must sift in order to prioritize which information was delivered to the president. Akaar had three young Starfleet officers charged with that duty for him, and they in turn received information from a larger pool of even younger officers who reviewed and arranged the incoming chaos into some semblance of order. When imagining himself toiling in such a thankless capacity, Akaar decided he would rather dive naked into an active volcano. It would be a less painful torment, with an ending far more merciful than being sentenced to that particular flavor of administrative purgatory.

"The president's ready for you," said th'Priil, leading the way from the foyer and past the outer offices where assistants and other staff members worked. Th'Priil's own office was the last one, and Akaar noted the cluttered desk and large viewscreen segmented into eight different displays, each broadcasting feeds from different news organizations either on Earth or other prominent Federation planets. There was time for little more than a cursory glance before he found himself standing before the ornate wooden double doors through which he had passed more often in the last year than the rest of his career. Standing with th'Priil, he waited as they were scanned by the door's locking mechanism and cleared for entry by the room's prestigious occupant. Once the doors opened, th'Priil gestured for him to enter first.

"Good morning, Zha President," said Akaar, striding into the room and moving toward the wide, curved desk at the room's far end. Behind it, framed by the bay windows behind her and the breathtaking morning view of Paris it offered, stood Kellessar zh'Tarash, President of the United Federation of Planets.

Extending her hands in greeting, zh'Tarash offered a practiced, professional smile. "Admiral Akaar. Thank you for coming on such short notice. I hope I haven't disrupted your schedule too much, but I thought this a conversation best conducted in person."

As usual, she presented herself as unfailingly polite and considerate of those around her, which had the virtue of being a true reflection of her personality. In a realm where kindness and concern for others could be viewed as weakness by more opportunistic souls, Akaar found zh'Tarash's warmth and refined manner refreshing. In many ways that had nothing to do with her political views, she had much in common with her predecessor, Nanietta Bacco.

Yes, Ishan Anjar was her immediate predecessor, but he doesn't count.

"I appreciate you asking me to meet, Zha President," said Akaar. "It's always good to see you. I only regret that we have to meet under such troubling circumstances."

With th'Priil now standing next to Akaar, the doors to the office closed, leaving them in perhaps the most secure room on the planet. Sensors along with scattering and other inhibitor technology prevented any conversations held here from being monitored or the room itself from being scanned. Deflector shields protected the entire building and surrounding grounds, and the executive level was a series of self-contained, fully protected compartments with its own environmental control system, and emergency supplies to last for days in the event of some unforeseen yet appropriate need. Akaar chose not to dwell on what form such an occurrence might take.

Zh'Tarash gestured toward a sitting area that included two sofas, a quartet of low-slung chairs, and a round short table cast from a piece of polished obsidian glass. "I should tell you that I asked Attorney General Louvois to meet with me later this morning. I wished to get her perspective on the situation as well, but wanted to give both of you the ability to speak freely." She selected one of the chairs and took a seat, and Akaar waited until she was settled before lowering himself into the chair nearest hers.

"I assure you I have no concerns speaking with the attorney general," he said, "or in her presence. We've both been working together on this from the beginning, and I want that to continue. I think that approach is best for the Federation."

Reaching across the gap separating their chairs, zh'Tarash placed a hand on his arm. "I did not mean to imply otherwise, Admiral. I simply want to hear both viewpoints without either influencing the other. I have no doubt that you both will be as forthcoming with me as you have always been."

These days, such a level of trust was hard to acquire. The current climate did not lend itself to trusting anything or anyone in a position of authority. Even as uncertainty and anger permeated the civilian populace on worlds across the quadrant, Akaar knew it was even more rampant within the halls of Federation and Starfleet leadership. Though he would never admit as much out loud, Ozla Graniv's startling revelations had shaken his own faith in these stalwart institutions.

Shaken, not broken, he reminded himself. *Don't ever forget that.*

Zh'Tarash turned in her seat so that she now faced Akaar. "What more can you tell me about the incident with Admiral Ross?"

"Our follow-up investigation is in line with our initial report, Zha President." Akaar had spent the previous evening reviewing the complete analysis as provided by the Federation Security Agency prior to transporting from San Francisco to Paris. "It was an unfortunate lapse in security that allowed Officer Margo Dempsey to be anywhere near any of the suspects we've taken into custody. She took active steps to circumvent the procedures that would have identified her as having an obvious conflict of interest with respect to Ross and any other alleged Section Thirty-One operatives. This included removing any information connecting her to her husband, Officer Clark Dempsey, who was killed by agents of Thirty-One. This prevented various cross checks from flagging her once the list of operatives and alleged victims was made public."

"I saw that in the initial report." The president lowered her gaze, shaking her head in obvious sadness. "I cannot imagine what she must have been feeling after finding out her husband was murdered, rather than falling victim to a simple but still terrible accident."

Th'Priil said, "So, Officer Dempsey took deliberate steps to ensure she would not be removed from any security detail overseeing any Section Thirty-One operatives currently in our custody."

"That's correct," replied Akaar. "We interviewed several of her coworkers and close friends. None of them reported any significant change in her behavior after she would have learned the truth. One of her fellow officers who served with her, Jonas Voight, said she displayed the shock you'd expect, said that she only seemed to burrow deeper into her work, taking on extra shifts and even rearranging duty rosters to ensure she was present when Admiral Ross was removed from maximum security and transferred to the interview room for his meeting with Attorney General Louvois. According to the computer logs, she started making changes to mask her personal history as soon as it was announced we were taking Section Thirty-One people into custody. And it looks like she started planning to kill Ross from the day his interview with Louvois was announced."

"What will become of her?" asked zh'Tarash.

Sighing, Akaar replied, "She'll be tried for murder, and most likely sentenced to a penal settlement. New Zealand, I imagine." He shook his head. "I can't say I approve of what she did, but I can certainly understand it." Capellan culture would laud Dempsey's act of vengeance on behalf of her slain husband, but his heritage was not always in keeping with forthright Starfleet and Federation values.

"It is a terrible tragedy, for all involved," said zh'Tarash. "I only wish there was something we could do, but her actions leave us no choice. Now more than ever, we must adhere to our principles if justice is to truly prevail. The public's faith in us is tenuous, at best. So far as this matter of prosecuting Section Thirty-One operatives is concerned, we must adhere to transparency and open honesty with our citizens in everything we do. Anything less will only serve to further damage our credibility."

"Agreed, Zha President." That much was obvious from Akaar's attempts to stay abreast of the news broadcasts, which weeks later continued to report on Ozla Graniv's Section 31 revelations. They were impossible to ignore, with programming available around the clock not just from outlets on Earth but other planets as well. Then there was the constant speculation about the ramifications of what the rogue agency's actions meant for every Federation citizen. Some of the theorizing was at least carefully considered, while far too much more seemed to originate from the realm of sheer fantasy and paranoid conspiracy mongering.

"The most difficult part of this entire affair is having to acknowledge just how much influence on all our lives that artificial intelligence exerted." Settling back into her seat, zh'Tarash released a long sigh. "I have spent many sleepless nights trying to comprehend the scope of what it all means, Admiral. That program wove itself into the very fabric of our society, at the most granular level. It has thrown into doubt every decision made on behalf of Federation security for the past two centuries. Were our actions justified, or the result of manipulation for an agenda we may never fully understand?"

Akaar said, "I refuse to believe that everything we've done for more than two hundred years was solely due to some computer pulling all our strings. I reject the notion that our values—the things that define us as individuals and as a society—were given to us by a collection of ones and zeroes cobbled together by some naive engineer before there even *was* a Federation." He tapped his chest. "My behavior wasn't dictated to me by a computer. I am responsible for the choices I've made and the actions I've taken, for better or worse."

"Ultimately," said zh'Tarash, "most people will realize they believe just as you have stated it, Admiral; we remain freethinking beings driven by the fundamental right of self-determination. However, there can be no denying the pervasiveness of the Uraei program, and its impact on many if not all of the major touchstones across Federation history. Lawyers, historians, scientists, and uncounted people across many different walks of life will spend years if not decades trying to put this entire affair into some kind of understandable context. Our very way of life demands that accounting, if for no other reason than taking such a long, painful look inward at ourselves is the best strategy for reaffirming the very values we claim to cherish. That is how we move forward from this stain on our history and legacy."

Akaar said nothing, content to listen as she pleaded her case with the same conviction and passion that had helped her win over a Federation still reeling from the assassination of one president and the unmasking of another as a traitor. Despite being something of an outsider before her elevation to her current office, coupled with the tumultuous period of uncertainty that had accompanied questions, doubts, and fears over Andor's place in the Federation, zh'Tarash had convinced a skeptical public that she was the best person to lead them away from upheaval and uncertainty and back to the path envisioned by the Federation's founders. Akaar harbored no doubts she was still the leader he and every other citizen needed to guide them through this new time of uncertainty.

"If I may offer one piece of advice," he said, "it would be for you to never waver from that course. Two centuries of secrets and deception are a formidable obstacle, but I believe they can be overcome. It's the only way to earn back the trust the public has placed in all of us. I understand that I serve at the pleasure of the president, but I have every intention of seeing this through to the bitter end, and to pursue the truth wherever it takes us. If that means dragging every embarrassing skeleton from the darkness into the light, then so be it. If the truth reveals I am found to be complicit, even unknowingly, then I will submit myself to whatever punishment is deemed appropriate. On this, you have my word, Zha President."

Once more, zh'Tarash touched his arm. "You have always been a man of integrity and principle, Admiral, and I am grateful for your service and counsel. There will be no scapegoats in this matter. I will need you by my side in the days ahead, and I am comforted by the knowledge that you are here. We will see this through together, and I hold myself to the same promise you just made."

"Before we all offer ourselves up for ritual sacrifice," said th'Priil, earning him grateful smiles from Akaar and zh'Tarash for easing the solemnity of the past few minutes, "there is the matter of interviewing and prosecuting the suspects currently in our custody. In light of what happened to Admiral Ross, how will you proceed?"

Akaar replied, "Federation Security has already altered their procedures for detaining and transporting those suspects. Complete background checks on all FSA agents and officers are being conducted as we speak. Anyone with any connection to Section Thirty-One operatives or victims, no matter how small, is being flagged. Meanwhile, Attorney General Louvois is continuing to schedule and conduct her interviews, but security procedures for those are also being modified and enhanced."

Th'Priil said, "We need to exercise caution here. While augmenting security is a sound strategy, I can see it being used by conspiracy theorists to fuel speculation that we are attempting to obscure portions of the investigation from the public. I have already seen claims from some quarters alleging Admiral Ross's murder was part of a cover-up, and justification to drop a veil of secrecy over the proceedings."

"The only way to fight that perception is as the president has already suggested," said Akaar. "Transparency, and open dialogue, especially with the media. We should be able to truthfully answer any question put to us about any of this." He shrugged. "All of Section Thirty-One's secrets are already out in the open. We can only make things worse by denying or dodging the truth."

Leaning forward in his chair, Akaar rested his forearms on his thighs and clasped his hands together as he regarded zh'Tarash. "However, while we're trying to be honest and open with this investigation, there is another issue we need to keep in mind."

"What issue is that, Admiral?" asked the president.

Before he could answer, th'Priil said, "We have several Section Thirty-One operatives in custody, both here on Earth and at detention facilities on six other planets. All of them eventually will be brought back to Earth. Federation and Starfleet intelligence and security agents are continuing to hunt down others. Many of the people named in Ozla Graniv's report remain at large. Some of them are suspected of being key Section Thirty-One players."

"And you think they may try to do what Officer Dempsey did," replied zh'Tarash.

"Not just that," replied Akaar. "We can't rule out the possibility they may try to regroup in some manner."

Releasing a long breath, the president reached up to rub the bridge of her nose. It was but a momentary pause, and when she returned her attention to Akaar, he saw a new conviction in her eyes.

"Then we will fight any such attempt, Admiral. We will hunt them down and crush them. Never again will the citizens of this Federation be slaves, unwitting or otherwise, to such a corrupt entity as Section Thirty-One. On that, you have *my* word."

28

—•—

Emerging from his ready room, Picard moved not to his command chair but instead the front of the *Enterprise* bridge, positioning himself before the main viewscreen. Displayed on it was an image of the *Osijemal*, focused on the area of hull through which the *Utenla* had cut a hole with its laser torches. The Torrekmat salvage vessel was maintaining position several hundred meters from the ark ship, while its companion had taken up a parking orbit near the larger vessel's aft end.

"Any change?"

Worf, sitting in the command chair in the captain's stead, vacated the seat and moved toward him. "No, sir. Estimated time of arrival is less than one hour." He turned and nodded to Aneta Šmrhová, who once more stood at the tactical station.

"Fifty-seven minutes, fifteen seconds, sir," she reported. "All five ships are maintaining course and speed. So far as I can tell, they're ignoring our hail attempts."

"Are they communicating with Brinamar?" asked Picard.

At the science station, Lieutenant Dina Elfiki replied, "We've detected one communication attempt, but it was encrypted. I'm running it through our translation and decryption protocols, but it could take some time."

"Time we wouldn't have if not for your smart thinking, Lieutenant," said Picard, glancing to the science officer and then Šmrhová. "And yours."

Elfiki and the security chief had both hit on the idea of deploying a trio of sensor buoys away from the *Enterprise* and the *Osijemal* because of the interference generated by the ark ship's hull. Once free of such limitations, the automated drones were able to carry out a full spectrum of unimpeded scans and relay that information back to the ship. It also allowed the *Enterprise* to remain on station near the *Osijemal* and ready to assist the away teams and Nejamri personnel currently scrambling to restore the ark ship's power.

"Status of Commander La Forge's repair efforts?" asked Picard.

Worf replied, "The runabout has been positioned, and he and his team are already working with the Nejamri engineers to connect it to the *Osijemal*'s power systems. They are encountering challenges in linking our technology to theirs."

It was an expected facet of the operation, La Forge had explained prior to his departure. Despite all the work Worf and the first away team had accomplished in understanding the Nejamri ship and its systems, there remained many unanswered questions and concerns as to whether the two disparate technologies could be connected without introducing new problems or even dangers to the ship. Casting a shadow over the entire effort was the *Osijemal*'s computer complex and the sixty thousand lives it embraced and protected. Any unanticipated problem carried the risk of damaging—perhaps irreparably—the systems responsible for maintaining the Haven and consigning the Nejamri to oblivion.

"Lieutenant Šmrhová, hail the *Utenla*."

A moment later, the *Osijemal* disappeared from the viewscreen, replaced by an image of Brinamar. To Picard, the Torrekmat ship captain looked tired, and perhaps even stressed. Her lavender skin seemed paler, somehow, and there was a reddening to her yellow eyes.

"*Captain,*" she said.

"Brinamar, we have been unable to establish contact with the approaching vessels. We know they're receiving our hails, but are choosing to ignore them. I was hoping you might help me to understand what's happening."

"*I have had only limited communication with them, myself, Cap-*"

tain. They are proceeding here under orders from the Jirol Salvage Guild to take possession of the Osijemal. *Of course, they're basing this decision on the report Senthilmal sent after his confrontation with you, which means the guild also wants to know more about your ship.*" She scowled, clearly unhappy with the present situation. "*So far as I have been able to determine, they have no knowledge of my reports to the guild, so the leader of the group now approaching was unaware of the Nejamri when he accepted the assignment.*"

Picard said, "But you have been communicating with him."

"*I have, but the lead ship captain seems 'unconvinced' about what I am telling him. He says he prefers to assess the situation for himself upon his arrival.*" Brinamar stepped closer to the screen. "*Do not trust him, Captain. I know Crelin. He is a mercenary of the worst sort. He will do whatever he feels is necessary to secure anything he views as a valid salvage claim, including your ship if he decides it can command a fair price.*"

Worf said, "Even though this ship is not abandoned or adrift? At least, Senthilmal could not be faulted for not knowing the *Osijemal* was inhabited, but no such confusion exists with the *Enterprise.*"

"*Crelin will not be bothered by such things,*" replied Brinamar.

"This Crelin," said Picard. "Is he not a member of your guild? Is he not required to follow whatever rules and regulations you have pertaining to asserting salvage rights?"

For the first time, Brinamar offered a small, humorless laugh. "*The guild in actuality is a rather loose association of salvage and other specialists. It has a leadership and a structure as well as a very long list of its own rules and regulations it makes genuine effort to enforce, and we are pledged to abide by the various laws governing salvage work. However, it also employs a large number of contractors—freelance salvage operators—who do not always represent the guild's best interests. Ultimately, the guild's main priority is receiving its share of whatever profit one of its ships garners after a salvage claim.*"

Picard said, "Meaning the guild will look the other way so long as there's a way to plausibly deny knowledge or involvement in anything illegal."

"Yes, exactly."

Picard asked, "Does that include murdering the passengers and crew of a ship they decide to salvage? Surely the guild cannot simply ignore such a grievous crime."

Brinamar looked away, and Picard heard a muffled voice just out of range of whatever passed for an audio pickup on the *Utenla*. Reaching up to rub her forehead where the elaborate tattoo adorned it, she nodded at the apparent report from one of her subordinates before turning back to the screen.

"If someone undertakes a job and makes some . . . questionable . . . choices with respect to how that task is accomplished, and the details never reach guild leadership, such things are treated as if they never happened. The guild has gotten quite proficient at presenting a facade of legitimacy in the eyes of our government, at least while operating within the confines of our star system. Out here, well away from scrutiny and anyone who can corroborate any outlandish story?" Her expression fell. *"There are even greater opportunities to remain blissfully unaware of the harsh realities of salvage life."*

"Is there any way you can reason with them?" asked Picard.

"I can certainly appeal to their desire to earn a profit with a minimum of risk and expense in time and resources on their part." Brinamar closed her eyes and rubbed her forehead once more before adding, *"You were very generous with me earlier. Perhaps a similar offering might suffice."*

As a gesture of good faith to help establish their working arrangement and in addition to transferring Senthilmal's boarding party to her ship, Picard had instructed Worf to prepare a consignment of metals and other raw components Brinamar listed as having value within the Torrekmat economy. Indeed, the care package represented a sizable bounty, according to Brinamar's estimate upon its receipt. Such materials were easy enough to produce with the *Enterprise*'s replicator systems, but he saw no reason to share that information with his new partner.

"I'm certainly willing to make such an offer," he replied, "particularly if it will prevent our meeting with them from turning unpleasant."

Brinamar gestured toward the screen. *"I would suggest preparing that offering, Captain, but I cannot promise it will prevent Crelin from seeing it as just a portion of the much larger profit to be had from your ship."*

Suppressing a grunt of annoyance, Picard instead replied, "We'll deal with that situation if and when it becomes necessary. Thank you, Brinamar." Once the connection severed, he turned to Worf. "Your assessment, Number One?"

The first officer clasped his hands behind his back. "She seems genuinely troubled by the other ships. Given the assistance she has provided us thus far, it is possible she may be at odds with this Crelin when he arrives."

"But do you trust her?" asked Picard.

"Not yet. It is also possible that when pressed, Brinamar will side with her fellow Torrekmat in any offensive action taken against us or the *Osijemal*." The Klingon almost appeared to regret the observation, casting his eyes toward the bridge deck. "That would be most unfortunate."

Picard said, "Agreed, but it's a possibility for which we'll be ready."

"Captain," replied Worf, stepping closer and lowering his voice, "if we are forced to take action against the Torrekmat ships, the numbers may well work in their favor, despite the *Enterprise*'s superior weapons and defenses."

"I'm well aware of that, Number One," said Picard. Despite the somber outlook, he at least had the knowledge that the starship's main deflector array was back online, and its shield generators were functioning at peak efficiency.

The captain directed his gaze back to the viewscreen and its image of the ark ship. "Of course, having the *Osijemal* at something more than minimal operating capacity would certainly even the odds. Let's just hope Commander La Forge and his team can pull off another of their miracles."

Pieces of the *Araguaia*'s hull and onboard systems littered the room's deck. Chen watched as members of Commander La Forge's engineering team stepped over and around various components, dragging lengths of optical data cabling and larger, more robust shielded power cables between the partially disassembled runabout and the collection of conduits, access ports and panels, and control consoles packing the room.

"What exactly is this place again?" asked Chen. Once more ensconced in her environment suit, she moved about the floor while doing her best not to step onto or into anything. Even though the atmosphere had been removed from this part of the ship, artificial gravity remained active.

Wearing his own EV suit and kneeling next to a large, squat rectangular piece of equipment to which were connected several cables strung from the runabout's port side, Taurik replied, *"This is one of several distribution hubs that divert energy from the* Osijemal's *primary power generators. It is also one of two that are in close proximity to those generators. With the assistance of the Nejamri engineers, we are attempting to convert this facility so that it can provide at least some power to the ship, allowing the primary plant to be repaired without fear of impacting the onboard computer."* He gestured to the equipment he was inspecting. *"Commander La Forge and I have reconfigured this portable generator to act as a flow regulator for the actual distribution hub to which we are connecting. If our plan is successful, we will be able to channel energy from the runabout's warp engine directly to the* Osijemal's *power grid."*

Chen had tried to catch up with at least some of La Forge's pre-mission briefing before boarding the *Araguaia*, and now felt sheepish about how many of the minor details had escaped her review. After being released from sickbay, she had wanted nothing more than to crawl into her bed and sleep for three days. She almost asked Doctor Crusher to keep her in sickbay for a little while longer so she could take advantage of the relative quiet. But there was no way she could let her shipmates carry out this daunting task without trying to contribute in some manner.

"Sounds like a plan," she said. "How can I help?"

Taurik replied, *"Our modifications are nearly complete, and I have finished my safety checks. The next step is a controlled test of the connection to ensure system compatibility."* Rising to his feet, he said, *"Taurik to Commander La Forge. We are ready to proceed."*

"Same here, Taurik," replied the chief engineer. *"The Nejamri engineers are making some final adjustments of their own, and we should be set."*

At the room's far end, just beyond the *Araguaia*'s nose, La Forge and a Nejamri, each protected by environment suits, emerged from an open hatchway into which a large cable, easily a half meter in diameter, snaked from the runabout. The engineer and his companion stepped over the cabling, making their way across the equipment-strewn floor. While La Forge proceeded toward the ship, the Nejamri stopped at a console set into the room's far bulkhead, where two other members of his engineering team were working.

"I don't know if it's the neatest job I've ever done," said La Forge, *"but it should work, at least long enough to get the* Osijemal *running under its own power again."*

"Even a runabout's warp core isn't big enough to handle the job?" asked Chen.

La Forge replied, *"It's not about the size or even the power output. The key here is regulating the energy consistently so it doesn't disrupt the main computer core or trip any of a few dozen security protocols built into the ship's automated processes."* He gestured around them. *"Even with the Nejamri able to monitor almost everything from in-*

side the Haven, they couldn't fix problems that required their physical bodies."

"The first power transfer from the Enterprise *stabilized their systems to a point that allowed them to dispatch a small number of engineers to assist us,"* Taurik added, *"but it, along with damage from the destroyed Torrekmat vessel, had a detrimental effect on their remaining energy reserves. Our current strategy will provide greater stability for the ship's critical energy needs while permitting us to work without haste and risk potential carelessness in our actions."*

"Assuming those salvage ships let us do that," said Chen. According to the last report from the *Enterprise,* fewer than fifty minutes remained until the new group of Torrekmat vessels arrived. Everything now under way was a gamble, for Captain Picard, the away team, the Nejamri, and even Brinamar and her two ships that had been aiding in the relief effort.

La Forge said, *"If we can stabilize the power, the Nejamri will have enough energy for more of their weapons. That should help the* Enterprise *if things get dicey, but let's hope it doesn't come to that."*

Stepping away from the control console his companions were overseeing, the Nejamri engineer in his cumbersome environment suit made his way toward them. His plump, orange face was little more than a broad smile as he approached. Chen recognized him as Kersis, Yidemi's assistant. Portly in appearance, he seemed almost ready to burst from his suit, but his movements were fast, graceful, and confident as one would expect from someone skilled in extravehicular activities.

"Commander La Forge," he said as he stopped before them. *"Our final adjustments are complete. We are ready to proceed."*

The chief engineer moved to the reconfigured generator, and Chen watched him give it one final check before calling out, *"La Forge to Faur. Bring the warp core back online."*

Over the comm channel, the *Enterprise* flight controller replied, *"Copy that, Commander. Reengaging primary systems . . . now."*

Even through her suit, Chen felt the slight rumble in the deck as the *Araguaia*'s warp engine, disconnected from the rest of the runabout's systems without being powered down, reasserted itself. The squat nacelles that also functioned as landing gear flared to life, pulsing with vibrant blue-white energy yearning to be unharnessed. Within seconds, energy transferred from the ship made its presence known at the field generator turned flow regulator, as that component's various displays and indicators flared to life.

"Here we go," said La Forge.

Chen followed Taurik, who along with Kersis stepped away from the makeshift regulator and made his way to the console along the compartment's far wall. The engineer had dispatched his two companions through the open hatch, ostensibly to check on something there, but Chen could not see anything through the portal.

Consulting his tricorder, Taurik said, *"Kersis, I am detecting fluctuations in the flow rate as it reaches the distribution hub."*

"We anticipated some initial deviations during this first test," replied the engineer. *"Adjustments will be necessary before we increase the rate of transfer."*

Based on lessons learned from the *Enterprise*'s first attempt to direct energy to the beleaguered *Osijemal*, Chen knew that La Forge's insistence on finding a means of controlling the rate and intensity of this next try came with good reason. It was hoped such measures would avoid the sort of issues the ark ship had taken to protect itself from a perceived assault on its systems.

"I am detecting a response from automated oversight processes," reported Taurik. *"Similar to what hindered the previous energy transfer. The* Osijemal*'s security protocols are quite formidable."*

Kersis, his attention on the workstation, said, *"I do not understand. According to our tests, we addressed and bypassed those processes. This should not be happening."*

"Then we obviously missed something," replied Chen. "Or maybe the damage was worse than we thought, and that's having an effect?"

Before Taurik or Kersis could respond, more than a dozen of the console's alert indicators flared to life, flashing and blinking for attention. Despite all of the messages and other advisories being rendered in Nejamri script, it was obvious to Chen what was happening.

"I am picking up a massive feedback pulse," said Taurik. Turning from the console, he waved toward La Forge and the *Araguaia*. *"Commander, discontinue the transfer."*

Chen watched the chief engineer reaching for something on the regulator at the same time she heard in her helmet, *"Faur, cut the pow—"*

Interrupting himself, La Forge turned and with sudden, even frantic speed began lumbering away from the regulator, seeking the room's only nearby shelter: the *Araguaia* itself. He made it perhaps five meters before the regulator came apart, consumed by a tight, focused explosion that ripped out its innards and propelled them in all directions across the room.

Feeling herself pulled to the deck as Taurik yanked on her arm, Chen fell in a heap atop Kersis as the Vulcan covered her with his own body. Rolling to one side, she saw La Forge tossed toward the *Araguaia*, thrown off his feet until he slammed against the side of the runabout's hull. His left arm bent at an unnatural angle and she saw his entire body go limp before falling toward the deck. Then her eyes widened at the sight of white vapor escaping the engineer's suit helmet.

"Chen to *Enterprise*! Lock transporter on Commander La Forge! Emergency beam-out to sickbay. Now!"

29

There were days when Brinamar loved the choices she had made. Giving up a military career in favor of a civilian occupation often resulted in a less than favorable transition, bringing with it stress, depression, even anger. Despite an uneven start to such a transition, she had persevered.

Not that the change was without challenges. Just as she was cautioned when submitting herself to the interminable boredom of being processed out of the service, consumption of mood-altering beverages and other illicit substances was a risk, as was engaging in all manner of questionable if not dangerous behavior. Brinamar had certainly partaken of her share of such behaviors. Too much time spent in bars, casinos, brothels, and other disreputable establishments defined her life in those early days following her transition. It might well have ended that way for her if not for the timely intervention of a friend and former comrade-in-arms, Dovat. He gave her an alternative, employing her aboard his salvage ship and teaching her how to survive and thrive in an occupation that rewarded hard work and punished those who lacked the conviction to succeed. When Dovat opted to retire, he gave her this ship, the *Utenla*, to command and chart her own path to prosperity. Choosing to accept such a gift and the living earned since then had never given Brinamar any cause for regret.

Until today.

"It is not supposed to be like this," she said, not realizing she had spoken the words aloud until her assistant captain, Cipal, turned away from his console at the rear of the *Utenla*'s command deck and regarded her with an expression of concern.

"Brinamar?"

Embarrassed at her lapse, Brinamar offered a dismissive gesture. "I apologize. I was wallowing in my own thoughts."

"That seems to be a common malady," said her friend, indicating with a wave the salvage vessel's cramped command deck. Here, five other members of her crew, three females and two males, worked at the room's various consoles or, in one case, crawled into the space beneath and behind one station to make repairs.

"It may be a sign that we are all well overdue for an extended rest," Cipal continued, "preferably somewhere warm with lots of sun and the ability to swim in an ocean. I have a particular penchant for those resorts where random servers just bring you food before you even know you're hungry, and they ensure my hand is never far from a tall, strong drink."

Brinamar smiled. "I have a fondness for such destinations, as well."

"If we leave now, we can be on a beach within three cycles."

"Do not tempt me." Brinamar eyed her friend. "It takes only a moment to plot a course."

Taller than her, Cipal was of leaner build, appearing too thin for the monotone coverall garment he preferred to wear while aboard ship. An engineer by trade, he did not hesitate to crawl into any conduit or access crawlspace in order to diagnose or fix some problem, no matter how far it required him to delve into the *Utenla*'s darkest, dirtiest recesses. Brinamar had known him since her first days working under Dovat's tutelage, and over time the engineer became her closest friend. Upon her own promotion to captain of the salvage vessel, she gave thought to no one else serving as her assistant captain.

"Has there been any further communication from Crelin?" he asked.

Closing her eyes, Brinamar rubbed her forehead. The ache behind her eyes was stronger than it was just a short while ago, and the pain-relief medication she had taken from the small medical kit in her cabin was proving ineffective.

"No. He is receiving our transmissions, but is simply electing not to respond."

It was frustrating, but Brinamar had no idea what to do. Annoyed at the continued failure of her fellow shipmaster to acknowledge her communication attempts, she had recorded a message detailing the situation here and programmed the *Utenla*'s computer to continue broadcasting it until otherwise ordered. She had also included information about the consignments provided by Captain Picard and the promise of there being more in the offing, should the Torrekmat choose collaboration over confrontation. At this point, all she could do was hope Crelin would tire of hearing about the repeated calls until he surrendered and gave her a chance to speak.

"Crelin has a reputation for operating outside of guild rules," said Cipal.

"True, but until now I have never known him to flagrantly defy the laws," replied Brinamar. "And certainly not when it amounts to piracy." Jirol Salvage Guild rules about illegally seizing ships not deemed to be derelicts were strict and unforgiving, but as with any such regulations, their power came from how well they were enforced. Once more, the truth was the Nejamri ship was well away from the Torrekmat home star system and definitely beyond established or even infrequently traveled extra-solar merchant routes. Who was to say what happened out here, far from guild rules and those who cared about them?

Cipal said, "He is an opportunist, to be sure. Once he sees for himself what the newcomers have offered, even Crelin will realize this is a relationship from which we can derive much profit." He paused, gesturing to one of the command deck screens that now displayed an image of the *Enterprise*. "Besides, would we rather have them as an ally or an enemy, especially with a fleet of ships such as that?"

It was a question Brinamar had asked herself. In particular, she had considered it just before and soon after their first encounter and resulting skirmish with the *Enterprise*. The brief battle was enough to tell her that even outnumbered, the other ship carried more than enough firepower to destroy all three of her vessels. Instead, the newcomer captain had displayed surprising restraint and even mercy, offering assistance with repairs and injuries among her people when it would have been so much easier to simply end what she had so unwisely started. Brinamar declined the offers, motivated more by stubborn pride than any other reason.

Still, she knew from her own military service that the ability to demonstrate grace and understanding while still wielding such strength was a quality to be admired, not dismissed. Instinct and experience told her Captain Picard was someone she could trust, and that feeling only strengthened as she and her crew turned to the task he gave them and prepared the *Osijemal*'s hull for access by the smaller transport craft. Once this immediate situation was resolved, she and her people stood to make a handsome profit, and there was plenty of it to share with Crelin and those who traveled with him. She had only to convince him and anyone else harboring similar doubts that her instincts were correct.

The time Brinamar needed to do that would soon be gone, leaving her with an even more troubling prospect: turning against her own people.

Please, Crelin. She wanted to scream her plea across the void of space. *Please do not force me to make such a choice.*

"He's going to be fine."

The words greeted Picard just as he stepped through the doors into the *Enterprise* sickbay's treatment area. His gaze locked on Geordi La Forge, lying atop the bed at the room's center, before shifting to see Beverly Crusher standing on its far side and staring at him. She nodded, her narrow, angular features brightening with a small, relieved smile.

"Captain," said La Forge, who was conscious and seemingly alert as Crusher and Doctor Tamala Harstad hovered over him. The engineer's environment suit had been removed, leaving him with its standard undergarment. His entire left arm was encased within a cylindrical diagnostic and treatment sleeve. "Is everything all right, sir?"

Picard replied, "That's my line, Commander."

Despite the time crunch and with the new group of Torrekmat ships with unknown intentions still on approach, he felt compelled to venture down from the bridge to check on the engineer. Thirty or even twenty years earlier, would he have done such a thing while preparing to face a possible crisis situation? Would the burdens of command have taken precedence above all else, without exception? That likely was the case, Picard conceded, but it was not twenty or thirty years ago, and he was no longer that man. The gulf of time separating that person from the man he now saw every day in the mirror had changed him, taught him to cherish the things that truly mattered. Just as the *Enterprise* was his home, so too had its crew—particularly his senior staff— become his family.

He looked to Crusher. "Doctor?"

"A fractured left humerus and a torn ligament that we'll have back where it belongs and knitted in no time," replied the chief medical officer. "Some bruising along his shoulder and chest from the impact, which likely hurt worse than they look. He also has a minor concussion, which I'm monitoring. I don't see anything more serious, though."

"I don't feel a thing," said La Forge. "That could be Doctor Crusher's medication, though."

The humor was welcome, and Picard placed a hand on the other man's uninjured arm. "No effects from his suit's breach?"

Harstad replied, "No, sir. His helmet didn't shatter, but it was on its way." She pointed to where La Forge's suit had been discarded near one of the other treatment beds, and Picard saw the large, wide crack in the helmet's transparent shield. "His oxygen levels were already down to critical levels when Chen called for the emergency transport . . ."

She let the rest of the sentence trail away, and Picard took his hand from La Forge and placed it on her shoulder. He said nothing, but Harstad still responded to the gesture and offered him a grateful nod. He was well aware of the romantic relationship she shared with his chief engineer, and also knew it was difficult for anyone to set aside emotions and focus on one's responsibilities when it involved a loved one. Despite the brief pause, it took Harstad only a moment to regain her composure, and offer him another silent look of thanks before returning her attention to her patient.

Behind him, the sickbay doors parted again, this time to admit Taurik and T'Ryssa Chen. Both had removed their environment suits and now wore standard duty tan coveralls. Chen's face was slick with perspiration and her dark hair flattened across her head. Meanwhile, Taurik appeared only slightly disheveled, following what Picard guessed was nothing short of a sprint from the transporter room.

"Is he okay?" asked Chen by way of greeting.

Crusher replied, "He will be, thanks to you."

"Fast thinking on your part, Lieutenant," added Picard. "Well done."

La Forge, his words still sluggish, asked, "No one else was hurt, were they?"

"No, Commander," said Taurik. "However, the flow regulator we constructed was completely destroyed. Lieutenant Faur was able to sever the link to the *Araguaia* before the feedback pulse could damage its warp engine or other onboard systems."

"We'll need to rig another one," replied the chief engineer. "That won't be easy, and it also won't matter if we can't figure out what's tripping the pushback from the *Osijemal* side of things."

Taurik said, "The Nejamri engineers have been working to diagnose the issue, and have arrived at a working theory. According to their internal scans, they believe there is yet another override protocol still in operation. It is partially overseen by the ship's main computer, but there also are physical components including power relays, overload switches, and distribution points between the hub we are using and the junction that services the bulk of the ship and the computer core. The scans indicate these processes are operating as originally designed, to protect the core and the sensitive data storage arrays from corruption or other damage due to power surges or other outside threats."

"So," said Picard, "the process is essentially working too well for its own good?"

Pausing a moment as though to consider the captain's words, Taurik nodded. "Colloquially expressed, but accurate, sir."

"Okay, so what do we do?" asked La Forge.

Crusher placed a hand on the sleeve encircling the engineer's wounded arm. "We aren't doing anything, Geordi. At least, not until I finish your arm and verify your concussion isn't more serious than it looks."

"Do not be concerned, Commander," said Taurik. "I have already instructed our team to begin making the necessary modifications to a substitute generator and to inspect and replace any equipment that may have been damaged. Once that is complete, Yidemi and his fellow engineers stand ready to assist us."

Chen added, "But, there's just one problem."

This was taking a worrisome turn, Picard decided. The last thing they all needed at this juncture was an unexpected complication that might hinder or even thwart their efforts. A glance at the chronometer on the treatment bed's bio-monitor told him the approaching Torrekmat ships were now less than thirty minutes from arrival.

"What is it?" asked La Forge.

"The equipment and processes causing the issue are located in an area of the *Osijemal* that is not readily accessible, sir," replied Taurik.

"At least, not by anybody in physical form," said Chen.

Picard crossed his arms, drawing a long breath as he considered the new report. An uneasy feeling was beginning to form in the pit of his stomach. "You wouldn't be here telling us this if it only involved Nejamri engineers from inside the Haven."

"No, sir," replied Chen. Her expression betrayed her reluctance to say what Picard knew was coming. "While the area can be accessed using the remote processes the Nejamri have developed, there's still uncertainty about how our technology interfaces with theirs. There likely will have to be several adjustments made to their equipment if we're hoping to avoid what just happened. Somebody with knowledge of our technology is needed. Inside the Haven."

It was Harstad who responded to that, just beating Crusher. "You mean, go back inside . . . inside that computer? We're still not sure if doing that's done any permanent damage to you."

"I feel fine, Doctor," said Chen. "Even the dizzy spells are pretty much over. Yidemi explained to me that mapping our neural pathways was a little different from theirs, but now that the computer knows what to do, it shouldn't be a problem this time, at least for me."

Picard said, "Making you the logical choice to go."

"I don't like it," replied Crusher. "We haven't had the chance to run enough tests."

Though he understood the simple facts of the problem before them, none of that realization eased Picard's growing anxiety at this potential new course of action. "Even if there are no detrimental effects to your transitioning back to this Haven, there remains the power issue. If we're unable to fix that problem, particularly before the Torrekmat arrive—"

"I know, sir." Then, realizing she had interrupted him, Chen said, "Apologies, Captain. It's a risk, but I think it's one we have to take. If we don't, then the Nejamri are in trouble." She shrugged, forcing a small smile. "I am the contact specialist, after all, and I do keep complaining there are never enough opportunities to do my job."

Despite her attempts to ease his concerns, Picard felt nothing but anxiety. Over the course of a long career, he had sent members of his crew into dangerous situations, knowing on some of those occasions that those brave men and women were undertaking what amounted to suicide missions. It was an unpleasant yet necessary duty of any starship commander, but not one he took lightly. Only after careful consideration and with the full knowledge that no acceptable alternatives were available did he commit to such decisions.

Here, he saw no other way.

Trust your people, Jean-Luc. It was a simple plea, one Picard often employed when reminding himself about the capabilities and convictions of those under his command. *They know their jobs, and they know what they're asking to do.*

"Very well, Lieutenant," he said. "Make it so. Is there anything else you need?"

Chen's expression turned uncertain. "Well, now that you mention it, sir, there is just one thing."

30

—◆—

"I can't believe I let you talk me into this."

Dina Elfiki's were the last words Chen heard before a pair of white-blue energy beams lanced out from the sphere hanging from the control room's ceiling. Then the light enveloped her, washing away everything else and drowning all other sounds in a rush of noise that filled her ears. Unlike her prior transfers between her physical body and her digital doppelganger, Chen this time tried to maintain awareness of the actual transition process, taking in every possible detail. Could it just be her imagination, or was there a fleeting yet still perceptible moment where she existed in a realm that was neither physical nor virtual? Was she alive, yet untethered? A roaming consciousness? A free spirit?

Seeming to last an eternity and yet between beats of her own heart, the transit was over, and Chen found herself once more surrounded by darkness.

"Dina?"

To her right, Elfiki replied, "I'm here. I think. Are we sure this worked? I don't feel any different."

"Don't worry," said Chen. "This happened before. It's sort of a power-saving move on their part."

No sooner did she speak the words than the darkness began to fade, replaced by what at first seemed to be nothing more than a motley collection of immense conduits, oversized access and control panels, and equipment she did not recognize. As the scene continued to coalesce around her, more such components appeared, filling in gaps and slices of darkness and light with more and more detail. Everything seemed enormous, and she was gripped by an abrupt, unsettling feeling of insignificance.

"This is so weird," said Elfiki, and Chen realized the science officer was beside her as she beheld the scene around them.

Chen asked, "Do you feel all right?"

Nodding, Elfiki replied, "I think so. There was a little disorientation, just for a few seconds, but it's gone." She looked down at herself. "What, no cute dress?"

Only then did Chen notice that like Elfiki, she still wore her Starfleet uniform, just as they had before the transition.

"Interesting." Chen had almost come to miss the comfortable gown given to her in lieu of her environment suit during her previous visit. "Maybe we can get you one when this is all over, and we can check out whatever passes for a Nejamri nightclub."

After Captain Picard approved her plan, which included bringing Elfiki with her back to the Haven, both women returned to the *Osijemal*. There, Yidemi and Taurik awaited them in the control room found by her and the original *Enterprise* away team. Even with the ark ship's energy reserves nearing dangerous levels, Yidemi reported that Alehuguet and the other Conclave members agreed the plan to bring Chen and Elfiki into the Haven was necessary if there was to be any chance of restoring power.

"T'Ryssa," said a new voice, Alehuguet's. She was simply there, standing with them in the now very crowded chamber. With her was Yidemi. Unlike when she had last seen him on the *Osijemal*, the Nejamri engineer's dark, single-piece coverall garment was clean and missing the tears on one sleeve that were products of the work he undertook after having returned to his physical body.

"Alehuguet," said Chen. She gestured to Elfiki. "This is my friend Dina. She's here to help me if I get into trouble or come across something I don't understand."

The Nejamri leader regarded Elfiki. "I know who you are. We observed you and your companions when you first arrived aboard our ship. It was your efforts that allowed my people to understand yours. Thank you for helping us."

"We're certainly going to give it our best shot," replied the science officer.

Gesturing to Yidemi, Alehuguet said, "Yidemi is one of our specialists who is most familiar with the systems you will be accessing."

Chen asked, "What's the *Osijemal's* current status?"

"Our power reserves are nearing critical levels," replied Yidemi. "We have already been forced to deactivate most of the Haven environment. Only those processes deemed absolutely necessary to the repair effort are being allowed to continue operating."

"That tracks with our readings," said Elfiki. "If the drop-off persists at the current rate, the battery storage arrays will be exhausted within two hours." She added nothing more to her report, and Chen knew why. Along with everyone else, they both knew what would happen at that point. Nothing more about that needed to be said.

Instead, Chen offered, "All right, then. Let's get to work. Taurik, are you there?"

"I am here, T'Ryssa," replied the Vulcan's disembodied voice. *"Kersis and I have returned to the* Araguaia *and are completing our final adjustments to the new flow regulator."*

"I'm here, too, Lieutenant," said the voice of Commander La Forge. *"In a manner of speaking, anyway. Doctor Crusher is letting me oversee everything from sickbay."* Chen decided he sounded much more alert than the last time she saw him.

Despite the current circumstances, she could not help herself. "Tamala's going to kill you for that, sir." Chen could almost hear the chief engineer's smile coming through the communications link.

"She's already given me an earful. I'm sure I'll hear more after this is all over."

Elfiki said, "I'm going to want to be around for that, and I

still want to see this Haven for myself. Let's get on with this."
She paused, looking around them at the dense conglomeration of
equipment, conduits, and circuitry before turning to Yidemi. "I
hope one of you has a map to this place."

The Nejamri engineer took a moment to process her comment,
but then he nodded, his orange face breaking into a wide smile.
"Oh, yes. I can guide you."

"It's pretty cramped in here," said Chen. "How do we get
where we need to go?"

Alehuguet replied, "Remember, T'Ryssa. This is the Haven."

Before Chen could reply to that, everything around her vanished.

Over the open communications channel piped into his helmet,
Taurik heard Rennan Konya's litany of groans and sighs. Turning from the field generator to which he was making one last set
of configuration changes now that it had been converted into an
improvised energy flow regulator, he regarded the security officer.

"Are you all right, Lieutenant?"

Konya replied, *"Sorry, Commander. It's just been a while since
I've spent so much time wearing one of these things."* He gestured to
his environment suit, a match for Taurik's. *"I mean, we train just
so we can learn to be comfortable moving and even fighting in them,
but I've never been a big fan of them."* Apparently resigned to the
fact that he could neither pull nor stretch the suit to be any more
comfortable on his body, Konya returned to his final check of the
open access panel on the side of the *Araguaia*. Thick cabling was
attached to various connectors inside the panel, snaking from the
runabout to the newly improvised regulator.

"The last time we were required to wear environment suits for
an extended period was during our investigation of the planet
Ushalon," said Taurik. Keeping his attention on his tricorder
while tending to the regulator's final set of configuration inputs,

he added, "Of course, the dimensional shifting that world experienced only added to our difficulties."

"Not a chance I could forget that," replied Konya, looking over his shoulder and away from his work at the runabout's open hull panel. *"I still wonder what our counterparts in those other realities might be like, or what they're doing."*

Discovering the rogue planet, alone in space and at the mercy of an unending, randomized sequence of abrupt transfers between three different dimensions, was one of the more interesting missions in which Taurik had taken part since joining the *Enterprise* crew. Ushalon and its unwilling inhabitants, a team of scientists and other members of a previously unknown race called the Sidrac, were victims of a technology experiment gone awry. Working from a theory postulating the existence of other universes and planes of existence, the Sidrac designed and constructed a massive complex to test their hypothesis and attempt a bridge to another dimension. The scientists lost control of their experiment, and only with assistance from the *Enterprise*—along with a version of the *Enterprise*-D from another dimension and time period as well as the crew of a Romulan warship pulled from yet another reality and era—were Ushalon and the Sidrac returned to their own universe.

"I also have given that much consideration," replied Taurik. "The possibilities are quite intriguing. However, I believe now is not the best time to engage in such speculation. Once our business here is concluded and the Nejamri's situation is secured, I would be interested in revisiting the topic. Perhaps we can do so in a social setting, such as the Riding Club."

"Taurik," said Konya, *"are you suggesting we grab a couple of drinks after work?"* The Betazoid turned from his work at the *Araguaia*, his smile clearly visible even through the slight tint of his helmet's face shield.

Despite the illogical nature of the current conversation, Taurik knew it was a means of easing tension in some humanoid species.

In Konya's case, the Vulcan suspected it was a method of coping with the fact that his romantic partner, T'Ryssa Chen, was once more undertaking a risky mission while working to help the Nejamri. The lieutenant was not in a position to help her, and so therefore was attempting to maintain control of his own anxiety.

Using one gloved finger to enter a final set of instructions to the regulator's control pad, Taurik said, "I believe it would be a stimulating conversation, and I have no objections to you enhancing your participation by consuming spirited beverages. I suspect T'Ryssa would enjoy taking part as well."

"We could make it a double date," said Konya, his tone now more boisterous. *"Who will you bring?"* As soon as he asked the question, his expression changed. *"I'm sorry, Commander. I didn't mean to—"*

Taurik replied, "No apologies are necessary, Lieutenant." He suspected Konya's sudden discomfort stemmed from the fact that prior to her romantic partnering with him, Chen and Taurik also shared an intimate relationship. Though that coupling had ended and he remained friends with her, Taurik also understood that not all humanoids viewed such interactions with the same degree of objectivity or logic.

"Okay, Commander," said Konya, his tone turning more serious. *"I've completed my final checks. Ready to go on this end."*

An indicator flashing on his tricorder informed Taurik his last set of instructions to the regulator had been processed, and he returned the device to its holster on his right hip. "T'Ryssa, the regulator has been configured and we are standing by to connect to the Nejamri power systems."

"All right, Taurik," replied Chen, with the help of the Nejamri technology allowing her to interface and communicate using the frequency shared by the rest of the away team.

Konya, already climbing inside the *Araguaia*'s open hatch, disappeared from sight but his voice was still clear over the channel.

"I'm ready to bring the mains back online at your order, Commander."

So far as Taurik could tell, all that could be accomplished from this location was completed. Nothing else could be done until Chen and the Nejamri did their part. Though he was not prone to such things as superstition and other bizarre points of human interest, he understood the comfort it brought his friends. It was therefore logical to invoke it during times of stress or uncertainty.

"Good luck, T'Ryssa."

Five ships, largely identical to the previously encountered Torrekmat salvage vessels save for assorted modifications or signs of repair, were centered on the *Enterprise* bridge's main viewscreen. Arrayed in a loose wedge formation, one ship moved at the head of the group while the other four trailed behind it to either flank, alternating between flying above and below the lead ship's plane of approach. It was a grouping from which various other, more aggressive tactical options were available, depending on the situation. As a Starfleet Academy cadet a lifetime ago, Picard learned to pilot smaller craft participating in such formations, or defending against them. For someone possessing even modest strategic skill, it was a simple configuration to employ and from which to launch any number of offensive gambits.

Standing just behind the conn and ops stations, Picard studied the oncoming craft. "Weapons capabilities?"

Behind him at the tactical station, Aneta Šmrhová replied, "More or less the same as the other Torrekmat vessels, sir. One to one, we outmatch them, but the numbers favor them in any prolonged engagement."

"We're not going to let it get that far," said Picard. "Place phasers and quantum torpedoes on ready status. As soon as those vessels are within range, target each of their engine sections and be ready to fire on my command." He was still hoping to attempt reasoning with the new arrivals, but if that proved impossible, then he had every intention of ending any resulting skirmish as quickly as possible.

At his left side, Worf asked, "A preemptive strike, sir?"

"We've gone through this twice now, Number One. They've had every chance to see that we don't want a confrontation. If this Crelin insists on fighting despite Brinamar's apparent attempts to convince him otherwise, I don't plan on giving him the first punch." Stepping forward, he placed a hand on the flight controller's chair. "Conn, you've seen how these ships perform. Be ready for offensive maneuvers on my order."

Back at her station following her brief sojourn to the *Osijemal*, because Picard now preferred her along with the rest of his alpha shift bridge officers to be at their stations, Lieutenant Joanna Faur replied, "Aye, sir. I'll be ready."

"Captain," said Šmrhová. "We're being hailed by the lead ship."

Exchanging glances with Worf, Picard replied, "On screen."

The image before him shifted to that of a large, muscular Torrekmat male. Unlike his counterpart, Senthilmal, this specimen had no hair on his head, and his yellow eyes stared out from beneath a heavy brow. Behind him, members of his crew worked at various stations in a well-worn bridge. Ripped upholstery on chairs and scuffed and disassembled consoles were evident, and Picard could even see refuse scattered on the deck. As for the Torrekmat before him, like Brinamar he also sported an intricate white tattoo stretching across the lavender skin of his wide forehead. The design was different from Brinamar's, but Picard thought he noted some commonalities. Was it perhaps a religious or some other ideological marking?

"Crelin, I presume?" he asked.

The Torrekmat glowered at him. "*I am. You must be Captain Picard. Brinamar has told me a great deal about you, and I have also reviewed the report Senthilmal dispatched before his ship was destroyed."*

"A regrettable tragedy, I assure you." Picard stepped closer to the viewscreen. "Believe me when I tell you it is an incident I don't want to see repeated. We have already struck an arrangement with Brinamar and her crew, including a handsome payment for her assisting us with the *Osijemal.*"

Crelin appeared unmoved by the comments. *"You refer to the derelict, to which Senthilmal staked a valid claim under our law."*

"I have no doubt Senthilmal believed his claim was legitimate at the time he discovered the ship, which indeed was adrift and seemingly abandoned. Only later was the truth about its crew and passengers revealed."

As before, Crelin offered no hint of understanding or caring. *"Yes, I am familiar with Brinamar's rather surprising tale. I admit I find it all very hard to believe, but she mentioned you were quite generous with your payment for her services. I can appreciate someone who conducts business with integrity."* He leaned forward, his expression taking on an air of menace. *"For that reason alone, I offer you one opportunity to take your vessel and leave. Senthilmal was my friend, newcomer, and I mean to honor his claim on this derelict. If you interfere, then I will claim your ship, as well."*

Picard gestured as though pointing toward the *Osijemal.* "There are over sixty thousand people aboard that ship. We are attempting to help them, and Brinamar is assisting us in that effort. If you do the same, then I am more than happy to arrange payment just as I did with her."

"Whatever you have to offer cannot be worth more than that ship, Captain." Crelin's eyes narrowed. *"Even your own vessel does not appear to approach its value, but I am content to seize it and find out. As for the derelict, we will determine the truth about its crew, if indeed they exist, and proceed from there."*

Shaking his head, Picard said, "Senthilmal and Brinamar said the same thing. Brinamar realized the error she committed, but

Senthilmal didn't, and we both know what happened. Learn from your friend's mistakes, Crelin. We do not need to be enemies here."

"I gave you your chance, newcomer." The muscled Torrekmat leaned toward the screen, glaring at Picard. *"You wish to defy me. Very well. I will claim your ship for my friend, and see to it that his family is given some small compensation for his loss."*

The transmission ended, returning the viewscreen's image to that of the approaching Torrekmat ships.

"Damn," said Picard, scowling. It was all so stupid and wasteful, and potentially life-threatening with respect to the Nejamri. "We don't have time for this nonsense. Lieutenant Šmrhová, how soon until they arrive?"

"Eleven minutes, forty seconds, sir."

Turning to Worf, Picard released an irritated sigh. "All hands to battle stations, Number One."

31

So, this is what a moth feels like.

The errant thought almost made Chen laugh as she, along with Elfiki, Alehuguet, and Yidemi, moved as if flying between rows and planes of electronic circuitry. Relays, junctions, switches, ports, indicators, and myriad other equipment seemed gigantic as they moved deeper into the Haven's virtual representation of the *Osijemal*'s systems. She was reminded of stories about the first generation of computers on Earth during the twentieth century, with their assortments of vacuum tubes and panels of electrical wiring that attracted, along with dust and other irritants, small visitors. Drawn by the light and hum emanating from the tubes, curious moths and other winged insects often met unfortunate ends in such circumstances, and on occasion even caused the computer to malfunction.

Let's hope we have better luck, Chen mused.

"This is incredible," said Elfiki, her expression conveying her obvious wonder in response to their extraordinary tour of the ark ship's innards. "Imagine the uses technology like this could have for science, exploration, medicine. Doctors already use holographic representations to get more informed views of their patients' internal organs. But being able to put yourself right at the site of an operation, no matter how small, and do the work as if you're actually there? Or being able to examine some ancient artifact or piece of alien technology. We can do that with holodecks, but you're still not interacting with the actual object."

Chen smiled. "Don't get too caught up in all of this. We still have some work to do, and not much time to do it." Taurik's last reminder warned her and Elfiki that fewer than ten minutes remained until the Torrekmat vessels arrived. According to her friend, Captain Picard believed there would be another confrontation with a group of aggrieved salvage merchants. Despite the *Enterprise*'s larger size and more formidable weaponry, five against one were long odds. Plus, Chen was not yet fully convinced Brinamar and her crew along with that of her companion ship would—at the moment of truth—opt to side with the *Enterprise* rather than maintain allegiance with their fellow salvage merchants.

Captain Picard's handling it, she reminded herself. *You just do your job.*

"We are here," announced Alehuguet, even as Chen sensed her forward motion slowing. They had moved to float before a massive construct onto and into which numerous conduits and other components converged. Even though the size differential was vast, she still recognized the pattern of Nejamri electronic circuit pathways and relays from the equipment she studied during her first visit to the *Osijemal*.

Likewise, the sections of melted composite materials and the ominous patch of black scoring that covered a large portion of the hub were also familiar. She and Elfiki had studied a diagnostic schematic of this system prior to their transport into the Haven. What was a small mark on a display screen now appeared more than a dozen meters in diameter, the center of its irregular shape hinting at the origin point for the fault that had disabled this component.

"I swear," said Chen, "this is like crawling around inside one of the *Enterprise*'s warp nacelles."

Elfiki replied, "I can't say I've ever done that."

"You should hang out with me more often. It's one of the benefits of being a contact specialist aboard a starship that spends weeks or even months between first-contact situations." Chen offered her friend a wry smirk. "Worf and Commander La Forge are always finding odd jobs for me to do." Rather than resent the additional duties, Chen had come to enjoy the opportunities to learn about various shipboard systems unrelated to her primary responsibilities. Her increased knowledge and expertise in a number of different areas enabled her to help find solutions to more than one problem and even the occasional crisis or two.

And it makes you the perfect candidate for crazy ideas like this one.

"We will have to revise the processes overseeing this portion of the relay system to bypass the damaged elements and reroute intact connections through this point," said Yidemi, gesturing toward filaments—which to Chen appeared thicker than the *Enterprise*'s warp core—running to and from the marred component. "My analysis indicates this can be done via reprogramming and without the need to replace physical components, at least until a proper repair can be made. We simply have to correctly choose the new pathways linking the relays."

"Sounds easy enough," said Chen. "What's the catch?"

The engineer regarded her with skepticism. "In theory, it should be a simple task, given our ability to directly interface with the ship's various autonomous systems from within the Haven. However, considering the widespread problems across multiple *Osijemal* systems and the still uncertain nature of linking your technology to ours, we must exercise care if we are to avoid inflicting further damage."

"If I understood you correctly at your briefing," said Elfiki, "this isn't a single fix. We may have to make adjustments on the fly even as the power transfer gets under way."

"That is correct, Lieutenant."

Chen tried to lighten the moment. "Sounds like fun." The comment earned her a befuddled expression from Yidemi and a playful slap on the arm from Elfiki.

"Okay," said the science officer. "What do we do?"

Without replying, Yidemi turned to face the damaged components. As Chen and Elfiki watched, he closed his eyes and his body went limp as energy coalesced around him. It formed a cylinder with the engineer at its center, darkening almost to black as smaller strings of energy began cascading through it. The streams rushed past like a blur, some pausing before resuming their fall while others separated and moved from string to string, or created still more filaments of their own.

"It's an interface," said Elfiki. "He's accessing and reconfiguring the computer's underlying programming code." She shook her head. "I mean, sure, it's happening somewhere inside this box or whatever, but it's still him interacting directly with the rest of the machine."

Awestruck by what she was witnessing, Chen looked closer and saw what Elfiki had recognized. The strings were actually scrolls of small blue script in what Chen recalled as one of the written Nejamri languages they had seen on console displays. Only now, watching the streams of text flying at a rate that was almost too fast to follow, she realized she was starting to see shifts from indecipherable text to words, figures, and other terms she could identify. Indeed, the more she studied the chaotic display, the more it seemed to slow, allowing her to read and comprehend.

"Oh my . . ." Her words caught in her throat.

Yidemi's gaze was not on her but instead on various strings of data. He said, "You understand, yes? Entering the Haven means your consciousness is now a part of the system. This allows you to communicate and access all the information it contains. Your own translation protocols have helped us to understand you, and in return aided in forming a bridge between our languages, which is why what you now see appears familiar to you."

As the Nejamri offered his explanation, Chen's eyes widened in response to a similar column of energy forming around her. Within seconds she was surrounded by falling strings of information, even now more understandable than just moments earlier.

Peering through the streams moving past her gaze, she saw Elfiki confronted by her own interface.

"This is incredible," said the science officer. "Why can't I have my tricorder with me in here?"

Chen held out a hand and, as though by her unspoken command, the swirls of data halted their movements, allowing her to focus on one series of filaments that caught her eye. "Is this it?" she asked, already wondering how she might show Yidemi or Elfiki what she was seeing.

"That is a part of the larger process," replied the Nejamri engineer, and Chen could see from her vantage point that he now was focusing on the same segment of code. "It is one piece we will have to modify."

Elfiki said, "Good eye, Trys."

"I have no idea what I'm even looking at," replied Chen, but that was not entirely true. Not anymore, at least. The longer she scrutinized the strings of data, the more comprehensible they became. "I feel completely useless in here."

"You have good instincts," said Yidemi. Having resumed his review of the data streams before him, he turned his body to examine the filaments scrolling past behind him. A moment later, he called out, "I have found our point of entry." Pausing the flow, he reached out until he made contact with the energy column, and segments of different data filaments glowed in response to his touch. Where gaps appeared, he moved his fingers into those areas and new bits and pieces of pale blue script materialized to fill those gaps.

Beyond the column surrounding her, Chen watched as indicators on the massive, scarred relay component began flashing in what at first appeared to be random, unrelated sequences. Some blinked in rapid succession while others were slower, cycling just once or twice before either remaining steady or extinguishing altogether. Whatever Yidemi was doing, it was already starting to have an effect.

"Something's happening," said Elfiki, echoing Chen's thoughts.

Chen nodded. "Yeah, but is it happening fast enough?"

Standing with Kersis at the workstation, Taurik studied the console's readings and compared them to those from his tricorder. He had configured the device to provide him with immediate updates on the status of the makeshift flow regulator, and for the moment everything indicated operation at full efficiency. He had wanted to move the repurposed device closer to the console so he would have easier access to both, but the unfortunate fate visited upon their first regulator insisted he refrain from pursuing that course. This left Taurik with his tricorder and the simple act of walking between the station and the regulator.

"We are ready," said Kersis. As he spoke, he tapped various controls on the console, prompting changes in the different displays and other information routed to the workstation from the depths of the *Osijemal*'s computer. Despite the cumbersome gloves of his EV suit, the Nejamri's fingers moved with surprising dexterity and confidence.

"You seem to possess considerable experience working in situations that require you to wear an environment suit," said Taurik.

Turning from the console, Kersis smiled. *"Before leaving Nejahlora, I worked as a construction engineer, helping to build ships like the* Osijemal. *These vessels were assembled in orbit above our homeworld, as they were far too large to construct on the planet's surface and then lift them to space."* He tapped his suit's scuffed and dented breastplate. *"I spent many, many cycles wearing one of these."*

"Many of our starships are built in similar fashion," replied Taurik, "though I myself have never contributed to such an effort."

Satisfied that the workstation's assorted indicators communicated positive feedback from the system, Taurik moved back to the regulator, which like its predecessor was a conglomeration of cabling and conduits along with a few components scavenged from other equipment. According to his tricorder, everything was still optimal.

"Taurik." It was T'Ryssa Chen, her voice filtering through his helmet speakers. *"Yidemi has started his modifications. You should be able to see some changes."*

Making his way back to the console, Taurik was in time to see Kersis calling up a new set of technical schematics. The resulting images took over most of the station's display space, and the Nejamri engineer traced his gloved fingers across the screen to enlarge the readout.

"This is a diagram of the affected system," said Kersis. *"Yidemi is reconfiguring the software overseeing this process."* He pointed to one area of the screen, which displayed a large, rectangular shape. *"This is the component from which he is setting up a new pathway for the incoming energy flow, away from the damaged junctions."* He tapped another part of the schematic. *"Toward this series of operational relays. It is a time-consuming process."*

Taurik opted not to state the obvious, but the unfortunate truth was that time was not their ally. Less than two hours remained before the *Osijemal* exhausted its remaining power reserves. The situation was growing more dire with every passing moment, to the point Captain Picard had already suggested the Nejamri transfer as many of their complement as possible out of the Haven and back into their physical bodies so that they could be transported to the *Enterprise*. It was not an ideal solution, but rather an unpleasant contingency, a final attempt to save as many of the ship's passengers as could be extracted before the ark ship's systems failed for good. Taurik knew that attempting to move even a small number of Nejamri would only accelerate the power drain to such a degree that only a fraction of the *Osijemal*'s community could be saved. As expected, the Nejamri leader, Alehuguet, informed Picard that no one would be taking advantage of his offer. Instead, her people preferred to stay with their families and friends, regardless of what might happen in the hours to come.

For Taurik, there was but one solution to their problem: solve the *Osijemal*'s power issues and save the Nejamri. No other option was acceptable. He knew from a logical standpoint his outlook was improper, but he did not care. The simple fact was that due to the current circumstances, other outcomes were possible and even likely. However, a life and career lived among species with lesser control over their emotions had given him the ability to appreciate their resolve in the face of adversity. Humans in particular seemed to thrive in such situations, defying logic and even reason in order to fight their way to a desired goal. While it was intriguing to observe, it took on an even greater degree of fascination when he found himself participating in the pursuit of such a quest. Though his Vulcan instructors might admonish him for holding such a stance, he had grown to admire this quality in humans, and especially those he called shipmates and friends.

"*It is working,*" said Kersis, pointing to the console screen. Additional indicators were flaring to life, and Taurik now could see representations of power flowing in new directions and configurations across and through modified relays and pathways.

"Lieutenant Konya," he said into his helmet communicator. "Stand by to bring the runabout's warp engine online." He turned toward the *Araguaia*, and saw the security officer waving through the craft's cockpit canopy.

"*Just say the word, Commander.*"

Chen's voice chimed in, "*Almost there, Taurik. I wish you could see this. It's incredible.*"

"Perhaps another time." Standing next to Kersis and with his attention now on the workstation, Taurik watched as still more reconfigurations manifested themselves as though of their own volition rather than the efforts of Yidemi from somewhere inside the *Osijemal*'s vast computer.

"Enterprise *to away team*," said the voice of Captain Picard. "*Commander Taurik, our time's almost up. The Torrekmat vessels have arrived.*"

32

Red alert klaxons wailed even before Aneta Šmrhová could make a report. Red lighting panels pulsed to life, shoving aside the *Enterprise* bridge's standard illumination and casting the room in veils of crimson and shadow. The effect was only momentary before the security chief rescinded the alarm and restored normal lights.

"They broke formation as soon as they dropped out of warp," she said. Bent over her tactical console, she was inputting commands as fast as her fingers would allow. "Estimated time to intercept sixty-three seconds."

Picard, realizing his fingers already were taut on the arms of his command chair, loosened his grip. "Weapons status?"

"Phasers and quantum torpedoes at your command, sir." Šmrhová paused before adding, "The other complement of torpedoes is also ready."

"Glinn Dygan," said Worf from where he sat next to Picard. "Route power from nonessential systems to the shields."

At the operations station, the Cardassian officer nodded. "Aye, Commander."

"Tactical inset on viewer," Picard ordered, and within seconds Šmrhová pulled up a computer-generated, two-dimensional schematic of the immediate area as interpreted by the *Enterprise*'s sensors. The new image occupied the viewscreen's lower left quarter, with a blue Starfleet insignia representing the starship at the screen's center. Smaller red triangular icons depicted the positions of seven other vessels, the Torrekmat salvage ships. Two of these hovered near a large white circle the computer had designated as the *Osijemal*. Picard noted how the enemy vessels were separating, with the computer providing information as to their distance, speed, and angle of approach along with elevation above or below the *Enterprise*.

"Conn, move us away from the *Osijemal*," he said. "I want some maneuvering room."

Acknowledging the order, Lieutenant Joanna Faur guided the *Enterprise* on an arcing course down and away from the ark ship. The tactical inset depicted the five incoming Torrekmat ships altering their approach vectors to compensate.

"It is a simple envelopment maneuver," said Worf.

Picard had already seen it as well. A common opening attack, the scheme was intended to put an enemy between two or more sources of fire. Even if one was the target ship, there were ways to counter such a strategy.

Wait for it, Picard cautioned himself. *Not yet*.

"What about the *Utenla* and the other ship?" he asked.

Šmrhová replied, "They're maintaining station near the *Osijemal*. No indications of weapons coming online."

"And Brinamar hasn't responded to any of our hails?"

"No, sir."

What was she planning? Though Brinamar had committed to helping him and his crew to assist the Nejamri, would she stand with Crelin and the other new arrivals now that they were here and spoiling for a fight? Five against one promised favorable odds of success for the Torrekmat if they elected to fight the *Enterprise*, but seven against one marked a considerable upping of the ante. Picard had already decided that if either of her ships made an aggressive move, there would be no choice but to attempt disabling them. For now, though, he had more immediate concerns.

"Targets acquired on all five ships," reported Šmrhová. "They're still moving to envelop us."

Picard said, "Fire phasers."

Both the viewscreen's tactical plot and the main image depicted the results of his order, with multiple phaser beams launching from the arrays along the top and bottom of the *Enterprise*'s saucer section. All five incoming Torrekmat ships received hits to their deflector shields even as the starship maneuvered farther away from the *Osijemal*.

Worf, dividing his attention between the main viewscreen and the console next to his chair, said, "Two of the ships are breaking off and attempting new approach vectors. The other three are maintaining course and trying to pin us between them."

"Don't let them have it, Conn," said Picard. "*Enterprise* to away team. What is your status?"

Over the intercom, the voice of Lieutenant Commander Taurik replied, *"The Nejamri are in the process of reconfiguring their power relays in preparation for the power transfer, sir. I do not have an estimated time of completion."*

Keeping his eyes on the viewscreen and its tactical schematic, Picard said, "I don't know how much time we have out here, Commander."

"Understood, sir."

Behind him, Šmrhová warned, "Incoming fire."

Heartbeats later the viewscreen image flared as disruptor energy collided against the *Enterprise*'s deflector shields, followed in rapid fashion by a second impact. Picard felt the slight tremble in the deck beneath his feet, but he knew the attack was little more than a pair of glancing blows. Faur's deft maneuvering of the starship had spared it from falling victim to the worst of the initial assault, and she was already bringing the ship up and around in a bid to help Šmrhová return fire.

"Shields at ninety-three percent," said Glinn Dygan from ops.

"They're all angling for a shot," reported Šmrhová. Her words were punctuated by a cascade of alerts indicating the *Enterprise* was firing its own weapons. Šmrhová had given the ship's computer responsibility for targeting the Torrekmat vessels in accordance with Picard's directives about disabling rather than destroying the attacking ships. This gave the automated fire control system freedom to engage as opportunities presented themselves and do so far more quickly than even Šmrhová could respond.

"Hits on two of the ships," reported the security chief. "Their shields are below seventy percent." A moment later, she added, "Additional strikes on the other ships. Shields are between eighty-five and ninety percent."

Weighing his options, Picard knew the short term favored the *Enterprise* but the longer this dragged on, the chances of their adversaries finding and exploiting some advantage only increased.

"Captain," said Ensign Oliver Trimble, the junior officer once again manning the science station while Dina Elfiki was off the ship. "I'm picking up increased energy readings aboard the *Osijemal*. It's the *Araguaia*'s warp engine coming back online. I think they've started the power transfer, sir."

It was a welcome bit of good news delivered at just the right time. Buoyed by the report, Picard shifted in his seat as he contemplated his next move. On the viewscreen, the tactical plot showed him how the Torrekmat ships were maneuvering to mount another attack.

"All right, everyone. We need to buy our friends just a little more time."

"Incoming fire from multiple ships," called out Šmrhová.

The effect this time was more pronounced, with the *Enterprise* shuddering as its shields fought to absorb the combined attack. Alert indicators flashed on consoles around the command well and bridge officers turned to the new alarms.

"Shields are down to seventy-four percent," said Glinn Dygan. "I'm registering fluctuations in the aft shield generators."

Picard said, "Conn, pick a ship and head for it. Lieutenant Šmrhová, punch us a hole, but I want to reposition this little party on our terms." He had no intention of remaining at the center of a multipronged attack. "They'll get the message or they won't."

"Engineering to bridge," said the voice of Geordi La Forge.

"Captain, I'm routing power from the warp engines to help shore up the aft shields."

"Mister La Forge?" asked Picard. "You're not in sickbay?"

"I figured I was of more use down here, sir."

Worf said, "I suspect Doctor Crusher will not be happy with him about that."

Picard almost smiled. "With either of us. Geordi, take power from wherever you can find it, but keep those shields up."

"Aye, sir."

A little more time, Picard reminded himself. *Just a little more time.*

"Something's not right here."

T'Ryssa Chen, still encircled by the column of streaming information that was her window into the *Osijemal* main computer's core software, reached forward to stop the relentless cascade of data. With both hands she highlighted and enlarged a section of native Nejamri script, which with the aid of the computer's translation protocols quickly morphed into a decent approximation of Federation standard.

"What is it?" asked Dina Elfiki, from where she hovered within her own cylinder. "I'm not seeing anything."

To Chen's right, Yidemi said, "T'Ryssa is correct. Our modifications are not yet complete. I believe we missed reconfiguring one of the pathways." As he talked, he halted his own data stream and excised a portion of blue computer script.

"Do we need to halt the power transfer?" asked Elfiki.

Upon completing the initial configuration repairs, Yidemi—with some assistance from Chen and the science officer—had instructed Taurik to initiate the transfer process from the *Araguaia*. For the first few minutes and with the process moving ahead at a minimal pace, everything appeared to be functioning as expected. It had taken only seconds to register an uptick in the

Osijemal's power reserves as energy flowed from the runabout's warp engine to the ark ship's vast battery storage array. Satisfied with the distribution hub's new settings, Yidemi had ordered the rate of transfer increased. Within seconds, Chen noted the first anomaly, and she was already echoing Elfiki's concerns, at least to herself.

"If we blow the new flow regulator," she said, "we won't be able to get another one over here and modified in time." Chen tried not to dwell on the fact that the *Enterprise* and her shipmates— her family—were engaged in a pitched battle, doing their best to provide cover for the *Osijemal* long enough for this power transfer to work.

You can't help them. You need to do your job.

"Do not halt the transfer," said Yidemi as he continued to work. Chen watched him pull and push at the isolated segment and even remove some portions in their entirety. With a wave of his hand, new text appeared in that space, which Yidemi shoved back into the information strings as the flow resumed.

"I'm seeing some changes here," said Elfiki.

The Nejamri engineer's modifications were reflected by a new surge of energy flowing to and from the reconfigured panel that still loomed before them. The burned protective cover was gone, revealing the component's labyrinthine innards. Chen could see that his new corrections were pushing the incoming energy flow into a new pattern away from the area of the relay that had triggered her concerns. There was only a brief surge of power as the new pathway was initiated, after which the flow evened out and resumed its former intensity.

"The transfer is progressing," said Taurik's disembodied voice. *"At this rate, I estimate the* Osijemal *can begin reactivating primary systems within ten minutes. Faster, if we increase the transfer level."*

"Hang on!" said Chen, almost without realizing it. "Something's still wrong." It was fleeting and she almost lost it in the nonstop onslaught of information, but she was certain she had seen another anomaly flash past in her peripheral vision. What was it? Reaching for the scrolling data strings, she extracted first one then another segment for closer inspection, but whatever had caught her attention now seemed keen to elude her.

"T'Ryssa," said Taurik. *"We are detecting a new fluctuation in the energy flow. It may be building toward a feedback surge."*

"I don't think it's this relay," said Chen. "It has to be something else."

Elfiki asked, "Another override or protection protocol that we missed?"

His face all but buried within the rush of data streaming past him, Yidemi replied, "That seems a logical deduction, but I have run a check on the relevant systems and I am not finding such an event."

"Then it's somewhere else." Zeroing in on a segment of code, Chen pulled it from its home filament and enlarged it. With her left hand she held it in place while using her right to push past more of the data stream. Growing more comfortable with every passing second as she immersed herself within this astonishing interface to the *Osijemal's* computer, she was seeing greater detail and even subconsciously noticing things that would have been alien to her mere moments earlier. Was it an effect of her brain's direct connection to the machine as a consequence of this bizarre noncorporeal state?

Having moved beyond the boundaries of the software overseeing the systems they were trying to repair, Chen found herself drifting among new strings of data. It continued to scroll past her eyes, and she realized she no longer needed to stop or even slow it in order to read and comprehend it. Her movements now were one with the information, and it responded to her thoughts without her conscious control.

There.

A fragment of script was out of sync with the data surrounding it. Chen caught it in her hand, freeing it from the cascade and illuminating it. "I think I found it," she said. "Yidemi, am I reading this right? Is this a secondary overload or protective pathway of some kind?" The text before her at first resembled all of the other characters encircling her, but its responses to her access attempts made her think there had to be a fault here. "I think this segment is corrupted."

Yidemi, now scrutinizing his own view of the targeted section, replied, "It is part of an independent management process. Though not specifically tasked with monitoring the areas we are attempting to repair, I believe it may have automatically corrected itself in response to the larger, system-wide damage the *Osijemal* incurred earlier. In doing so, it acquired additional oversight of areas not normally within its sphere of influence."

"Okay," said Elfiki. "Can we fix it?"

"I believe so," replied the Nejamri.

Taurik's voice boomed once more. *"T'Ryssa, power fluctuations are increasing. If it continues, we will be forced to abort the transfer until repairs are completed."*

"No!" snapped Chen, then softened her tone. "Sorry, Taurik, but you know we don't have time to take baby steps. The *Enterprise* needs our help, so it's now or never. Yidemi?"

Entranced by the work before him, the Nejamri said nothing. He seemed oblivious to everything save the information tumbling past him.

"Yidemi?" she repeated. "Really not the best time to tune us out, friend."

Before she could say anything else, fresh plumes of harsh crimson alert indicators flashed all around her.

"Uh-oh," said Elfiki.

His tricorder seemed to be emitting every alarm bell and light it possessed, and Taurik briefly wondered if the device was about to suffer its own overload. Moving toward the flow regulator, he deactivated the tricorder and returned it to its holder on his right hip. He no longer needed it to ascertain the stopgap contraption's current status.

"The feedback is increasing," reported Kersis. The Nejamri engineer, continuing to monitor the power transfer from the workstation, pointed to the technical schematic on his console. *"They are attempting to reconfigure that area of the system, but it is more complicated than first believed."*

Taurik, examining the regulator's control pad, replied, "The power transfer is continuing unimpeded, at least for the moment." At the present rate, the *Osijemal*'s primary systems would be available for reactivation in less than nine minutes. He was certain that left unchecked, the feedback surge currently building within the Nejamri power distribution hub would take far less time to inflict its damage, nullifying all of the effort expended to this point.

"Lieutenant Konya," he said. "Prepare to disengage the transfer and take the runabout's warp engine offline."

"Standing by, Commander," replied the Betazoid security officer, his voice echoing in Taurik's helmet.

"Wait," said Kersis, and Taurik heard the alarm in his voice. *"Something else is happening."* He tapped several controls on his console. *"It is not a feedback surge. The battery array is discharging its stored energy."*

Moving closer to the console, Taurik asked, "How is that possible?"

"Another damaged circuit elsewhere in the system," replied the Nejamri. *"It has activated a maintenance protocol designed to drain the batteries so they can be serviced. Under ordinary circumstances, we would only take such action against a small number of the batteries, and never all at once."*

Taurik examined the console's schematics. "The rate of drain is accelerating. If this is allowed to continue, the entire storage array will be powerless in minutes. We have to discontinue the transfer, or we risk the regulator suffering possibly irreparable damage even with the additional safeguards we have installed."

Having learned from the first regulator's fate, Taurik had incorporated a pair of surge protection relays into this modified generator. The new configuration had survived a simulated test with this tricorder, but even his best attempt could not anticipate the uneven nature of the power transfer between these two diverse sets of technology.

Of course, in a few moments, none of this would matter.

"T'Ryssa," he said. "You and Lieutenant Elfiki must withdraw from the Haven immediately."

"Taurik, wait." It was Chen, her words spoken at a higher octave than was normal for her, and which he surmised was due to the stresses she currently endured. *"Yidemi's almost there. Just a few more seconds."*

A host of new alerts flashed across the console, and despite his emotional control, Taurik's eyes still widened as he studied the new messages. "The power drain is increasing, T'Ryssa. In less than one minute, all power will be exhausted, and the computer will shut down. You need to—"

Chen's voice was frantic. *"I said wait!"*

33

His eyes closed, Yidemi's hands moved as though guided by divine will. Far too fast for Chen to follow, the Nejamri was scrolling through showers of data while pulling, replacing, or inventing new pieces to take their place.

"Is he all right?" asked Elfiki, who had realized that merely walking through the cylinder that wrapped around her made the entire interface disappear. She now stood in front of Yidemi, watching him. "He looks like he's in a trance."

Electing to remain within her interface, Chen was continuing to sift through the relentless progression of information. The new problem had arisen as if from nowhere, demanding Yidemi's attention and forcing him to abandon the final set of adjustments he hoped to make for the power transfer.

"I'll say one thing for their software," muttered Chen as she kept scanning the flood of data, her voice tight. "It's as tenacious as it is adaptive. One system is damaged or taken offline, and another steps in to cover the gap. It's intuitive, modifying itself as needed to minimize disruption and ensure continuous operation."

Elfiki replied, "Given what's at stake and what the system is protecting, I suppose that makes sense. But there's such a thing as too smart for one's own good."

"It's not the software's fault," said Chen. "It's only adapting as best it can based on what's available, including circumventing the systems damaged during the ship's voyage or thanks to the Torrekmat attacks." The result of the latest modification had somehow tripped what under normal circumstances would be a routine maintenance procedure designed to aid in the servicing and fine-tuning of the ark ship's battery storage array. Instead of individual batteries, the program execution had affected the entire affair, and the system had so far not identified the error, let alone tried to correct it.

"T'Ryssa." It was Taurik. Despite the single word, Chen heard the barely restrained worry in her friend's voice. *"We are running out of time."*

"I have located the source of the problem," said Yidemi. Chen looked over to see the Nejamri holding a large section of computer code before him. Several segments flashed in erratic fashion, but at the center a block of script remained still and steady. "The problem exists at two separate points. I do not know how to repair one without disrupting the other; not while the system is active."

Chen, having located the same section of code via her own interface, removed it from the data stream. The characters danced in her vision, taunting her and daring her to find the solution hidden among their chaos.

Wait.

"I see it!" she called out.

Elfiki, moving to stand before her, stared at her through the cascade. "See what?"

"We're looking at this the wrong way," said Chen. Pulling other segments of code from the screen, she set them aside and retrieved the first isolated segment, reworking various characters in rapid succession. "The system wants to adapt to protect itself. We're trying to get around that instead of . . . well . . . going with the flow."

She inserted her modified code segment and was rewarded with a flash of white light as the data stream resumed its frantic scrawl.

"I'll be damned," said Elfiki, who had turned to look at the relay and its associated components. Every pathway was illuminated. All alarms were gone. The entire distribution hub pulsed with power.

Yidemi said, "The power drain has stopped, and the transfer is once again progressing without interference. There is no sign of the feedback surge. All readings appear normal."

"Taurik! I think we got—"

Everything around Chen vanished.

Darkness pressed in around her, forcing away the maze of relays and their circuits glowing with new energy, leaving her to float alone in an unending void. She neither saw nor heard anything. It was as though the blackness wormed inward to engulf each of her senses.

Hello? Dina? Yidemi? Was she speaking the words or merely thinking them? Chen could not tell.

Before panic could take hold, brilliant white exploded in her vision, almost blinding her before shapes and colors materialized around her. Chen watched as the village courtyard and surrounding buildings solidified and stretched away from her in all directions, returning to the forms she remembered from her first visit to the Haven. Sunlight bathed the buildings as well as the vibrant trees and foliage filling parks and the undeveloped countryside at the settlement's outskirts.

All around, far more Nejamri than she saw the first time she was here surrounded her. They crowded the parks as well as the roadways and walking paths weaving through the village. Unlike her initial visit, when everyone appeared to just be going about whatever passed for their everyday lives, now everyone—adults and children alike—seemed to be taking in the world around them with a sense of wonder. Many looked up toward the beautiful green sky, and even it seemed brighter and more full of life than Chen remembered. So clear was her view for kilometers in every direction, she now thought she could see hints of other villages, mountains, and even a sprawling city in the distance. None of that was there before, was it?

"Oh, wow," said Elfiki, who stood beside her. "Is this . . . ?"

Chen nodded. "Nejahlora. Their homeworld, at least as it used to be."

"I guess that means it worked?" The science officer raised her hands, still acclimating herself to her new surroundings. Closing her eyes, she tilted her head toward the sun and smiled. "This is incredible. I can feel its warmth on my face."

For the first time, Chen realized the other Nejamri were taking notice of her and Elfiki. No one said anything or even moved toward them, but it seemed that dozens of pairs of eyes—no, hundreds if not thousands—were now staring at them. Everyone in the village square or on nearby walking paths, standing in windows or on balconies, was focusing their attention on the strangers in their midst. Chen felt neither uncertainty nor fear from the mass scrutiny. If she was able to sense anything at all, it was a single, simple emotion.

Gratitude?

Before Chen could say anything to acknowledge the newfound attention, she realized Alehuguet now stood beside her, appearing once again as though from the ether. The Nejamri leader, like everyone else, regarded her with an expression of welcoming and thanks.

"You and your friends have saved us, T'Ryssa," she said, reaching out to place a hand on Chen's shoulder. "You have saved us all. We can never repay such a tremendous act of kindness."

Elfiki replied, "Actually, we could use a hand helping our friends."

"We are aware of the battle. Your ship is defending itself admirably, but the Torrekmat do have the numerical advantage. As our power reserves increase, we will be able to render greater assistance."

"Taurik, can you hear me?" said Chen.

"I am here, T'Ryssa."

"How did we do?"

The Vulcan replied, *"The regulator's power readings are stabilizing. We are detecting no sign of fluctuations or feedback. We should now be able to safely increase the rate of transfer."*

Elfiki smiled. "Nice job, Trys."

"You too." Chen turned to Alehuguet. "And to Yidemi, wherever he is."

Alehuguet replied, "He is continuing to oversee the repairs and modifications you made, to make sure we encounter no other unexpected difficulties."

"We are increasing the transfer rate to maximum," said Taurik. *"The* Osijemal's *battery storage array is at fifty-six percent and rising. I estimate the array reaching capacity within three minutes."*

"We're out of time, and the *Enterprise* needs our help, Taurik," said Chen. "Push it right to the wall."

"Brinamar?"

Sitting in her chair on the *Utenla*'s command deck, she looked up to see Cipal staring at her with obvious concern. Trying to keep up with the nearby battle that continued to unfold had captured her attention to the near exclusion of all else. How long had her friend been standing there, trying to gain her notice? Brinamar shifted in her seat, embarrassed by her lapse as she looked away from the pair of screens attached to her chair's arms.

"Has Crelin responded to our communication attempts?"

Cipal shook his head. "No. The only signals we are receiving are those transmitted between all our vessels. We can monitor the battle, but nothing else."

She had elected to keep her vessel and the *Badak* out of the fight, citing for Crelin's benefit the damage sustained by both ships during their own skirmish with the newcomer ship. However, Brinamar and her crew were able to stay informed as the current battle continued thanks to the encrypted communications frequency used by all of the salvage ships under her counterpart's command. While Crelin had not addressed her or the *Badak*'s captain, Sigeta, neither had he thought to scramble the frequency so they could no longer hear. Brinamar suspected he was occupied with greater concerns just now.

The screens on her chair afforded her a direct view of the data collected by the *Utenla*'s various scanners. From her seat, she had an overview of the entire battle as it continued to unfold. So far, the *Enterprise* had been successful in holding off the worst of Crelin's coordinated attacks, but scans showed the newcomer ship was beginning to show signs of wear as the engagement proceeded. It was easy to reason why the skirmish was taking this turn. The newcomer captain, Picard, was trying to force an end to the fight without inflicting catastrophic damage to any of his adversaries, whereas Crelin had no such reservations. Were Picard to unshackle himself from whatever morality informed his existence, this battle likely could be over in mere moments and with devastating results.

"Brinamar," said Radaena, the crew member currently assigned to oversee the ship's scanner suite. An older male, he had been with her since she first took command of the *Utenla*. He pointed to his instruments. "All of Crelin's ships have taken severe damage to their shields, as has the newcomer ship."

"Show me," she replied, pushing herself from her chair. She advanced across the command deck until she stood before the central display screen, which now depicted a computer-realized schematic of the battle. The five Torrekmat salvage ships under Crelin's command were swarming around the *Enterprise*, advancing and retreating in various sequences designed to keep their adversary on a defensive footing and allowing no opportunity to mount any meaningful counterattack. Each time it appeared Crelin's ships might gain an advantage, the *Enterprise* extracted itself, but Brinamar knew this could not last. Eventually, superior numbers would work against the newcomer ship.

"The derelict," said Radaena. "Scans are registering an increased power reading aboard it."

Brinamar nodded. "The *Enterprise* did send personnel over to attempt restoring the vessel's power."

"I believe they were successful."

On the viewing screen, Brinamar watched as the *Enterprise* maneuvered away from another attack from two of Crelin's ships. Disruptor beams clashed against the newcomer ship's shields, and Brinamar was not certain but she thought she saw one of the beams slam into the vessel's hull.

"The *Enterprise* shields are weakened," said Radaena.

Enough, Brinamar decided.

"Signal the *Badak*," she said. "We are moving. Full power to the shields. Move to intercept."

Worf looked up from the console next to his seat. "The *Osijemal*'s power levels are rising. Our sensors are detecting an increased rate of energy flow throughout the entire ship. It should be at full strength within ninety seconds."

Picard felt his heart rate speed up in response to the welcome report. "Outstanding. We just need to hold on for that much longer."

On the bridge's main viewscreen, the tactical inset continued to provide Picard with real-time information about the status of the battle. The Torrekmat ships were not as aggressive as during the skirmish's outset, having suffered enough damage to their own shields to make Crelin and his fellow ship captains wary. Their previous attempt to attack with all five ships was nearly two minutes ago, with the intervening time devoted to single- and double-prong assaults while the others hung back, likely so they could assess the situation. Picard was doing his best to thwart that strategy, directing Lieutenants Faur and Šmrhová to take the fight to the lurkers the instant any opportunity presented itself. If he could not disable the enemy ships, he decided, he could at least stall for time until his people carried out the power transfer to the *Osijemal*. Now it seemed that strategy was just about ready to pay off.

"Captain," said Ensign Oliver Trimble at the science station. "The other two Torrekmat ships. They're moving away from the *Osijemal* and headed in our direction."

Picard said, "Glinn Dygan, our shield status?"

"Forty-nine percent, Captain," replied the Cardassian operations officer. "If they manage another coordinated assault on a weak point, it could prove effective enough to overwhelm the generators."

Exchanging worried glances with Picard, Worf asked, "Weapons?"

"Both ships have armed their weapons and raised their shields, sir," said Šmrhová. "Our scans are still showing damage from our previous engagement they've not finished repairing."

"Damn," Picard said. The odds were now solidly swinging in the Torrekmat's favor. Dragging out this squabble only served to give them the advantage. "We're going to have to up our game, Number One. Glinn Dygan, have engineering route emergency power to the shields. Conn, stand by to—"

"Sir," said Šmrhová. "The *Utenla* and *Badak* aren't moving to join the other ships. They're moving to *intercept* them. Sensors are picking up targeting scans."

Pushing himself from his chair, Picard turned toward her. "Are you certain?"

"Absolutely."

Worf also rose to his feet. "Captain, look."

On the viewscreen, the image now showed the *Utenla* angling toward one of the other salvage ships, approaching from a plane above the other vessel. Without warning the *Utenla* opened fire, with multiple strikes from its disruptors slamming into the other vessel's shields. The effect was immediate, as Picard watched the screen's tactical plot update to show the small armada of five Torrekmat ships break off their various attacks in response to the new, unexpected threat. Already two of the ships were maneuvering for an attack on the *Badak*.

"I'll be damned," said Lieutenant Faur. The flight control officer was already plotting maneuvers to exploit this new advantage and moving the *Enterprise* into better position to seize the initiative before the Torrekmat could recover.

Picard offered silent thanks to whichever deity or omnipotent super being might be listening while being insufferably pleased with themselves for orchestrating this turn of events. That settled, he looked to Worf.

"It's our turn to come to the rescue, Number One. I think it's time we gave them something they haven't seen yet."

The first officer nodded, and the barest hint of a small, satisfied smile crossed his face. "Agreed."

"Lieutenant Šmrhová," said Picard. "Deliver our little surprise."

"Aye, sir. Dropping shields and deploying quantum torpedoes."

At Picard's order, Šmrhová enlarged the tactical plot so that it covered the entire main viewscreen. His attention on the icons representing the *Enterprise* and the seven Torrekmat ships, he silently counted off the seconds he knew would pass before the strategy he and Worf devised took effect. Right on schedule, a host of new, smaller circular indicators appeared on the schematic. Green in color and ordered into small clusters of four, they materialized in a concave formation in the flight path of each of Crelin's five attacking ships.

"Shields back up," reported Šmrhová. "Triggering simultaneous detonations now."

Each indicator represented a quantum torpedo transported from the *Enterprise*'s arsenal. No sooner did they appear than they began vanishing, and all five of the salvage vessels altered their approach vectors away from the *Enterprise*.

"Simultaneous detonations complete," said Šmrhová. "All ships are showing less than fifteen percent total shield strength. Two have lost them altogether. They're breaking off their attack."

Worf asked, "What about the *Utenla* and *Badak*?"

"They're out of immediate danger," replied the security chief.

On the viewscreen, the tactical inset returned to the corner of the image, leaving the rest of the display to show three of the Torrekmat salvage vessels as they moved away. One of the ships appeared to have suffered some hull damage near its aft engine ports, while its two companions maneuvered closer as though to provide cover.

"Any signs of hull breaches or fatalities?" asked Picard.

Šmrhová said, "Nothing on sensors, sir." A tone sounded from her console, and she shook her head. "The other two ships are coming around again, sir. One of them is Crelin's. Both have minimal shield protection, but they're definitely moving into attack vectors."

"Warn them off," said Worf.

After making the attempt, Šmrhová replied, "No response, Commander."

Shaking his head at the stupidity of it all, Picard resigned himself to the unfortunate inevitability of this entire affair. The only way to end the confrontation was to take away Crelin's ability to continue fighting.

"Target their aft shields, Lieutenant," he said. "Quantum torpedoes. Aim to disable."

From the science station, Ensign Trimble called out, "Captain, the *Osijemal*. I'm picking up massive power readings."

"And weapons," added Šmrhová. "A *lot* of them."

"Visual," Worf ordered.

On the viewscreen, the image of the *Osijemal* had been reduced so it now fit entirely within the frame. This did nothing to diminish its size or stature. Along its enormous length, energy coursed along its hull, manifesting itself in ports and along lines designed to enhance its silhouette. Cradled within the ark ship's large aft primary hull section, the massive sphere flared to life. A swirling globe of pulsing green-blue energy cast light across the vessel's dark, smooth hull, highlighting pits, scars, and other damage to its skin and also bringing attention to the numerous weapons turrets positioned along that section of the ship. All along the main hull and its trio of spires, more placements were coming online, moving independently of one another as each turret searched for a potential threat.

"They're not screwing around, are they?" said Lieutenant Faur.

Ignoring the comment, Picard asked, "Ensign Trimble, what's the *Osijemal*'s status?"

The junior science officer replied, "Its power reserves are at eighty-nine percent and rising, but they have more than enough to operate every functional weapon turret."

"And with the *Araguaia* continuing to transfer energy," Worf said, "they have power as long as that connection is maintained."

Šmrhová said, "The Torrekmat are taking notice, sir. Scans show the *Osijemal* is targeting each of Crelin's ships with multiple weapons." She looked up from her console. "It'll be a shooting gallery out there, sir."

"But the *Osijemal* isn't firing?" asked Picard.

The security chief shook her head. "No, sir. Not yet, anyway."

"It is likely Commander Taurik or another member of the away team convinced the Nejamri a show of force was sufficient," said Glinn Dygan.

Worf asked, "What about Brinamar's ships?"

"They're not being targeted, sir. Both vessels are returning to their former station-keeping orbit near the *Osijemal*."

His gaze still locked on the viewscreen and the now even more impressive ark ship, Picard said, "Hail Crelin's ship. Let's see what he thinks about all of this."

Before Šmrhová could respond, a new tone sounded from her console, and she offered Picard a wry smile. "They're hailing us, sir."

"No kidding," said Faur, looking over her shoulder from the conn station. "If I were him, I'd be standing on the hull waving a white flag right about now."

Crelin appeared on the main viewscreen seconds later, and Picard saw he was not even trying to hide the anxiety he had to be feeling now that the tide of battle had turned so far away from him. The Torrekmat ship captain held up his long, lavender hands in an obvious gesture of submission.

"Captain Picard, I have called off our attack. Your weapons have all but crippled our defenses, and my ships stand no chance against . . . against that vessel."

"Quite right," said Picard. "Is this your way of telling me you rescind the Torrekmat's claim on the *Osijemal*? Will the Nejamri be free to proceed on their journey without further action from you?"

Crelin nodded. *"Agreed. The claim is rescinded, and will be so recorded with the Jirol Salvage Guild. Brinamar will be able to confirm this for you. On behalf of my ships, I offer you our surrender."*

Allowing the other captain to stew for a moment, Picard eventually relented. "Very well. I accept your surrender. You may take your ships and return to your homeworld in peace. Let both our peoples learn from this unfortunate encounter so that it isn't repeated." He stepped closer to the screen. "However, I will know if your or another Torrekmat vessel attempts to interfere with the *Osijemal* again. Do we understand each other?"

"We do, Captain. Thank you."

The connection severed, leaving Picard with a view of the five salvage vessels as they began moving away. Returning to their loose formation, they banked toward the viewscreen's lower left corner before disappearing from view. Only when they were gone did Picard allow himself a sigh of relief.

More than enough excitement for one day, I think.

34

For the second time in as many days, Phillipa Louvois found herself admitted into the office of President Kellessar zh'Tarash. As with the first occasion, her arrival was in response to a summons. It was phrased as a request with all the politeness and flourish one might expect from the highest elected leader in the entire Federation, but it was uncommon if not unheard of for anyone to refuse such an "invitation" for any reason that did not involve grave illness on the part of the invitee, or perhaps their sudden or imminent death. Louvois had none of those excuses working in her favor, and neither was she required to travel vast distances across interstellar space to honor such a request. With an office in the Palais de la Concorde a mere handful of floors below the executive suites, there really was no place for her to hide.

If ever there was a better incentive to avoid government work, she could not readily think of one.

Entering the president's office, Louvois found zh'Tarash standing in the middle of the room, and she was not alone. Also waiting for her was Admiral Akaar. Both of them stood before the president's desk, framed by the massive windows that formed her office's back wall and the always inspiring view of Paris beyond the transparent barriers. While Akaar wore his standard Starfleet duty uniform, zh'Tarash was dressed in a colorful, flowing gown Louvois knew was a favorite fashion trend on the president's homeworld of Andor. The vibrant hues and looser fit were at odds with the more conservative ensembles she wore for her official appearances and daily duties. Louvois decided it made her appear more relaxed, as the colorful garment highlighted her bright blue skin and stark white hair. Given that it was just before noon on Sunday in Paris, a quick calculation told Louvois that the admiral had either been roused from slumber to transport from San Francisco for this meeting or else was working the latest in a long string of late nights. As that was the current state of her own exhausting life she could sympathize, and the two shared a nod of greeting and understanding before Louvois turned her attention to zh'Tarash.

"Zha President," she said, hoping her smile didn't look tired or forced. "If we keep meeting like this, people are going to start talking."

Akaar replied, "Anyone with access to my transporter logs is probably thinking I'm moving my office here."

For her part, zh'Tarash smiled. "We all know our various meetings and activities have provided no shortage of material for endless speculation and gossip-mongering. It is not something I particularly enjoy, but I came to accept it as a byproduct of the job."

"It's also one of the barometers of a free society, Zha President," said Louvois. "Letting the media pundits and conspiracy theorists have their say is one way to remind the public that the government doesn't seek to curtail their liberties."

"And given our current troubles, it doesn't hurt to be reminded of such things from time to time," added Akaar.

Zh'Tarash smiled. "Agreed, for all of us."

She gestured toward the sitting area in the corner of her office, and both Louvois and Akaar waited until she chose her seat, a straight-backed chair positioned between two sofas and a low-rise table, before opting to sit across from each other on the couches.

"Thank you both for meeting me today," she said once they all were settled. "I know it is a Sunday and you both certainly deserve at least an opportunity to rest, but even at the best of times I find myself lacking the ability to have anything but brief and often terse discussions with the numerous people I encounter on a daily basis. That has only worsened in recent weeks, and I find myself going further and further outside my official schedule if I want to have any sort of meaningful conversation. I hope you'll both understand that given my role, the list of people with whom I feel comfortable talking is frankly quite short. I value your counsel and not just because of your professional responsibilities, but also because I know I can trust you."

Glancing to Akaar, Louvois replied, "We appreciate that, Zha President."

The admiral said, "Your faith in us is humbling, madam. How may we serve you today?"

"I imagine no one knows more than the two of you that this business with Section Thirty-One is not going away at any point in the near future. There are still so many questions to be answered, and the answers we have found beget even more questions. In and of itself, that part does not concern me. The public has the right to pose such questions, and I believe it is our responsibility to answer them to the fullest possible extent."

Where is she going with this? Louvois considered the question in silence, opting for now against giving it voice, but it was obvious zh'Tarash had something on her mind, was uncertain how to proceed, and was working her way toward asking for whatever advice or assistance she thought she needed.

"So far," continued zh'Tarash, "news outlets have been content to report on the facts of the matter and have largely done a remarkable job refraining from baseless speculation. I believe a good deal of that can be attributed to the open nature of your current investigations. You have both been most forthcoming at every turn, and for that I am extremely grateful."

While Louvois believed and even championed a high level of transparency—taking into consideration appropriate and practical matters of security not just with information but also the people involved—she knew there was a price to be paid. Almost from the moment Ozla Graniv's initial report was released, media outlets across the Federation began conducting their own investigations into the information provided by the now celebrated journalist. Both Louvois and Akaar, the most easily recognizable figures representing the Federation and Starfleet as the joint investigation progressed, had agreed to more interviews in the past month than either could easily count. The media sought any angle, searched for any witness, heretofore "person of interest," or nugget of previously buried information that might provide new insight and, more importantly, material exclusive to their respective broadcast networks and publishers.

Elsewhere, the scandal was fueling other, often fascinating, developments. A scan of the news told Louvois no fewer than five dozen books, each purporting to be "the real story" behind Graniv's startling revelations about the "mysterious" Section 31 and its cabal of operatives, were due for publication within the next two months. Each was being written by someone promoting themselves as an "insider" or "expert" on the subject, which Louvois found amusing given that none of their names appeared anywhere in the information exposed by Graniv, and neither were they individuals of interest in either the Federation's or Starfleet's official investigation. Some of the books were even about the investigations themselves, as told by hard-hitting investigative journalists supposedly benefiting from access to those "deep in the halls of power" where the secrets were kept and the bodies were buried. At first she found such tomes concerning, but peeks at draft manuscripts and advance copies of the finished books told her the authors behind these would-be exposés were either horribly misinformed or else were exploring their talent for crafting fiction.

Regardless of the agenda driving such publications, Louvois knew they would contribute nothing to the public discourse except uncertainty and distrust if left unchallenged. With that in mind, she saw it as her sacred duty to ensure that the truth—or at least as much as could be safely shared—was made available to that same public. If that meant she lost a lot of sleep while conducting interviews, then so be it. The truth deserved nothing less.

It did not, however, make her job any easier or less stressful, and it certainly did not make her any less tired.

Akaar said, "Zha President, all we can do is what we've been doing: conducting our investigation in as forthright a manner as we're able. That comes with costs we all likely imagined, even if we didn't anticipate just how high the price might be in some cases." He paused, casting his gaze to the low, polished table between them. "I wonder if Admiral Ross knew."

"He knew," replied Louvois.

Clearing her throat, she looked away from zh'Tarash and Akaar and toward the windows behind the president's desk. Even from where she sat, Louvois still could see the Tour Eiffel, reaching toward the cloudless blue sky. The ancient monument remained an inspiring sight, but it did little to soothe her as she recalled those last moments with Ross before Officer Margo Dempsey's phaser beam cut down the admiral and Captain Rebecca Steeby. She mourned the woman, a dedicated officer given the difficult and thankless task of ensuring the man charged with a litany of heinous crimes against Starfleet and the Federation received the vigorous defense that was his right under due process of law. Louvois doubted Steeby, who swore the same oath as every other Starfleet officer, ever seriously expected to give her life in defense of that promise and the values it represented. As much as anyone, she deserved the unrelenting efforts of Louvois and everyone else to see that justice was done.

Returning her attention to the president and Akaar, she said, "Based on everything I've dug out of Ozla Graniv's report and the information she released, Ross was one of the top figures—if not *the top figure*—within Section Thirty-One's leadership structure. Despite it being decentralized to a staggering degree, far too many data points in various Thirty-One operations lead back to Ross. Maybe he didn't even know he was the top dog, or as close to one as the Uraei program allowed while he was in Starfleet."

"With him out of the picture," said Akaar, "cooperation from people like Alynna Nechayev and Tujiro Nakamura becomes even more important. More than anyone else we've interviewed to this point, those two along with Ross looked to have been dug in pretty deep. This could get more serious as we start moving toward trials and courts-martial."

While the civilians indicted by the Section 31 reveal would be tried in Federation courts, Starfleet officers were facing tribunals. Depending on the individual officer, the charges were such that determinations had to be made as to which type of legal proceedings the suspect would face. It was just one of numerous headaches currently plaguing Louvois.

"It's because of what happened with Admiral Ross that the Federation Council is now considering holding its own independent investigations into the entire affair," said zh'Tarash. "This isn't public knowledge, of course, so I would appreciate you keeping this conversation between us. I have received reports from several council members expressing concern over what Ross's assassination represents. They worry other prominent suspects we currently hold in custody might also become targets."

"I suspect there are other motivations behind these concerns," said Akaar. "Not to be indelicate or speak out of turn, Zha President, but not everyone on the council is your best friend. I'm betting at least a few of the people bringing these complaints see this whole affair as a means of advancing their own careers and agendas."

Zh'Tarash rose from her chair, and in response Louvois and Akaar also stood. Waving them back to their seats, the president moved behind her desk until she stood at the window. Only a long wooden credenza separated her from the transparasteel barrier. Her attention seemingly on something neither of them could see, she said nothing for a moment. Then her shoulders seemed to sag, and she leaned forward until she could rest her palms on the credenza. Even her antennae seemed to droop as she leaned against the table.

"Investigations by my colleagues on the council do not concern me," she said, without looking away from the credenza. "Neither does media scrutiny or public disapproval that we do not move fast enough for their liking. Finding the truth is all that matters."

Straightening her posture, zh'Tarash turned from the window and crossed the office back toward them. "I believe staying the course we have set will allow us to weather this crisis, and perhaps even come away from it wiser and more protective of the values we cherish and have sworn to uphold. If there are those who see this as an opportunity to foment disruption or dissent, we will deal with them as appropriate, but not at the expense of the truth. Indeed, I believe when historians write about this tumultuous period, it is precisely how we conduct our search for that truth which will define our legacy."

Simply listening to zh'Tarash speak, not from a prepared speech but here in this unguarded moment, was enough to make Louvois's spirits soar higher and with more conviction than she had felt in far too long. It reminded her that she was perhaps too caught up in this business of searching for the truth and bringing to justice those responsible for this terrible crime against every Federation citizen. The necessity of the work had, for a time, blinded her to the reasons for it, not just in service to the law but also those for whom the rule of law provided the society promised to them and their ancestors more than two centuries earlier. Hearing zh'Tarash's words reminded Louvois of the greater, far nobler purpose to which she had committed herself.

"The course we now chart impacts every Federation citizen," the president continued. "Not just by what has been revealed but also by the actions we take going forward; yet we must also not lose sight of those who watch from afar and wait to see how we act. This is why I have brought you here today, my friends."

Returning to her chair, zh'Tarash sighed. "What I am about to tell you I have not shared with anyone else, not even the Federation Council. I have no intention of keeping this from them, but before I enter that arena, I wanted your counsel on how best to proceed. I have received an encrypted message by just such an . . . interested party. Much to my surprise, we appear to have an ally in all of this, from the most unexpected of quarters." Turning from Akaar and Louvois, she said, "Computer, replay encrypted message zeta-tango-two-zero-zero-one. Authorization: zh'Tarash, three-nine-five-five."

On the wall opposite the president's chair, a large viewscreen activated, displaying the Federation seal. After a moment, it was replaced by the imposing figure of a male Klingon. He wore a hybrid ensemble of military uniform and the robes of an elected official complete with a large assortment of awards and other vestments. His long mane of dark hair was streaked with gray, and his already intimidating countenance was enhanced by the patch of puckered, scarred flesh where his left eye used to be.

"Chancellor Martok," said Akaar.

"President zh'Tarash," said the leader of the Klingon High Council. *"I offer greetings on behalf of the Klingon Empire. I trust this finds you well, but I suspect you are enduring a great deal of turmoil. Perhaps the trials the Federation now faces are outgrowths of its own hubris and naiveté, but one thing I know is that you are one who leads from integrity and honor. For that reason alone, I offer this: I stand with you."*

Louvois could not help saying, "I'll be damned."

"There are those within the Empire who do not see things as I do," Martok continued, *"just as I am sure you have your own dissenters. I believe they operate from positions of ignorance and perhaps even cowardice as they seek to reap personal benefit from this chaos. Whatever their motivations, they are detrimental to the greater good. For the Empire to move beyond the uncertainty this entire affair has wrought, so too must the Federation. Let us work together to accomplish that goal. I await the opportunity to meet with you, Zha President, and discuss how we best serve both our peoples."*

The message ended and Martok's image faded, leaving Louvois

and Akaar to stare in stunned silence at zh'Tarash. Akaar was the first to find his voice.

"He's taking an enormous risk. It's no secret he has enemies on the council. Someone there will use this as an opportunity to challenge his place as chancellor. This could have serious repercussions throughout the Empire."

Louvois replied, "And yet there he is, pledging to work with us."

"There will be members of the Federation Council who won't like this," said Akaar. Then, attempting a smile, he added, "I don't think they'll challenge you to a death match for your office, Zha President, but these days nothing would surprise me."

Zh'Tarash returned the smile. "Let us hope things do not proceed to that point." She gestured to the screen. "But, as you can see, our problems are much larger than even we thought. We are not merely acting in our own best interests, but also as an ally. Despite the troubles that have entangled the Federation and the Klingons, Martok was elevated to lead the High Council *because* he represents a bold new vision for the Empire."

"Of course he'd pledge his support now," said Louvois. "He's always championed a stronger alliance between us, and that has placed him at odds with hard-line traditionalists on the High Council. Our biggest concern all along was how the Klingons would respond now that the truth about Zife and Tezwa is public, but Martok's telling us he stands with us, and he's fighting to get his people to go along with him. He needs our help as much as we need his."

"Coming to the aid of an ally who was once our sworn enemy," said zh'Tarash, and to Louvois's surprise the president smiled, and her antennae even perked up. "What better way to demonstrate our values and how we have learned to put aside differences in pursuit of common prosperity can there be? Is that not the very essence of what those who founded our Federation envisioned all those years ago?"

"I admire your optimism, Zha President," said Akaar. "Of course you know you can count on my full support."

Her expression warming, zh'Tarash turned to Louvois. "And you, Madam Attorney General. What do you think?"

"It's a bold goal," replied Louvois. "For both our peoples. It's certainly easier said than done, but anything worth doing usually is."

How that was to be accomplished was anyone's guess, Louvois knew, but any day that began or ended with the Klingon Empire declaring itself a friend rather than a foe had to be a good day, right?

So much for today, she thought. *Let's see what tomorrow brings.*

35

The coliseum was immense, reminding Picard of venues on Earth and other planets where large numbers of spectators assembled to watch sporting events or other entertainments. Tiered viewing stands encircled the bowl-shaped structure, descending toward a lush green field that was unadorned except for the large circular dais at its center. It was here that Picard stood, trying not to feel too much on display before an audience of more than sixty thousand Nejamri.

"Captain Picard," said Alehuguet. "On behalf of my people, I thank you for agreeing to meet with us today so that we may offer you our sincere gratitude for all you have done to assist us. If all the people of the Federation you represent are like you and your crew, then we hope we are taking but the first steps along a long, enduring path of mutually beneficial and prosperous friendship."

When she spoke it was in a normal tone, and she made use of no visible microphone or other device to augment the volume of her voice. Nevertheless, applause and cheers erupted from all around the coliseum. Turning in place to review the massive audience, Picard saw most if not all of the Nejamri rising to their feet. Though this was not his first time standing before a large gathering, rarely was the occasion when he was the focus of attention on this scale. Even with Geordi La Forge, T'Ryssa Chen, Dina Elfiki, and Beverly Crusher with him, he still felt more than a bit overwhelmed by the circumstances.

"Everybody loves a hero," said Beverly, gently poking him in the rib cage.

"Aren't you glad you came?" asked Picard, sharing a playful look. "And you were so worried."

Only upon Alehuguet's insistence did Picard accept the Nejamri leader's invitation to partake in these proceedings, despite the unusual logistics involved. With sixty thousand people hoping to show their gratitude to Picard and the *Enterprise* crew, few ready options presented themselves. Though the *Osijemal*'s power issue was no longer a dangerous concern, and with repairs to the ark ship's primary energy generation facilities now well under way, it simply was not practical to transfer the entire Nejamri population back to their physical bodies. Complicating matters was the simple if amusing fact that despite the *Osijemal*'s size, there existed no single area within its confines capable of accommodating the ship's entire complement.

It had taken some convincing on the part of Chen and Elfiki, but eventually Picard relented, accepting Alehuguet's invitation to transfer into the Haven. Doctor Crusher had voiced her expected objections and reservations, but her scans of both Chen and Elfiki revealed no detrimental effects resulting from their own experiences within the virtual realm. Now that the Nejamri had complete information on human physiology—and human-Vulcan variances, thanks to Chen—any uncertainty of the Haven being able to care for them had vanished. Other species represented by the *Enterprise* crew would take a bit longer, but for now the progress allowed Picard and a small contingent to join the Nejamri. With her concerns addressed, Crusher declared there was no way she was letting her husband have all the fun, and insisted on accompanying him.

"Thank you," he said, remembering that he also did not need to raise his voice. As Alehuguet explained, the Haven took care of ensuring everyone in the coliseum heard his words as though he were standing directly in front of them. There was not even the echo of his voice being channeled through a public address or other communications system. The effect was to give the entire experience just enough of a surreal quality to remind him that he was not occupying physical space.

"It is a great honor to be with you today. We know that you have already made a long and dangerous journey, and that you still seek a new world to call your own. Members of my crew, working with your own representatives, have reviewed our star charts. We believe we have identified several worlds that show great promise. According to our information, all are uninhabited, and all possess environments similar if not identical to the world you left behind. Once your repairs are complete, you will be ready to resume your voyage, and it is my sincere hope that one of these planets will suit your needs."

He paused, taking a short respite from his prepared remarks as the audience offered more cheers and applause.

"The man knows how to work a room," said La Forge, earning him chuckles from Crusher as well as Chen and Elfiki. Picard's only response was to offer the other man a sidelong glance.

Recovered from his injuries, the chief engineer had stepped away from overseeing the remaining repairs to the *Enterprise* in order to get his own look at Haven. More than any of the others, Picard wondered how the transition had affected La Forge, given his ocular implants and their substitution for his lack of "normal" vision. As it turned out, the answer was as interesting as the question.

"Who needs eyes when the computer generates everything for your mind to see?" he said upon their arrival. His excitement only grew as he explained to his companions that the Haven was giving him the equivalent of normal sight, at least so far as his brain was concerned. With no need for the data received by his implants to be interpreted and processed so that he could "see," the Haven merely did what it was doing for everyone else: it tied his neurological activity directly to the computer's matrix so that he saw and interacted with the environment the same as his companions.

Once the crowd settled again, and at Alehuguet's prompting,

Picard continued, "To reiterate Alehuguet's words, I hope that this is the first of many meetings between our two peoples. The mission my crew and I have accepted is to venture forth from the confines of the Federation and seek out new civilizations with whom we hope to form lasting friendships. We cherish individual liberty and diversity, but we also see the value in common pursuits. The universe is vast, with room for all of us, and we believe it is the right of all beings to live without fear of enemies. However, the reality is that enemies do exist, but by coming together we are stronger than if we faced adversity alone. In time, after you find your new home, it is my hope that we might welcome you into our Federation, which represents hundreds of worlds and billions of people. We stand ready to greet you with open arms and add your voice to ours. Until that day, I wish you a safe and prosperous journey. Thank you."

Renewed applause greeted his words, and Picard said nothing. So intense was the outpouring from the audience that it almost felt like a physical force pressing against him from all directions. It was humbling to be the focus of such attention, and despite his best efforts, he was unable to prevent the heartfelt emotion driving the crowd from affecting him. He could only hope that the future brought with it fulfillment of his fervent desire for the Nejamri to begin their civilization anew, and for them to realize the potential of what he had promised.

It took Picard a moment to realize the applause and cheers were fading, along with the coliseum itself. Everything around him was disappearing into blinding white light. Seconds later, he found himself standing with his officers and Alehuguet in what she had termed a transit station, one of the platforms employed to transfer Nejamri to and from the Haven. Though it bore a superficial resemblance to a transporter such as those on the *Enterprise*, the platform possessed a ceiling but was open on all sides, with a curtain of energy generated by power nodes above and below where a transferred subject stood. Picard and his people along with Alehuguet fit onto the platform with more than enough room to spare, and there was nothing indicating an individual pad on which to stand. This suggested the platform could handle many more subjects than the "normal" transporter systems with which he was familiar. The transfer completed, the cylinder of energy encasing the platform dissolved, and Picard could not help placing a hand on his stomach as though to verify that his entire body had made the transition.

"Remarkable," he said, more to himself than anyone else as he and the others moved off the platform.

Chen still heard him. "That gets more fun every time I do it, sir."

"Is it different from your previous transfers, Lieutenant?" asked Crusher.

"I think so, but it's hard to explain, Doctor." Chen frowned. "It sounds odd, but I think it was . . . smoother?" She shook her head. "I don't know."

Alehuguet said, "Our actual transit stations are specifically designed for moving to and from the Haven. As such, they possess all of the scanning and protective systems to ensure a safe transfer. We were able to replicate most of those functions for the improvised transfer emitters we modified in our remote access arrays, but it was not a complete substitution."

"As long as it works, I'm happy," said Elfiki.

La Forge added, "Amen to that."

"I am pleased that our desperate tactics did you no harm," said Alehuguet, "but I am content not to rely on such measures from now on."

A new voice said, "I only wish that I could have seen it."

Picard turned to see Brinamar standing near the platform. The Torrekmat wore clean clothing, better fitting and not nearly so bedraggled as the last time he had seen her. She moved around the platform, crossing her wrists before her chest and bowing.

"Captain, it is good to see you again."

Returning the greeting, Picard replied, "And you as well, Brinamar. Thank you again for your assistance."

"Thank you for yours. My crew and I appreciate everything you have done to help us with our repair efforts and for the consignment you offered." She turned her attention to Alehuguet. "And to you."

Alehuguet replied, "We are grateful for your help as well. Thanks to you, my people and I are able to resume our journey with renewed purpose."

"You have also given me a new outlook." Brinamar smiled. "This experience has been . . . most informative and inspirational. I have much to think about, as I am sure I will have much to answer for upon our return home. I hope the Jirol Salvage Guild sees things the way I now do."

"My offer to meet with your government's leadership stands," said Picard. "As I told you before, we have no desire to make enemies out here, but we are always hoping to meet new friends."

"I shall carry your message home, Captain. Until we meet again, I bid you and your crew safe journey." She repeated the gesture with her arms. "And to you, Alehuguet."

"Travel in peace, Brinamar."

With a Nejamri engineer standing ready to escort her, the Torrekmat turned and left, on her way to the landing bay and a transport craft back to her vessel. Picard watched her go, wondering how the message she planned to deliver would be received.

Friends, not enemies, he reminded himself. *One can only hope.*

"Mister La Forge," he said after a moment. "Are we on schedule?"

The chief engineer nodded. "Yes, sir. At last report, Taurik and Yidemi said that the repairs to the *Osijemal*'s primary power generation systems should be finished in a few hours." He looked to Alehuguet. "After that, you'll be free to continue your journey."

"The closest of the planets we've identified is about three months away at the *Osijemal*'s top warp speed," said Elfiki. "That should give you plenty of time to finish up any other repairs or maintenance tasks you want to tackle before you get there, and to conduct long-range scans and prepare a survey plan. With your systems and defenses back to full operational capacity, I doubt you'll run into any more trouble along the way."

Alehuguet smiled. "I am anxious to make that journey and to see what awaits us. Would it not be wonderful to find a new home so soon after benefiting from your assistance? And then to make contact with any of our other ships? Of course, perhaps they have found worlds of their own, and are attempting to locate us? The possibilities abound, I think."

"Now that we know there are other ships like yours somewhere out here," said Chen, "we can certainly be on the lookout. On the other hand, space is pretty big."

"Indeed it is," replied Alehuguet, "and the journey can be a lonely one, but perhaps less so when made with friends. Captain, might you consider traveling with us? After all, the vast majority of my people have not yet had the chance to meet their saviors. There is much we could learn from one another along the way."

Picard conceded it was a tempting notion. "The opportunity to learn from you would be extraordinary."

"A chance to learn more about your technology?" asked La Forge. "I could spend the next few decades crawling around in this ship."

Elfiki added, "He's not even kidding. Same goes for me, by the way."

"And I have to wonder," said Crusher. "If you do find a suitable world, how will you and your people handle the eventual transition back to your physical bodies." She gestured to indicate the ship around them. "I mean, you've lived within the Haven for centuries, far beyond a normal Nejamri life span. Can you resume a 'normal' life?"

Smiling, Alehuguet nodded. "We are eager to do so, Doctor. The trouble with immortality, or as close to that state of being as technology will allow, is that it stifles any real incentive to make the most of one's otherwise temporary existence. Within the Haven, we lived secure in the knowledge that, barring extreme circumstances, there would always be a tomorrow, and as many tomorrows as were needed to achieve our ultimate goal. It was comforting, but perhaps ultimately detrimental."

"Life is for living," said Chen.

"Indeed it is." Stepping toward her, Alehuguet placed a hand on Chen's shoulder. "We believe our reason for being is to make a difference, rather than simply marking the passage of time. We have done quite enough of the latter, and thanks to you, we are able and ready to regain our lives and continue pursuing our true beliefs."

The words and the conviction behind them prompted Picard to recall a similar conversation, shared years ago with Will Riker, as he and his former first officer stood on the wrecked bridge of the *Enterprise*-D.

Someone once told me that time is a predator that stalks us all our lives. I'd rather believe that time is a companion who goes with us on the journey, and reminds us to cherish every moment, because they'll never come again.

"What we leave behind is not as important as how we've lived." He smiled at the memory. "After all, we're only mortal."

"Yes," said Alehuguet. "Exactly." Taking Chen's hands in hers, she said, "Thank you, T'Ryssa Chen, for all you did to help us. We will not forget you." She looked to Picard. "We will not forget any of you. May you all travel in peace."

"Travel in peace, Alehuguet."

36

—◆—

"I can never keep these things straight. Is it morning or evening for you out there?"

Picard forced himself not to smile at Admiral Akaar's attempt to open their latest conversation on a casual note. He started to reach for the teacup and saucer resting next to the computer terminal on his desk, which took up most of the space in the small area he had established as a work area in the quarters he shared with Beverly Crusher and their son. Thinking better of the tea, he instead straightened himself in his chair as he regarded the admiral's image on the terminal's screen.

"Late evening, ship's time, Admiral. Gamma shift will begin within the hour. After a stressful couple of days, we're finally getting back to a normal routine." Before he could continue, a sound from the other side of the room caught his attention, and he glanced to the small couch positioned against the wall opposite his desk. There, curled into a ball with a padd cradled in his arms and partly draped by a thick, dark blue blanket, was his son. René Jacques Robert François Picard, barely five years old, was already an accomplished snorer. The boy had taken the liberty of relocating the blanket from his own bed to the sofa as was his habit when he wanted to read or play a game yet not interrupt his father working at the desk. As was also customary, he had fallen asleep on the sofa, content with the knowledge that he soon would be carried to bed by one of his parents. His snores, light and steady and quite unyielding, brought a sort of calm to the room that Picard rather welcomed.

Returning his attention to the computer terminal, he said, "I apologize for the short notice, but I felt this wasn't something that could wait for my next scheduled report."

He knew without asking that it was almost 0500 hours local time in San Francisco. Akaar appeared to be sitting at his own desk in his office at Starfleet Headquarters, and darkness shrouded the view outside the row of windows behind him. The admiral looked tired, Picard decided. Deep circles were visible beneath the Capellan's eyes, though the eyes themselves still burned with their normal intensity.

"I've already reviewed your preliminary report about the Osijemal *and the* Nejamri. *So far as I'm concerned, you handled the situation exceptionally well. Despite trying circumstances and no shortage of challenges and obstacles, you and your crew took care of everything just as you always do. I'm looking forward to your final report."*

Though their recent conversations had lacked the fire and fury of their confrontation following the release of Ozla Graniv's bombshell Section 31 exposé, Picard was not expecting the admiral to offer such effusive praise so soon after that much less pleasant meeting.

"They're very much open to the idea of our reestablishing contact once they're settled on their new world," he said. "There is much we can learn from the Nejamri, Admiral, and it certainly wouldn't hurt to have another ally out here."

Akaar nodded. *"My thoughts exactly. The time you and the* Enterprise *have spent in the Odyssean Pass has reaped great benefits for Starfleet and the Federation, Captain. Of course, I was confident that would happen."* To Picard's surprise, the admiral even offered a small smile, but it was fleeting before his normal, impassive expression returned. *"However, something tells me you didn't contact me this early to talk about the Nejamri."*

"No, sir." Pausing, Picard cleared his throat. "It regards . . . the other matter."

"I'm guessing you've been keeping apprised of the latest news on that front."

"Indeed I have, Admiral. It's obvious that you and Attorney General Louvois are taking every precaution to ensure the proceedings are as fair as they are transparent. There can be no understating the impact of Section Thirty-One on all our lives, and those responsible for allowing that cancer to spread unchecked must be brought to justice. That is why I can no longer allow distance or mitigating circumstances to shield me from the fallout. And while I sincerely appreciate your candor and your efforts, I also can no longer permit you to shield me from it, sir."

Akaar was silent for a moment, and Picard watched as he settled in his chair. His left forearm lay across his desk, and Akaar began drumming his fingers along its smooth surface.

"Louvois was right, damn her."

Frowning, Picard asked, "I beg your pardon?"

"She said you'd never sit back and allow others to take the heat for something you did, or were accused of doing. Didn't matter who the target was. Didn't matter whether you knew them or even liked them, but you would never stand by and allow someone else to take any blame or punishment you believed should be directed at you. Conscience and honor, and sense of duty, would always win out, regardless of the cost." He shrugged. *"For what it's worth, I knew that was true, too, but I especially knew she was playing with fire when she dragged Riker into her office. If anything was going to get you running this way, it'd be something like that."*

"Will Riker is quite simply one of the finest officers with whom I've ever served. He has no involvement in any of this, and I won't stand to see his record or his reputation tarnished. There are plenty of people to share whatever blame and punishment will come from all of this, but you need officers like him at your side, Admiral—particularly now."

Picard knew the only reason Riker had even agreed to a meeting with Louvois about any of this was out of loyalty to him. As for Louvois, despite whatever personal history Picard himself might have with her, she was a consummate professional driven by the pursuit of truth and justice rather than personal feelings and vendettas. He could admit that he may not always have been appreciative of that drive, especially when he was her target. That much was true during his court-martial years ago after losing the *Stargazer* in battle, and later when he found himself acting as defense counsel to Data in the hearing that ultimately defined his status as a sentient being and Federation citizen. Louvois's only goal was to find the truth above all else, but Picard could not allow her to use Riker's loyalty to him as a cudgel against his friend.

His gaze wavering for a moment, Akaar's features softened as he seemed to consider Picard's words. When he returned his attention to the screen, it was with a new determination.

"We both thought you'd say that too. It has the virtue of being correct, of course. Rest assured, Riker won't suffer consequences from any of this, but you understand that we had to be sure. Louvois had to be sure, not for her own sake or even mine, but for the official record, and you know why. There may be a couple of freshman cadets over at the Academy who might not yet be up to speed, but pretty much anyone else with a pulse knows about your friendship with Riker. Not just your missions together, but also the lengths he'd go to on your behalf. I don't need to tell you that he never wavered in his convictions so far as you were concerned."

Leaning forward in his chair until his face all but filled the screen, Akaar pointed at Picard. *"You and I both know you can't buy or trade or even ask for that kind of devotion. It has to be earned, and nurtured. Riker was ready to stake his career and—so far as he may have thought at the time—his freedom rather than see your name sullied. In my experience, very few people are worthy of that sort of undying respect."*

"Respect and trust are gifts that must not be squandered," replied Picard. "Particularly when offered by those under my command."

It was an edict he had learned as a young officer, under the guidance of men and women who harbored similar attitudes regarding leadership. His former captain on the *Stargazer*, Daithan Ruhalter, had engendered such respect, doing so in a manner as to make it seem effortless. It was this strength of character that emboldened Picard, then a lieutenant commander and serving as second officer aboard the *Stargazer*, to take charge of the ship after it was severely damaged and many of its crew killed. Ruhalter had been among the casualties, and with the first officer, Stephen Leach, also wounded and out of commission, it fell to Picard to take the actions necessary to save the ship and its remaining personnel.

That had catapulted Picard to the center seat at the young, relatively untested age of twenty-nine, launching him on a career trajectory he could scarcely have imagined in those far-off days. Even now, more than fifty years after that incident, Ruhalter was not far from his thoughts, and Picard on countless occasions had asked himself how his former captain might handle any of the situations in which he and his crew—first the *Stargazer* and later the *Enterprise*-D and its successor—had found themselves.

What would he have thought of all of this?

"I live my life striving to be worthy of those gifts, Admiral. I know that my actions with respect to President Zife have eroded the confidence you've felt toward me, and I am not proud of that, but to have weakened it in the eyes of my crew is something for which I am unlikely to ever forgive myself. Were I again faced with the same circumstances and choices, I honestly do not know if I would make a different decision."

Akaar sighed. *"To be honest, when this news broke, the only reason I didn't order your first officer to throw you in the brig for the trip home is because you* are *Jean-Luc Picard. I know it sounds ridiculous when I say it out loud, but it's the truth. After everything you've done, I figured you deserve the chance to be heard, to tell us in your own words what happened. We've gotten explanations from* the others—Nechayev, Jellico, Nakamura—but they all have at least some involvement with Section Thirty-One. Ross, especially."

"I was sorry to hear about Admiral Ross," Picard said.

"I would've been fine with him spending the rest of his life in a penal colony," replied the admiral, *"but the bigger issue is that when he died he took with him whatever secrets he had about Thirty-One. Without him, getting a handle on the real list of operatives and agents became that much harder. I have no doubts some if not most of those people had escape plans, fake identities, and other contingencies in place for just this sort of thing. It could take us years to hunt them all down."*

He paused, staring for a moment at something offscreen, before continuing, *"You, however, are the anomaly, having crossed paths with them once or twice over the years while somehow managing to never run afoul of them."* Returning his gaze to the screen, his features warmed into a humorless smile. *"I don't know how much of that is your generally incorruptible nature, or the Uraei program deciding it needed you where you were to best carry out its master plan to rule the entire universe, or whatever the hell it was doing."*

The smile faded, and Akaar slumped back into his chair. *"The point of all this is when everything shakes out, there will be bodies everywhere and damage that will take years to fix. Some of it might be beyond saving. People will be looking for something—anything—that might provide any sort of relief from the daily storm of sins and secrets revealed and the basic undermining of everything they believed, learned to trust, and took for granted their entire lives. And that's before we get to the trials, convictions, and prison sentences. You'll just be one more entry on a list of names that's already far too long. These wounds will be a long time healing."*

If anything, the admiral's words only strengthened Picard's convictions. "But my name is on that list, along with all those others. For these wounds to truly heal, there can't be even the slightest hint of impropriety. Starfleet in particular can't be seen as covering up or obfuscating anything. I must submit myself to the process and let matters take their proper course."

Akaar said nothing for a moment, as though weighing the futility of whatever response he might bring. Then, as Picard knew he would, he offered a final observation.

"Even if you got under way right now, it's more than two months before you get back. All of this could be over by then."

"I think you and I both know that's not true."

"You're probably right."

Sighing, Picard nodded. "And I appreciate that, sir, but we both know this is something that must be done. It's something *I must do.*"

His eyes moved from the screen to where René slept. In the years to come, how could Picard attempt to instill anything resembling an appreciation for morals and principles without demonstrating their value through deed as well as word? How could he even bring himself to look the boy in the eye without feeling guilt or shame?

The first duty of every Starfleet officer is to the truth.

Picard recalled the words with which he had confronted a young, naive, fallible Wesley Crusher so many years ago. The young man, himself a Starfleet Academy cadet, had found himself involved in a scandal involving a daring, prohibited flying maneuver, the accidental death of a fellow cadet and member of his flying team, and lying to the Academy's board of inquiry about the tragic incident. Compelled to follow the team's charismatic leader, Wesley found himself caught between the often dueling principles of loyalty to one's friends and loyalty to the truth and one's self. Picard, unmoved by the cadet's inner struggle, reminded Wesley that upholding the truth was the basis of everything it meant to be a Starfleet officer. To do anything else was anathema to the organization's bedrock principles.

If you can't find it within yourself to stand up and tell the truth about what happened, you don't deserve to wear that uniform.

The words now echoed in Picard's own ears. Righteous and powerful at the time he used them against a scared young man, they now rang hollow as he contemplated his own hypocrisy.

The first duty, Jean-Luc. There is only one answer here.

As though surrendering to the inevitability of the situation, Akaar raised his right hand, touching his temple in salute. *"Very well, Captain. Safe journeys."*

The communication ended, leaving Picard alone. Settling back in his chair, he closed his eyes and tried to draw comfort from the silence of his ready room, but his sanctuary refused to provide even temporary solace. He knew that such respite would only come after he did what was necessary.

What I should have already done.

Exiting the turbolift, Picard paused just outside the car and regarded the *Enterprise* bridge. Alpha shift was just beginning, and his senior staff was well represented. Worf was already vacating the captain's chair, but Picard waved him to stay where he was.

"As you were, Commander."

That was enough for everyone on the bridge to turn toward him, and Picard waited until they all were looking to him. He noted the concern, curiosity, and expectation as reflected in their various expressions, except for Worf, of course. As always, the Klingon's face was unreadable. Even his body language as he stood before the captain's chair offered no hint as to his inner thoughts.

Following his conversation with Akaar, Picard had given himself the rest of the evening to contemplate his decision. Though sleep eluded him, he was content to sit on the sofa, allowing René to use his lap for a pillow. Only when Beverly found them both did Picard realize he had finally lost himself to a brief, fitful slumber. The short respite had done nothing to give him cause for reconsidering his decision. If anything, having that extra interval only served to strengthen his convictions.

"I know many of you have harbored questions about my involvement in the scandal surrounding President Zife. I've done my best to be as forthcoming as possible, and some of you have brought your questions to me. Those discussions have reminded me that many, many more people have similar questions, and it's time for me to answer them."

He paused, waiting to see if anyone might take the opportunity to respond or ask their own questions, but no one said anything. Their silence was made all the more intimidating by the background sounds emanating from various stations around the bridge and the omnipresent hum of the *Enterprise*'s engines. What he did note was the subtle shift in some of their expressions, the slight melting away of worry and perhaps even the hint of accusation he thought he saw in some of their eyes.

"You've all sworn a solemn oath to represent with honor and integrity the values we hold dear. Additionally, you've made a commitment to me as a member of this crew and to your shipmates, to carry out your duties with utmost professionalism and in the finest tradition of those same values. On this, you have never wavered, and it has been my honor to serve as your captain. Now I must honor you, by submitting myself to the proper authorities so they can take whatever action they deem necessary, also in defense of those values. Anything less would be a further betrayal of our oath and the trust you've placed in me."

Walking to the center of the bridge, he stopped before his chair, taking the opportunity to study the faces of his officers. All of them were riveted upon him, and he sensed their desire to say something—*anything*—that might alleviate the tension now permeating the room.

"We're behind you, sir," said Aneta Šmrhová, punctuating the statement with a single nod. "Whatever happened, we know you didn't do it lightly and wouldn't have done it without a damned good reason. Maybe we can help them see it our way."

One by one, Joanna Faur, Dina Elfiki, Glinn Dygan, and the

other members of the bridge crew verbalized their support, until only Worf remained. Picard turned to face his first officer, whose expression remained implacable.

"Number One?"

"You possess more honor than far too many Klingons I have known during my lifetime. Wherever you lead, I will follow."

It was enough that Picard's reply stuck in his throat, and all he could do was nod. He placed a reassuring hand on Worf's arm, leaving it there for a long moment before returning his attention to the others.

Regardless of the good if misguided intentions on the part of people like Admiral Akaar, Picard knew he could no longer remain in the shadows. It was time for him to step into the light. Whatever his next decision might bring, he would face it just as he had confronted every other obstacle and adversary throughout his life and career: head-on.

"Mister Worf, set a course for Earth."

ACKNOWLEDGMENTS

Heartfelt appreciation is extended to my editors, Ed Schlesinger and Margaret Clark. I've been doing this "writing *Star Trek* thing" for quite a long time now, and it's in large part thanks to these two individuals. They've provided numerous opportunities, unflagging support, and they even let me run off-leash every so often when I get a harebrained idea. Thanks for continuing to let me play in the sandbox.

Which brings me to the keeper of said sandbox: John Van Citters. A short while back, we realized that he started working for what has since morphed into CBS Consumer Products right about the same time I was writing my very first *Star Trek* novel for Simon & Schuster. He's always been a fierce defender of *Star Trek* as well as a staunch advocate of S&S's *Star Trek* publishing program, and he's always handled the demands of that role with grace and humor.

Then there's David Mack, friend and fellow word pusher. I was given the task of taking the baton he held out with his *Star Trek: Section 31* novel *Control*, so he and I ended up having a few conversations on how best to handle the fallout from the events of that book. As is often the case, there was much scheming as we figured out how to tackle the next chapters of this ongoing story-telling train that's been laid out over the past several years. This sort of spirited collaboration has always been one of the things I've most enjoyed about writing *Star Trek*.

And I can't overlook Will Nguyen on Facebook, who gave me the idea on how to insert one particular Easter egg. Good luck finding it.

Finally, there's you, dear reader: You're never far from our thoughts when we sit down to write these books, and we certainly couldn't keep doing it if not for you. Thanks for reading!

ABOUT THE AUTHOR

Dayton Ward: Author. Trekkie. Writing his goofy little stories and searching for a way to tap into the hidden nerdity that all humans have. Then, an accidental overdose of Mountain Dew altered his body chemistry. Now, when Dayton Ward grows excited or just downright geeky, a startling metamorphosis occurs.

Driven by outlandish ideas and a pronounced lack of sleep, he is pursued by fans and editors as well as funny men in bright uniforms wielding Tasers, straitjackets, and medication.

Dayton is believed to be working on his next novel, and he must let the world (and his editors) think he *is* working on it, until he can find a way to earn back the advance check he blew on strippers and booze during that one wild weekend in Las Vegas.

Though he currently lives in Kansas City with his wife and two daughters, Dayton is a Florida native and maintains a torrid long-distance romance with his beloved Tampa Bay Buccaneers.

Visit Dayton on the web at www.daytonward.com.